# Iain

# Crichton

# Smith

*Critical Essays*

edited by
Colin Nicholson

Edinburgh University Press

© Edinburgh University Press 1992

Edinburgh University Press
22 George Square, Edinburgh

Typeset in Linotron Garamond 3
by Photoprint Ltd, Torquay, and
printed in Great Britain by
Hartnoll Ltd, Bodmin

A CIP record for this book is available from the
British Library.

ISBN 0 7486 0340 9

The publisher acknowledges subsidy
from the Scottish Arts Council
towards the publication of this volume.

## Contents

|  | Foreword by Sorley MacLean | v |
|---|---|---|
|  | Introduction | x |
| One | The Gaelic Poetry<br>Derick S. Thomson | 1 |
| Two | The Necessity of Accident: The English Fiction<br>Cairns Craig | 11 |
| Three | Ways of Losing: The Radio Work of Iain Crichton Smith<br>Stewart Conn | 26 |
| Four | Double Man at a Culloden of the Spirit: Reflections on the Poetry of Iain Crichton Smith<br>George Watson | 37 |
| Five | The Wireless Behind the Curtain<br>Douglas Dunn | 51 |
| Six | Law and Grace: A Note on the Poetry of Iain Crichton Smith<br>Gerald Dawe | 73 |
| Seven | First the Footprints, then the Unfathomable: Writing, Difference and Death in the Later Poetry<br>Stan Smith | 82 |
| Eight | 'Deer on the High Hills': A Meditation on Meaning<br>Colin Nicholson | 102 |
| Nine | The Real Poem<br>Carol Gow | 122 |
| Ten | The Double Vision: Imagery in the English Poetry<br>J.H. Alexander | 131 |
| Eleven | Iain Crichton Smith: Cockerel From the Dawn<br>Alastair Fowler | 144 |
| Twelve | Iain Crichton Smith: A Rare Intelligence<br>Lorn Macintyre | 154 |
| Thirteen | Leaving Oban High School: *Hamlet in Autumn* and *Mr Trill in Hades*<br>Ann E. Boutelle | 165 |

| | | |
|---|---|---|
| Fourteen | The White Horse: Design and Grace<br>*Christopher Small* | 176 |
| Fifteen | Uirsgeul Mhic a' Ghobhainn:<br>Iain Crichton Smith's Gaelic Fiction<br>*Richard A.V. Cox* | 190 |
| | *Notes on Contributors* | 200 |
| | *Select Bibliography* | 203 |
| | *Index* | 205 |

# Foreword

## Sorley MacLean

In the very early days of *Lines*, when I was on its editorial committee, Sydney Goodsir Smith asked me to read all the contributions which he had received for a certain issue of the magazine. There were very many of them, and I had a few days to consider them all, I think very carefully, and told Sydney that easily the best of them were two short poems by one Iain Crichton Smith. There was nothing in either poem to indicate who the author was or where he was from, or any geographical clue of any kind. I knew that the name Smith was quite common in Lewis, but I had never heard at that time of the name Crichton in Lewis. Besides, there was, as far as I remember, nothing in either poem to appeal to political or social or linguistic prejudices of my own. Little did I know that I was then recommending the work of one whose imaginative and creative fertility and energy were to become the wonder of literary Scotland. In spite of at least one most moving novel, *Consider the Lilies*, several generally fine volumes of short stories like *Trial without Error*, many brilliant plays both in English and in Gaelic and much reviewing and lecturing, Iain Crichton Smith is primarily a poet even if he spends more time at the other literary work than at poetry. His range as a poet is great and the body of his very fine poetry is astonishing, even if some say that he publishes too much even of poetry.

I think Iain Crichton Smith is more a contemplator of the world than one who, like Shelley or Hugh MacDiarmid or Alexander MacDonald, aspires to change it; but the contrast is full of dangers and misunderstandings, for the great humanity that is everywhere, or almost everywhere, more than implicit in his poetry is itself the most powerful of pleas for most of the qualities that have for ages and ages been accepted as evidence of the god-like in the human being, and I know that Iain's practice is in accordance with the implicit preachings of his utterance. His faith is not without its works, even if it is the faith that expects nothing in return and is without petty pride or the kind of pride that is necessary in most people even if its necessity is implicit. I find so much of this in Iain Crichton Smith that what must be in some way or other a literary ambition in him does not seem any kind of ambition at all. It would seem to be a kind of compulsion to put his contemplation into words. If it is a compulsion, it has every mark of benevolence.

It is very often, if not generally, assumed that passion is necessary to great poetry, whether it is the passion of William Ross or of Mark Alexander Boyd. That is the passion of sexual love, or of half-sublimated sexual love, but it can also be the social passion of a Blake or Shelley or the religious passion of a George Herbert or Dugald Buchanan. I am not sure if Iain Crichton Smith has passion of any of those kinds, but he has the passion of the most profound feeling for humanity. More often than not, it is passion that causes in poetry what has been finely called the 'lyrical cry', which can often cry out in long poems like Wordsworth's *Prelude* or MacDiarmid's *Drunk Man Looks at the Thistle*, as it can in a lyric of Blake or William Ross. I sometimes think that the Gaelic word 'gaoir' would be a better word for this than the English word 'cry', for 'gaoir' has in it the sense not only of the cry but also of something like an electric shock or the frisson along the spine given by Housman's famous lecture, which is what also cries and shudders often in MacDiarmid's greatest lyrics and in Blake's. For such a 'lyrical cry', the metaphor is not necessary and nor is the conscious thought that betrays its consciousness, and the very sound is all-important, which is one reason why the fusion of words and 'music' in the old song is often something beyond poetry.

The Gaelic poem 'Tha thu air Aigeann M'Inntinn' ('You are at the Bottom of my Mind') is a poem of remembered passion. Its imagery is suited to its half-memories, a fusion of barely explicit thought trying to re-create an old passion, and because it is trying, it is failing, in which its failure is its triumph. It is a most remarkable poem, surely one of the finest that has come out of the 'Gaelic Renaissance', to which Iain's poetic contribution is greater than is sometimes admitted, partly because he has done so much in effacing himself to introduce others.

In Iain Crichton Smith's poetry, there is a great compassion; often the compassion is such that the lacrimae rerum is quiet, so quiet that there is no lyrical cry, nor 'gaoir', the word Housman would have used if he had known Gaelic. There is also sometimes a kind of deliberate anticlimax, which is as it were an acceptance of things as they are and

## Foreword

cannot be changed, a sort of acceptance without explicit approval or disapproval. The range of feeling, thought and imagery is, however, difficult to generalise. I am talking of the lesser bulk of his Gaelic poetry as well as the great bulk of his English poetry.

There was a time when I was not so sure of the language of his poetry in Gaelic as I was of his language in English. Probably that was due to dialectal differences between the Gaelic of Skye and that of Lewis, for the semantic differences are considerable, and there are even grammatical differences that jar on one until it is recognised that they are dialectal differences. For instance, I recognise that forms in Raasay are sometimes like the Lewis forms, not the Skye forms. Genders, datives and the use of genitives after verbal nouns are the chief points of difference.

Again and again, I have been struck by the impression which strangers who have never seen Iain Crichton Smith or heard him reading get of the man from reading his poetry. How right the impression is, certainly because the poetry is so honest and unpretentious as well as being so rich and varied in thought and imagery. The impression of the man and his work is always reinforced by seeing and hearing him. It is seldom that such honesty and unpretentiousness are enlivened by a lively, far-ranging intelligence and imagination. It is very seldom that genius is so wide and fervent in its sympathies and so lacking in egoism that it can be humorous without trying to be witty or clever. There are some people in the world who are not only good but also look good. Iain's poetry can afford to be sometimes even loquacious. His imagery can afford to be sometimes sought after and sometimes surrealist without a compulsive surrealism, but those 'weaknesses' are so few and insignificant in the astonishing richness and variety of Iain's poetry that it is invidious to mention them. The occasional image that is not significant, that is sought after, is so rare that it is not worth mentioning when the critic's dilemma is that he cannot draw attention to a tenth of the varied gems that gleam or glow in so many poems. Indeed, the great difficulty I find in writing about Iain's poetry is that, to do him real justice, it would be necessary to mention and to quote from so many poems. The concentration and economy of 'Aig Clachan Chalanais' ('At the Stones of Callanish') lie in the fusion of the prehistoric past of human sacrifices and the horror of Nagasaki, 'the beautiful blue ball like heaven cracking' and the 'children with skin hanging to them', all in eight lines. There are, too, the quiet conclusion of 'Aig a' Chladh' ('At the Cemetery'); the powerful surrealism of the second quatrain of 'Dè tha Ceàrr?' ('What is Wrong?'); the strangely effective surrealism of the last line of 'An t-Uisge' ('The Rain'); the metaphysical brevity of 'Neochiontas' ('Innocence'); the concentration of the nine lines of 'Mo Bhardachd' ('My Poetry') and of the twelve of 'Aon Nighean' ('One Girl'); and the reticent pathos of 'A' Chailleach' ('The Old Woman') with its magical last line, magical as a contrasting climax after the quiet, ordered pathos of the rest of the poem. The famous 'Na h-eil Thirich' ('The Exiles') has the magical dichotomies so frequent but so unobtrusive in Iain's poetry both in Gaelic and in English. The poignant poem 'Do mo Mhathair' ('To my Mother') has great imagery in the second verse, though the sea imagery seems too hectic at the end of the third verse, and the enigma of the last line is obscure to me. Nevertheless, the poem is a masterpiece that could have come only from Iain. 'A' Chlach' ('The Stone') is an impressive mystery to me, impressive with imagery that is powerful but to me somehow irrelevant. As a constrast, one could mention the lucidity of the 'simple' poem 'Nuair a Bha Sinn Og' ('When We Were Young'); and, as a contrast to that one, 'Air Oidhche Foghair' ('On an Autumn Night'). It has a strange, mixed metaphor in the antepenultimate and penultimate lines, but that may be due to a mistranslation if 'sniomh' means 'twisting' here instead of 'weaving'.

Iain has published so many fine poems in English that the critic has greater difficulty with them than with the Gaelic poems, for so many can be singled out for special mention that it would require a big volume to do justice to them. Fundamentally, the themes and attitudes are the same in English as in Gaelic. There is the same contemplation of the world sub specie Lewisiana, sub specie mundi and sub specie aeternitatis, the same pity and sympathy without condescension, the many-sided aspects of the human condition and dilemma, the same deep and far-ranging sympathies, the same modesty and sincerity.

On page 14 of the MacDonald Selection, there is the great, poignant poem 'Old Woman', and on page 18 the very different 'Sunday Morning Walk'. The two follow each other in the Carcanet Selection, the dying human being continuing to be the object of human love unconscious of her misery and the dead, rotting sheep subject to the ravages of flies and the object of human neutrality. Very different is the moderate poem 'By Ferry to the Island', and very different too the moderation of perhaps a great poem 'A Young Highland Girl Studying Poetry'. 'Two Girls Singing' has a splendid lift, and 'Old Woman (Your Thorned Back)' has its own great truth expressed in a spare language that is inevitable, for no other language would do.

I am not sure of 'At the Firth of Lorne', but I am sure of the quiet, almost implicit pathos of 'Old Highland Lady Reading Newspaper' and

*Foreword*

of the powerful dichotomy of 'Old Woman ("Overwhelmed with Kindness")'. 'Jean Brodie's Children' is neither here nor there for me, but 'Entering Your House' I find very convincing, even though I am sometimes dubious of Iain's hints about the 'righteousness' of the Free and Free Presbyterian Churches and of his apparent forgetfulness regarding their attitudes to those 'filthy rags' which were essentially 'filthy rags' but also necessary by-products of the saving grace from which came Justification, Adoption and Sanctification, after Effectual Calling. One requires to put against that fine poem a very different and fine poem, 'Of the Uncomplicated Dairy Girl', which describes one of the eighty-five or ninety per cent of a given Lewis Free Church congregation who would not be taking communion but who would be only adherents. What of her 'straight-backed brother [who] marched off to save the King'? I remember a very fine and very liberal Church of Scotland minister, Coll MacDonald of Logierait (an Iona man), who had been an army chaplain in the First World War, telling me that, in his experience, no men died better than Free Presbyterians. I suppose the same would be true of Lewis Free Church 'adherents', most of whom, like the Free Presbyterian 'adherents', could expect only the physical and mental Hell of their creed. It is over thirty years ago that I learned that, and I have wondered at it ever since. It was after Coll's youngest son, one of my greatest friends at the University, had been killed in the Second World War.

I open Iain's *Selected Poems* at random and find near the end 'Speech for a Woman', a poem of wonderful and intense imagination, and on the opposite page a very different and modest poem, 'My Brother'. I open another selection of his poems and find 'If You are about to Die Now', and I can only wonder at it. I leave 'Deer on the High Hills' to a younger, fresher and more percipient mind, but it is only one of many wonders, or, ought I not to say, one of many, many wonders.

# Introduction

This is the first collection of essays to address itself to Iain Crichton Smith's work. His formal and generic variety of production, to say nothing of its sheer volume – he is a popular novelist, a celebrated writer of short fiction, a radio dramatist, a literary critic and a poet of distinction – makes him a particularly interesting writer to come to terms with. As versatile in Gaelic as in English, the cultural pressures and determinations with which he articulates lend to his books peculiar and sometimes disturbing intensities and make of a writer born on the island of Lewis a representative figure of late twentieth-century *angst*. It is one of Crichton Smith's achievements to bring an island sensibility to the attention of the English-speaking world, thereby exposing the extraordinary divisions and self-divisions which the processes of cultural colonisation entail.

As he forges continuities with the Scottish diaspora, particularly its Canadian dimensions, he brings to light ways in which Scotland's compromised identity as a post-colonial society connects with international discourses of subjectivity and selfhood. In a world increasingly characterised by shifting frontiers and radical reformulations of hitherto assumed securities of ethnic and political definition, Crichton Smith speaks to us on several levels. The Hamlet-figure who stalks his poetry is one index of the complex imaginative responses he has developed to explore his own position as a native Gael increasingly prominent in anglophone literature. Feelings of betrayal and self-betrayal derive in part from an awareness of complicity in systems of cultural power which undermine native senses of origination. Similarly, the image of the island, another recurring trope in Crichton Smith's work, generates a pattern of complicated self-definition which is simultaneously a marker of existential and ontological uncertainty. So it seemed appropriate to

## Introduction

begin this volume, after Sorley MacLean's foreword, with a treatment of the Gaelic poetry and to end it with an essay on the Gaelic fiction, with various approaches to the English writing ordered in between. Derick Thomson's survey of the Gaelic poetry brings into focus the themes and concerns that occupy Crichton Smith across the body of his writing no matter which medium he employs: guilt, exile, an island complicatedly loved and left, the experiences of emigrant Highlanders in Canada and Australia, and the conflict in language which these tensions engender are established as recurrent *topoi* that give shape to the peculiar densities of expression and orientation in the Gaelic verse. Then, in a studied refusal to read the English-language fiction as simply a backdrop to the poetry, Cairns Craig reads a 'crisis plot' as typifying the novels. Exile and displacement also determine the narrative trajectories of this aspect of Crichton Smith's work, where a surface simplicity of utterance simultaneously masks and reveals the personal and cultural difficulty of discovering a language that might fit existential displacement. The friction between a shared language and what Craig calls 'solipsistic exile in a world of entirely private meanings' becomes a central problematic.

Given these contentions, it could hardly be surprising that ways of losing should also figure in Crichton Smith's radio work, and Stewart Conn's chapter suggests that while this area may hitherto have been considered peripheral to Crichton Smith's main achievements, it extends their concerns by composing an effective rearguard action against possession of the mind by spurious authority figures. In the poetry, such resistance is repeatedly expressed, and the antagonisms which Crichton Smith has to encounter and harmonise are given fluent voice. In an essay from which George Watson quotes, Crichton Smith has acknowledged that 'the very fact that I had to learn English when I went to school was probably registered in some obscure corner of my psyche as an indication that English was superior to Gaelic'.[1] Bringing to bear his own experience of a Northern Ireland childhood, Watson examines the evolution of Crichton Smith's voice from the cultural margins of England's dominating metropolitan discourse to its current position of authority and clarification. Watson traces the ways in which Crichton Smith's island upbringing helped to shape resonances beyond the boundaries of any local origin. Those positions of an alienated sensibility that it is the business of post-colonial literature in English to articulate and explore are deeply ingrained in everything the writer from Lewis has produced, and, as it elaborates them, Crichton Smith's poetry has good reason to carry within it a profound suspicion of the strategies of writing. In its quest for truths beyond the regional topographies of place, it deploys an often elemental imagery to encode a post-modernist awareness of the duplicity of metaphor.

Clearly, Crichton Smith's discovery of a sufficient poetic voice has been a difficult and painful process, and Douglas Dunn brings a writer's eye and ear to bear upon the tracking of its development. Beginning with a preliminary survey of early influences, Dunn examines the successes and failures of a poetry disconcerted by some of those English idioms it constantly refashions to project Highland purpose and place onto wider realms of experience. Initially denied a secure angle of approach, the poetry exhibits corresponding degrees of perplexity, with formal technique compelled to deal with cultural and historical instability. Out of these stresses comes a characteristic and often daring idiosyncrasy of expression. The American Robert Lowell's poetry is one of the influences mentioned by Dunn and acknowledged by Crichton Smith, and Gerald Dawe pursues the ways in which, for both poets, the relationship between 'community' and 'culture' in their writing lives is in turn deeply influenced by their religious upbringing and by the inherited assumptions which such an upbringing entails.

Given the insistent presence of the figure of Death in this writing and the sometimes cognate figure of a mother who died, Stan Smith's approach, beginning with *Love Songs and Elegies* (1972), combines the strategies of Jacques Lacan with the procedures of Derrida to construct a mode of textual psychoanalysis that is both pertinent and revealing. Cultural trauma finds its objective correlative in a peculiar compacting of the oedipal myth, and Crichton Smith's textuality becomes a paradoxical space where absence and emptiness are inscribed as an imaginary plenitude is envisaged. A scripted repossession of the figure of the mother creates the conditions for a process of recolonising which is hoped to be free from feelings of suffocation. In uncertain dialectic, dispossession vies with repossession. Douglas Dunn agrees that another American, Wallace Stevens, haunts 'Deer on the High Hills: A Meditation', a poem that Crichton Smith has more than once suggested slipped away from any conscious intention he may have had when he began writing it. Certainly, 'idiosyncratic' aptly describes this production, where suspicion of metaphor determines its formal unfolding and where history, perception and cultural genealogy mingle to particular effects, some of which I attempt in Chapter 8 to indicate.

'Deer on the High Hills' is a work that falls naturally within Crichton Smith's suggestion that 'sometimes the real poem is the dark companion travelling alongside the actually created one'. The remark prompts Carol Gow to explore what might be meant by 'the real poem' in these

# Introduction

contexts, and to examine ways in which the discovery of a self in the mirror of the poems is one of Crichton Smith's sustaining projects. Two chapters then analyse the poetry's distinctive imagery, with J.H. Alexander discovering the characteristic double vision constructed by Crichton Smith's habit of working with opposing or contrasting entities, so that conflicting ways of seeing can be investigated. Typically, a world dominated by severity, rigidity, hardness and law is set against one of gentleness, fluidity, fragile vulnerability and grace, with each world being defined and explored by connecting groups of persistent figures. Following a different procedure while still attending to paired oppositions in the writing, Alstair Fowler considers the gradual loosening of technical constraints which allows freer play to Crichton Smith's extraordinarily compressed tropes. In this reading, *A Life* (1986) and *The Village and Other Poems* (1989) appear as quantum jumps in accomplishment.

Both Lorn Macintyre and Ann Boutelle begin their chapters by registering personal affiliations with Iain Crichton Smith before setting off on their accounts of what the writing signifies for them. Beginning with the figure of the old woman, Macintyre sees connections between Crichton Smith's island upbringing and his subsequent interest in the existentialism of a philosopher like Kierkegaard. The path being traced here leads to the emergence of a nationally significant body of poetry. Boutelle recalls her own schooldays as one of Crichton Smith's pupils at Oban High School and reads *Hamlet in Autumn* (1972) in these contexts. Her discussion of the 1984 short story collection *Mr Trill in Hades* also brings to bear her memories of the characters and situations upon which some of the tales are based. Christopher Small brings the accounts of the English-language writing to a close with a different perception of features common to the prose and poetry before Richard Cox's survey of the fiction in Gaelic reminds us of the seemingly inexhaustible invention with which Crichton Smith works and reworks themes and circumstances that have inscribed the relevance of Lewis and the position of Gaelic character and event beyond their immediate locales. Crichton Smith's books resonate with significances that transcend their originations on the extreme territorial fringes of Europe.

NOTES

1. Iain Crichton Smith, 'The Double Man' in *The Literature of Region and Nation* (Aberdeen, 1989), edited by R.P. Draper, p. 137.

# *One*

## The Gaelic Poetry

## Derick S. Thomson

The post-war decade was a time of anticipation in Gaelic writing. It was clearly felt that there were, and should be, new initiatives. Not that it was a time for thinking 'Bliss was it in that dawn to be alive'. People were, instead, thankful to have the war behind them, and glad to get back to more positive activities. But the war years made a significant break with earlier attitudes. An early sign, in Gaelic writing, was the launching of the projected annual *Alba*, by An Comunn Gaidhealach, in 1948. This seemed a promising new outlet for Gaelic, but its organisational basis could not sustain it. To fill the gap, plans were laid in 1951 to launch *Gairm*, which began to appear in 1952. It was as though the time was by now right, and the organisation at least sufficient. Gaelic writing has not looked back since these early years around 1950.

It was just about then that Iain Crichton Smith was beginning to come on stream. His earliest writing was in English, but the existence of a Gaelic quarterly encouraged him to write more in Gaelic, which was his natural language. I can scarcely remember talking anything but Gaelic with Iain, on a one-to-one basis, until many years after this time.

Yet his early preference for English as a writing medium was not too unusual, and it was buttressed by the basic educational assumptions of the time and indeed of two or three previous generations. At school in Stornoway, for instance, our reading of English literature was quite wide, though it tended to stop at Georgian poetry, while in Gaelic, apart from poetry of a more traditional kind, there was not a wide range of reading easily accessible. In a fairly natural way, then, English influence became a strong factor in the development of the Gaelic writer who had gone through the educational system. If he had happened to take a University Honours English course, as several of us did, the opportunities, or pressures, were further increased.

Probably the earliest striking example of new influence on Gaelic poetry was a First World War poem by John Munro, 'Ar gaisgich a thuit sna blàir' ('Our heroes who fell in the battles'), which had been published in James Thomson's anthology for schools, *An Dìleab*, in 1932. By the late 1930s and the 1940s, new styles and preoccupations in Gaelic verse were appearing from a small group of writers, and eventually this movement was to create a new 'norm', making the more traditional styles, themes and metrics become almost old-fashioned. This process was going on steadily through the 1950s and 1960s, and could almost be said to have been completed by around 1970. This is not to say that there was no room for further development, and Crichton Smith's work itself gives the lie to such a thought. It is rather that the crucial acceptance had come of a new 'norm' of perception and practice in fashioning poetry in Gaelic.

Ten poems by Iain Crichton Smith appeared in *Gairm* in its first decade, and five of these were included in the verse section of his first Gaelic book, *Bùrn is Aran* (*Bread and Water*, 1960). The first of these to appear, in 1952, was 'Tha thu air aigeann m'inntinn' ('You are at the bottom of my mind'), a poem which has never lost its freshness or its depth. Two other poems which are significant in his Gaelic repertoire are 'A' dol dhachaigh' ('Going home', 1958) and 'Aig a' chladh' ('At the churchyard', 1959). The former of these gives us an early example of his slightly contemptuous use of stereotyped images. As he returns to his island (Lewis), he lifts a handful of soil, sits on a knoll of the mind looking at the cowherd and his cattle, while (he thinks desultorily) a thrush soars and 'a dawn or two' breaks. But behind these superficially reassuring images there is the great fire of Hiroshima and all the guilt and pity and perplexity that surround it. One of the early poems that does not appear in the 1960 collection is 'Airson Deòrsa Caimbeul Hay' ('For George Campbell Hay', *Gairm* No. 24, 1958), in which he expresses strong admiration for Hay's work:

> You don't talk about yourself
> but about your country, and Europe,
> and the world that is disappearing for ever . . .'.

And again,
> A great poet is enmeshed in his own poetry as water is in the burns.

Probably the other two most striking poems in *Bùrn is Aran* are 'A' chailleach' ('The old woman') and 'Do bhoireannach aosd' ('To an old lady'). Already here, he has set out the parameters of his lengthy engagement with the 'old lady' theme, which moves from family to national history, from verse to prose fiction, from anger to admiration, from appreciation to condemnation, but always with a sense of personal guilt in the background – guilt about the unfairness of life and society:

> You had not heard about Darwin
> or Freud or Marx or the other Jew,
> Einstein of the elegant mind:
> nor of the sense of the dream you dreamt
> last night, sleeping soundly in your room.
> . . .
> You had not heard how the lion sits,
> with its savage head, at the table with us.

And he wishes the old lady well:

> May your life go well with you
> as now you make your way home
> through streets white as a man's mind
> opened up by the sharp blade of the knife . . . .

He is concerned with other moral and intellectual dilemmas too, as well as psychological ones, as in the short poem 'Dè tha ceàrr?' ('What is wrong?'):

> Cò 's urrainn innse dè tha ceàrr?
> Bha mi aig lighichean is lighichean.
> Thubhairt fear ac' rium: 'Do cheann, do cheann,'
> 's fear eile, sgrìobhadh beag le peann,
> ''S e th'ann do chridhe, do chridhe'.
>
> Ach, aon latha, chunnaic mi
> sloc dubh an talamh gorm,
> gàirnealair a' pògadh dhìthean,
> cailleach 'na h-aonranachd a' bìogail,
> 's taigh a' seòladh air sàl.
>
> Chan eil fhios eil cànan ann 'son sin
> no ged a bhitheadh 'm bithinn càil na b'fheàrr
> a' briseadh mac-meanma 'na mìle pìos:
> ach aon rud cinnteach feumar fios
> fhaighinn air a' cheart tha ceàrr.

In Crichton Smith's own translation:
> Who can tell what is wrong! I went to doctors and doctors. One of them told me, 'It's your head,' and another one, writing small with a pen, 'It's your heart, your heart'. But one day I saw a black pit in green earth, a gardener kissing flowers, an old woman squeaking in her loneliness, and a house sailing on the water. I don't know whether there is a language for that, or, if there is, whether I would be any better breaking my imagination into a thousand pieces: but one thing is certain, we must find the right that is wrong.
>
> (*The Permanent Island*, 15)

So, already in that 'first decade', he is defining the range of preoccupations that are to characterise his work, although leaving ample room, of course, for later, deeper and more detailed exploration, especially in fictional works. The short stories in that Gaelic collection of 1960 mark out another of his favourite areas, with the themes of exile and return prominent.

His metrics, in this early work, suggest a slight preference for regular but lightly ornamented verse forms, with a readiness to experiment with freer forms, whether the six-line stanza of 'You are at the bottom of my mind', with its minimal rhymes and significant variations in line length, or the freer, more conversational rhythms of 'Going home' and 'To an old lady', both probably dating to the later 1950s. I have the impression that he moved rather earlier towards free verse in his Gaelic than in his English work, and this arouses some interesting reflections which are not pursued here (see e.g. Thomson, 1974, 1985).

In his first extended Gaelic collection of poems, *Bìobuill is Sanasan-Reice* (Bibles and Advertisements), published in 1965, he retains nine of the *Bùrn is Aran* poems, starting his collection with them. The rest of the collection is new, and shows significant development in the range of themes and techniques. The first of the new poems here is entitled 'Ochd òrain airson cèilidh ùir' ('Eight songs for a new ceilidh'). He picks up the Hiroshima theme here again, integrating the harrowing experiences of the twentieth century with the cosier Gaelic tradition of songs by sailors and exiles. In our new world of displaced persons and values, there are new stereotypes: Belsen, Pasternak, Venus (the planet, not the deity), Nazis, Guernica. His invitation to his sweetheart is to go with him to Japan:

> Am falbh thu leam, a rìbhinn òg,
> a null gu Japan far bheil ar ciall

# The Gaelic Poetry

> a' caitheamh anns a' bhoma mhòr
> a thuit air baile is air sliabh?

(Will you go with me, young maiden, over to Japan where our sanity is wasting in that big bomb that fell on town and on mountain?)

*(The Permanent Island, 17)*

This rather than the conventional invitation to go back to Uist or Lewis, or bid farewell to Fiunary, or go to a Glasgow or Edinburgh ceilidh to listen to Duncan Bàn Macintyre songs which are, he seems to suggest, irrelevant to our age.

The transition foreshadowed in the early poems has been made, and the new perspective is in place. Perhaps the poet's experience of Oban had helped to change the perspective too. The short sequence 'An t-Oban' makes stark contrasts between his traditional (Gaelic and religious) world and the world he now lives in, a world on which he puts the no doubt oversimplified tags of advertisements and circuses. He ends these reflections with the powerful, perhaps Yeatsian, section 5:

> Thòisich an clag mòr a' bualadh.
> Tha an eaglais air a fosgladh.
> Shuidh mi sìos innte 'nam inntinn
> 's chunna mi air an uinneig
> an àite Nazareth 's an Crìosdaidh
> talamh caithte is min-shàibh,
> leòmhann a' falbh air buaile
> spreadhte Phalestine gun tàmh.

(The big bell began to toll. The church has been opened. I sat down inside it in my mind, and saw on the window, instead of Nazareth and Christ, worn earth and sawdust, a lion moving in the explosive circle of Palestine without cease.)

*(The Permanent Island, 18)*

A number of short poems in this collection record impressions of a rather lonely existence, in a world dominated superficially by advertising images. The internal debate continues, surfacing in reflections about Freud and Calvin:

> Tha Calvin ag innse gu bheil sinn caillt'
> is Freud ag ràdh gu bheil sinn meallt',
> O mo làmhan tana caola
> carson a rèisd tha sibh a' sgrìobhadh?
>
> 'S a' cheist mhòr ud air chruth nathrach
> a' gluasad air crìochan m' athar,

O mo làmhan caola, tana,
bha an saoghal caillt' is mi 'nam leanabh.
Is am faileas fad ud 'na mo chnàmhan
on chiad latha a bha mi rànail.
Tha Freud is Calvin tighinn ri chèile
mar ainglean dubh' air feadh mo speuran.
(Calvin tells us that we are lost. Freud tells us that we are deceived. O my long thin hands, why then are you writing? And that great question in the shape of a snake moving on the lands of my father. O my long thin hands, the world was lost when I was still a child. And that long shadow in my bones from the very first day that I cried. Freud and Calvin come together like black angels and devils about my skies.)

(*The Permanent Island*, 31)

There are of course other reasons for the loss of the poet's early world, and even when these are very respectable intellectual reasons he seems to retain a sense of guilt, but the guilt is not smothered in nostalgia. This seems to be his preoccupation in a poem which he addressed to me, as his one-time fellow villager, 'Do Ruaraidh MacThòmais':

is sinne nis air feadh ar tìme
is solais gheala, solais mhìn oirnn,
is Steòrnabhagh cho beag ri prìne

is sìoltachan an t-saoghail mun cuairt oirnn
gun chrodh r'am faicinn air a' bhuaile

ach seabhag òir san adhar àrd ud
mar Dhia a' sealltainn ann an sgàthan.

(and we now in our time with white lights, smooth lights on us, and Stornoway as small as a pin [surrounded by the world's strainer, with no cattle to be seen in the field] but a golden hawk in that high sky like God, looking in a mirror.)

(*The Permanent Island*, 33
with a translation supplied for the penultimate couplet.)

In the final poem in this collection, the poet gives his pen to a raven, who is enraptured with this fresh opportunity. It is not a bad image for some of Smith's commentary on certain aspects of his experience and the tradition he relates to, though there is a dove there too at times.

The next Gaelic collection of poems did not come until 1974, and it was altogether lighter in weight and tone. *Eader Fealla-dhà is Glaschu*

(*Fun and Glasgow*) is mainly a series of very short poems, some of them in sequence, but for the most part picking up isolated aspects of a theme, and using the *haiku* form or variants of it. Many of the resulting comments are wry or satirical or humorous. The subjects may be Christmas, or odd encounters (as when a sea-monster rises out of the sea and asks 'Will you take a cup of tea?'), or glimpses of the moon, or glimpses of Glasgow like this one:

Nas bòidhche
air an oidhche
na air an latha
Glaschu
siùrsach aosda.
(Bonnier at night than in daytime, Glasgow, an old whore.)

Television is another source of image and comment:

    Cheannaich e 'War and Peace',
    Tolstoy, tha mi ciallachadh,
    an dèidh fhaicinn air on TV.
    (He bought 'War and Peace',
    I mean Tolstoy,
    after seeing it on the TV.)
    (*The Permanent Island*, 65)

The zany humour, irreverence and positive cultivation of a stance that is well distanced from a sense of *gravitas* accurately reflect certain aspects of the poet's personality and conversation, and make a refreshing interlude.

 This was followed, in 1983, with the collection *Na h-Eilthirich*, a series of forty-five short poems grouped round the general theme of the book's title: The Emigrants. Some of the poems are about conventional emigrants, to Canada or Australia; some are more generalised, and many focus on the homeland rather than the adopted country. The homeland is usually Lewis, at least by implication, and the emigrant is sometimes the author. These are for the most part bleak recollections, troubled by a sort of guilt and a rueful honesty, as where he writes about a former classmate, whose name escapes him, and who comes with his daughter seeking an autograph. Disillusionment with the traditional Presbyterian island religion often surfaces, as when he thinks of his classmates:

    Bha dùil am gun ùraicheadh sinn an saoghal.
    Ach gu h-eagalach dubh an-diugh
    tha sibh a' tighinn às a' choinneimh.

> (I thought we would revivify the world.
> But in fearful black today
> you come away from the [church] meeting.)

Some of the emigrants return and live a make-believe life as if nothing had changed. Others struggle with the generation gap. Some succumb to alcoholism, like the famous footballer:

> Thàinig a' Bheatha thugad
> cha b'ann idir mar centre forward,
> ball iomlan aig a chasan,
>
> ach le copan mealltach
> a thogas tu a-nise
> gu critheanach gu do bheul.

(Life came to you not like a centre forward, with a perfect ball at his feet,
but with a deceiving cup, which you raise now shakily to your lips.)

It is not a flattering or optimistic assessment of either the homeland or the emigrants, and it is no doubt one-sided, but from its perspective it is a truthful view.

*An t-Eilean agus an Cànan* (*The Island and the Language*), which appeared in 1987, is much more positive, if none too optimistic. It is as though a firmer perspective has been won, particularly in the 'Island' section. The items in the 'Language' section provide some commentary on contemporary language developments and attitudes, with a reference to

> Gàidhlig na stàit
> cho briste lapach

(the Gaelic of the State [i.e. courtesy utterances by Government representatives who do not know the language] so broken and halting),

or a poem about a Frenchman who is translating Gaelic short stories into French, and so on. These twenty poems are perhaps too much 'thesis' poems, on the general topic of bilingualism and biculturalism. It is a topic that has attracted Crichton Smith on a number of occasions, in both his English and his Gaelic writing. Some of these poems have perhaps the status of working notes for a thesis, and do not achieve a free existence of their own.

The much longer 'Island' section, with eighty-seven poems, seems to have a different perspective, a tighter structure and a freer imaginative sweep, though there is clearly an element of reportage in them too, and their relevance may be much greater for readers who know, and are

# The Gaelic Poetry

involved in, their background. These changes of approach and commitment are at once reflected in a different metrical structure, if metrical is the right word. They are more prose poems, with variable paragraphs rather than lines of verse. The subject matter becomes much more varied, and the author's zany interjections recur. In the Eden he remembers, there were oranges from Nazareth, and Adam plants potatoes with the seagulls around him. There are returned emigrants here too, and the author's thoughts oscillate between the 1940s and the 1980s, between Canada and Lewis. The images of some of these poems are more fluid in their sequence, less contrived or underlined, and so they create a kaleidoscopic sequence which is imaginatively fused:

> A' ghaoth, an cuan, na uèirichean meirgeach.
> An ceòl lom ud, an ceòl àraid ud.
> Tha na faoileagan a' teàrnadh às an adhar a' sgriachail, am bodach-ròcais air chrith.
> Tha an simileir a' seinn . . .
> (The wind, the sea, the rusted wires.
> That bare music, that strange music.
> The seagulls swoop from the sky, screeching, the scarecrow shakes.
> The chimney sings . . .).

In a couple of instances he 'reports' the unholy mixture of Gaelic and English that is sometimes used, very naturally, by islanders, and this can be quite hilarious, e.g. an account of a visit to Germany:

> Tha iad gu math spotless over there. Na gardens aca cho clean, na pavements as well.
> I liked it very much. In fact I would go back there.
> I went by plane, tha thu tuigsinn.

Or again:

> Aig Christmas bha mi fhìn is Sheila ann a Minorca.
> I'll tell you something, no more peats for me.
> Am faca tu a' video,
>   I was alone in New York?
> Bha mi bruidhinn ri Sasannach, 's *caomh* leis a bhith buain na mònach.

Perhaps all that need be translated there is the final line:
   'I was talking to an Englishman, he *likes* cutting peats'.

It is good to see these changes of perspective and technique, especially coming at a remove of twenty-two years from the publication of his main previous collection of Gaelic poems. Of course, Crichton

Smith has had to make his main writing career in English, for a Gaelic freelance writer could not survive, unless in the more luxuriant pastures of TV. But he has survived as a Gaelic writer as well, both in poetry and in fiction, as his recent novel *Na Speuclairean Dubha* (*The Dark Glasses*), published in 1990, testifies. Naturally there have been times when one language or the other, one form or another, seemed in the ascendant, perhaps Gaelic around 1960, and English for many years thereafter. There has always been a degree of movement between the two bodies of work, occasionally straight translation, more often adaptation or reworking. Perhaps it is a condition of his existence as a writer that he keeps both languages going, and both literary traditions, each of them in some degree energising the other.

BIBLIOGRAPHY

*Alba* (An Comunn Gaidhealach, Glasgow, 1948).
*Gairm* (Gairm Publications, Glasgow, 1952 onwards).
Mac a' Ghobhainn, Iain, *Bùrn is Aran* (Gairm Publications, 1960).
Mac a' Ghobhainn, Iain, *Biobuill is Sanasan-reice* (Gairm Publications, 1965).
Mac a' Ghobhainn, Iain, *Eadar Fealla-dhà is Glaschu* (Dept of Celtic, Univ. of Glasgow, 1974).
Mac a' Ghobhainn, Iain, *Na h-Eilthirich* (Dept of Celtic, Univ. of Glasgow, 1983).
Mac a' Ghobhainn, Iain, *An t-Eilean agus an Cànan* (Dept of Celtic, Univ. of Glasgow, 1987).
Mac a' Ghobhainn, Iain, *Na Speuclairean Dubha* (Gairm Publications, 1990).
Smith, Iain, C., *The Permanent Island* (M. Macdonald, Loanhead, 1975).
Thomson, Derick, *Introduction to Gaelic Poetry* (Edinburgh Univ. Press, 1990).
Thomson, Derick, *The New Verse in Scottish Gaelic: a structural analysis* (Univ. College Dublin, 1974).
Thomson, Derick, *Tradition and Innovation in Gaelic Verse since 1950* (Trans. Gael. Soc. Inverness, Vol. 53, available from Dept of Celtic, Univ. of Glasgow, 1985).
Thomson, James, *An Dìleab* (An Comunn Gaidhealach, Glasgow, 1932).

# Two

## The Necessity of Accident: The English Fiction

### Cairns Craig

Iain Crichton Smith the novelist has never been taken as seriously as Iain Crichton Smith the poet, despite the success of his early novel *Consider the Lilies*. That fitted too neatly, perhaps, into the tradition – as established by Neil Gunn and Fionn MacColla – of how one presented Highland experience; a 'fit' that was further encouraged by his concentration on much the same thematic material as earlier 'Highland' writers, in which the value of physical and spiritual delight has to be grappled from the clutch of the dour and negative repressions of Calvinist tradition. It is also tempting to look upon Crichton Smith's prose writing as the workshop of his poetic imagination – an outlet for a creativity which cannot cease from generating words rather than the mode in which his imagination truly seeks its expression – the hobby of the obsessive wordsmith rather than his vocation. So when images and ideas cross between poetry and novel, we are tempted to read the prose as 'background' to the more elliptical mode of the poetry: as, for instance, in the famous early poem 'Sunday Morning Walk', whose description of the dead sheep – 'The household air/ was busy with buzzing like fever. How quickly/ the wool was peeled from its back' – is repeated in *Consider the Lilies* when the protagonist, Mrs Scott, encounters just such a sheep as she travels to seek support from the minister against her coming eviction. But to treat the prose fiction as subsidiary – either to earlier models of Scottish fiction or to Crichton Smith's own poetic creations – is to miss the intensity of his commitment to the medium and the significance of his achievement in it.

For Crichton Smith, the novel has been the mode through which he has explored a particular and central theme of his own imaginative quest. However different they may be in dramatic setting or historical location, all of the novels have the same underlying structure — what one might describe as the 'crisis plot', in which the protagonists are forced to explore their pasts as a result of some present crisis which reveals just how repressed and repressive has been their previous existence. That 'crisis plot' almost invariably restricts Crichton Smith to a small, intensely-knit group of characters, whose familial interrelations provide the dynamic of the narrative. Indeed, outside this central plot structure, he loses interest entirely, and the broader sweep of social life does not exist for him at all. Even large-scale historical events are always focused through the lives of one or two intensely observed individuals, individuals who are much more significant to us than the social forces to which they are related. *Consider the Lilies* may be a historical novel, but it has none of the sense of history moving through a whole society that Scott sought or that is present in Gunn's *Butcher's Broom*. Crichton Smith's novels focus insistently on the consciousness of an individual, at the moment of crisis when that individual discovers the true extent of his or her isolation from the rest of the human community. It is this isolated consciousness, cut off from the rest of history and society, that is Crichton Smith's real concern in his novels — a consciousness usually aware of itself as sliding towards a solipsism which, unless it can be resisted, will be utterly self-destructive.

This 'crisis' situation on which his plots are based is related to a more general condition that all of his novels explore, the condition of exile. The protagonists of his novels are always exiles, displaced geographiically or spiritually from their culture and struggling to find a centre from which they make sense of their place in the scheme of things:

> I never really got used to the city, Martin was thinking. It was disparate, nothing had any connection with anything else . . . a feeling that in my very bowels I have been an exile, no matter how much at times I like the city, there has been a lack of . . . a lack of . . . centre, of meaning; it is a moving kaleidoscope but it has nothing to do with me at all, the deepest me. (*The Dream*, p. 125)

Conditions of geographical or cultural exile may bring on the crisis in which the self realises that nothing around it has any connection with that 'deepest me', but Crichton Smith's concern is not with the historical facts or causes of exile and cultural displacement; rather it is on the moments when the surface 'me' of society and history is stripped bare and the unknown, underlying 'me' has to be confronted or invented. The fundamental exile is not cultural or historical, but existential: the 'deepest me' has no place in the ordinary world, and it is

## The Necessity of Accident

only in and through exile that it comes to know of its own existence. Fundamental to all the forms of exile that Crichton Smith explores, in the novels as in the poetry, is the exile of language. But it is not, it is important to stress, the exile of the displaced speaker of a dying language; the situation of the Gaelic speaker is only a symbol of all languages, because no language can ever, for Crichton Smith's characters, make them 'at home' in the world. The spare simplicity of his own style merely emphasises the discordant ambiguities of his characters' inability to make their language connect with the world:

> Is this, too, a matter of language? And yet the city has its language, its winking semaphore, its signs, its advertisements, its alphabet which is not mine. (*The Dream*, p. 125)

Each of Crichton Smith's novels is the tracking of a character's consciousness through the crisis in which language ceases to correspond to a known reality – 'He was at the wrong angle to the world' (*The Dream*, p. 55) – and out of which the protagonist has to discover a new way of coping with the fragility of familiar – or at least accepted – modes of discourse.

It is from this central theme that there develops the fundamental irony on which all of Crichton Smith's fiction is based: he writes always in a grammatical and simple fashion, as though for writer and reader language *can* be taken for granted; but what we read about is his characters' struggle with the impossibility of any language fitting the nature of their experience. In his English prose, the novelist colludes with the reader in the idea of a common language, while the plot reveals the fragile contract upon which such communion of minds is based. The style of the novelist's language is like the world in which his characters move: deceptive in its simplicity, duplicitous in its intent, and yet unavoidable if we are not all to be trapped in our own private languages. Whether from the point of view of the linguistic exile – the Gaelic speaker in a world of English – or from the point of view of those who have ceased to believe in the possibility of any communication with their fellow human beings, it is on the conflict between a 'common' language and solipsistic exile in a world of entirely private meanings that Crichton Smith's fiction is focused. That dubiety is at the foundation of the terse inflections of his own prose: minimal, reductive, a deliberate limitation to what might possibly be a common ground where private meanings can become public – 'Yet their fragility was never in doubt' (*The Dream*, p. 53).

In Crichton Smith's 1987 novel, *In the Middle of the Wood*, the protagonist Ralph and his wife Linda, together with her mother, are on holiday in Yugoslavia. Linda recounts to him a dream she has had in which 'there was a record playing "Irene Good Night"'. A few paragraphs further on, we are told that 'two days later they were sitting in a restaurant in Porec and suddenly they heard tinnily played in a foreign intonation, the record "Irene Good Night", and Linda turned and looked at him, her face pale and overwrought: and he himself was startled as if the laws of reality had been broken' (p. 91). The law of reality which has been broken is also, of course, a law of fiction: novelists shouldn't construct improbable connections between their characters' private experiences and the public world in which they live; we shouldn't see the hand of the author disposing the 'reality' of his novel into patterns that will interconnect with the private worlds of the characters' inner lives, particularly by the use of coincidence. And yet Crichton Smith gestures to his own construction of the accident: it is necessary, and necessary that we should note it.

Accidents like this are always the turning points of Crichton Smith's fiction, because the accident which is a necessity of the plot, and the necessity of plot which can only be brought about by accident, focus the disparity between the apparently inevitable meanings of the 'common ground' of our social world and the entirely arbitrary and accidental foundations on which they are built. Ralph is a novelist, and the moment is a turning point in his journey into breakdown because it reveals for him the absolute separation between the structure of language and the nature of the world. In this foreign place, 'he was assailed . . . by the contingency of things, as if Yugoslavia was not a necessary place' (p. 64); cut off by language from the people of the country, he finds himself exiled from necessary meanings: 'So little he really knew about this land, its inner logic, its inner purposes' (p. 88). In exile, the world no longer communicates to him: he becomes trapped in a world which reflects back only the endless graspingness of a self that does not seek communication but only to consume: 'Yes, the whole world was a tourist centre, people seeking the final view, the final picturesque castle, the final experience. But as soon as one was seen, tasted, there was another waiting to be investigated, each in its lumpy dumbness . . .' (p. 71). The pre-packaged views of the tourist are like the accepted given of any language: it gives us back what we expected to find; it has no resistance; and it has nothing new to tell.

For Ralph, that sense of the irrelevance of language to reality leads to a linguistic alienation which gradually invades his relations even with

*The Necessity of Accident* 15

the people whose language he does speak – 'Ralph felt in a foreign country as far as Linda's mother was concerned. It was as if he couldn't speak her language nor she his' (p. 77) – until he descends into a terrible solipsism in which he 'sensed that he was being left behind, that the people who were lying roasting themselves on the rocks were ghosts from another country, that he himself was entirely alone and lost' (p. 81). Linda and her mother can both put themselves at the centre of this alien world, envelop it in their own meanings and patterns and defend themselves against its alienating effect, but Ralph is descending into a world in which there are only 'random flashes of chance' (p. 112), no necessary meanings whatsoever.

The pattern of *In the Middle of the Wood* is typical of many of Crichton Smith's novels. The characters are often grouped in threes – husband, wife, mother – and the three inhabit different domains of language. First, there is the domain of barricaded private communication that ignores the reality of the outside world: this is the domain in which Ralph's mother-in-law lives, the world of the tourists who carry meanings with them and never encounter the alien: 'As he listened to his mother-in-law it was as if they had been to two different countries. Yet what difference did it make. Yugoslavia, Czechoslovakia: Pula, Palma. Reality was what the tourists made of it' (p. 105). This is the world of the ordinary from which the protagonist is outcast. Set against it is the domain which increasingly threatens the protagonist: the world of absolute contingency in which no meaning is possible, in which nothing *makes sense* because everything is accident and chance. This is the world of characters like Douglas, the demonic mirror image of the protagonist in *The Search*: 'It seemed to him that Douglas was on the edge of madness, that he was entirely unpredictable' (p. 151); it is the world which Mrs Scott confronts in Patrick Sellar, whose words – 'But what had he just said? Something about the church being pulled down. That of course was untrue. He must be joking' (p. 22) – make no sense to her, though for him they are the inevitable outcome of the progress of the world. It is a world in which Ralph comes to depend more and more on Linda as his only connection to a pattern: 'With terror he imagined her disappearing and himself searching in alien police stations, among alleys, in formal offices, and not being able to find her' (p. 74).

That world of the absolutely contingent is where Crichton Smith's characters get lost; but often they get lost because they are in search of something else, its opposite, a world of absolute necessity. It is a necessity that is both cultural and natural, a necessity which is figured for Ralph in the Graeco-Roman remains that they visit: the amphitheatre is 'a vast empty vase of stone which hoarded the frightening power of the sun . . . There had been days of real life and real death in this ring. In the same way as the rabbit cowers before the weasel, before the dancing stoat, in its advancing playful iron rings of necessity, so too had the slaves watched the lions come' (p. 96). That Roman necessity is the necessity of tragedy: a world of inevitable but meaningful death, a world which 'would never have bothered about his mother-in-law with her swollen legs and varicose veins. They would never have listened to her banal stories, her death would not have troubled them. They would have been concerned with power, with the spear, with the javelin, with the march of the legions' (p. 81). In this inevitable world, there is no compromise; it is a world centred in necessity both culturally — a significant moment of 'history' whose 'light of brisk consciousness lit Rome, Greece, for a moment then passed on elsewhere' (p. 72) — and naturally: 'Here it was that true tragedy had begun and flowered, in the countries of the hot climates, not in the doubtful double countries of the cold and the ice' (p. 97).

Tragedy is one model of a world in which contingency has no place, and the idea of tragedy which hovers over European culture and drives the tourists into the amphitheatre for the smallest hint of its continuing existence has its own Scottish equivalent in Calvinism. Both make demands which are impossible for modern humanity — except as a ruin, a leftover, to be visited and consumed and turned back into the contingent and accidental which is our reality. The drive to escape Calvinist repression, which is so often taken to be the major theme of Crichton Smith's work, is matched by an opposite impulse, the unfulfillable desire to recover the world of necessity which is lost when one escapes from Calvinism.

These three levels — a privately imposed reality, absolute contingency, absolute necessity — form the structural basis for much of Crichton Smith's writing. His characters are continually assailed by the gap between the absolutely necessary and the absolutely contingent — a world of things full of meaning and a world full of meaningless accumulations of things; or are horrified to discover how personal and private and *imposed* are the meanings which they assumed to be inevitable. For some, to lose contact with the world of necessary meanings is a continual nostalgia, as it is for Martin, in *The Dream*, for whom the opposition between the city in which he lives and the island on which he grew up is an opposition between a world of 'random simultaneity' and a world of 'unity' (p. 125); but for others, like his wife Jean, it is the world of necessity which is destructive: the island represents to her a destructive enforcement of order that is the counterbalance to the contingency — the accident — of her own illegitimate birth. Lost in the world of contingency, Crichton Smith's characters seek the solace of the inevitable and necessary; trapped in the tragic pattern of the necessary, they seek escape into the contingent. The dialectic is endless and, in the end, unresolvable; but it is also unsustainable. The tradition of western novel-writing are founded on the possibilities of human beings learning to *see truly* and to distinguish reality from appearance. For Crichton Smith, however, that pattern is reversed: it is learning *not* to see that is important, learning to forget the apparent reality of the contingent or the necessary.

The dialectic of these opposing forces was there from the beginning of Crichton Smith's fiction: he drew it in *Consider the Lilies* in the conflict between Mrs Scott and both her husband and son: she tries to explain to her son that his father was irresponsible, 'just like a gipsy':

> This was the worst she could say about him. For gipsies wandered about, homeless. They lived in a world of their own and depended on others, for they were always stealing and frittered their time away. They had strange beliefs and wore bright clothes. They even had a language of their own. (*Consider the Lilies*, p. 62)

Theirs is the world of accident, a language without a home, the absolute antithesis of the harsh but necessary world of the Calvinist. And yet it is the purposiveness of that harsh and necessary world on which she draws when she refuses to leave her house or to betray the atheist Donald MacLeod. Those who live in the world of the necessary may seem without human sympathy, but they have a strength which is denied to those who have no such necessities to draw on. It is the temptation of an entry into that necessary world which forms the driving force behind Crichton Smith's central characters. They are all desperate to become part of, to inhabit and be at home in a world without contingency.

Salvation, for Crichton Smith's characters, comes therefore by a counter-redemption in which they come to accept the contingent as their true home, however 'meagre' (a favourite word) it is. Thus Martin, at the end of *The Dream*, comes to realise that he must annul the image of the 'three' — mother, wife and himself — which has obsessed him, a threesome which represents a cohabitation of the three perspectives:

> Without thinking, he went and pulled the curtains to block it out, that thin fragment [of moon] that floated on the edge of the sky. There were the two of them in the kitchen. He had wanted to bring his mother down here. That too was part of the dream . . . He had tried to pull his mother into his dream whereas she

> wouldn't have existed in that reality which was not for her a dream. (p. 166)

The necessity represented by his mother's world, the private enclosure of his wife's and the contingency of his own: in his dream of a return to a childhood island – but taking back with him his adult consciousness (and adult wife) – these dimensions could have fused together in a unified totality. But in the end, he has to recognise the falsehood of that dream and accept that where he sits is 'the bare negotiating table of reality' (*The Dream*, p. 167).

Martin's dream is, in effect, an effort to reconstruct his own life to have the complexity that Tom, protagonist of *The End of Autumn*, perceives in the poetry of T[om]. S. Eliot and the paintings of Picasso as he tried to explain them to his pupils:

> 'Eliot', he heard himself saying, 'can be compared with Picasso for he uses the same techniques. In the same way as in a Picasso painting we can see aparently unrelated images, such as heads of horses, candles, faces with three eyes, so we can find in Eliot as well images which apparently seem set down at random and without order.' But what did they know about Picasso and in order to tell them about Picasso he would have to . . . There was no end to the complexity and interrelatedness of the world – everything in the world must be talked of in terms of everything else. (*An End to Autumn*, p. 81).

At the moment that he tries to explain the aesthetics of the random, he comes up against the metaphysics of universal interconnectedness: the contingent dissolves in the necessary as the accidental of life ('heads of horses, candles') is turned into the inevitability of art.

As his novelistic practice has developed, Crichton Smith has become a more and more insistent challenger of the aesthetics of the modern for its assumption that it can impose the power of an aesthetic necessity on the terrible reality of the contingent. For Stephen Dedalus, exile and cunning are the routes to the discovery of the inevitable of art that can be made out of the flux of the real. For Crichton Smith, the trajectory is the opposite: exile and cunning are routes towards the overwhelming confrontation with the absolutely contingent. Crichton Smith's is an art which defiantly refuses us the central consolation that art has claimed for itself since the Romantic movement – the illusion of a higher order of meaning behind the banalities of our ordinary world. The minimalism and 'realism' of his narratives are not easy choices of the modes of popular fiction; they are strategic challenges to the aesthetics of the modern. For Crichton Smith, the necessary world is always the world of the elite: once it was the elite of the Calvinist elect, now it is the elite of the artists and intellectuals – people who know only by denying the meagre and compromising world of the ordinary which most people inhabit. So Tom, mouthing about Eliot and Picasso, watches 'what was going on outside the window, [and] saw a big yellow and blue machine with a long neck like that of a dinosaur . . .' This cubist machine is inhabited by a young man,

> And it suddenly occured to Tom to ask himself what the young man was thinking of, what his thoughts were at that particular moment. With great intensity he tried to put his own mind into that of the young man, and was repulsed again and again by a blinding darkness . . . And it came to him with utter certainty, as he watched the young man and the other one who was holding on to a bouncing pneumatic drill, that he didn't have any idea at all what the lad was thinking of, that he was as distant from the world of the young man as he was from the world of the pupils he was teaching. (*An End to Autumn*, p. 81)

Those who know the 'complexity and interrelatedness of the world' can connect with nothing in it; they are divorced from a reality which is subject to the accidental and the contingent by their commitment to a necessity that they alone can perceive. This is precisely the crisis that afflicts Ralph in *In the Middle of the Wood*:

> He had never understood 'ordinary' people. For instance they were very conscious of precedence: no one was more reactionary than an 'ordinary' person. Once on a train travelling to Edinburgh he had met a drunk who had said to him, 'I don't like you. You think I'm not good enough for you. But I'll tell you something, I'm far better than you.' The drunk had thrust his face at him like a damp torch and he had finally retreated to another compartment. Ordinary people were like another race: they read the *Sun* and the *Star*. (p. 137)

*Sun* and *Star* point to the traditional symbolic necessities of human experience, become degraded into the contingencies of a throwaway society: the elite artist writes about humanity but has no conception of the world in which it lives. The drunk who sozzles in the contingent is mirror-image to the artist who torches reality to create order and necessity. The protagonists of Crichton Smith's novels have all to be redeemed from the necessary into an acceptance of the ordinary, and therefore have to be redeemed from the aesthetics of the modern, with its high-flown belief in deep levels of meaning, into a humble acceptance of the 'meagre' but satisfying world of the real.

This is why *The Search* is a significant novel in Crichton Smith's development. It is a novel set in Australia, and the search is for a long-lost brother of the protagonist, Trevor, a writer who is visiting an Australian university for a short period. Australia, the word 'down under', is Eliot's *Waste Land* become real:

> On both sides of him was the monotonous, unforgiving landscape which hadn't tasted rain for months and on which the sun beat down day after day. His own days were now like that. In his work at Glasgow University his life had been a bookish routine, and now when that routine had been broken so brutally he couldn't cope. His failure irritated him as if it was of the deepest significance. If he didn't have the integrity to search for his own brother what did his lecturing signify. CALL IN AT JANET'S said a sign over a shop. I AM SAILING, said the voice on the cassette. (*The Search*, p. 83)

Whereas for Eliot the desert is the symbolic unifier of the disparate, revealing the true *significance* of the apparently random surfaces of life, this desert is the reverse: it is the very location of the accidental, in which 'signs' collide without context or order. *The Search* is an archetypal journey after the prodigal son, for the lost brother ('Musing upon the king my brother's wreck/And on the king my father's death before him'), drowned (Trevor thinks of 'Phlebas the Phoenician', not in the Eliotic sea but in alcohol; but it is an archetypal search exactly the reverse of Eliot's because it is its 'deep' significance which is illusory and which has to be continually undone by the banality of the actual.

Trevor constantly imagines his brother as a desperate alcoholic drop-out, possibly a child-murderer. The imaging is in part projected from his own guilt at having taken his brother's girlfriend (now Trevor's wife); he needs to imagine him thus in order to give himself the self-justifying heroic role of his brother's saviour: he will redeem his own guilt by redeeming his brother from his fallen condition. But, when he finally discovers his brother, what he discovers is the person he always was — Norman, Norm, Normal (p. 173) — an ordinary man who bears no grudges for the past and who has no deep significance to offer. He has already been *saved* in the most ordinary and banal way by his wife, Jean; Trevor's deeply significant search has none of the archetypal meanings which he, as a member of the meaningful elite, would wish to give it. His search tempts him with many possible, dramatic and oracular meanings: the demon, Douglas, is the *magi* of that meaningful world, but it is a world of illusions, dreams and fictions: the real brother is neither child-murderer nor fugitive, neither revengeful nor embittered, has no deep meanings to offer:

> Everything had come full circle, his brother was safe, he was not buried in a wilderness underneath an alien moon. And Trevor felt such piercing sorrow because of it. And yet why should he feel sorrow? Why should he not feel happy that his brother was living under a roof, with a job, and married? He didn't understand what was wrong with him. (p. 187)

What is wrong with him is the nostalgia for significance that he, as modern poet, inherits from Romanticism: what he has to learn is to live with his real brother, the real world, the Norm.

Trevor's discovery of his brother is an anticlimax – as the return to the normal will always be an anticlimax for those who seek a higher or a deeper meaning, for those to whom the desert must be an image of spiritual drought rather than simply a geological terrain inhabited by slightly unusual creatures: 'Norman hadn't needed to come to Australia to live like this' (p. 173). The world of necessity – 'Norman hadn't *needed*' – cannot accept the contingent pleasures and the accidental solutions of the ordinary. Not, at any rate, until it has returned home and passes through the corridor 'which said NOTHING TO DECLARE': he carries no baggage back from the archetypal journey; by not being lost and in need of redemption, Norman has allowed Trevor to return to *his* normal world, and to accept it.

This is why anticlimax is the mode of Crichton Smith's fictional conclusions: they refuse the aesthetics of necessary meaning, the demand for the discovery of significant conclusions. His protagonists are 'lost' not because they have failed to connect with the deeper realities of life, but precisely because they are in search of a deeper reality that makes them blind to the true value of the ordinary. For Crichton Smith, the business of the novel is to assert the value of precisely that surface, insignificant, ordinary world which the modernists condemned as banal and without spiritual significance. The world of the necessary is real only to those 'who have left the immediate, who have brooded . . . till finally it has become a haze' (*An End to Autumn*, p. 83); the world of our real existence is 'unpredictable, untidy, and in some sense inexplicable and finally perhaps holy' (p. 84). It is this contingent reality which is the true end of the spiritual search, not the ultimate, deep, hidden significances of the elite: self-discovery is the return to the ordinary, not the escape from it.

The paradox upon which this underlying conflict of the necessary and the contingent is built, of course, is that the world of the novel is itself a necessary world, one in which inevitability rules and in which the accidental and contingent cannot exist. But since the return to the accidental and contingent is the ultimate aim of the novels, it is from the denial of the necessary world of novelistic plotting that many of the characteristic effects of Crichton Smith's narrative style derive – effects which can look like blemishes of casual plot construction. Whereas in tragedy, the turning point of plot is founded on the recognition of the inevitable in a moment of *anagnorisis*, in Crichton Smith's novels the moment of revelation is the recognition of the decay of the inevitable – in effect, of the failure of plot. That is why, as his novel-writing has developed, the dénouement has been not the resolution of all the elements but an antithetical *deus ex machina*, an overthrowing of the divine power of emplotment in a return to the casual, the accidental, the deliberately trivial.

Compare, for instance, the end of *An End to Autumn* (1978) with *The Dream* (1990). *An End to Autumn* finishes with husband and wife reconciled in the coming birth of a child, and the mother-in-law who had come to live with them leaving to return to her own home. At the train station, the three family members *happen* to meet the other central character in their drama, a teacher called Ruth Donaldson:

> he felt her [Ruth Donaldson] burning, scorching, ugly and present. For a moment he thought that she was what Vera [his wife] might have become, and he suddenly took his wife's hand as if she had had a narrow escape in front of his eyes. His mother in black speeding through the countryside to her home and Ruth Donaldson were part of the one vision: they were on the rim of his world. (p. 154)

The emplotted 'accident' of the characters all being at the railway station at the same moment allows Tom to reinvent the 'centredness' of his own life, establishing a language which links himself and his wife together and shuts out the others, who 'were withdrawing into the reality and limits of [their] own life'. This is a world both of authorial and personal inevitability: the conclusion is structured by the author to allow the character a sense of inevitability of the pattern of his own experience. But at the end of *The Dream* there is a very different structure:

> And another story came into his head. It was one that Nina had told him. A friend of hers was suffering from senile dementia, and didn't recognise her own husband. She would say, 'Who are you? I

want to leave this house. I don't know this house.' And she would try to pack her things and leave . . . Her husband, who had been a seaman, used to make models of ships which he put in bottles and the wife would look at the ship for hours. The only pleasure she got was from the ship models. (p. 167)

The memory is casual and accidental for Martin; what it points to are the limits of the necessary (the ship model: art) and the contingent ('Who are you?') between which our lives are enacted. The accidentalness of the way in which the story occurs to him performs his release into a world in which the accidental is accepted: the desire for the necessary ends in illusion, madness, a forgetting and a separation. The novel therefore insists upon its own accidental and provisional conclusion:

Later he saw the moon through the window. It was a small fragment, nothing like the blaze it had once been. It was like the fractured rind of a fruit.

He thought idly before he feel asleep that if it had been a full moon he might have seen it as a ball that had flown idly over a fence and he would have gone to ask for his ball back. (p. 168)

The moon, symbol of the ideal, is reduced to a 'rind', to a child's ball. But the essential reduction is that it could have been either the 'fragment' or the 'full' moon: accident will decide: neither insists on a necessity which imposes itself on human beings unless they insist on interpreting the world in terms of the necessary.

It is for that reason that redemption in Crichton Smith's later novels comes through accident and through the acceptance of accident: it is the route back to the normal human world and out of the illusions of necessity or the threats of absolute contingency. Trevor, in *The Search*, is surrounded by Douglas' tales about his brother, and their intensity contributes to his own sense of the necessity of his journey; but in the end, as Douglas gives him the address that will lead him to his brother, he says: 'This time I'm telling you the truth. I found it out quite by chance' (p. 158). And what he is confronted with over the dinner table is the accident of his own identity: '"God knows" [Norman] said to his wife, "why my mother called him Trevor. It's not a Scottish name. She saw it in a book, I think"' (p. 180).

The plot of the novel – the necessity constructed by the author – has to be undone by the deliberately accidental. And this is why Crichton Smith's characters are so often caught up in plots, false plots or perceived but non-existent plots. The most extreme version is Ralph in *In the Middle of the Wood*, who, in his madness, comes to believe that everything that is happening to him is a plot constructed by his wife to have him incarcerated:

> The trickery went further than he had thought. They were all in the plot, not only Linda but the doctors and the nurses. Even the questions had been thought out in advance. There was a beautiful symmetry to the whole business . . . And of course Linda was behind it all, like a spider. (p. 114)

Confronted by the world of apparently absolute contingency, Ralph reverts to believing he is trapped in a world of absolute necessity, a necessity which accounts for every accident. But his determination to find the inevitable begins to break down on something that seems absolutely accidental (to us readers as well as the characters) – a Mexican hat adorning the lamp in his room: 'He was sure it wasn't a nurse's prank. There were too many wrong things, too many coincidences. But what was the inner meaning of leaving a Mexican hat? He was sure it must have some deep inner significance. An allegory, symbolism. But he couldn't work it out' (p. 130). Like the author and reader he is, Ralph must have everything become significant, be part of the plot; but Crichton Smith's plot reverses that demand and insists that it must incorporate the absolutely accidental, for it is only by the admission of the accidental that we can accept the relativity of our systems of meaning, their inevitable lack of completion.

That sense of being the centre of a necessary structure, of an emplotment over which they have no control, haunts all of Crichton Smith's protagonists, from Mrs Scott's son in *Consider the Lilies* who knows that he is surrounded by his mother's spies (pp. 89–91), to Trevor in *The Search* who feels 'himself at the centre of a devious intrigue which he was not equipped to unravel' (p. 64). The paranoia of a world organised in a pattern which controls and to which everyone else but you has access is never far from the characters' consciousness. But it is that emplotted world which they have to throw off in order to be liberated: they have to discover the necessity of accident, the incompletion of all systems of understanding, the provisional world of the ordinary. The problem, as Ralph discovers, is that it is very difficult to open oneself to the reality of accident:

> It occurred to him while the psychologist was talking that reality was far more fragile than he had thought, that whatever picture of reality one chose could be corroborated by information pouring in and being filtered, that a madman was the most rigorously logical of all beings. (*In the Middle of the Wood*, p. 183)

The desire and the need to deny contingency and to embrace inevitability run so deep that the actual can always be moulded to suit the pattern of one's desires: the protagonist of fiction is always the plaything of the author's desire to achieve that inevitability, and Crichton Smith's protagonists are always fighting off the plots by which their author surrounds them:

> He knew suddenly why Hamlet needed Horatio as a witness, why Horatio had to be left behind to tell the truth as he saw it, to explain the extraordinary pattern of events, the murders, the accidents. The most terrible thing of all would be to be in a world without witnesses. (*In the Middle of the Wood*, p. 183)

It is one of the major achievements of Iain Crichton Smith's novels that they act as witness not to the inevitability of art's patterns, but to the necessity of life's accidents.

# Three

## Ways of Losing:
## The Radio Work of Iain Crichton Smith

### Stewart Conn

Iain Crichton Smith is not a 'radio writer' in the sense of having written predominantly for the medium over the years. Nor do his radio pieces demand complex sound sequences or elaborate recording procedures: he is no more seduced by the trappings of the medium than impeded by its strictures. Against this, his frequent forays confirm that radio's potency resides in its intimacy and immediacy, rather than in any obligatory flaunting of 'technique'. His clarity, economy and sensitivity to speech nuances cater for the *inner* ear, as does his instinct for tapping the unease that lurks under what is said.

His first works broadcast in English other than poems and stories were a verse dialogue between Knox and Columba[1] and a solo-voice serialisation of 'Consider the Lilies'.[2] The novel observes, with deep psychological insights, the Old Woman at the mercy of the Clearances and betrayed by her Church. The veracity with which her self-awareness and mode of speech are conveyed stems, however, from a sustained simplicity, indeed purity, of expression true to her unsophisticated personality and way of life.

In their concentration on what is *said*, Crichton Smith's plays are themselves succinct and lucid. Indeed it can be difficult, not least given the hit-or-miss element in his scripts, to anticipate how effectively they might come off the page, i.e. to *hear* them. Their sparseness and brevity can seem dramatically slight, even facile. Only after rereading may it emerge that the speakers are not lacking in dimension but are stripped to emotional and linguistic essentials. He is not drawn to the spurious 'reality' of much radio drama, nor are his characters stylised so much as *crystallised*: he depicts all we need to hear from and know of them in order to identify them as moral beings and assess what the playwright, through them, is saying about ourselves.

Significant too is what remains *un*said. His silences are not 'empty' but eloquent and meaningful. Nor need those speakers who exist in a limbo of their own or his devising lack a social context. In *On the Bus*,[3] the driver's commentary, and the engine sound, punctuate and accompany a collage of exchanges among passengers who include a jaundiced mother and daughter and an irritable middle-aged couple. At one point, the bus stops and a Hermit appears, launches into a maudlin rendering of 'The heather-scented hills o' Bonnie Doune', then passes round his tin. They resent his being not 'real' but a tawdry fake, out of tune with the romantic landscape they are passing through but from which they remain conveniently remote. His presence disturbs, even threatens them, because he is disillusioning. The tour resumes. Tentative attempts at new relationships fail; the girl's hopes wilt; a disgruntled passenger buries his head in a book. By the next stop, they have reverted to isolated, disparate units:

[*Movement as they leave the bus*]

*Frank*: Let me help you with your coat, Irene.

*Irene*: Yes. Thank you.

[*More movement*]

*Harry*: A big plate of chips, eh, Martha? D'you no' fancy that?

*Martha*: Ssh! What'll people think of you? Chips? And they all look so la de da.

*Harry*: With vinegar. Plenty of vinegar. Just as in the old days, love. Just as now, too. [Laughs. They both laugh] Driver, tell me, do you ever get tired of us?

*Driver*: No, can't say I do. No, can't say I ever do.

*Martha*: Well now, Harry, if that isn't the best compliment. Don't forget your raincoat. It may rain.

*Harry*: But it's blazing down.

*Martha*: You never know, dear. Just take your raincoat. Things can change.

[*Lost atmosphere*]

For them, no change or development seems likely: they remain cocooned by inhibition, by petty and inverted snobberies and the routine trivia of their lives.

Among the most accessible, and to me the most mellow of Crichton Smith's conversation pieces is *By the Sea*.[4] A genteel elderly couple meet on the seafront of a small resort. The background which each lays claim to is revealed as a sham: he is not a retired naval officer but a pensioner on an old folks' outing; her memories of horse-riding as a child in India are invented:

>*Woman*: My father was, as I have said, a colonel.
>*Man*: A brigadier.
>*Woman*: Pardon?
>*Man*: You said a brigadier.
>*Woman*: Oh, of course. Your mistake is quite natural. At first he was a colonel and then he was a brigadier. When we were growing up he was a colonel . . . I don't like seagulls much, do you?
>*Man*: I'm afraid I don't know much about seagulls.
>*Woman*: I would have thought that being a naval man you would have had much contact with seagulls.
>*Man*: I didn't have much time. There was much paperwork as well.
>*Woman*: I see. [Pause] Anyway as I was saying, when I was growing up in Edinburgh we were a very musical family. Mozart has always been one of my favourite composers. Beethoven I have always found very noisy. We do not like noise in Edinburgh.

He buys ice-creams, and they exchange addresses with a view to meeting next summer. Each refrains from exposing the other's frail masquerade:

>*Man*: Tell me one last thing. Is it true that you visit the Edinburgh Festival?
>*Woman*: I'm afraid that . . .
>*Man*: I see. You are indeed a good story-teller.
>*Woman*: And you. I shall look forward to very interesting letters. Till next summer then.
>*Man*: Till next summer.
>   [*He walks briskly away*]
>*Woman*: [To herself] Next summer.
>   [*She sits there. From the distance comes the sound of laughter and fairground music. 'I'll be seeing you always'. It plays on, then fades to silence*]

With the minimum of props, *By the Sea* is a poignant study of loneliness. Crichton Smith neither satirises the couple nor deprives them of dignity. This is true to his belief that 'people erect a fence to protect themselves. If you break it you could really destroy them. And everyone, not just the old, needs illusion — so I don't make fun of them'.[5] The wistfulness of the dialogue is aurally 'framed' throughout by the fairground music, rising and falling on the breeze.

In 1978, Radio Scotland commissioned six half-hour dramatic monologues under the heading 'In the person of . . .'.[6] In the first, a librarian returns at night to his empty premises:

> [*feet echoing hollowly on floor and then chair being pulled back and someone sitting down*]
>
> Well here I am.
>
> Midnight again. Nice to have the key and sit here, in command of everything. In the quietness.
>
> Like a king on a throne. In command of all the books, the whole library.
>
> Wordsworth over there. Kant over here. Annie S. Swan by the door. The whole public library under my dominion . . .
>
> [*laughs*]
>
> I don't know why I keep coming back here at night. Even though I am the Head Librarian and I have the right to. There's no law that says that I can't come back at night. I might be working late, checking the tickets, what homes have got chickenpox and the mumps, and maybe the Black Death.

Soon his peaceful universe is disrupted by a drunken refrain, real or in his mind, of 'Flower of Scotland'. The second speaker, a General, is haunted by the screams of those dead soldiers whose forgiveness he begs. The world in his head is that of Mons and Passchendale:

> I feel funny tonight. The moon, it's so bright. Perhaps I should draw the curtains. It doesn't matter, I never see anybody, it's only the screams I hear. They're too careful to show themselves. Maybe we taught them that, to use camouflage . . .
>
> They've grown very cunning, all those years.

The disjunctive phrases, with their mundane detail, assume a mesmeric significance. So do the more tortuous syntax and terms of reference of the Actor, who first sees himself as Hamlet, clad in Elizabethan collar and hose and encased in a hall of mirrors; then his whole world a Conspiracy of Players: an extension of Shakespeare's metaphor, 'All the world's a stage'. Like Hamlet too, he finds everyone against him. Trapdoors open at his feet. Even Catherine, his loved one, when she says 'I love you' and 'till death do us part', is only acting. Seeing 'no street down which we can go after we have been in the theatre which is not itself part of the theatre', his solution is to change the ending of the play: tired of killing the King night after night, he will at that point kill *himself*.

*Napoleon*, in contrast, opens with deceptive informality:

> [*Sound of Sea*]
> I don't like it here. I never liked it here.
> I look at it and it reminds me of things.
> Like Villeneuve for instance. He was no good.
> He failed me. Nice chap but he failed me.
> The world is full of nice chaps and they fail you. And some of them
>    betray you.
> Like . . .
> Someone else I can't remember.
> Someone like Josephine but not Josephine.
> [*Pause*]
> That seagull now. It's got a beak like Wellington. White.
> White coat. Everything white.

The speaker is not Napoleon, but is locked in the obsessive pretence that he is. In what could be a soliloquy from a madhouse, he flees from rows of Cossacks dressed in white, steps into the sea and is engulfed — still wearing his crown. The last two monologues presage Crichton Smith's subsequent plays. A Schoolteacher's farewell address develops into a tirade against the system, as he accuses his colleagues of the treason of the clerks. And a terminal Patient berates those in his ward and the wife whom he decrees must gain nothing from his will, 'signed by me in the sign of Capricorn now just before I go away from them all to the fields of asphodel or such . . . Just before . . .'.

Paranoia stems, throughout, from the break-up of Order. The Librarian was brought up in a private world of books:

> I would read them all. There I was holding the fort with my
>    Foreign Legion cap on. It was difficult going in to tea after
>    that. After I had been in the desert, after I had saved the
>    *Hispaniola*. With the salt water still on my lips. That is why I
>    became a Librarian, I think. That was why I took the
>    responsibility. Of holding the fort.

The Teacher's guilt is overwhelming:

> We have gone wrong. We have taken the wrong path. We have
>    done what we should not have done, as St Paul said. We
>    should have been stronger than we have been. I have been in
>    this school now for forty years and what have I seen? I have
>    seen strength give place to weakness . . . We have sold our

# The Radio Work

souls for a mess of pottage. We have abdicated our responsibility and our strength.

As custodians as well as purveyors of learning, the Schoolteacher and the Classics Master shoulder a double burden. In the fragmentation of Society, they detect the disintegration of a cultural order – and of the mind. Despair seeps from an awareness that *neither* fort can any longer be held. Each monologue, in its selected idiom, bears Crichton Smith's imprint, depicting with intensity and delicacy, and at times visceral insight, a mind at the end of its tether.

His outrageous comic energy and stylistic versatility register very differently in *Goodman and Death Mahoney*.[7] A spoof western, its raunchy lyrics have a delicious insouciance and rhythmic verve. It opens:

> So he rode out of the hills in his black hat, black boots and black shirt, wearing a black gun and humming a black tune. The drunken bum sat up when he saw him coming, the drunken judge stopped playing draughts, the crooked saloon owner ran to meet him . . . The pianist played faster and faster, the dancer danced more dizzily, the paunchy sheriff looked into his eyes that were as black as dominoes.

There is room (remembering the title of his early collection of poems *The Law and the Grace*) for a favourite *leitmotif*:

> I learnt you to draw to be the Law
>     and do the Devil down
> So take your place by God's own grace
>     as the Shinin' Light of the Town.

Goodman's reply, before shootin' up the town, is a further reminder of the almost manic prodigality of his wit:

> Dear Ma, you are a terrible bore
>     and you're pretty ugly too
> you shut me up like a fly in a cup
>     so I didn't know what to do.
>
> Accordin' to Freud I've a pure unalloyed
>     Oedipus complex, so
> I aim to abjure all that and abjure
>     your boring calico.

As for a moral, the spitoon-happy old Cowpuncher sums up:

> All I know is, Goodman was as bad as Death Mahoney. ''cept when he shot you he usually had a reason for it, but that didn't do you no good if you was the one who was bein' shot.

We return to a world of dark undercurrents in a trio of short plays, self-contained but with overlapping themes.[8] *The Voices* starts early on Christmas morning. A man hears an echoing cry from space, saying 'L . . . o . . . v . . . e'. When he records this and plays the machine back, nothing is there. He receives a letter seemingly from his wife, driven to suicide by the pain of cancer. Helpless, he howls like a wolf. Children sing carols. Snow falls. An obsessive music of the spheres absorbs him, resonating within the play's formal framework with a scarcely communicable sense of loss:

> *Wilkins*: You can't go on like this, sir, listening at windows and doors.
> *Man's voice*: There's nothing in there, is there, Wilkins? In the cupboard?
> *Wilkins*: No, sir.
> *Man's voice*: Her face . . . her voice . . . where is it? I missed her. I missed her all the time. The pain, Wilkins, it's everywhere. Never such pain. Is the Universe made of pain, Wilkins?
> *Wilkins*: Goodnight, sir . . .
> *Voice*: L . . . o . . . v . . . e.
> *Man's voice*: Ssh, it's not my voice. It's there, isn't it? Surely it's her voice. No, it's not mine, it's hers. Surely?
> [*Silence*]

In *The Letter*, a small girl's homework triggers off her mother's long-nursed suspicions over a wartime letter which her husband received from France – signed 'Claire'. At the time, she had spent a retaliatory night with a man now dead. Things were not, however, as she thought: he had merely protected Claire from a German soldier. Not only that, but the girl, only sixteen when the letter came four years later, had been a mere child at the time. They continue to talk not so much to as *across* one another. His innocence, and the wife's having not after all been unfaithful, fail to bring them closer. Too much has been irredeemably lost:

> *Frances*: So it wasn't really important after all.
> *Jack*: O, but it *was*. That's what you don't see. It was very important.
> *Jean*: [Distant] La table . . . la fenêtre . . . la table . . .

In *Murdo*, derived from a published story, a former bank clerk, now a would-be writer, faces that 'mountain of white', the blank page. Sifting through his life, he encounters his former Bank Manager. At the local library, he asks for *War and Peace* by Hugh MacLeod, or failing that *The Brothers Karamazov* 'about three brothers and their struggle for a croft'.

His father appears on 'a fine *blowdy* day', to talk himself into a dram. 'Keep off the corned beef,' Murdo warns: 'it has a strange poison in it, from the east, which attacks old-age pensioners.' 'Go and drown yourself' is the reply. Murdo's mind is slipping: he sees blood on the walls and a vampire in the house, fails to recognise his wife and applies for a job in London as a shepherd. Ultimately, he is reconciled to confronting the mysterious White Mountain — and to climbing it. The play's logic is delightfully anarchic, its inconsequential conclusion giving it the flavour of an *aperitif* sharpening the appetite for more.

Deploying a variety of acoustic and other effects, *The Smile* is 'a record of an odd evening, merging into night'.[9] The philosopher Kant muses on the categorical imperative ('a bell, that rings through the Universe'); a young lady who offers him a 'good time' steals his watch; and a ranting Christopher Columbus figure arrives in the throes of emphysema. The duplicity of language is again explored. Illusion gives way to delusion, to the predestined illogic of our Universe. The *smile* is on the face of a sick woman whose husband, convinced she is dying, preserves suspicions that she has had a relationship with a student:

*Man*: So I asked her.

*Kant*: And what happened?

*Man*: She smiled. But what was the meaning of that smile? Did she mean it was silly to ask her such a question at such a time? Did it mean . . . remembering that student . . . ?

*Kant*: Look up at the heavens: the Categorical Imperative is smiling.

*Man*: I don't understand.

*Kant*: The smile is the smile on the face of the Universe. I think, sir, that the smile meant that she did not betray you.

*Man*: Goodnight. God bless you.

*Kant*: The Categorical Imperative bless you. [*The Man goes*] Maybe she *was* lying. Laughing at him. It is the ultimate irony.

The central figure from the novella-length *Mr Trill in Hades* re-emerges in one of two conversation pieces commissioned by BBC Radio 3.[10] It opens with Mr Trill's obituary:

[*Close: sound effects of wine bottle being opened*]

*Joyce*: [Off mic.] O, listen, Dave, Mr Trill's dead.

*Dave*: Mr Trill? Mr Trill? *Of course*, Mr Trill. How old was he?

*Joyce*: It says here [pause] seventy.

*Dave*: Yes that would be right . . . I worked out that he would be about that much older than us. That's why . . .

*Joyce*: Can't hear you. What did you say?

>    *Dave*: That's why I thought it strange he wasn't in the war.
>    [*Joyce comes into the same room*]
>    *Joyce*: Don't you remember, Dave, his voice. [*She imitates him*] Of course it is important to get the absolute ablative right, Simmons. Even in time of war.

During the War, their crossword-compiling classics master had, despite heart trouble, been a code-breaker, not the coward Dave assumed. In retrospect too, he becomes warmer and more dignified than either ever suspected. Dave is chastened by the memory of his assumptions and mockery of Mr Trill. The pair of them round things off by toasting this new realisation of him and his beloved ablative absolute.

*The Visitor*, with its glint of the supernatural, is a less playful indictment of bourgeois complacency. Late at night, Mr Harris (yet another schoolteacher) rehearses his retirement speech to his wife. The doorbell rings. Enter 'Mr Heine', who claims to be a former pupil of Mr Harris. Now working with an advertising agency, he comes out with jocular jingles, but this is a prelude to claiming that in the old days, with their red-haired son as ringleader, his classmates had regularly bullied him, beating him up in the boiler-room when the janitor was away, and chanting:

> Dirty Jew, dirty Jew,
> they stuck your body on with glue.

The parents ridicule this. Heine recalls Mr Harris deriding his efforts at poetry with 'a long disquisition on the advantages of rhyme' – now his strength. When Mr Harris enquires why Heine is visiting them in the first place, the reply is that he wanted to contribute to the presentation. As Mr Harris insists he put away his chequebook, Mrs Harris adds chillingly: 'And that pen, Mr Heine. We do not want your Jewish money'. The visitant departs. An owl hoots . . .

>    *Mrs Harris*: Let's go to bed then.
>    *Mr Harris*: Yes dear. Let us go to bed. [*In a sudden access of rage*] I haven't rehearsed my speech.
>    *Mrs Harris*: It doesn't matter, dear.
>    *Mr Harris*: I shall think of something. I'm sure I shall think of something. Will you switch the light off or shall I?
>    *Mrs Harris*: [*recedes*] You do it, dear.
>    [*Sound of owl hooting*]
>    *Mr Harris*: That' bloody owl.
>    [*Fade on hoot of owl*]

One reviewer, calling the two pieces 'delicious interludes', expressed the view that 'so long as writers like Crichton Smith continue to ply and perfect their art, we can be confident that words can still be reclaimed, any time we choose, for that beauty, economy and truth-bearing significance that they so often seem to have lost'.[11]

I see his radio output, while peripheral to the grandeur of his major achievements, as an invigorating complement to them. His plays probe states of mind and areas of loss, unerringly exposing human foible and vulnerability. Their rearguard action against possession of the mind by spurious authority figures is consistent with his distaste, expressed in a Radio 3 feature, for 'any form of ideology'.[12] At the same time, in his handling of human relationships, he restricts himself to the tip of the iceberg, leaving us to deduce what lies below. On the evidence of the plays, this constitutes love, bounded by pain and suffering; yearning to be infinite, but stoically conscious that it cannot be. I see their true arena, in keeping with the themes central to his poetry, as that tremulous and vulnerable territory, the exiled human heart.

Ultimately too, everything hinges on the tone and texture of his dialogue. Eschewing the sensuousness of his earlier verse in particular, the plays — in the accuracy and integrity of the *language* through which his compassion expresses itself — appear pared to the bone. One of his essays says, of Lewis, that it gave him 'images of the sea, and the bare mind'.[13] In relaying the austereness and moods of the former, and the bleakness of the latter, he is unimpeachably true to his origins and challengingly in tune with the times in which we live.

NOTES

1. *St Columba and John Knox* in 'Three Poets': 09.01.66/SHS.
2. *Consider the Lilies*, abridged in seven parts: reader Bryden Murdoch: from 02.07.67/SHS.
3. *On the Bus* (30 minutes): 21.03.68/SHS.
4. *By the Sea* (30 minutes): 30.03.76/R4S, repeated 15.09.87/R3.
5. ICS, speaking to Joy Hendry: in 'Radio Times' 17.09.87.
6. *In the Person of . . .*, comprising *The Librarian, The General, The Actor, Napoleon, The Schoolteacher* and *The Patient*, for performance by Tom Fleming (30 minutes × 6): from 23.11.78/R4S.
7. *Goodman and Death Mahoney*, with commissioned music by Robert Pettigrew (30 minutes): 08.07.79/R4S, repeated 20.01.80/R3.
8. *The Voices, The Letter* and *Murdo*, as *Ways of Losing* (60 minutes): 29.12.81/RS.
9. *The Smile* (35 minutes): 23.04.85/RS.
10. *Mr Trill* (25 minutes) and *The Visitor* (25 minutes): 26.08.88/R3.
11. Joyce McMillan in 'The Glasgow Herald', 27.08.88.
12. *The Island is Always With You*, compiled by Andrew Mitchell (45 minutes): 27.11.88/R3.

13. 'Between Sea and Moor' in *Towards the Human*: Lines Review Editions (Macdonald Publishers, 1986).

[*The Letter* and *Murdo* directed by Patrick Rayner; other programmes directed by Stewart Conn.]

[SHS: Scottish Home Service; R4S: Radio 4 Scotland; RS: Radio Scotland; R3: Radio 3; R4: Radio 4]

# Four

## Double Man at a Culloden of the Spirit: Reflections on the Poetry of Iain Crichton Smith*

### George Watson

Iain Crichton Smith is an exemplary poet: exemplary in the honorific sense as one of Scotland's best poets in both English and in Gaelic, and exemplary also in that his work as a whole — the poems, the short stories, the novels and the essays — focuses issues of great interest and significance to anyone from Scotland, Ireland or Wales (though even to invoke the Celtic fringe is to limit unduly the issues involved): cultural dispossession, the relation of language to cultural identity, the problems and challenges of bi-lingualism, the meaning of tradition, and the parish to the universe (to use terms familiarised by the Irish poet Patrick Kavanagh).

He writes about a great range of subjects and in a great variety of literary forms, and frequently shows himself intimate with and perceptive about the lives of the urban bourgeoisie, thus escaping 'that element of bravado which takes pleasure in the notion that the potato-patch is the ultimate'.[1] Freud and Hiroshima are just as likely to turn up in his work as Duncan Bàn Macintyre. Yet he occasionally betrays anxiety about being seen as 'merely' a Highland writer condemned to rehearse Highland themes. He should not worry. No single writer can give us all the world, and anyone who can so memorably give us a vital part of it deserves our gratitude. I propose in this paper to concentrate on his Highland — or island — poetry, however, and without apology or any imputation of restrictedness to Crichton Smith's vision. As he himself remarks of Hugh MacDiarmid,[2] one must look always in any writer for those elements where his imaginative and verbal energies seem most obvious; and I find these, and what Seamus Heaney calls the 'watermark' of this particular sensibility, in those peoms which deal with Lewis and the Highland experience in general.

* This chapter first appeared in *Verse* 7 (no. 2), Summer 1990.

The strengths and appeal of that poetry are obvious, but perhaps need to be emphasised in a day and age when the groves of Academe are encroaching perilously on Parnassus, and where, as a result, poetry is too often valued for its TPQ (thesis-producing qualities) or for ER (explication ratio). TPQ and ER may be related to culture-babble, the factitious noise generated by and surrounding contemporary metropolitan centres. The last thing I want to suggest is that Iain Crichton Smith is a kind of Robinson Crusoe; the point is rather that the consistency and integrity of his imagination (and even his scruples about that consistency, his anxiety about repetition) mark him, and his poetic world, as, mercifully, from London far, and as free of the dangers of the steady Manhattanising or Los Angelisation of the imagination.

What Crichton Smith's poetry at its best offers us is an elemental world seen through an elemental imagination – as he says himself, Lewis gave him 'images of the sea, and the bare mind': a bare, stripped-down experience, 'life without art, the minimum' (*A Life*, Carcanet, Manchester, 1986, p. 11). It is fitting that 'Poem of Lewis' should stand at the beginning of the *Selected Poems, 1955–80*:[3] its imagery of barren rock, open skies, gales and the heave of the sea recurs through his volumes. Here is a world with no place for arabesques, for the baroque or the rococo, either in living or in art. 'Face of an Old Highland Woman' is superbly characteristic:

> This face is not the Mona Lisa's
> starting from a submarine
> greeness of water. There's no grace
> of any Renaissance on the skin
> but rocks slowly thrust through earth
> a map with the wind going over stone
> beyond the mercies of Nazareth.
> Here is the God of fist and bone
>
> a complex twisted Testament
> two eyes like lochs staring up
> from heather gnarled by a bare wind
> beyond the art and dance of Europe.

At least as far back as Edwin Muir, the sense that Scotland missed out on the European Renaissance, to her detriment, has been a familiar theme.[4] It is appropriate that Crichton Smith should so concentrate and personalise the large aspects of cultural history, and further, in the poem's own sinewy spareness, imply his own trust in the desolation of this particular rock-bred reality, greater than that in the seductive, watery graces of the Renaissance.

# A Culloden of the Spirit

A poet cannot smother or disown – even should he want to, as Yeats bemoaned the popularity of 'The Lake Isle of Innisfree' – his most anthologised pieces; and if 'Sunday Morning Walk' is one of Crichton Smith's most anthologised poems, this is because it encapsulates perfectly what I have called the elemental qualities of his art. How perfectly timed, in the fifth stanza, into the wonderfully evoked *dolce far niente* of a summer Sunday's nicely classicised eroticism, comes crashing the grim symbol of *memento mori*:

> And occupied thus, I came where a dead sheep lay
> close to a fence, days gone. The flies were hissing and buzzing
> out of the boiling eyes, wide open as day . . .
> Three crows famished yards off. Live sheep grazed far
> from the rotting carcass. The jaw, well-shaved, lay slackly
> there on the quiet grass. The household air
> was busy with buzzing like fever.

Except, of course, that it isn't 'a symbol' of *memento mori* – it is the thing itself: bare, unaccommodated dead sheep (one can only admire the quiet brutality of the unadorned 'days gone' and the grimly comic realism of 'household air').

It may seem paradoxical to say that this most compelling of Crichton Smith poems is, perhaps, not representative of the bulk of his poetry. One can place certain poems beside it – 'In Luss Churchyard', 'Entering Your House' and 'At the Sale' – all different poems, but sharing with 'Sunday Morning Walk' a basis in incident, vividly remembered and visualised. They all seem to be what he calls, unduly disparagingly, 'poems of the moment';[5] on the whole, his poetry is more meditative and 'philosophic'. However, one can only respect the integrity of a mind which turns aside from such aesthetic and emotional poetic victories, not, in his view, sufficiently comprehensive. For Crichton Smith, the moment is not enough; the condition must be explored.

In one of his essays, he praises the 'immediate sensuousness' with which his fellow islander Derick Thomson can evoke the world from which they both have come. Given 'Poem of Lewis', 'Face of an Old Highland Woman' and 'Sunday Morning Walk', one might boggle at the implication that Crichton Smith lacks the same touch; but it is true that in his work there is a deeply-rooted suspicion of what he calls the 'glitteringly aesthetic'. In a paragraph where he shows an easy familiarity with the great Russians Turgenev, Tolstoy and Chekhov, he remarks of Nabokov's undoubted talent: 'can we not say that he is a writer at play dealing only with dilettantish enigmas?'.[6] Crichton Smith believes in 'poems morally shaped',[7] and is wary of what Seamus Heaney has spoken of to the present writer, 'the lasciviousness of the word'. Let me quote Crichton Smith's sturdy view:

> Metaphor can sometimes be used to conceal insoluble contradictions in life, and Yeats's poem 'Easter 1916' did not solve the Irish crisis, it only clarified it. In the end society lives and works outside the metaphor, and to think that the metaphor solves anything except the problems set by the poet would be silly and unrealistic. Beyond the poems of Seamus Heaney, beautiful though they are, the masked men will stand above the draped coffins saluting an empty heaven with their guns.[8]

The poetry underwrites the critical position. It is frequently in favour of plainness, for the empirical reality, and against large gestures of an emotional or rhetorically grandiloquent sort. As he writes in 'Deer on the High Hills: A Meditation' (XIV):

> There is no metaphor. The stone is stony . . .
> The rain is rainy and the sun is sunny.
> The flower is flowery and the sea is salty . . .
> The stars are starry, and the night nocturnal.

There is an unflinching quality in Crichton Smith's imagination, and what might, on first sight, seem like banality in the poem just quoted, comes to seem a rock-like (for once the cliché is justified) integrity of vision, as in 'On Looking At the Dead':

> This is a coming to reality.
> This is the stubborn place. No metaphors swarm
> around that fact, around that strangest thing,
> that being that was and now no longer is . . .
>     Nothing more real than this.
> It beats you down to it, will not permit
> the play of imagery, the peacock dance,
> the bridal energy or mushrooming crown
> or any blossom. It only is itself.
> It isn't you. It only is itself.

One is back to the dead sheep; yet one cannot deny the poetic force which Crichton Smith manages to squeeze from such, literally, dry bones:

> You must build from the rain and stones
> till you can make
> a stylish deer on the high hills,
> and let its leap be unpredictable!
>     ('Dear on the High Hills', V)

# A Culloden of the Spirit

All this distrust of metaphor, the uneasiness before 'the play of imagery, the peacock dance', lends a dramatic tension to all of Crichton Smith's poetry – in his work we see very clearly enacted the old, never-ending battle between moral *gravitas* and the irresponsibility of the flighty Muse. To be a poet, yet to be so aware of the dangers of the aesthetic attitude is a problem which, yet again, he faces uncompromisingly, as in two poems from a recent collection, *The Village and Other Poems* (Carcanet, Manchester, 1989). 'Slowly' belongs to the exclusively abstract side of his art, a poem which proposes that aesthetic categories may overlap unhealthily with political and moral categories:

Slowly we are adopted by the words . . . slowly we are other.
We are the aesthetic critics, not the ethical.
The play is a playful event.
Even agony becomes beautiful.
Even the broken heads are questionable.
Even the dictator's talent is in doubt.

Crichton Smith's distaste for 'aesthetic critics' in that poem, though obvious, never comes to poetic life; however, 'Girl and Child' perfectly brings together, in finely-judged dissonance, the scuffling world of Thatcher's Britain and the perfectly chiselled and marmoreal world of Homer:

Trudging through the air of Homer for a sight of the bruised
girl with the child
who stops at kiosks to wait for a telephone to ring
with his voice out of the clouds that have grown suddenly callous
and a ring which she has not yet sold winking on her finger,
and the child's blue eyes staring out of its temporary nest,
I found only the scene where Andromache holds her child
up to Hector
and with small fingers it touches the big shadowy helmet
before his death in a whirl of vulnerable dust.
And the battle is different and for the girl there is no Homer
and there is no memorial among the slums and lights of the city
as she stares into the windows at the bridal dresses and the furs
and slowly licks her lips as if she was tasting the last of her milk.

Crichton Smith clearly does not trust the way in which the seductions of lyric poetry can prettify reality; occasionally, one senses that he – for good reasons to be discussed – distrusts language itself, and this love-hate relationship with his very medium of words does produce what Roderick Watson has finely called his 'visionary existentialism'.[9]

Now, clearly all this can be linked to the Calvinism which is Crichton Smith's inheritance; but it would be insultingly reductive to tie it solely to that. In the face of life's grimness, many poets have expressed their sense of guilt at the incongruity between the brute facts and the capriciousness of the imagination in handling those facts (one could make an interesting list of poems more or less on this subject, from Keat's *Hyperion* down to Heaney's 'Exposure' and 'Sandstone Keepsake' — and of course, to Crichton Smith's lyrics). And, from a different angle, one might be tempted to ask if the guilty — or the doubters — may not have a case. A recent book, Leo Bersani's *The Culture of Redemption* (Harvard, 1990), is, for once, quite well described by its blurb, which says that his book

> does battle with a pervasive view in modern culture: the idea that art can save us from the catastrophes of history and sexuality . . . The art that thinks it can redeem life — make it whole, correct its errors, sublimate its passions — trivialises both life and, paradoxically, art.

One can imagine Crichton Smith nodding at least a guarded assent to this.

One cannot mention Calvinism and not discuss further its relation to Crichton Smith's poetry. It is not surprising that he should stress the narrowness of the Calvinistic ethos, its fundamentalism, its dismissiveness of art, its tenacity and inescapability (see 'Poem of Lewis', 'About that Mile', 'The Law and the Grace', 'I Build an Orange Church', among many other poems). What is characteristic is his willingness to see the strengths of an ethos which, fundamentally, he dislikes. 'The Good Place' describes a bourgeois paradise — 'the adults friendly and the children happy . . . cardboard yachts heel[ing] stiffly round the bay', yet acknowledges that something is missing:

> You'd say it was a good place except that sometimes
> a wish for terror and for lightning strode
> down the great mountains to the village rhymes
> to find in lakes the wicked face of God.

Fundamentalism has its problems; but at least — and by definition — it mocks superficialities.

While Crichton Smith's 'Note on Puritans' accuses 'these men of singleness and loss of grace', it also admires, however ambiguously, a kind of ultimate bravery in them:

> That was great courage to have watched that fire,
> not placing a screen before it as we do

> with pictures, poem, landscapes, a great choir
> of mounting voices which can drown the raw
> hissing and spitting of flame with other fire.

He also appreciates, however regretfully, the wider socio-cultural role of the church in some of the island communities, in terms which can be easily transposed to the Irish context. He regrets that 'one of the "gifts" of this religion has been a weakening of the will, a fatalism', yet acknowledges that the church 'at least offers stability in a shifting world':

> If we should mock the rigidities of such a religion we must also remember that rigidity is the price one pays for insecurity: if there is no real home than an unreal one will be provided.[10]

While his poetry memorably conveys the lived experience of Lewis, I wish to turn now to the wider cultural and linguistic problems and issues enacted – often passionately – in Crichton Smith's writing. His analysis of the cultural situation of the islands and Highlands is perceptive, comprehensive, and comprehensively pessimistic. It is strengthened to precisely the extent that he refuses to idealise: he recognises the claustrophobia (especially in the religious sense) of the islands, their conservatism and hostility to change, and their distrust of individuality, and rejects the obvious, oversimplified stereotype, in remarking 'the islands were never an Eden from which we were thrust by the sword of economics: it may have been a home but it was never an Eden . . . To grow up on an island is a special . . . but . . . not an ideal experience'.[11] At the same time, he is passionately aware of the strengths and positives – the sense of community, rootedness, and of the freedom from the pressure of perparing a face to meet the faces that you meet, which is one of the greatest penalties of exile: 'When one is in harmony with the community then one's identity is reflected back from the others by a plain mirror and not by the exaggerating or attenuating mirrors that one sees in fairs'.[12] And, since he sees these positives as not only outweighing the negatives, but further, as greatly threatened, the major tone of Crichton Smith's writing is one of lament.

For Iain Crichton Smith is the same man as Ian Mac a' Ghobhainn, whose first languge is, and much of whose writing is in, Gaelic, which he sees as in possibly irreversible decline. As he writes in his own translation of 'Am Faigh a' Ghàdhlig Bàs?' ('Shall Gaelic Die?')

> Advertisements in neon, lighting and going out, 'Shall it . . . shall it . . . shall Gaelic . . . shall it . . . shall Gaelic die?'
> He who loses his language loses his world. The Highlander who loses his language loses his world.

While he writes with great and justified anger of 'the waste, the dreadful waste of our island humanity'[13] resultant upon emigration and exile, and is very perceptive about the psychological distortion of false consciousness in the exile's nostalgia for and sentimentalisation of his first world, the decline of Gaelic remains for him the fundamental tragedy, underlying everything else, since language is seen as the absolutely core constituent of cultural identity. As he puts it in his major 1986 essay, 'Real people in a Real Place', p. 20:

> if there is no Gaelic left, will not the islander live in a disappearing landscape, as an Englishman would if his language were slowly to die? . . . For we are born inside a language and see everything from within its parameters: it is not we who make language, it is language that makes us . . . for Gaelic to die would be for the islands to die a more profound death than economics could bring. The imperialism of language is the most destructive of all . . .

The intensity of Crichton Smith's feelings about the place of Gaelic is compounded by a personal sense of guilt at the fact that he himself, perforce, frequently writes in English. In his moving address to the conference on the literature of Region and Nation, at Aberdeen University in 1986, it was clear that the problem of Gaelic was of no mere academic concern to him, but a kind of inescapable schizophrenia:

> there are too few openings in Gaelic for me to make a living from writing exclusively in that language. Economic factors govern cultural ones to an extent greater than we often dream of. And thus I am a double man riddled with guilt . . . The complexities are enormous, mind-breaking. Only those who have lived through or are living through them can fully understand them. And it is not even a question of understanding it, it is a question of feeling them on the pulse.[14]

This general cultural situation which Crichton Smith lives out on his pulses has its inevitable effects on the literature of Gaelic. Obviously, there is the problem of the small audience or readership ('fit audience though few' is all very well, but only as a deliberate choice); more seriously, perhaps, are the dangers in what Derick Thomson[15] calls the 'reservation mentality', in which certain themes and references – such as Crichton Smith's own references to Freud and to the nuclear threat – may be considered 'not Gaelic' or 'boastfulness'.[16] Gaelic, says Crichton Smith, 'does not have the strength to allow explorations into language beyond itself . . . Thus the creative writer is constrained by the weakness of his own language, and his adventurousness becomes treachery'.[17] Above all, Crichton Smith seems to feel the constraints on

# A Culloden of the Spirit

the tone of Gaelic poetry imposed by the cultural situation. Speaking of the Gaelic poetry of Donald MacAulay and Derick Thomson, and, by implication, of his own Gaelic work, he sees their undoubted energies somehow transmuted into what he calls 'paralysis', into an elegiac tone of defeat:

> It is with a sense of shock and shame that we see such energies continually breaking as at an invisible Culloden of the spirit, perpetually falling back on elegy, when they should be building from confident axioms . . . Behind the haze of falsity imposed on the islands, both by outsiders and naive exiles, lies the brokenness which will not allow writers the confidence that others can have, who when they write do not feel their subject matter disappearing before their eyes.[18]

The Irish experience of linguistic loss or dispossession is frequently in Crichton Smith's mind, as analogue or grim warning. Thus the essay 'Real People in a Real Place' is prefaced by a lengthy quotation from Daniel Corkery' *Synge and Anglo-Irish Literature* (1931), in which Corkery famously laments the anglophone education and literature imposed on Irish schoolchildren, and describes the results:

> Everywhere in the mentality of the Irish people are flux and uncertainty. Our national consciousness may be described . . . as a quaking sod. It gives no footing. It is not English, nor Irish, nor Anglo-Irish.

In 'For Poets Writing in English Over in Ireland' (in *The Exiles*, Carcanet, 1984), Crichton Smith wryly measures the distance between himself and some young Irish poets who, against the background of a ceilidh with traditional Irish music and dancing, confidently discuss the work of Philip Larkin and of Douglas Dunn:

> I turn a page and read an Irish poem
> translated into English and it says
> (the poet writing of his wife who'd died):
>
> 'Half of my eyes you were, half of my hearing,
> half of my walking you were, half of my side.'
> From what strange well are these strange words upspringing?
>
> . . . Inside the room there's singing and there's dancing.
> Another world is echoing with its own
> music that's distant from the world of Larkin.
>
> And I gaze at the three poets. They are me,
> poised between two languages. They have chosen
> with youth's superb confidence and decision.

'Half of my side you were, half of my seeing,
half of my walking you were, half of my hearing.'
Half of this world I am, half of this dancing.

Perhaps it is true that — as the gentle ironies of this poem suggest — Ireland is further down the road to monolingualism than the Western Isles, and that the anguish of the division in which Crichton Smith lives and writes is, for the Irish, more muted. No Irish person, however, can read his work, or consider the general issues which he poses so squarely, without a sense of unease or even of discomfort. The integrity of his vision, and of his position, challenges most powerfully that current in contemporary Irish intellectual life which — no doubt partly in reaction to the intractable and traditional bigotries of the Northern situation — makes virtues of pluralism, pragmatism and a revisionary ideology, all of which seek to cut Irish cultural identity free of 'the three-leaved shamrock of race, language and Catholicism which were an imposition by nineteenth-century nationalists'.[19]

My own unease in reading Iain Crichton Smith has complicated roots. The town in Northern Ireland in which I was born was overwhelmingly Protestant and Unionist in political complexion, and the schools — Protestant and Catholic — and playing fields, the street games and the comics we read, were all correspondingly suffused with what might be called the reference points of British popular culture. So, for me, until the age of eleven, the passing of the famous 11+ examination and the entry to secondary school in another (overwhelmingly Catholic) town ten miles away, it was all Stanley Matthews and Tom Finney and Portadown FC, who played at Shamrock Park in the Irish (*sic*) League, and cricket and Wimbledon, and the *Beano* and *Dandy*, and Flash Gordon and Enid Blyton, and trips to cinemas in Belfast with names like The Regal and Her Majesty's. However, not that I was even conscious of it, I considered myself absolutely Irish. The question of identity, when it did surface, confirmed my natural assumption: in boyish sectarian encounters, my brothers and I were told we were Fenian scum, and to get back to the bogs of the west.

It is thus a paradox that it was the encounter with more specifically Irish culture, or perhaps more accurately, with a certain attitude to and presentation of that culture, which first shook my sense of identity. My secondary school in Armagh was intensely nationalist. There was a kind of unwritten scale, or league table, of 'Irishness', which at its simplest level was based on your town (or townland) and your name. Boys from Portadown and Lurgan started well down below boys from Pomeroy, Aughnacloy and Crossmaglen. If your surname was Watson, the Quinns

## A Culloden of the Spirit 47

and the O'Kanes and the O'Fiachs had a perceptible advantage. As for a Christian name of 'George' . . . Gaelic games were not only compulsory: in accordance with the Gaelic Athletic Association's famous ban on foreign sports, the playing of soccer, tennis or 'English cricket' was an offence against your school, your country and – by extension – your God. (I was punished for starting a small five-a-side soccer league on the grounds that I was 'corrupting the Gaelic morale of the school'.)

And, of course, there was the Irish language, very much linked with the exclusivist sports attitude. It was a patriotic duty in the Catholic schools of Northern Ireland to study Irish, and I was quite happy to do so. But as with the sports, so with the language; among the boys, there was a small and – I found – unpleasant core of *gaelgeóirí*, or linguistic authoritarians, who wore the gold *fáinne* (a ring which identified you as an Irish speaker) as a kind of threat, and regarded an interest in Shakespeare as fairly conclusive evidence of *seoinínism* ('West Britonism'). This was all very problematic, because while Irish may be my mother tongue, English is my native language. The learning of Irish thus became associated in my mind with an authoritarian nexus of nationalism, cultural morality and racial purity, which was extremely conservative and very hostile to any vision of Ireland not based on the rural, Gaelic-speaking districts of the west. If this was 'true Irishness', I began to doubt whether I qualified despite having a mother who was a Connemara native speaker (non-authoritarian), and, in Joyce-fuelled adolescent sullenness, I cast the Irish language from me, emotionally at least, if not far enough to stop me passing my A-level in it. But that was very much a labour, rather than a labour of love.

I doubt if my experience, at least in general outline, was untypical. The bungling, and bungled efforts of the various governments of the Irish Free State (later the Republic) to make Irish once again the national language, have scarred generations of Irish schoolchildren with memories of incompetence, authoritarianism and, above all, hypocrisy.[20] (Even an Irish schoolchild, toiling over the irregular verbs in Irish, does notice when the Minister of Education is speaking, on the radio, in English). The Northern Irish situation was different, of course, but cultural and political pressures can have the same power as the compulsions of law.

I use these personal but perhaps representative memories because Iain Crichton Smith's work makes me so uncomfortable with them and about them. He is no linguistic authoritarian, and no laws have been passed to help the survival of his language or his culture. The power of his poetry, stories and essays about the threatened Gaelic world makes me ask myself, as I should better have done all those years ago in that school in Armagh: what have I lost, and how much have I lost, in my emotional monolingualism? (for my binlingualism is merely technical). Perhaps what has been lost has been too comprehensively lost for me even to be aware of the scale of it — which would be part of Crichton Smith's point.

Yet I must ask — and I admit, somewhat defensively — how far language is the sole constituent of a valid cultural identity? How true is it that the death or serious illness of a language is a terminally morbid condition for a culture? I think of Brian Friel's play *Translations*, which concerns the imposition of English placenames on Irish places in the nineteenth century, and with the imposition of the anglophone National School system — in short, through these examples, with the anglicisation of Ireland. Towards the end of the play, the old schoolmaster Hugh accepts the inevitability of the triumph of English. Pointing to the new book of English names, he counsels his community to reclaim in and through the English language that which has been lost to it. 'We must learn those new names,' he advises sombrely, 'we must learn to make them our own, we must make them our new home.'

In a sense, Friel's Hugh is defining the project of nearly all twentieth-century Irish writers in the English language. The task has been to refashion in a new tongue the lineaments of an indigenous cultural identity. And when one thinks of Yeats, Joyce, Synge, O'Casey, Beckett, Heaney and many others, can one really say that the project has been a failure? While, on a famous occasion, Joyce's character Stephen frets under the shadow of the imperial language, feeling that his English interlocutor's speech will always be for Irish Stephen 'an acquired speech', Joyce's own achievement in tilting and shaping English aesthetic models and the English language itself towards Irish materials surely justifies Seamus Heaney's remark that, in his use of English Joyce took an imperial humiliation and reforged it as a native weapon.[21]

It is with some irritation of spirit that one reads Denis Donoghue's essays in the volume *We Irish: Essays on Irish Literature and Society* (Alfred A. Knopf, New York, 1986) alongside Crichton Smith's work. Donoghue is the holder of the Henry James Chair of Letters at New York University, and perhaps the spirit of the Great Pretender lurks behind his remark that 'the real trouble is that our [Irish] natural experience has been too limited; our history has been at once intense and monotonous' (p. 150). This seems to me to partake of that common

# A Culloden of the Spirit

error which assumes that Irish history is freakish and that a kind of mid-Atlantic haute-bourgeoise culture is the norm, when in fact — alas — Ireland's history is much more representative of the history of many peoples throughout the world. I prefer Crichton Smith's passionate objection, in defence of his islanders, to 'the idea that they are somehow sheltering from history, who have seen so much of it, far more than the bureaucrats in their offices'.[22] However, Donoghue does point out that, while Irish literature is a story of fracture ('the death of one language, so far as it is dead or dying or maintained as an antiquity, and the victory of another' — *We Irish*, p. 145), it is possible that these fractures are good for literature, if bad for other purposes. One does not want, of course, to sound like a Hibernian RSM yelling at Highland wimps to pull themselves together; but that 'brokenness', that 'invisible Culloden of the spirit' of which Crichton Smith speaks in relation to his own culture and his own literary tradition, need not produce only the elegiac tone, or reflect only an inevitable marginalisation. Of Crichton Smith's work, and that of his fellow island poets, it might be said that, like William Faulkner, or the Australian poet Les Murray (to use deliberately two very constrasting examples), they realise our perspectives on the whole of human culture precisely because they see it from the edge. For the Gaelic speaker, the example of Ireland may be depressing; for the writer, it surely must be positive. Thomas Kinsella, one of the best contemporary Irish poets, and distinguished translator of the *Táin Bó Cuailnge* and of *An Duanaire* (*Poems of the Dispossessed 1600–1900*), admits in a famous essay that the death of a language is 'a calamity'. But he finishes his essay:

> pending the achievement of some total human unity of being, every writer in the world — since he can't be in all the literary traditions at once — is the inheritor of a gapped, discontinuous, polyglot tradition. Nevertheless, if the function of tradition is to link us living with the significant past, this is done as well by a broken tradition as by a whole one — however painful it may be humanly speaking. I am certain that a great part of the significance of my own past, as I try to write my poetry, is that the past is mutilated.[23]

The writing of Iain Crichton Smith certainly gives us, memorably, that human pain of which Kinsella speaks; it anatomises the 'broken tradition'; but it surely links us living with a significant present as well as past in an art where one language shadows another in a genuinely moving human and cultural drama.

NOTES

1. Patrick Kavanagh, 'The Parish and the Universe', in *Collected Prose*, London, MacGibbon and Kee, 1967.
2. 'The Golden Lyric: The Poetry of Hugh MacDiarmid', in *Towards the Human: Selected Essays*, Edinburgh, Macdonald, 1986.
3. Published by Macdonald, 1981. Except where indicated, all quotations from the poetry are from this volume.
4. See, for example, Muir's *John Knox* (1929).
5. 'Between Sea and Moor', in *Towards the Human*, p. 81.
6. 'Real People in a Real Place', in *Towards the Human*, pp. 48, 62.
7. 'Between Sea and Moor', p. 81.
8. 'Real People in a Real Place', pp. 48–9.
9. 'Internationalising Scottish Poetry', in Cairns Craig, ed., *The History of Scottish Literature*, Vol. 4, Aberdeen Univ. Press, 1987, p. 328.
10. 'Real People in a Real Place', pp. 51, 53.
11. ibid., p. 18.
12. ibid., p. 23.
13. ibid., p. 49.
14. 'The Double Man', in R.P. Draper, ed., *The Literature of Region and Nation*, London, Macmillan, 1989, p. 140.
15. In his 'Introductory Note' to *Towards the Human*.
16. 'The Double Man', p. 138.
17. 'Real People in a Real Place', p. 21.
18. ibid., p. 35.
19. K.D. O'Connor, 'Ireland – a nation caught in the middle of an identity crisis', *Irish Independent*, 20 July 1985' cited in J.J. Lee, *Ireland 1912–85*, Cambridge University Press, 1989, p. 658.
20. See J.J. Lee, op. cit., pp. 658–74.
21. 'The Interesting Case of John Alphonsus Mulrennan', *Planet*, Jan. 1978, 34–40.
22. 'Real People in a Real Place', p. 49.
23. Thomas Kinsella, 'The Irish Writer', in *Davis, Mangan, Ferguson? Tradition and the Irish Writer*, Dublin, Dolmen, 1970, pp. 57–66.

# Five

## The Wireless Behind the Curtain

### Douglas Dunn

The poet is a maker, not a retail trader. The writer today should not be so much the mouthpiece of a community (for then he will only tell it what it knows already) as its conscience, its critical faculty, its generous instinct. In a world intransigent and overspecialised, falsified by practical necessities, the poet must maintain his elasticity and refuse to tell lies to order. Others can tell lies more efficiently; no-one except the poet can give us poetic truth. (Louis MacNeice, *Modern Poetry*, 1938).

Even more than in the politicised 1930s, poetry has been responding to a broad-ranging, oddly amorphous, yet powerfully insistent set of pressures. Many of them are political in various ways, whether the usual politics of Left or Right, or else they stem from the politics of gender, sexuality, race and other sources of oppositional feeling and belief. Over half-a-century later, MacNeice's sneer at 'a world intransigent and overspecialised' seems understated. So much has happened since then that the traditional verities of poetry can appear to have been enfeebled by the 'practical necessities' of commitment to one thing or another. Priorities other than those of poetry itself have led to the neglect, or dislodgement, of poetic truth as primary in the experience of trying to write poetry, and to the reading of it. A generation of readers is growing up with a highly imperfect knowledge of what poetic truth is. They may even be sceptical as to whether it exists at all. Or it could be suspected of amounting to little more than a stunt calculated to pin poetry to a harmlessly aesthetic realm and nowhere else.

It is through the idea of poetic truth that I want to approach Iain Crichton Smith's poetry. Over forty years of writing, he has gnawed obsessively at the possibility of poetry possessing its own autonomous existence in relation to the writer's mind and imagination, and to the society in which he lives. First, though, a tentative definition, beginning with a negative. Poetic truth is not merely a poet's success in convincing a reader that the beliefs and statements embodied in a poem are true. As everyone knows, a 'suspension of disbelief' can be negotiated by a reader for the sake of the other qualities of a poem. However, it is a momentary arrangement, even when repeated many times. Poetic truth, therefore, ought not to be considered absolutely immune to the reader's right to challenge its departure from fact or ethical veracity. It might best be defined as poetry's exercise of freedom within its intuitive principles as these are revealed acceptably in the work of an individual poet. To claim that is to do more than insist that a poet should have a sentient, instinctive intelligence adequate to the task of avoiding 'bad truth' or humanly untenable points of view. More positively, it is to claim that some poets are in touch, or, at the least, concerned, with the *essence* of poetry as opposed to the occasion of a poem; and the essence of poetry is truth of its own kind, which the poet makes truth of 'our kind', the matter of life and spirit expressed beyond all doubt on that particular occasion and as far as the poet is concerned. But poetic truth is under no obligation to accord with quotidian reality, or to diverge from it. A well-schooled disinterestedness may be what is required, on any subject under the sun, whatever its sorrow or delight. That should suggest how difficult it is, and it could be that poetic truth is an aspiration of poetry, only sometimes to be fulfilled when a poet's courage permits images and narrative to go where they want instead of towards a conclusion pre-plotted by the 'practical necessities' of taking sides or other kinds of intervention.

In naming it 'poetic truth', not only is 'truth' qualified or described on faith, but it is also elevated and isolated in order to say that poetry approaches in a different way what is commonly known as truth. It identifies poetry with more than a celebrated or notorious struggle with the meanings of words. There is implicated in it, too, somehow or other, the awkward notion of failure, an exalted futility. It is not that poetry seeks to improve on the truth. How could truth be bettered? Well, by putting it in a poem, perhaps . . . But by showing a demonstrable truth, or a truth created by a poet, by exposing it to realms of thought, imagination and feeling which others do not share to the same degree, perhaps by drawing truth from these realms, then the poet shows the difference between poetic truth and truth pure and simple. It is not just truth heightened by the techniques of poetry. It *wants* to be a better truth, and hence poetry's courting of the ideal and the impossible. Part of the reason why poetry risks its own dismissal is that what it says is very often opposed to the expected case. Its lustre, mystique and breadth are almost always drawn from unpredicted relationships with the average or commonly known or widely believed. Poetic truth is almost always a matter of surprise. However, to look for constant surprise in a poem would be a waste of time. 'Poems very seldom consist of poetry and nothing else,' A.E. Housman once wrote. Narrative, argument, descriptive scene-setting and so on can be poetic or, at least, unobtrusively prosaic. Poetic truth is likely to occur momentarily when what a poet is saying is a coincidence of imagery, rhythm and meaning – the imagination made visible, audible and interesting. Certainly, it is not imagery and figurative language alone which stimulate an imaginative response in the reader. Imaginative pleasure in this special kind of veracity is encouraged by cadence, sound and meaning. The experience of poetic truth is one in which as many as possible of the five senses are invited to participate.

Crichton Smith's childhood and youth occupied the years before the Second World War and the war years themselves. On the evidence of his prose reminiscences, several poems (especially those depicting old women), or an essay such as Hector MacIver's 'The Outer Isles', it is hard to see Crichton Smith's background as 'modern'. Using 'provincial' to mean a degree of alleged backwardness relative to metropolitan up-to-dateness will not suffice, either. No doubt Lewis's remoteness in the 1930s could be overstated, but it seems to have irritated a young man whose reading afforded him glimpses of life elsewhere. Oppositional anxieties in Crichton Smith's early poems are therefore linked to a self-aware rummaging for apt and modern styles of poetic expressiveness. 'Poem of Lewis', for example, begins with a statement which movements of feeling in contemporary poetry have made to seem ambiguous:

> Here they have no time for the fine graces
> of poetry, unless it freely grows
> in deep compulsion, like water in the well,
> woven into the texture of the soil
> in a strong pattern.

Another Lewisman, Crichton Smith's elder contemporary, Derick Thomson, has turned that image of the well ('An Tobar') into a self-aware source of cultural renewal. In the early 1950s, however, Crichton Smith felt himself obliged to be negative before the virtues of communally approved or traditional poetry and its values. Indigenousness is seen as excluding the elegant freedoms of imagination. He might have been trying to reject more than he could deal with – the place itself, and its past and present. Inherited values are shrugged off as out of step with the concerns of a poetic personality already familiar with modern poetry and its options as well as a university syllabus in English literature. 'The material of thought', 'lightning', swiftness, 'the bursting flower' and 'the great forgiving spirit of the word/ fanning its rainbow wing' are all expressions identified with a fulsome appreciation of poetry itself. Others, cleaving to Lewis, are associated with aridity and mental attitudes for which the poet has neither use nor sympathy. 'The black north', 'the barren rock', a sea that 'heaves/ in visionless anger over the cramped graves' come across as the targets of Crichton Smith's farewell. Right at the start of his career, Crichton Smith revealed the inevitability of what was already known as 'interior exile' or the state of being an 'inner emigré'. That is, home might have been loved, but it was understood to prohibit poetry on the poet's own terms. Especially remarkable, though, is the image in these lines, and its implications:

> The two extremes,
> mourning and gaiety, meet like north and south
> in the one breast, milked by knuckled time,
> till dryness spreads across each ageing bone.

The influences of Eliot and Muir seem detectable there, as well as some raw reading of the Apocalypse poetry of the late 1930s and 1940s. However, these 'two extremes' would become an essential part of the cultural stress which Crichton Smith's poetry has had to contend with. Meeting in the 'one breast' makes it clear that he did not absolve himself from these 'extremes', one of which is surely implicated in the grim evocation of permanence and death with which the image closes.

Mention of Edwin Muir is not beside the point. Another early poem, 'The Good Place', states its Muir-like title, and then proceeds to stand expectation on its head. Its manner reaches for something like the tone of mid-1950s English verse. Rhymes like 'happy/ sloppy' and 'winter/ painter' show that whatever impact The Movement might have had on Crichton Smith, he was less than prepared to take it as seriously as its admittedly vague prescriptions invited, although it might be a case of having intuited some of its procedures rather than sympathised with them as momentarily instructive.

At any rate, *English* poetry has never been thought by Crichton Smith to be alien. His Gaelic-speaking background might even be implicated in how he seems to have fantasised Englishness as a schoolboy who was not to leave Lewis until he went to university in Aberdeen in his seventeenth year. In his essay 'Real People in a Real Place' (in *Towards the Human*, 1986), he says:

> Though I was brought up on an island where Gaelic was the dominant language, my reading was much the same as if I had been schooled at Eton . . .

He then mentions a lucky access to copies of *Penguin New Writing* (and poetry by Auden, Spender etc.). In another essay, 'Between Sea and Moor', his list of early reading includes detective stories, westerns, Keats, Shelley, P.C. Wren, *Chambers' Journal, The Tatler* and *The Listener*. Lying in bed with asthma or bronchitis, he dreamt of 'some other world that wasn't this one, a world inhabited as much by English public schoolboys as by my own friends'. Later in the same essay, he says:

> I did not feel myself as belonging to Scotland. I felt myself as belonging to Lewis. I had never even seen a train. I had never been out of the island in my whole life. Glasgow was as distant to me as the moon. I had hardly read any Scottish writers, not even MacDiarmid. Most of the writers I had read were English.

For a Scottish writer, Crichton Smith's memory of his early reading seems refreshingly free of retrospective tampering. He admits that his background did not include a native perspective on literature and poetry, and this left him ready to associate the poetry that matched his temperament with that of places other than Lewis or Scotland as a whole. 'Not even MacDiarmid' could be an unnecessary admission. Older than Crichton Smith by about eight years, Edwin Morgan has said in interview that he did not read MacDiarmid in the 1930s. Morgan's early work, too, is uncertain and imitative. Unsettled beginnings to what have turned out to be major careers could be explained, albeit tentatively, by the lack of local and national guidance of the sort that can be radiated by a poetically powerful and productive figure. Literary chronology asks us to accept MacDiarmid in that role, but the influence of his work was clearly withheld by a provincial climate and, it seems possible, by prejudice working against the discussion that would have made his work better known.

Throughout his writing life, Crichton Smith seems to have depended on one transitory 'influence' after another, perhaps as a consequence of how, at the start, no single influence was sufficiently meaningful as to determine most of the direction his work would take. A writer can feel grateful for circumstances that leave the future open and full of fluid options. It might be possible, too, to feel regret at the absence of an early and impressive force against which subsequent writing can contest its newer priorities. Crichton Smith, however, is an intensely literary poet, and, at the same time, one for whom 'real people in a real place' matter to his artistic vision. Auden has been an abiding affection, although only rarely could Crichton Smith's poetry be said to be Audenesque – 'End of Schooldays' could be a virtually self-conscious example. Through the 1960s, there are some pretty obvious signs of an interest in contemporary English and American poetry. Lowell is an American poet whom Crichton Smith acknowledges, while 'At the Sale' owes a debt to Larkin. A relatively early poem like 'Sunday Morning Walk' has a famous near-parallel in Baudelaire's 'Une Charogne'. Wallace Stevens haunts 'Deer on the High Hills' but without leaving an indelible mark on later work. Poems in *Love Poems and Elegies* (1972) hint at the condensed verse associated with *The Review* in the 1960s and early 1970s. East and Central European and other poetry in translation also appear to have been picked up by Crichton Smith's sensitive antennae. With something like fervour, he has ransacked what Larkin dismissed as 'the myth kitty'. At one time, the glamorous passion and recklessness of classical heroes amounted to his supportive image of the need for action in the face of a lethargic and dying local society. Shakespeare enters his poetry as a subject, and, again, as a touchstone of active imagination. He writes about poetry and song more often than most poets. Limiting reference to *Selected Poems* (1985) alone would seem to show a disproportionate number of poems concerned with poetry, poets and philosophers, while others are drawn from literature, especially 'Chinese Poem' and the extracts from *The Notebooks of Robinson Crusoe*. Laying too much stress on Crichton Smith's literariness, however, could misrepresent the instictive reasons why he is so literary a poet. It would also tend to blur the socially critical dimension of his work.

Poetic truth is not a notional event for Crichton Smith. It was born out of experience which denied its existence.

> It's law they ask of me and not grace.
> 'Conform', they say, 'your works are not enough.
> Be what we say you should be . . .'

The controlled anger of 'The Law and the Grace' is potent and real. When he asks himself if he should submit to presbyterian dogma and 'bring the grace to a malignant head', he is hazarding nothing less than the selling-out of poetry and its truth for the sake of conformity. He does not sell out, but just as in 'Poem of Lewis' there was room, if only just, for the poet to associate himself with everything he meant by 'mourning and gaiety', he establishes a connection between the enemy term 'law' and the poetically benign idea of 'grace'. It is a complication which the poem then attempts to resolve to poetry's satisfaction. 'Grace' is moralised perhaps more than a poet ought to chance when its unambiguous release might have served him better.

> Do you need, black devils, steadfastly to cure
>
> life of itself? And you to stand beside
> the stone you set on me? No, I have angels. Mine
> are free and perfect. They have no design
> on anyone else, but only on my pride,
>
> my insufficiency, imperfect works.
> They often leave me but they sometimes come
> to judge me to the core, till I am dumb.
> Is this not law enough, you patriarchs?

Moralising 'grace' turns out to be justifiable as a thrust against 'law'; but it is also deeply ironic in that 'grace' is disclosed as 'law enough'. Poetry and its truth ('free and perfect') are shown as disinterested and autonomous but exactingly judgmental on the practitioner of the art which it is part of Crichton Smith's purpose to defend. Gaelic traditions might even be mocked in the process, for 'the stone you set on me' could be the slab or boulder lowered onto the chests of ancient bards as an inducement to write well and write quickly. What adds to the poem's rage, and its ironic disorder, is its awareness of imperfection; he is a poet who admits to the in-built failure of his art even when it is working with noticeable success. It is not a tactic. Nor would it be worthy of the poem to see it only as a judicious, formalised discharge of grievances. Instinctive responses to issues which are fundamental to Crichton Smith play a much more important role in his work than the versification which he has often used to convey them. Verse sentences, line endings, caesuras and his typical punctuation make it clear that he writes quickly and under something close to the daily pressure of the subjects and feelings from which his poetry rarely departs. It would be difficult to say of Crichton Smith, as R.P. Blackmur said of Conrad Aiken, that 'He sings by nature and training out of the general body of poetry in English'. Educated and literary as Crichton Smith is, a trained, well-rehearsed, culturally *secure* angle of approach would seem to have been denied to him by circumstances, by that curious, intuitive design that the work has on the writer as much as the writer is able to direct to the work. When he writes through formal versification, it can seem at times as if stanza, metre and rhyme are being used to fix that elusive security to the voice and the page. However, the impression can also be one of trying to domesticate an imagination that is more indignant, wild and associative than Crichton Smith's other concerns are prepared to tolerate.

Above all, there is the complicating matter of Gaelic. Crichton Smith's earliest published work (*The Long River*, 1955; his contribution to *New Poems*, 1959; and *Thistles and Roses*, 1961) is in English, but his first collection of poems and stories in Gaelic, *Bùrn is Aran* (*Bread and Water*) appeared as early as 1959 and was followed by *Biobuill is Sanasanreice* (*Bibles and Advertisements*) in 1965. His first published poem in Gaelic appeared in *Gairm* in 1953. It seems right, then, to bear in mind that, throughout his writing life, Crichton Smith has written and published in two languages. As he says in a lecture given in 1986, 'I am a linguistic double man'. He adds to that remark:

> I write in an English which is probably, in some ways unknown to me, a Highland English. It is comprehensible, but is it allowing my whole personality to function as is absolutely necessary for the writing of poetry? Probably not. (*The Literature of Region and Nation*, ed. R.P. Draper, 1989)

Painful honesty and self-lacerating candour are drawn out of Crichton Smith by an unfairness that is a consequence of history more than a gasp of gentle or irritated modesty.

Perhaps the most intriguing as well as the most mysterious aspect of poetry is its involuntary arrival in at least some passages of writing and sometimes in whole poems. 'There was, and there still remains, the mystery of *inspiration*', Valéry wrote,

> which is the name given to the spontaneous way speech or ideas are formed in a man and appear to him to be marvels that, of and by himself, he feels incapable of forming. He has, then, been *aided*. (*Paul Valéry: An Anthology*, selected, with an Introduction, by James R. Lawler, Routledge and Kegan Paul, 1977 p. 166)

A poet whose life-circumstances have made bilingualism inevitable may well experience, at a very deep level, an anxiety stemming quite naturally from the doubled poetic burden that it is its lot to carry. It is likely to be even more the case when one of the poet's two languages is that of a 'minority' culture vulnerable to actual and poetic extinction, and the other language is the competitor, or invader, which has brought that threat about. Gaelic, then, might be seen (confusingly) as resistant to modernity, the language of a 'defeated' culture, but the poet's own. English might be seen (again, confusingly) as hospitable to modernity (although I doubt if it is) and the language of a 'victorious' culture (again, doubtful).

Poetry is as unchosen as a poet's language, or, in Crichton Smith's case, his two languages. He was born to both, and, obviously, to one more than another or both equally, although the weight of that 'or' could be an issue on which Crichton Smith is never likely to come to a decision, or to want to. It is where he differs from Sorley MacLean and Derick Thomson, whose unchosen language is Gaelic and for whom English has become a language of translation and reading, as far as their poetry is concerned, and of necessary conversation. But when a poet lives in two languages, the choice between them could be a daily dilemma. A degree of perplexity could easily arise. In which language is the involuntary pressure of inspiration to be recorded? Presumably the conscious poetic mind can deal with the practical issues of bilingualism – although it could be a lot to take for granted. What, though, of the unpremeditated imaginative events and chance perceptions of poetry which, to an extent that no-one can measure exactly, arise from the nature of language and which might even be suggested by its phonology and rhythms? To handle *two* mediums of involuntary purpose or inspiration seems either fortunate and astounding or bad luck and a cause for sympathy or contempt. It is a different kind of phenomenon to the influence of poetry from other languages on a poet more or less monoglot in the sense of being devoted only to the language of the poet's writing. It is a kind of poetic bigamy; but I should think that Crichton Smith has only one Muse.

The consequences of being bilingual impinge on Crichton Smith's English, especially in his early work. In 'The Good Place', for example, his 'certain kind of poet/ who wrote in miniature' is said to have 'listened with patience to a crashing bore'. While the idiom of the poem as a whole sounds removed from a Scottish accent of any kind, 'crashing bore' sticks out as a phrase fantasised from books. A line like 'some angel somewhere who might land perhaps', from the otherwise admirable 'Old Woman', over-enacts the meaning of 'maybe' like a caricature of some of the dithering English verse of the 1950s. 'One might see' in the same poem, or 'One simply doesn't/ know enough . . .' in 'For the Unknown Seamen of the 1939–45 War Buried in Iona Churchyard' uses the English indefinite pronoun with a frequency which most Scottish writers usually seek to avoid. One doesn't say 'one' very often, in prose. Does one? One was brought up to say 'you' or 'we' or to take a chance on 'I'. 'One' sounded as if you were trying too hard. It was infected with class associations. As a classless island in Crichton Smith's younger days, Lewis might have been free of inhibitions of that sort. What he calls 'Highland English' could be closer to the diction of English English than to the English spoken and written in the Lowlands outside the usual thickly imitative circles.

Crichton Smith's reliance on literary, philosophical, historical and mythical figures, and the general literariness of his poetry, indicate a temporary unsureness and a need to take refuge within poetry while simultaneously asserting the writing of poetry as an authentic art. 'Lenin', for instance, purges the possibility of dismissing the 'infinitely complex' as a by-product of 'admiration for the ruthless man' or the saint, extreme forms of action or contemplation. It sets free

>     the moving on
> into the endlessly various, real, human,
> world which is no new era shining dawn.

As in 'Two Girls Singing', a benign openness begins to emerge which is willing to express life as the sum of its possibilities and poetry as its own pretext ('larks for no reason but themselves'). Poetry and song are put across as instruments of disinterested but socially significant truth:

> It was the human sweetness in that yellow,
> the unpredicted voices of our kind.

In several of these earlier poems, a rhetorical tendency argues the issue with a freer, more colloquial and individual experience of language and rhythm. Larkin, however, can be heard in 'Schoolroom Incident':

> Why the paralysis
>
> on my own mind in guilt?
> Too, I suppose, sensitive. And so
> I dream all night . . .

*The Law and the Grace* (1965) also includes 'Poem in March', 'The Clearances' and 'Envoi' as well as 'Two Girls Singing', the title poem and 'Lenin'. All six are characteristic, but the first three possess a more daring idiosyncrasy. 'Poem in March' begins:

> Old cans sparkle. Tie slaps at the chin.
> The mind puts on its sword.
> This is the country of the daffodil
> and the new flannels, radiant and belled.

That chin-slapping tie and new flannels show up like Crichton Smith's fingerprint on the page, particularly when set among old cans and daffodils, or that typical line 'The mind puts on its sword'. Equally true to the unexpectedness of Crichton Smith's imagination is this image from 'Envoi':

> I in my plates of frost go
> among the falling crockery of hills . . .

'The Clearances' is an angrier poem, but it goes about its disclosure of feeling with a similar naturalness and eccentricity. Compared to these, other earlier work can sometimes look as if it had been too deliberately prepared in advance of writing. 'Lenin' and 'The Law and the Grace' state conclusions which are essential to Crichton Smith's poetry. While memorable in themselves, their importance might lie in what they attempted to put behind him, and the poetry they made it possible for him to write later. 'The wandering senses/ are all, are all', a phrase from 'Deer on the High Hills', has to be seen to be deserved through a poet's negation of social responsibility and the earning of its purely poetic counterpart, to which it is sometimes related. There are few 'wandering senses' in 'Lenin' and 'The Law and the Grace', but what they argue with looks for an opportunity to set them free.

Hawing set up that possibility, Crichton Smith's next collection, *From Bourgeois Land* (1969), charged off in precisely the opposite direction. Instead, he chose to write *about* the oppositional loneliness of poetry and the poet in a society that cares for neither. Some individual poems will prove to be exceptions; but on the whole the book illustrates the difficulty which Scottish poets experience when getting away from a direct poetry is technically and imaginatively feasible but, as often seems to be the case, thematically ill-advised. It is as if the potential freedom of a Scottish poet is constrained by silent accusations. Precedent has a large following in Scotland, and is a sore discourager to any poet who wants to give his or her assent to a poetry which is not one of direct address and thoroughly vernacular in spirit. *From Bourgeois Land* assails the reader. However, it does so with the reader's preferred manner of verse. There is not enough ironic awareness of Crichton Smith's part to say that he knows what he is doing, that is, enough irony to subvert the manner. The opening poem, for example, is pointed at Germanic *Bürgertum* (a different phenomenon to the French *bourgeoisie* and the Anglified middle classes). Iambicated indignant chatter turns out to be about the bureaucracy of the Holocaust. The subject is too important to be fudged by simplified history or affronted verse. Of a horrid clerk toting up timetables of death-trains, morbid statistics and the 'accountancy of murder', he writes:

> Perhaps it's possible to see him drive
> from his bourgeois home to his office, bright with glass,
> sit at his desk, consider how (alas)
> the times are changing, it's imperative
> to get some typists who are not so crass,
>
> pencil an entry in his calendar,
> a party or some fishing or some golf,
> a spot of carpentry (say that kitchen shelf)
> a game of chess, an evening at the fire
> with his wife and/or his children and himself.

Crichton Smith decides that his near-empathy (caricatured though it is) demands more imagination than the clerk granted to the lives reflected in his arithmetic of the dead.

> it is simpler and more close to reason
> to say at last when everything has been said:
>
> 'Such human beings are conceivable
> if, being dead, one can be said to live,
> if to the plague I answer "I forgive",
> if to the stone "You are forigivable",
> if one could say, "I will forgive you, grave"'.
>
> But otherwise, you clerk who hated error
> more than the sin that yet involves us all,
> I say, 'You are so monstrous I would call
> the bells of hell, gassed faces in the mirror,
> to enliven age on age your bourgeois soul'.

You can see why Larkin never wrote about the Holocaust. Whatever his conscience, his technique would have been capable of not much more than a confused sermon either. Crichton Smith's poem, however, is not without its effectiveness. Rhyme and rhythm in the penultimate stanza are less routine than usual. But the poem is marred by how it lives in the history of 'I suppose'. All the evidence points to anti-Semitism in Germany and elsewhere as an irrational but devoutly cultivated hatred that crossed and still crosses class barriers. Among those who perpetrated Nazi horrors were men and women who would be described accurately as working-class. A relatively lowly clerk is hardly an example of the *bourgeoisie* no matter what the nationality under consideration. The unreasonable appeal of anti-Jewish feeling might even originate – as it did in Germany and Austria – from a busy envy directed at Jewish '*bourgeois*' success in material and cultural life by their

# The Wireless Behind the Curtain

*bourgeois* competitors and others lower down the pecking order. Crichton Smith's poem is too unsubtle to comprehend the horrors it confronts.

Although some poems in *From Bourgeois Land* are titled, all are numbered, so it seems clear that the book is meant to be read as a sequence. The second poem involves the Free Church in Crichton Smith's rattled anti-*bourgeois* mish-mash. Again, though, the poem is speculative. The 'I suppose' of the imagination turns up a retrospective prayer for a girl who looks like Emily Brontë in an oval frame 'staring from the peril/ of commandments breaking round her'. 'And I pray/ that she was happy' he says, before bursting into a polite exclamation – 'How little beauty conscious sins allow!' Is that line 'Highland English'? It doesn't seem to be. It sounds more like a form of English English poeticised from or encouraged by a surrender to the iambic frame. Could it be that, as Crichton Smith was writing, the metrical stencil which he chose to follow was one which led him to an echoic Englishness which worked against the release of a more appropriate language and its poetry?

Versified prose arguments get in the way of the poetic in *From Bourgeois Land*. Quarrelsome attitudes are allowed to take the upper hand so that the tone becomes disdainful or hectoring more than poetically criticial. No 12 begins:

> My Scottish towns with Town Halls and with courts,
> with tidy flowering squares and small squat towers,
> with steady traffic, the clock's cruising hours,
> the ruined castles and the empty forts,
>
> you are so still one could believe you dead.
> Policemen stroll beneath the leaves and sun.
> Pale bank clerks sit on benches after noon
> totting the tulips, entering clouds in red.

The second 'with' in the first line pads it for the sake of a pentameter, and so do the next two in lines two and three. Even the two definite articles in line four could be criticised as redundant. Disdain sits up and begins to scowl in the first line of the second stanza – and there's that 'one' again. That aspect of the poem gets worse. There is a price to be paid for peace, and it is not just the dangers of provincial complacency and fatigue. Part of the cost is that a poet can come along and sling accusations at it.

> And yet from such quiet places furies start.
> Gauleiters pace by curtained windows, grass

absorbs the blood of mild philosophers.
Artists are killed for an inferior art.

Gauleiters? Mild philosophers bleeding to death? Murdered or executed artists? All of a sudden, somewhere like Forfar, or Dingwall, or Selkirk, has been whipped off to somewhere else and drowned in what MacCaig calls 'filthy history'. Nightmarish nastiness is evoked and listed in the following three stanzas; but the poet is not content to leave his affront in its time and place or to probe only into darker currents running beneath the stagnant waters of an identifiably complacent Scottish society. 'Gauleiters' has suggested too much to him; the poem has to end on 'And distant Belsen smokes in the calm air'. Scottish history is bad enough without associating it with the blame for the worst of somewhere else's.

Appropriately enough, 'At the Sale' is as cluttered with the detritus of old-time acquisitive habits as salesrooms used to be before junk became valuable. The 'we' of the poem stroll through this resting-place of middle-class cast-offs as the poet wonders about their original owners or what worn-out household technology was actually for. The poem's atmosphere is one of a convincing bemusement and fear. It is among the best of Smith's formal poems. 'How much goes out of fashion and how soon!' intrudes Larkin's voice-print, as does 'that gap-toothed piano'. 'O hold me, love, in this appalling place' sounds like Robert Lowell or Ian Hamilton. Yet the nervy, disconcerting and threatening vision of heaped, inanimate objects is Crichton Smith's own. An old machine is transformed by imaginative description into a metaphor of mindless routines. Unlived life, leading to death ('and the flesh itself becomes unnecessary'), is seen as a consequence of mechanical deeds and which the sequence as a whole associates with the Bourgeois Land of the title. Interestingly, though, Crichton Smith reaches for this vision of domestic and public grimness by means which transcend literal description. In a passage of twenty-four lines, prosaic argument and narrative become secondary to the poetry that they are able to set free.

> We walk around and find an old machine.
> On one side pump, on another turn a wheel.
> But nothing happens. What's this object for?
> Imagine how we will
> endlessly pump and turn for forty years
> and then receive a pension, smart and clean,
>
> climbing a dais to such loud applause
> as shakes the hall for toiling without fail

at this strange nameless gadget, pumping, turning,
each day oiling the wheel
with zeal and eagerness and freshness burning
in a happy country of anonymous laws,

while the ghostly hands are clapping and the chairs
grow older as we look, the pictures fade,
the stone is changed to rubber, and the wheel
elaborates its rayed
brilliance and complexity and we feel
the spade become a scoop, cropping the grass,

and the flesh itself becomes unnecessary.
O hold me, love, in this appalling place.
Let your hand stay me by this mattress here
and this tall ruined glass,
by this dismembered radio, this queer
machine that waits and has no history.

Sixteen-line sentences are uncommon in contemporary stanzaic poetry, but the rush of Crichton Smith's utterance cumulates effectively, and it is its anxious passion which convinces the reader that quibbles directed at obvious stepping-stones and links in the syntax are unnecessary. Crichton Smith here is writing poetry, whereas in much of *From Bourgeois Land* he is complaining about the social, political and historical affronts which make poetry difficult, and whose truths contrast with poetic truth only to its alleged embarrassment. Significantly, though, his transformation of the queer, historyless machine into a representative image of pointlessness as well as one of humanity held captive by conventions and the quotidian can stand almost symbolically for the obstacle faced by the poet's urge to create and by poetry itself in the post-second World War world.

Equally provocative, however, is the presence of a radio. In the essay 'Between Sea and Moor', he writes that

> There was one radio in the village (it was called a 'wireless' in those days, though it had wires) and curiously enough it was in a thatched house. Every night I would go and listen to it. It was perched on a shelf with a white curtain around it, and before the news began the curtain was pulled aside, almost as if to reveal to us an idol speaking with a godlike voice.

It is an apt image for the beginnings of Crichton Smith's search for a modern idiom. However, his view of modernity is double-edged. While he quite clearly revels in styles of writing capable of releasing poetry from hidebound and traditional expectations, his attitude to the modern world is usually one which recoils from vulgarity and squalor and other deformations of 'law' which inhibit 'grace'. Urban life is observed frequently in his work only to be shown as miserable and inadequate.

There is an irony, too, in that the news which Crichton Smith listened to as a boy was news of war. There is a lot of war in his poetry. Another, paradoxical this time, is that the radio on the shelf behind the white curtain is an image of the modernity that Crichton Smith would come to find ambivalent, a source of artistic release but also of work, tedium and grief. It is an image which seems to portray the outside world as esoteric.

'Only the poet can give us poetic truth', MacNeice wrote. However, its disinterestedness is difficult to achieve without a poet sensing a departure from social responsibility for which it is possible to feel ashamed. Either way, whether devoted to poetic truth or to social, political or historical truth in poetry, he or she is on a hiding to nothing. Poetic truth can be accused of neglecting social reality, while a socially descriptive or critical poetry can be charged with forgetting the disinterestedness of which poetry is capable. That, though, is a crude simplification. It need not be as bold a dichotomy as the essential dilemma suggests. Writers respond to *both* pressures, and, in doing so, evolve a 'mixed' style, which can be more than a matter of High and Low, of cultivated rhetoric and demotic speech, or a lyrical register and another closer to the literal. Different parts of a poet's idiom comment on each other and on the levels of awareness that they represent. In No. 31 in *From Bourgeois Land*, Crichton Smith writes of a lawyer:

> The great waters pour
> at his small dapper feet. He feels at home
> by the sea's phased formalities.

'Small dapper feet' and 'the sea's phased formalities' contrast not only two different registers of writing, but also different kinds of perception. Were a poem to be written entirely in the idiom represented by 'small dapper feet' and nothing else, a reader would be disappointed. Cast wholly in the idiom of 'the sea's phased formalities', then a reader equally alert to nuance, or, rather, its absence, would be alarmed, and might smell a fake, the sort of posturing which happens with the donning of latter-day singing-robes. Such garments are in Crichton Smith's wardrobe, but they are no sooner put on than taken off again. Of necessity, a contemporary poet has become a quick-change artist. He or she has more than one role to perform. It is the only way in which reality and what might be perceived beyond it can be contained by a writer for whom literal and poetic truth actually matter while permitting a proper, maximum freedom to both. Crichton Smith's poem, then, depends for its success on rapid contrasts of tone and image. Some pretty rough light verse is practically obliged to coexist with Eternity, God and the sea.

> The sea is rather extravagant and defiant
> but nevertheless God is a cunning client
>
> with an eye for the small print, a love of fences,
> brutal litigation, tough expenses,
>
> and, above all, a language more obscure
> then even a lawyer's.

By the end of this brief but intriguing (and also amusing) poem, the two idioms blend into an eccentric unity:

> A dream
> of happy carbons repeats busy Nature
> on an immense harmonious typewriter.

Other examples from the same collection are Nos 34 and 35. In the first poem, the grating, possibly self-pitying or defensive complaint of the opening lines — 'What's your Success to me who read the great dead? . . .' — is lifted from argumentative whinge into poetry's own truth:

> Over terraced houses
> these satellites rotate and in deep spaces
>
> the hammered poetry of Dante turns
> light as a wristwatch, bright as a thousand suns.

Obviously, the first simile is demotic and reductive, the second rhetorical and fulsome.

Poets younger than Crichton Smith have enjoyed an easier access to what seems a necessary displacement of both lyrical and rhetorical registers by demotic, argumentative and narrative styles, and *vice versa*. Larkin is perhaps the older figure whose work has been instructive. But poets like Seamus Heaney, Derek Mahon, Craig Raine, Robin Fulton, Michael Longley and several others all write as if by now it is taken for granted that sublime, transcendental or spiritual passages of experience can be deserved only if there are *other* passages in the same poem which acknowledge the conscious mind as well as imagination confronting visible reality and anything and everything within it. It seems fair to see the drama of Crichton Smith's poetry as an attempt to establish a right, instinctive balance between the imaginative and the social, the literal and the mysterious, the private and the public; it has been a restless, sometimes uncertain, and possibly even an anguished heave of his gift against its obsessive material.

For any one poet to articulate an epochal, harmonious proportion between the social and the spiritual, a true balance for the Age, a contemporary symmetry, is probably asking too much. A large part of the interest of recent poetry lies in discovering the achieved degree of coordination between these literal and imaginative extremes in an individual poet's work. After all, what it amounts to (or so it could be claimed) is how far a poet can integrate his or her temperament with the nature and demands of poetry and if he or she can do this to the extent of making poetry happen.

It is what Crichton Smith succeeds in getting through to consistently in his recent work. *A Life* (1986), for example, goes over subjects, places and people already familiar from earlier collections. But the book is not an opportunity for revision as much as a rewritten retrospective – new poems on old or permanent subjects. Why should he have done this? Part of the answer might be the need to have gone over ostensibly well-trodden areas of experience made unfamiliar by an enhanced understanding of his own work and the mind responsible for it – the kind of understanding that perhaps only the poet himself can really know very much about. Noticeable in *A Life* is how argument and narrative, while almost always present, tend to become secondary to the importance of imagery. In the best poems, saying becomes embodied almost seamlessly in a clash of candour with impersonality. Several ingrained attitudes and convictions remain, however. 'By the Sea', a sequence which appeared in *Selected Poems* (1970), is an impressive work flawed by how his observations of people and places on the Firth of Clyde encourage an excessive distaste for the vulgar, tawdry and wilfully secular and anti-poetic. But Crichton Smith's eye is sharp and the writing vivid as a result, so that the sequence creates an unsettling portrait of a solitary poet's disenchantment increasing poem by poem as he witnesses trivia in the context of a nuclear naval base's capacity for destroying the world.

Material life and the objects with which people ornament or assuage a possibly misplaced hunger for happiness have always filled Crichton Smith with a disdainful horror close to repugnance. Parts of *A Life* reflect a similar contempt; others seem to atone for it. 'Oban 1955–82', for example, consists of fourteen poems, many of them about schools and teachers. In the tenth poem, Crichton Smith acknowledges that the distractions with which the young are faced turn into contemporary ideals which neither literature nor education in general can shift. Fashionable attitudes to this kind of subject could look on these lines and find them chancy in how they risk condescension:

> The girls yearn
> for glamorous hairdressing, where helmets burn
>
> as if on space men. Through neglected terms
> they dream of dances and of wavy perms.

In one sense at least, the ratty consciences of the Left would be right in feeling that Crichton Smith is patronising schoolgirls. Yearning and dreaming are hard to ascribe to anyone other than yourself without begging the question, 'How do you know?' In 'By the Sea', Crichton Smith registered his dislike of popular chimeras and left it at that. Here, though, he turns against his own disdain. 'Sir, we are the stupid ones,' the school footballers say in the last poem of the series. 'Who has taught/ the inner rhythms of this outward play?' the unphysical poet asks. It is a dangerous pitch for a middle-aged poet. A touch of classical mythologising makes it even riskier:

> The English master with the grey moustache
> watches from the touchline. 'Fodder, these . . .
> But after all they rescued Rome and Greece
> for the lucid talkers who turned pale as ash.'

Auden fidgets in that phrase 'the lucid talkers'. What follows next – 'Bewildering gyrations!' – sounds like Larkin in his rhapsodic mood. Crichton Smith's style is curiously hospitable to other writers' habits; but the phrase introduces a beautiful image of goalkeeping:

> A ghost with gloves protects their universe.
> The net behind him is a complex thing.

The last quatrain delivers Crichton Smith's liberal compensation or apology:

> O graduate from this to Tennyson!
> We fail at fences which the others raise.
> We are practitioners of choice ideas.
> It is our turn to listen and to learn!

'Taynuilt 1982 – ' shows the imaginative and stylistic space he has been making for himself. It is a poetry which can speak more freely of

> so many owls
> sucking to their eyes

> the moon-struck mice
> in the leafy classroom,
>
> and the world a skirt
> turning a corner
> altering pleat by pleat
> its breezy sculpture.

Or, in the first poem of the Oban sequence,

> The War Memorial burns.
> One soldier helps another through the stone.

Poetry as confident and achieved as in these extracts has appeared in Crichton Smith's work from the beginning, usually in shorter poems where a notional metrical framework has been disavowed, or in metrical poems where a hot but almost always negative passion led him to dismiss the inherited terrors which threatened his work. In 'Envoi', he writes of how

> the punctual dead visit us, rise
> bird-voice from the grass,
> and the owls
> are scholars of the woods.

Hamlet (a frequent voice and visitor in Crichton Smith's work) is speaking to Horatio. Literariness, however, is cold-shouldered by the spoken movement of the poem's language and imagery. While still a 'literary' poem, 'Envoi' holds together and balances the several strands of a poetic personality that can at times be content with maladroit technique and a fragmentary disclosure of emotional states. It is recognisably a poem by the author of these lines from 'On a Summer's Day':

> This it is.
> There is much loneliness
> and the cigarette coupons will not save us.

A similar oddness or individuality occurs in the last lines of 'Envoi', expressing what he means in that line from his poems about Oban in *A Life*: 'We fail at fences which the others raise'. He is impatient of Tragedy, but at the same time he refuses to fall for a reductive pessimism or elevating optimism. 'The endlessly various, real, human world' ('Lenin') which he stated early on is fulfilled admirably as the poet's embrace of everyone and everything as the probable concerns of art.

> None is the same as another,
> O none is the same.
>
> And that none is the same is not
> a matter for crying.
>
> Stranger, I take your hand,
> O changing stranger.
>
> ('None is the Same as Another')

Hamlet, then, says in 'Envoi',

> Tragedy is
> nothing but a churned foam.
> I wave to you
> from this secure and leafy entrance,
> this wooden
> door on which I bump my head,
> this moment and then,
> that.

In *The Village* (1989), unexpected lyrical phrasings occur with satisfying frequency. In the last lines of 'Listen', for example, the sociable and the numinous become part of the same voice. Notice how the lines have been cleansed of redundant articles and conjunctions which form the over-lavish padding of his metrical verse. He writes of

> a resurrection of villages,
> townspeople, citizens, dead exiles,
> who sing with the salt in their mouths,
> winged nightingales of brine.

No-one else in Scottish poetry creates such lines, phrases and images, or releases a lyricism of the same kind or of comparable rarity and excellence. It is an achievement earned at the cost of having had to pave the way with indifferent and even bad verse, as in the tetchily programmatic *From Bourgeois Land*.

Something about Crichton Smith's patience, distractions and devotions is reminiscent of Rilke's image of Cézanne sitting in his garden like an old dog, 'the dog of this work that is calling him again and that beats him and let him starve'. Poetic truth, the disinterested purposiveness of poetry's veracity, a verisimilitude that relates to imaginative as well as literal reality, is indispensable to poetry. Without it, all that is left is one kind of easily described verse or another. But it is not easily obtained; it is not acquired by effort or choice or by technique, although a predisposition to a belief in its existence and importance, and the technical means adequate to its presentations, are both necessary. In modern times, however, poetic truth has become controversial as well as elusive. Whipped-up, self-willed vatic states of mind won't help, nor will down-home, nose-in-the-gutter, equally determined sniffings on the trail of the demotic. Both, in more or less exaggerated forms, are essential, but poetry insists on both, and that is the point. That seems instructively clear in the battered and distracted progress of Crichton Smith's poetry. Unfortunately, the phenomenon of poetic truth — which is often left unspoken and undiscussed — seems to have become identified as the illusory objective of those for whom society and its political and other concerns are to be avoided like the plague or treated with lofty scorn. It has become associated with flowers, the moon, the gods of this, that and the next thing, empty landscapes and preciosity of diction.

Whatever the path taken, and the routes are surely plural, the consequences for a serious artist are likely to be as Rilke suggested. On the one hand there will be what he means, metaphorically, by a beating, and, on the other, what he means by starvation. The dog of art never lets an artist go. Poetry's cost is always exorbitant. In Crichton Smith's poetry, there is a very distinct sensation of struggling towards a time when his poetry can win through to the perfection of which it dreams. As Sartre said in *What is Literature?*, there are no victories in poetry; no-one wins. It is not depressing. Or, rather, it is depressing only to those whose materialist casts of mind demand applause, triumph and reward.

# Six

## Law and Grace:
## A Note on the Poetry of Iain Crichton Smith*

### Gerald Dawe

It should come as no surprise that the two poets whom Iain Crichton Smith singled out for mention in the *Agenda* magazine 'State of Poetry' (Vol. 27, No. 3, 1989) symposium were W.H. Auden and Robert Lowell. Both poets avoided what Crichton Smith called 'an inescapable parochialism in contemporary writing' and their work was 'adventurous, risk-taking, exciting'. To his own question as to whose books he waits for 'with tingling excitement today', Crichton Smith responds: 'In poetry, no-one since Auden and Lowell'.

The stated concern for this preference, and the implied disenchantment with contemporary poetry that lies behind it, revolves around the inability of contemporary poetry to address 'the important issues of our time'. Auden and Lowell achieved this stature. There may also be a further, if hidden, association in Crichton Smith's mind with Robert Lowell since, like him, Crichton Smith has struggled as both poet and critic, with his immediate cultural and religious background. He has fought, as Lowell did, and Auden before him, with a recalcitrant, introverted, separate background that, in religious terms at least, presented itself as hostile to the imaginative life.

New England and the Isle of Lewis are literally poles apart, but, to the poet, they are both inspiration *and* obstacle. Similarly, the obscured 'England' which Auden re-imagined, and to some extent created out of diverse cultural and historical fragments, parallels the poetic focus to which I would like to draw attention in this chapter.

For if Auden knew by heart the moral, cultural and geographic dimensions of post-First World War England, the Scotland which

---

* Part of this chapter was previously published in the *New Edinburgh Review* (Summer, 1984).

Crichton Smith's poetry embodies is defined as much by religion as it is by the Gaelic culture and language in which he was brought up; both worlds defined by immense, incipient threat of extinction. It is a conflict rooted in much of what Crichton Smith has said about his own self-image as a writer:

> sometimes I feel that there are Free Church or religious elements in me which are in conflict with my art. I feel this conflict a great deal . . . Now, my attitude to Free Church and religion is very ambivalent. You see, in one sense I think of it as constricting, and, in another sense, I admire the people who belong to that church because they represent, in a very strong and almost unquestioning way, things which I find very difficult and very complex. One of the things I have had to find out as a poet is how to release the complexities within myself, not to find simple answers, because I think it is easy, coming from an island where religion is so strong, to think that you can find simple spiritual answers. So, religion is very important to me as a kind of force that I react against. (*Seven Poets*, 1981) pp. 42–3.

This is temperamentally close to the notes of Robert Lowell gathered together in *Collected Prose* (1987) and published as 'New England and Further'. In his piece on Hawthorne, Lowell describes the great nineteenth-century novelist as

> an ironic allegorist, therefore shady and suspect as a moralist. A being of such intermingled gloom and brightness, his mood is hard to find. One of his virtues, possessed by few of his forebears, is that he knew how to dislike, not the lawless and ungodly, but the simple, the tedious, the absurd. He fought off the Puritans, whose shades he partly invented, that they might sober his dark, imperilled repose. (p. 189)

The same ambivalence, the intermingling of 'gloom and brightness', licence and restraint, love and hate, law and grace, discipline and freedom determines the 'imperilled repose' of Iain Crichton Smith's poetry. Not only is Crichton Smith unenamoured with contemporary poetry, but one also senses in his writing a deep-seated unease with the contemporary world and, specifically, the poet's ability to confront it. There is a yearning for grandeur in Crichton Smith's poetry, a passionate melancholia at the state into which the art has fallen coupled with a shrewd realisation that other options on offer are more often than not wasteful dreams. The false vision of a restored Romanticism or the heroic rehabilitation of some mythical Gaelic order hold few attractions for Crichton Smith. Instead, one finds in his work as a poet and also in the critical essays he has collected in *Towards the Human* (1986) a steely grasp on what has become of the modern world.

From a state of island innocence, Crichton Smith experiences the fragmented and alienated urban society such as present-day Britain without flinching and with no faddish self-indulgent *angst*:

> the impression of sordidness that [one] gets from travelling through British cities, the breakdown of transport, the graffiti which shows the aggression of the 'homeless', the language of hatred, ferocious and misspelt, the feeling that one has of an urban world breaking down: the rushing from late trains to vandalised telephones, as if this was a land where people no longer feel at home.
>
> ... Where is the home of the urban dweller now? And if he looks into his mind what does he see but images of aggression and violence, beggary and greed, hatred and envy?
>
> ... It is against such a failure that one can set the idea of community, the idea of a culture. (*Towards the Human*, pp. 42–3)

This is the world too of Robert Lowell's New York — a violent, disintegrating life linked, by comparison, to the inert yet stable Boston, very much in the same way that Lewis is perceived in Crichton Smith's poetry as a familiar, secured place. Both poets, albeit in quite different ways, counterpose the available realities of social life against the (unexamined) idea of a fuller, more enriched community and culture, mediated through the knowledge of their own 'places' as an experiencing of 'the self'. It is quite literally a balancing act.

With Crichton Smith and Lowell, the relationship between 'community' and 'culture' in their own writing lives is deeply influenced by their own religious upbringing[1] and the cultural assumptions that such an upbringing brought with it. One need only recall the early poems of Lowell's such as 'The Protestant Dead in Boston'[2] or, from *Lord Weary's Castle* (1944) 'At a Bible House', where the portrait of the 'Mennonite/ Or die-hard Doukabor,/ God-rooted, hard' is echoed in poem after poem. With Crichton Smith too, the harshness of his landscapes underlines the tenacious self-righteousness of the dominant Protestant religion of his upbringing. Take 'A Note on Puritans'[3] for instance:

> That was great courage to have stayed as true
> to truth as man can stay. From them we learn
> how certain truths can make men brutish too:

>  how few can watch the bared teeth slow-burn
>  and not be touched by the lumps of fire they chew
>
>  into contempt and barrenness. I accuse
>  these men of singleness and loss of grace
>  who stared so deeply into the fire's hues
>  that was all fire to them.

The accusation recurs in different guises throughout Crichton Smith's poetry because the 'singleness' means 'loss of grace', and *that* loss is the greatest sin in Crichton Smith's book. It excludes, denies, represses and effectively destroys the possible communion of the individual life as found in art:

>  They have no place for fine graces
>  of poetry. The great forgiving spirit of the word
>  fanning its rainbow wing, like a shot bird
>  falls from the windy sky. The sea heaves
>  in visionless anger over the cramped graves
>  and the early daffodil, purer than a soul,
>  is gathered into the terrible mouth of the gale.
>
>  (Poem of Lewis)

As a poet, of course, Crichton Smith has attempted to overcome this 'loss of grace'. On the one hand, this has meant his waging a kind of war on the 'men of singleness', all the while harbouring an envy of the very thing he despises in them: their adamant belief that they are right. On the other hand, he must question his own self and where he stands in regard to what, after all, *made* him. This double bind is neatly summarised in what Crichton Smith has written about himself as being intellectually a free thinker but emotionally stained by the religion he rejects:

>  I do tend to be analytic. I don't know whether this is a bad thing or not. When one talks about the heart I begin to get very suspicious because I think a lot of Scottish poetry has . . . in the past suffered from too much emphasis on what might be called the heart . . . I think myself that I would prefer to be an analytical poet, rather than poet of the heart considered simply.

This ability of Iain Crichton Smith's to question his own past is particularly noteworthy, since it has an objectivity about it which is rare in contemporary poetry in English. Crichton Smith's clarity as a poet has an Augustan sense of compassion, satire *and* intellectual scrupulousness which neither diminishes its accessibility nor undermines its own artfulness in the interests of 'relevance'. He has been meticulous too in his use of autobiography, fearful, all the time, as he remarked of Lowell's later poems, of writing 'a rapid diary of events' (*Agenda*, p. 14).

Instead, Crichton Smith produces a perceptive concentration that transforms the domestic, everyday and mundane into something special, as in 'Tinily a Star Goes Down', which I quote in full:

> Tinily a star goes down
> behind a black cloud
>
> Odd that your wristwatch still should lie
> on the shiny dressing table
>
> its tick so faint I cannot hear
> the universe at its centre.

Or he embraces, with sympathetic scrutiny, the facts of history as these have been lived out in the poet's own name:

> All our ancestors have gone abroad.
> Their boots have other suns on them. They died
> in Canada and Africa with God,
>
> their mouths tasting of exile and spray.
> But you remained. Your grave is in Argyll
> among daffodils beside a tree
>
> feathery and green. A stream runs by,
> varying and oral, and your will
> becomes a part of it, as the azure sky
>
> trembles within it, not Canadian but
> the brilliant sparklings of pure Highland light.
>       (All Our Ancestors)

There is just the right degree of distance within this poem between the poet and his 'subject' to ensure that it is not a sentimentalised picture, nor is the experience merely an occasion for abstract rhetoric. The fine balance is the expression of an exact imagination and one that can also sustain a long but consistent meditation like 'Deer on the High Hills' or create, out of the most elementary moment, a line of reasoning such as 'The Glass of Water'. This means that even when Crichton Smith names names and calls out the standard and most available of images, the result is an actual poem and not a cypher for one, conventionalised out of existence:

> Stone and rain and mist on the mountains.
> The calm straits extend everywhere without sails.

> The minister in black drowses in his manse.
> Once they say there were thirteen hundred souls
> on Raasay. Now there are one hundred.
> The Isle of the Roe Deer is corruptly beautiful.
> Whose is the blind dog with the green eyes
> sniffing among the thorns? The silence is cruel.
> It makes the old faces thin and pale.
> Here time munches comfortably. Look out to sea.
> A live sheep, deep in the brine, stands with drenched wool.
> (Skye)

The cinematic zooming and documentary detail is only half the job; perversity rears its head in the blind dog and in a moment of imagined time that is literally terrible, were it not for that 'live sheep', human-like, 'deep in the brine'. What might have been a 'mists and heather' *cliché* becomes the genuine article. There are numerous examples of Iain Crichton Smith's poetry which display this deceptively plain sight. Sometimes it can indeed be unrelieved when the view has not a sufficient object in mind and the imagination is neither drawn upon nor playfully engaged. But generally the poems are focused and in such a way as to lead unpretentiously into their inner and often deeply troubled selves:

> A classical sanity considers Skye.
> A huge hard lights falls across shifting hills.
> This mind, contemptuous of miracles,
>
> and beggarly sentiment, illuminates
> a healthy moderation. But I hear
> like a native dog notes beyond his range
>
> the modulations of a queer music
> twisting his huge black body in the pain
> that shook him also in raw blazing London.
> (Johnson in the Highlands)

It must be from this restrained self-knowledge ('I hear/ . . . notes beyond his range') that Crichton Smith's poetic understanding can embrace a culture such as the Russian without straining, under the effect, our awareness of the obvious and profound differences which separate the two cultures. 'Russian Poem' is introduced in the following way by 'How Often I Feel Like You':

> This space is far too much for us like time.
> Even the clocks have asthma. There is honey,

> herring and jam and an old samovar.
> Help us, let something happen, even death.
> God has forgotten us. We are like fishers
> with leather-leggings dreaming of a stream.

The naturalness of the image of fishers 'in the stream' metaphorically corroborates the cry of 'Let something happen' in a world where 'space is far too much for us like time'. In the ten sections of 'Russian Poem', Crichton Smith dramatises the situation from figures of modern Russian literature (Gogol, Dostoyevsky) to its violent history (Great War, Revolution), picking up again on an earlier poem, 'Lenin', where

> the true dialectic is to turn
> in the infinity complex
> . . . for the moving on
> into the endlessly various, real, human
> world which is no new era
> shining dawn.

In Section IX of 'Russian Poem', he writes of Lenin:

> His head is a bell tolling for theses,
> articles, students, appendices and
> 'questions'.
>
> He has simplified the world like an assassin.
> Where his barrel points is where evil is.

In common with Lowell and Auden, Crichton Smith's poetry has an intellectual vitality that is far from abstract and rarely prosaic in the negative sense of that word. He consistently maintains an active regard for the integrity of languge to *produce* the kinds of insight out of which poetry is made. There is, in other words, no complacency in Iain Crichton Smith's poetry. At times he broaches a surreal installation of how the world appears to be (in poems like 'The Torches', 'If Ever I Loved You'), or, in 'On an Icy Day', he draws out of Hamlet a fable for our own times such as Boris Pasternak did before him:

> And what is that face in the mirror? Is it Claudius?
> blowing his drunken trumpet, power at the source?
>
> The ordinary folk are sliding hither and thither.
> They never look in the mirror but straight
> ahead of them

towards the shrunken branches, baskets
clutched in their hands.

Crichton Smith's poetry embodies this open ground, an imaginary place where words form new associations without losing face. This combination of ease and formality, in the shifts from colloquial fluency to lucid elegance, is all the more impressive because it conveys what has been described by Stan Smith as Iain Crichton Smith's belief in the 'strenuous demands of the intellect and the puritan conscience'.

If I read him at all well, Crichton Smith is committed to pursue a middle course, as it were, between the ostensibly exclusive in-house games of latter-day post-modernism (whatever about the Masters themselves) and the prickly briars of a self-consciously nativist or regionalist art. This middle course relates to the public image of the poet which emerges from Crichton Smith's poetry.

Again Pasternak comes to mind in what Peter France and Jon Stallworthy have described as his 'artistic asceticism' and the rejection of 'the romantic manner by which [Pasternak] meant principally the insistence of the "I" of the writer, who is set off in a spectacular way against the mass of ordinary people' (Pasternak: *Selected Poems*, 1984)

Pasternak's emphasis upon the responsibility and modesty of the artist would, I imagine, find a sympathetic hearing in Crichton Smith's court. What is of special interest here is the way Iain Crichton Smith explores the cultural dimensions of the artist in the context of his own and his country's past, probing the extent of imaginative freedom and the depth of inherited inhibition. Crichton Smith may not go far enough for some tastes in pursuing the effects of this relationship and the political significance of the fact that this culture was (and still is to a large extent) pre-eminently Protestant.

From these grounds, however, other questions proliferate. Does the contradiction between island-son and city-boy that works through so much of Crichton Smith's poetry account for the insistent sense of estrangement from the pieties of his past which the poet cannot reasonably accept any more, but cannot dismiss either without losing a substantial part of himself? Is there a fundamental conflict between the 'Protestant' (Calvinist) moral and spiritual code and the poet's ordering of reality into a form of art? Is it possible for a rejected religious background to intervene so persistently in the very make-up of a writer's vision as to inherently determine it? What chance has the imagination?

One thinks of Beckett as a possible comparison. Is there a damning hostility in the experience of the Protestant faith and ritual when it aligns itself with and conforms to an unstable, ideologically limited and sexually repressive social system? Beckett fled. So too, in different material and cultural circumstances, did Lawrence. In such a situation of inherent and inherited social and cultural antagonism to the life of the imagination, is the poet's language and artistic ambition likely to be negatively circumscribed? Can a writer, finally, transform this inheritance into a creative one without having to accept limitations to his or her art, or can he or she defy such conditions as if they did not matter? Can there ever be an Eden for the writer?

Iain Crichton Smith's response is to engage with the demons of his own particular time and place and make out of them a poetry of vigilant lucidity and independence:

> No, I have angels. Mine
> are free and perfect. They have no design
> on anyone else, but only on my pride,
>
> my insufficiency, imperfect works.
> They often leave me but they sometimes come
> to judge me to the core, till I am dumb
> Is this not law enough, you patriarchs?
> (The Law and the Grace)

The question embodies the full vigour and grace of Iain Crichton Smith's poetry as art takes on life.

NOTES

1. The fact that Robert Lowell converted to Roman Catholicism underlines the need he felt to distance himself from Protestantism only to discover, as he remarked in an interview with Ian Hamilton: 'Catholics and Calvinists I don't think opposites; they are rather alike compared to us in our secular sprawl. From zealous, atheistic Calvinist to a believing Catholic is no great leap. We overhammer the debating points. Yet Calvinism is a too-conceived abstract-expressionist Church of Rome' (*Collected Prose*, p. 277).
2. Ian Hamilton, *Robert Lowell: A Life* (1983), p. 76.
3. Poems by Iain Crichton Smith are taken from *Selected Poems 1955–80* (1981).

# Seven

## First the Footprints, then the Unfathomable: Writing, Difference and Death in the Later Poetry

### Stan Smith

THE STUBBORN PLACE

In a 1971 interview, Iain Crichton Smith observed that 'everything I have ever done is really eventually coming to this question. What is death? What is a dead person, and in the end what is the value of writing when one is confronted by a dead person?' In Crichton Smith's poetry, writing is repeatedly 'confronted by a dead person'. Death is not an abstraction consummately addressed on the initiative of the poem. Rather, the actual presence of a dead body thrusts itself abruptly upon textuality, its oxymoronic bluntness questioning our basic assumptions about identity and self-presence: for if a 'person' is defined by subjectivity, as a writing, speaking self, how can this *thing* relate to the subject it once was?

In the earlier verse, death is regularly troped, even in its shocking presence, as the morbid figure of other kinds of loss, lack and absence in a dying and haunted culture, where the wreck of the Iolaire, the carcass of a dead sheep, or the mythic and fictional necrophilia of Orpheus and Hamlet provide scope for meditations of a more general nature. In *Hamlet in Autumn* (1972), in the words of one poem,

> Death was everywhere, it was a plague.
> The reasonable man became obsessive.
> ('Oedipus and Others')

What is remarkable in these powerful poems, in retrospect, is the control which the 'reasonable man', the writing subject, exercises over his death-obsessed creations, declaring along with Creon '"The king must rule, that's what a king is for"', refusing even as he acknowledges the 'ecstasy of longing' in which Antigone dies. If the poet's *anima*, in the Jungian terms also appropriate to *Orpheus and Other Poems* (1974) where the lost bride merges with the dead mother, figures itself forth as Antigone here, choosing to die herself in loyalty to the recently dead, Creon represents that strong voice of the superego decreeing that the show must go on, the voice of a 'wise Athens' where

> The light burns fiercely on a public stage.
> They're all proud germs the theatre must kill.

The assumption of the Hamlet persona in this volume is significant. The intellectual prince is half in love with easeful death, yet also rages impotently at the murderous interruption which has cut short his own real plot and forced him to take on a melodramatic role in an outmoded parental theatre, a fate to which he adjusts by re-enacting the primal drama upon a public stage, rendering all things theatrical, including grief. The Freudian dimension summoned up by Oedipus and Hamlet alike is not accidental, though it may be less than intended, for what these poems offer in a particularly pure form is a series of meditations on the intertwining of *eros* and *thanatos* which invites the intervention of a Lacanian reading.

For Jacques Lacan, the trauma of the child's separation from the Mother, under the shadow and in the name of the castrating Father, inscribes loss at the heart of a subject who comes into being *as a result of* this rupture. In this moment of scission, the child for the first time becomes aware of itself as another, difference from the Mother (the 'Mirror Phase'). It enters, that is, the Symbolic, the order of language, which is also the order of difference and non-identity. The Imaginary is constructed in the same moment as the retrospective fantasy of that lost union with the Mother. All subsequent separations, in varying measure, revive the terrors of that original schism. Since this was the originary moment of the subject, such rites of passage are always perilous and fraught, shot through with an anxiety where selfhood and loss of self are paradoxically intertwined, and the death-drive is charged with libidinal energy.

The mother's death, the theme of many of Crichton Smith's poems in the 1970s, reawakens all these ancient traumas, with a profound shock to the subject's confidence in its own rootedness, mobilising guilts, anxieties and disturbances that rock its foundations, it at once seeks to identify with the absent site of fulness, the mother's body, completed in death, and to recover, Orpheus-fashion, that lost imaginary plenitude by an act of restitution and restoration. In order to overcome its terror, the subject has to rewrite itself into the record as autonomous and self-constituting, turning its back on loss, lack, deprivation. The power of the literary imagination then acts not only to confront but also to displace, defer, the enormity of death. Love, as in the *Orpheus* sequence, almost but not quite reclaims the beloved Eurydice from the underworld, but, in failing to do so, reinstates the bereaved self as a source of power, agency and authority, a language-marking subject, mastering disturbance by an appropriative writing, in the Name of the Father.

This chapter does not intend to psychoanalyse the biographical Iain Crichton Smith. It attempts, rather, a *psychanalyse du texte* which explores the primal drama of which Crichton Smith's poems are the site. There are, nevertheless, biographical over-determinations which prepare his writing for this confrontation with the body of death. After his father's early death, Crichton Smith's mother inevitably came to combine both parental roles, in a peculiar compacting of the Oedipal triangle. Crichton Smith has himself written of the smothering closeness and solicitude which he experienced in childhood as 'suffocating', a condition psychosomatically translated into bodily form in recurrent attacks of bronchitis and asthma. It is no accident, then, that the trauma of his mother's death should be relived in *Love Poems and Elegies* (1972) in images of suffocation, or that the cause of her death from 'lack of oxygen' ('You Told Me Once') in these elegies should, in a powerful transference, cross over to the love poems, 'Poems for S.', as a metaphor of lonely asphyxia in the airless depths of space which figures forth the loss of love.

Through this shared trope, the love poem 'The Dream' links with the elegy 'The Space-Ship'. In the former, the poet suffers the metaphysical loneliness of the astronaut, a drifting, abandoned Eurydice whose oxygen supply is running out. In the elegy, it is more conventionally the mother at the point of death who is Eurydice. But the power of analogy works to conceal her disappearance by transference to the abandoned but still dependent figure of the astronaut-child, his umbilical link to the mother ship severed, dying for lack of a nurturing oxygen:

> I think of you and then I think of this
> picture of an astronaut lacking air
> dying of lack of it in the depths of space.

The real death drifts off into a metaphoric space where both mother and son, the 'I' and 'you' constituted in thought in the opening line, disappear into a third-person narrative in which the death of a sun 'exploding with tremendous light' mirrors the explosion of the spaceman's suit. This vertiginous loss of self, dispersed into 'the crystal of unnumbered stars' in the 'limitless azure' of the abyss, is enacted in the disappearance of personal pronouns. The death of the mother is thus both evoked and evaded. The lack of which she died becomes a figure of what she is: lack itself, pure absence. The separation of death re-enacts that fateful primal rupture in which, in Lacanian terms, entering the Symbolic, the child learnt of – that is, invented for itself – the always-already lost Imaginary where it was one with the mother. As in all those poems about old women in his earlier books, the mother is the figure of lack precisely because the maternal body is also the site of fulness, of that homely plenitude which is the goal of Antigone's longing and of Oedipus' and Hamlet's desire. Yet the loss is curiously consoling. At this moment of final sundering, the son repossesses in the Symbolic order the body of the mother, enfolds her in his gaze, preserves her as a speaking subject who 'told me once' and now will be retold in a writing which recreates her. The dead mother and the bereaved son are reunited in a shared linguistic space where selfhood is absorbed into the Oceanic experience of the womb, void becoming fulness.

The strategy whereby literature recuperates death lies at the heart of 'You Told Me Once'. The poem opens by recalling his mother's account of her younger brother's drowning at sea, singing a psalm to guide would-be rescuers to him. It then shifts abruptly, across the stanza divide, to her own death in the bumpy and belated ambulance, fulfilling by her lights a destiny as predetermined as her brother's. The transition between these two moments inserts a literary self-consciousness into the poem:

> One cannot hide,
> you would have said, from destiny. So here
> there are two meanings working side by side.
>
> You died of lack of oxygen . . .
> I thought that moment of the psalm as guide
> beyond our vain technology.

The two meanings are the two lives (and deaths) overlaid in the text as in memory, replete with all the resonances of vanity. They are also the two narratives, human and divine, here both coincident and at odds in this third, poetic narrative. On the one hand, there is the personal life of wishes and desires, that used the psalm pragmatically to guide the rescuers, in which the nature of the song was irrelevant (anything might have done as well). On the other, there is the narrative of divine providence which has already shaped his end and is present in the very *content* and *original purpose* of the psalm. But Crichton Smith's poem also self-consciously multiplies its double meanings. In contemplating one death, it reaches out to another, and beyond that to another, the poet holding his mother's death in personal memory as she held her brother's and as her brother's in turn called up the psalmist's, in a *mise en abyme* which takes us back to the origin of things. At either end of this process, then, is a text, whether the psalmist's or the poet's, both walking in the valley of the shadow of death. But encompassing both is the storyteller constituted by the title and the opening line. It is the mother, the absent author of the poet's being, whose voice is vicariously reinstated as the author of the poem by 'You told me once'.

The indirect reported speech, however, though it gives priority to the 'You' of the imagined addressee, does not really supersede the writing 'I' of the poet. He may feel himself 'tossed aside' like those blankets (mortal coils) which the mother casts off in the moment of death, but his survival is the very premise on which this narrative is founded. The two meanings side by side are those of the *énoncé* and of the *énonciation* simultaneously. Death is not denied by these multiple literary displacements; but its sting is drawn by a story-telling which inscribes resurrection in its opening premise, uniting mother and son in a single discourse as its end prefigures the death of the author.

Throughout *Love Poems and Elegies*, a tender Orphic eroticism suffuses the elegies, as a plangently funereal tone pervades the love poems, many of which could refer equally to the lost mother as to the departed lover. (The actual sequence of elegies and love poems in the book reverses the order of the title, overlaying grief and desire to the confusion of genre.) 'No One At Home', the opening poem of 'Poems for S.', is an almost gruesome evocation of a beldame-sans-merci who is never at home when he calls, who prowls the streets restlessly with a brain full of snakes, and is 'as white as an eel . . . upright in the water, almost dead'. She is 'an angel whose bubbles are all gone' (like the mother's oxygen), associated with a music that records '"there is no place as terrible as home"'. Again, 'I Thought I Saw You' could refer either to dead mother or absent lover. The poem evokes a double absence, moving at once into the imagery of haunting, asking 'What receives your ghost?' and acknowledging that 'The mind has tricks that we are desperate for'. The poem asks difficult questions about the object of desire figured by the maternal body: 'How can we turn away? there is no home/ other than it'. 'Resurrection, equally confuses living lover and dead mother, as she 'rise[s] from the dead ghosts of last night's party'.

Everywhere in these poems, textuality is a paradoxical dimension which inscribes absence and emptiness as it constructs an imaginary

*First the Footprints*

plenitude. The stark lines of 'On Looking at the Dead' sum up the paradox. Ostensibly they proclaim the obduracy of the real, beyond and unassimilable to language, stress the need to go beyond metaphor, in 'confronting a dead person':

> This is a coming to reality.
> This is the stubborn place. No metaphors swarm
>
> around that fact, around that strangest thing,
> that being that was and now no longer is.
>
> This is a coming to a rock in space
> worse than a rock (or less), a diminished thing
>
> worse and more empty than an empty vase.

The dead are empty. But then the living are not, conversely, full. Indeed, the dead have a kind of fulness, since they are totally at one with themselves. It is consciousness which inserts distance and difference through the intervention of a language which everywhere estranges the Real. The Real here seems to be identified with a Death which, as 'Shall Gaelic Die?' observes, 'is outside the language. The end of language is beyond language. Wittgenstein didn't speak after his death.' Only 'God is outside language, standing on his perch', an empty signifier projected into the void, ironically giving us back our own words as nonsense, like a parrot. Here, however, the living man still speaks. Grief itself is a register of survival, and survival occurs within the estranging order of language.

PHANTOM OF A BOOK

'On Looking at the Dead' denounces metaphor, repeating a motif of 'Deer on the High Hills': 'There is no metaphor, the stone is stony'. The denunciation is troped and trumped as it is uttered, for the literal concept of 'metaphor' is metaphorically transformed into flies around the poem's cadavre, filling the deathly silence with the buzz of words. The body of the Real is an ineluctable presence, a corpse seen as in some ways *more* real than the self-conscious subject it once was, than the still-living subject who now grieves over it. Yet, *identical with* itself, the corpse is also not *present to* itself, does not know that gap in being between self and other, consciousness and body.

It is at this very moment of schism that the 'devious mind' of the bereft son can repossess the body of the mother. Even to attribute stubbornness to the inert body is to restore will and volition to it. As the 'it' of a general condition turns into the specific 'it' of the corpse, so the 'you' of the poet, reflexively self-addressed in antithesis to it, merges with the 'you' of a mother who was once living, to create a 'we' united by the possessive plural of 'our stony gaze', fusing the blank stare of the dead with the grief-numbed stare of the survivor. Mother and son are reunited in a grammatical confusion which abolishes separation. The stubborness is as much that of the devious mind as of the intransigent body:

> The devious mind elaborates its rays.
> This is the stubborn thing. It will not move.
>
> It will not travel from our stony gaze . . .
>
> and this is real, nothing more real than this.
> It beats you down, will not permit
>
> the play of imagery, the peacock dance,
> the bridal energy or mushrooming crown
>
> or any blossom. It is only itself.
> It isn't you. It is only itself.

The eyes of the mother return nothing. The son's gaze has now become the originary centre of things. But, standing in this centre, he is displaced in a long, final sentence which never finds the main verb that would centre him as its articulating subject. A metaphor from astrophysics focuses the paradox of a centre which is not fulness and self-presence, but a void that sucks all meaning into itself, abolishing it in the process. In her death, the nurturing mother becomes one with the voracious absence which has engulfed her, and thus obliquely identified with the devouring mother of fable and Freud:

> To face it where it is
> to stand against it in no middle way
> but in the very centre where things are
> and having it as centre, for you take
> directions from it not as from a book
>
> but from this star, black and fixed and here,
> a brutal thing where no chimeras are . . .

The idea of the book, of textuality, even negatively evoked, rebuffs the black hole of meaninglessness. The last of the elegies, 'The Earth Eats Everything', expands the motif of a devouring maternal earth, and sets up in opposition the tombstone as the text in which the son traces his

*First the Footprints*

survival, inscribing and deciphering his own succession in a recurrent forgetting and recall:

> The earth eats everything there is.
> It is a year and a half now since you died.
> Your marble tombstone stands up like a book.
> The storms have not read it nor the leaves . . .
> I have forgotten it over and over.
> Life is explainable only by life.
> I have read that on paper leaves.

To outlive is to go on reading — redemptively *re*-reading that which is expunged. Writing is at once as temporary as the leaves of a tree, and as obdurate as marble. The same image is troped in a love poem also preoccupied with the absence of the beloved body, 'Where Are You Tonight?':

> Sometime long ago we were sent to bed
> and held the page up like a tombstone,
> which later was our fascination and our pride . . .
> I see you bowed in the rain over
> your green and humming leaves forever
> child, reader, insatiable sister,
> phantom of a book, holding a book in your hands.

The poem constructs a purely verbal 'we' as the subject of its sentence, putting the lovers to bed together in an *imaginary* shared childhood, in the process making the bridal bed a place both of reading and of death, the two merged in the idea of *inscription*. The woman is the 'phantom of a book', formed by back-formation from the book she holds and reads. This is a peculiarly self-involuted trope — an involution echoed in that transgression of the incest taboo which recreates her metaphorically as an 'insatiable sister', standing in, in the signifying chain, for the devouring mother and the voracious maternal earth. This insatiable reader/lover also devours writers, reducing them in the process to shadows of men, 'facsimiles of other men's thoughts,/ footnotes explainable by scholarship'. There is a remarkable condensation in the simile which expands this idea: 'We are like asterisks in the shady sky/ and more translatable than poetry'. The pun on *aster*, a star, recalls the black hole of 'On Looking at the Dead'. It suggests that 'translatability' is also a figure of death, the living body translated as in the myth of Astraea into a sign in the heavens which registers an absence, as the asterisk indicates what is missing in a text, or signals its displacement elsewhere, to the foot of the page, the end of the book.

The phrase 'no middle way' in 'On Looking at the Dead' recalls T.S. Eliot's meditation on mortality in 'East Coker', 'In the middle, not only in the middle of the way/ But all the way, in a dark wood'; and Crichton Smith's black hole may update that same poem's vision, shortly after, of 'The vacant interstellar spaces' into which the dead proceed, 'the vacant into the vacant'. Both poets in turn recall Dante's phrase at the start of his own Orphic descent, 'nel mezzo del cammin'. The phrase is taken up in the title of Crichton Smith's last volume of the 1970s, *In the Middle* (1977), which in one poem postulates a comparison between Crichton Smith's Scotland, where 'the people walk with . . . newsprint over their bodies', and Dante's Florence, with 'newsboys shouting out his latest verses', body mysteriously conjoined to textuality.

A jacket note for this volume wilfully casts the poet not as the masterful author of his own words but as the surprised reader, finding them to be other than he thought:

> Reading them, I find that what they seem to be about is the strangeness and eeriness of reality. I had wanted to write about simple things, the traffic of day to day, but found that overwhelming these was a cry or scream of mortality. Now and again, the world of the scholar and the 'elitist' enters, but with diminishing force. It is as if these poems – perhaps too simple – were telling me of the horror which closes Conrad's *Heart of Darkness* but that in the end – as in the last poem – we must celebrate change which is the source of the horror.

This is a striking comment. Not only does it displace the author from determining authority over the meaning of his texts; it also speaks of ends ('in the end – as in the last poem') which return us to the origin — a source, as in Conrad's novella, which is the place of horror where all begins and ends in a cry or scream that overwhelms the speaking, 'rational' subject, the 'elitist' superego. It is the poet as reader, secondary to the text, and not as writer, prior to and author of it, who *finds* these things, as if for the first time, in a text in which his self is externalised as *other*. The relation between writer and reader figures for Crichton Smith the pattern of all intersubjective relations, in which we are all in our exchanges secondary to the text which constitutes us, phantoms of a book.

LOST FOREVER TO THESE FABLES

The title poem of *In the Middle* places the poet 'in the middle' of opposing forces. But the significance of the title has perhaps less to do with Dante than with the Aristotelian prescription for storytelling, which should begin not at the beginning but 'in the middle of things'.

It adds a modern twist to this idea: we are all born *in medias res*, and this is also where we die, for death cuts short a narrative the true conclusion of which, for the experiencing subject, is perpetually deferred. The last poem of the volume, to which Crichton Smith refers in his jacket note, 'None is the Same as Another', is pre-eminently about this saving *différance*, its ambiguous title proposing both identity and difference at the same time, depending on how we construe the verb 'is' and its relations to the concepts 'none', 'same' and 'another'. Language constitutes a discourse in which the subject is perpetually estranged from itself, displaced, superseded, endlessly shifting. But the Other, the object of perception, also perpetually changes. Otherness, difference, is inscribed right in the heart of the self. We read a text we have written and it is strange to us, estranged from us. We are at once and irreconcilably the text as *énonciation* and as *énoncé*. In life, too, we are other to ourselves and other to another, and this, paradoxically is both 'matter for crying/ since never again will you see/ that one, once gone' and also 'not/ a matter for crying', so that the poem concludes with a welcoming of that difference in which being and significance are forever deferred: 'Stranger, I take your hand,/ O changing stranger'.

The three volumes of the 1980s, *The Exiles* (1984), *A Life* (1986) and *The Village* (1989), take their cue from these lines. Thus the first poem of *The Exiles*, 'Returning Exile', echoes the last words of *In the Middle*, addressing a 'beloved stranger' who remains unnamed but who is readily identified as Odysseus, known by his old dog when his wife, the putative speaker of the poem, fails to recognise him. The note is one of initial reproach turning to a welcome which requires no substantiating narrative:

You who come home do not tell me
anything about yourself, where you have come from . . .

Do not tell me where you have come from, beloved stranger . . .

In the opening poem of *A Life*, the poet himself has come home like a returning child to reproachful questioning not from a patient wife but from a dying mother, who asks, fixated on separations, 'When did you come home? When are you leaving?' The second poem of the sequence repeats the temporal doubling of 'You Told Me Once' with its image of a mother who in her sleep 'calls on her dead mother, her live son', hanging on to a 'frayed thread of being' which is also a thread of narrative like that which sustained Theseus against death in the labyrinth. She becomes, in the peripeteia of the poem's ending, the child of her own son. This is the pattern of the whole sequence in which, like Stephen Dedalus at the end of *A Portrait of the Artist*, the poet reforges his forebears as fictive children. *The Village* continues this impulse in a drive to recover the *present*, to evoke the ordinary world around a poet who has, like Odysseus, finally settled in one dear perpetual place. It is, nevertheless, a poetry of place shot through with intimations of elsewhere, of other places where the world unravels its stories.

While in no way a formal trilogy, these three volumes interact among themselves to tell a story of sorts. Echoes of language and image, recapitulations and premonitions, bind them together into a coherent group. Even their parsimonious titles, moving from the general to the particular and from displacement to place, organise a life into its synchronic and diachronic dimensions. *The Exiles* extends widely in time and space, telling the separate tales of many different exiles and returns, from the *Nostos* of Odysseus, through the Highland crofters despatched to Canada or Australia in the eighteenth and nineteenth centuries, to the Nazi war criminal in 'The Man Without a Name', assuming a new identity in America, ironically converted into a 'Wandering Jew'. Conjoined in the book's single space, all these separate lives are bound together by its collectivising definite article in a community of exile, where displacement of one kind or another becomes the very model of being-in-the-world. *A Life* then offers a diachronic account of one particular version of this general exile, the poet's own, tracing in its departures and returns a common destiny. *The Village* finally situates this life synchronically, in the real place it nominates as a provisional home, and it looks in on some of the other lives congregated in this same space, each with a past and future of their own.

'Home', however, is not a secure concept in Crichton Smith's work. As 'Autumn' tells us, 'exile, parting, is our earthly lot', though 'Art feeds us, famished' with delusions of belonging. 'Next Time' picks up the story of Odysseus once more only to see in its endless rereadings a model of a life in which 'return' is the delusion of a consciousness that yearns for closure in a world where all true narratives speak the language of exile. The poem moves from the instruction to 'enter the boat/ and leave the island/ for there is no return' to consider Penelope's narrative threadwork as a model for all plots: 'let the tapestry be unfinished/ as truthful fiction is'. As 'No Return' insists, 'really you can't go back to/ that island any more . . ./ the fairy stories/ have gone down to the grave in peace'. Heraclitus rules on Lewis as on Helicon, and

> You can't dip your mouth in the pure spring
> ever again or ever again be haunted
> by 'the eternal sound of the ocean'.

## First the Footprints

This island home was never an 'objective' reality, always only a bundle of fairy stories told by 'The old story-telling people' who 'have gone home to their last houses' so that the island is left bare, with a sly play on 'composed',

> itself alone in its barren corner
> composed of real rocks and real flowers
> indifferent to the rumours and the stories
> stony, persistent.

In 'The Legend', the poet speaks of receiving a letter from an old schoolmate in which 'I am returned to what seemingly I was'. This is, though, no simple Odyssean 'return'. What he once was ('seemingly') remains problematic, a site of repression, blankness, and loss:

> I can remember nothing. Was I like that?
> The anthology of memories of the other
> is a book I hadn't reckoned on. My fear
>
> or rather hope is that I am put back
> further and further in that clutch of tales
> till I am lost for ever to these fables,
>
> O false and lying and yet perhaps true . . .
> without a title, a great blank behind me,
>
> and only a real future ahead,
> myself with a caseful of impersonal poems.

The self here is dispossessed from a past which is supposedly its own but which actually belongs in the narratives of another. He is, or wishes to be, 'lost forever to these fables' in a double and a contradictory sense: both taken over, appropriated by their urgent narrative insistences, finding by surrendering himself; but also disappearing into them – simultaneously totally available to the stories and not available at all. What both conditions share, however, is loss of self-presence. These multiple texts all proclaim the death of that subject who speaks for and of himself, and the very poem in which he writes of the process has itself already become, by the time we read it, a fable to which the real author is forever lost. For, as we read this poem, the author has become no more than the traces of an absence in somebody else's text, reduced from living body to a fabular writing punningly 'without a title', 'returned to what I was' as a mere 'clutch of tales'. Every text is a tombstone, every poem an epitaph, in which we read of the death of the author.

### THE WAKES ARE FOR EVERYONE

Writing the self, or having it written by another, alike recall the speaking subject to its earthly mortality. In 'When My Poetry Making

Has Failed' (*The Exiles*), volatility and loss of self grip a subject whose identity and origin are always elsewhere, in a place where language touches the real at its source, divining 'the water that runs . . ./ from some place that I have been and cannot remember/ where the words stand around like rocks'. The poem which follows this begins with the idea of writerly mortality, 'Always in the same way the poets die', with the simultaneous crossing and closing of horizons, and ends with a recurrent image for the pattern of both a life and a text, lights trembling in 'the unmown wake' of the late evening water. The wake is a key concept in all three volumes of the 1980s, its ambiguity (a death wake, the wake of a boat) central to their ambivalences.

Elsewhere in *The Exiles*, the topos is again associated with reading/ writing. 'Reading Shakespeare' speaks of an author who 'always remains' amid 'changeable' weathers, in a world full of departures. But in fact all we have of 'Shakespeare the man' are the writings which inscribe his absence. Like the poet in the anthology of his friend's memories, Shakespeare is precisely *not here*. To underline this point, this poem is followed by 'Speech for Prospero', which turns from *reading* to *rewriting* Shakespeare. Following Auden in *The Sea and the Mirror*, it extends *The Tempest* beyond its final speeches, to put words into the mouth of a fictive Prospero who has left the island of his exile to return to a different exile in Milan. The ship's *wake* is here a central image, both the trace of abandoned meanings, 'shining and fading' and, like an umbilicus, the 'cord of a new birth', linked ambivalently to 'the telephones . . . ringing with messages from the grave'.

The 'wake' metaphor recurs with a complicating ambiguity in *A Life*. There, at the end of the Lewis childhood section, he recalls the annual visit to Stornoway and the cinema. The poem deploys a repertoire of film allusions, from Laurel and Hardy to Errol Flynn, as the discourses within which the boy constructed his ideas of being-in-the-world, including the North Pacific island which was the setting of one such war film:

> On Wake Island
> we left the wakes behind, and strode, blinded,
> into the brittle sunlight. This town is
>
> too small for both of us, bowlered minister.
> The colours of the cinema warmer than
>
> your plain clear window. Till we reach our homes
> we ride the gulches of the starved fields.

The ambiguity of the word 'wake', underline by the play on the island's name, alerts us to other innuendoes. Complex Oedipal adjustments are taking place here at the level of the text's unconscious: coming out of the dark cinema into unexpected sunlight (metaphor of a birth to selfhood), the rebellious son is metaphorically blinded like Oedipus for an unwitting parricide refigured in the re-enacted gunfight with the minister. Modelling a sense of self on cinematic images, the emergent boy rides the gulches of a cowboy film superimposed in imagination on the starved fields of home. Selfhood is constructed out of renunciations which are then reproduced in the opening line of the next section ('The glitter of the water and the wake'), where the seventeen-year-old, leaving home for university in Aberdeen, experiences the pristine freshness of a world in which 'I see the train/ for the first time ever steaming from the Kyle'. That 'for the first time ever' hovers beautifully, though we are not fooled, between the seeing and the thing seen, just as we can infer an innuendo of sexual initiation in the way the landscape 'unwinds/ its perfect symmetry' for him.

These Oedipal adjustments, in which the self enters into separate identity by re-enacting in a positive mode that trauma of separation from the maternal body, explain the intensity with which the adolescent responds to the blind beggar on Aberdeen station. This encounter with the real is obsessively replayed in Crichton Smith's writings, the literal event transformed by its repetition into a powerful imaginative trope. It is usually associated with recollections of his mother's impoverished widowhood, saved from beggary by a nurturing community. Although an intensely 'real' occasion, the incident has its textual precedent in a famous passage of Wordsworth's *Prelude* (Book VII) where the young poet, similarly fresh from the country, thrown into the disorienting world of the city, finds himself 'As if admonished from another world' by a blind beggar on the street, wearing on his chest 'a written paper, to explain/ His story, whence he came, and who he was'. The young Crichton Smith, like the young Wordsworth, finds his joy in his new-found independence darkened by this brutal return of the repressed, in which the beggar, figuring forth subliminally his own dead father, bestows on him his birthright of mortality:

> Should I freely give?
> Or being more shameful than himself refrain?
> His definite shadow is the day's black stain.
> How in such open weakness learn to live?
>
> I turn away, the money in my hand,
> profusely sweating, in that granite blaze.

>     Unknown, unlooked at, I pick up my case.
>     Everything's glittering and transient.

In this moment of metaphysical vulnerability, the future poet is rescued by the alternative *textual* father (also blind) to whom he instinctively clings: 'I hold my Homer steady in my hand'. It is in the mystical succession of writing and reading that the subject resists its own erasure. But at the same time, writing as trace is what testifies to that very erasure as, in another image in *A Life*, 'The jet plane leaves a trail in the blue sky', announcing thus that it is already 'far from us// in another country, almost another time'. 'The trail I leave is far more tortuous', the poet remarks, 'invisible and quite tentative'. That trail both inscribes absence and affirms the possibility of presence, of a community which can exist only in *language*.

At the end of *A Life*, the morbidity of Mathew Arnold's 'To Marguerite' and 'Dover Beach', in which the sea is an image of estrangement and separation, is rejected in the name of a solidarity in which 'we are not estranged/ by the salt billows', and 'There is no island/ the sea unites us', restoring even the drowned, the exiled, the effaced, 'the homeless ones/ forever rowing'. The poem integrates the two meanings of 'wake' in a single image which metaphorically overcomes the lonely exile of the self in the world:

>     The wakes
>     are for everyone
>     and the large sun
>     glints on the excised names
>     of the exiles.

But if the dead are reincarnated in the bodies of the living, 'precious ones/ whose flesh is my own,// and who arise each day / to a new desert', what reclaims them from *erasure* ('excised names') is precisely *writing*, as their 'inscribed faces/ burn out of the brine'. This is not any mystical return but, as a poem in *The Village* makes clear, an embodied, biological one. 'It is true that the drowned return to us', says 'The Drowned', for their legacy is encoded, written into the genes, and we are the traces, the wake in which they reawaken:

>     articulating
>     sons and grandsons of themselves, stumpy
>     authentic chimes,
>
>     echoes, reflections, shadowy
>     waves that speak through the new waves,
>     underwritings, palimpsests,

> a ghost literature behind another one,
> carbons that have faint imprints on them.

Living and dead alike in the next poem, 'Villagers', are 'bone of my bone', while in *A Life* the poet in the very act of writing acknowledges that bodily death which inscribes him in the community: 'Peasant that you are, realise/ that you belong with them/ . . . when the epauletted one/ ticks off on his register/ their names'. In another poem, the dead poet will 'arise from the dead', resurrecting himself as he resurrects others in a writing which spurns death's register:

> Your hand is the script of millions, of the dumb.
> In you they live. Through you their blood returns.

Solidarity is indeed the keynote for outstaring death in these volumes, translating the wake as trace into the wake as commemoration, a collective *re-membering* of community. Poetry reinstates in its narratives those people identified in the last pages of *The Exiles* as 'The Survivors', 'The "Ordinary" People', who 'sing on the edge of the grave' and 'walk through [tragedies] clutching food, bottles', teaching us that 'there is no such thing as tragedy,/ that the hero has deceived us . . .'. The final poem of *The Exiles*, 'Envoi', reveals Hamlet committing his tale to the survivor Horatio, advising him with belated wisdom that 'Tragedy is/ nothing but churned foam', the wake of a disturbed passage, while the mortal sea continues to roar 'at the edge of/ all things'.

THE AUTHOR DIES

The unthinkable: one's own death. To be 'confronted by a dead person' is to realise the paradox implicit in the oxymoron. Death is outside the language. Its bodily *presence* means the *absence* of a person, the end of all the grand narratives in the death of the author. That death is, in fact, the real theme of *A Life*. The particular life exists only in the context of the death which prescribes its limits. As a caricatured Grim Reaper says directly in *The Village*, 'Without me, they would not exist/ without my sickle and scythe/ without my empty circles'. Supersession is the guarantee of authenticity. *A Life* plays on the tension between the written 'Life', one of many possible readings, and the real, unique, particular life it addresses, which is simply *a* life, one among millions.

Everywhere in this volume, writing consorts with the body, linking death and sexuality in a common corporeality. There is, for example, the fellow National Serviceman whose suicide the poet discovers on the barracks floor, his blood spread over the Dracula comics he reads, so that in both text and life 'the victim bubbles gently'. But there are also 'the unpredictable flashes of girls' knees' contrasted with the 'careful bureaucratical fine prose' in a poem about schoolteaching. And there is the fictional Sancho Panza, telling the fictional Don Quixote that a true knight in old romances never needed to pee, since there is no written account of him doing so – which is a scrupulous reminder of the difference between text and body. In the library, another poem tells us, while the writers 'scribble// their transient names', there are bodies which, overwritten with tattoos, 'scandalise the Forms' of an abstract Neoplatonism. Writing and materiality struggle in complex, confused relation in these poems, only in utopian fantasy to be united *somewhere else*:

> Somewhere I see my pent
>
> bourgeois persona, individual,
> thornily investigate the rose which
> raggedly pushed through pale slabs of prose.
> The human flesh and the reflective jewel
>
> to be combined and unified! The fixed
> and unpredictable to sing as one . . .
> and Venus smiling from her marble text!

In fact, text and body mutually disconcert each other, and 'The terrible/ agonised cry infects the page'. The world itself is a corpus of material texts. Of summer he can say punningly that there is 'no end . . . to the freshness of your plots'; of winter snow, that it transforms the world 'as from graffiti into origins', creating, as if for the first time, in 'the whiteness of eternity . . . a book with no print'.

The title of the last section of *A Life* inscribes a joyful incompletion full of intimations of mortality ('Taynuilt, 1982–') to address the sense of an ending in both literary and real life. Setting out to write in poem 1, the poet in 2 finds himself reading instead, and what he reads is the brief lives of others, *Aubrey's Brief Lives*, their insistent brevity inscribing finitude, so that when he returns to his work table it rises towards him 'containing white sheet after sheet' of papers which in their blankness seem like shrouds. Fiction disposes of endings, poem 5 suggests, endlessly renewing its tales:

> The joy of the author is beyond speech.
> His characters come dancing back to him.
> They sing in the morning in his happiness.
>
> Like the morning stars they are innocent,
> enigmatic, diamond-like, without denouement.

This endless deferral of conclusion by a perpetual return to beginnings presupposes, though, an imaginary 'supreme author' to whom the mortal poet defers, seeking 'justification' in a mode which hovers between John Knox and Wallace Stevens:

> Are you happy with us, supreme author,
> as other authors are in the evening
> who scrupulously dine with their imaginings?
> [. . .]
> Life is a sublime gift, supreme one.
> What can it be compared to? Nothing.
> Your stars are like the words that burn on carbon.

The metaphor (stars, writing, carbon paper) works a significant change on that in 'The Drowned': carbon is the base of all organic life; it is produced in the burning of stars; trees convert sunlight into carbon; they can be converted into the paper on which our *Brief Lives* are written; burned, these *Lives*, like those lives and leaves, are translated back to carbon ash. Life can be compared to a 'Nothing' best glossed by reference to the last line of Stevens's 'The Snow Man', both absence and void, 'Nothing which is not there, and the nothing which is'.

The preceding 'Oban' sequence had opened right into such gulfs, equating 'extravagant presence' with an abyss which is all empty extension, recalling the ambiguity of Stevens's sea in 'The Idea of Order at Key West', a major intertext of these poems. *The Exiles, A Life* and *The Village* all end with images of the sea. Here, a bridal death waits in the margins of both text and abyss:

> O I see you, bride,
> Gaelic, mysterious: and this radiance is
> the extravagant presence of the sea's abyss
> extending to Iona and its graves.

Only in the empty traces of the text, 'inscriptions of our happiness' in the 'wide/ ocean' of event, can the mortal subject imagine itself

> To be centred in a place where the pure tide
> renews its treasures: and each misty hill
> is real yet poetic. There abide
> the famous dead who walk the promenade
> at watery evening when the world is still.

Every time that the text reaches towards images of plenitude, fulfilment and centredness, it finds itself displaced to the underworld of the famous dead, like Odysseus, Orpheus and Dante. This is indeed the pattern of the volumes which Iain Crichton Smith has published in the 1980s. Poem 7 of the Taynuilt sequence in *A Life* spells out a careful correlation between the narratives of life and fiction, the peculiar liaison of writer and reader, with art prefiguring life in its sense of an ending:

> I think you will die easily.
> You have been a book reader all your life.
>
> You will not fight the imagination.
>
> There have been so many deaths, *dénouements*,
> resolutions of plots,
>
> and marriages at the ends of books.
> We are always told of them
> especially in the empire of Victoria.
>
> So your death will be like a marriage,
> as a return of the lost boy
> to the house where he originally belonged,
>
> after he had been punished in an orphanage,
> forced to climb sooty chimneys,
> to put varnish on coffins.

Death is here converted through an idea of literary endings into a Dickensian return of the lost boy to his originary place, a nuptial reunion in insistently Freudian terms with the body of the mother from which he had been orphaned. We cannot in life go back to the beginning and rerun the narrative. The poet promises himself a death like those of fiction, 'the pages quietly finished,/ the last disentangling chapter// putting all the characters in their places', resolution blossoming from 'the final arranged words'. But the subject, living in the endless deferral of significance, cannot be put in his place except by that death which closes the gap between signifier, signified and referent. Poem 6 had warned, echoing Lawrence:

> Never trust the author, trust the tale.
> Out of the autumn mist it swims out to us,
> a strange exhalation from the past
> which is the tale remembering itself . . .
>
> The author is not important, the author dies.
> The tale lives on.

This is something of a Cretan paradox, since it is the author who thus advises us. But the point is craftily made. The tale becomes self-sufficient, without authorship, unauthorised. Even the text, then, lacks self-presence, is a trace of itself, self-remembering. 'Strange' here involves estrangement, a gap between the *énoncé* and the *énonciation*, in which there is no writing without reading, and the wake of the poem's passage is the funeral wake for the passing author, for all of us.

'The Story' in *The Village*, is a poem about interrupted endings, discontinued lines which restore us to origins, traces in that *tabula rasa* of snow left by a little girl who suddenly becomes invisible as she runs. This touching *anima* figure, Antigone or Ophelia to the insistent male ego of Oedipus and Hamlet, reappears in the course of the poem as self-authoring, 'no more a child,/ but adult, unperplexed, her own mother', a return already prefigured by that maternal Muse who is the real and ultimate author of the poet's tale-tellings, interrupting all the grand narratives of male discourse. The texts in which we live by inscribing our difference are in the end no more than traces, footprints in the unfathomable which record our passage and our absence. The author, like the reader, dies *in medias res*, in the middle of a good poem which will never be finished, which is both 'hiatuses' and 'a bridge . . ./ into the rich ignorance of the future', the narratives of a collective story-telling taken up by others who in turn end in incompleteness:

> Like the reader who leaves off reading the page,
> Like the dying who still have some way to go.
> There are first the footprints, then the unfathomable.
> The Muse hasn't finished the good poem.

# Eight

## Deer on the High Hills: A Meditation on Meaning

### Colin Nicholson

> There is a logic of the imagination as well as a logic of concepts.
> T.S. Eliot
>
> The final belief is to believe in a fiction, which you know to be a fiction, there being nothing else. The exquisite truth is to know that it is a fiction and that you believe in it willingly.
> Wallace Stevens

When one of the founding fathers of American 'New Criticism' anathematised 'the heresy of paraphrase'[1], he exposed the sacerdotal pretensions of what became in effect a dominant priesthood in America's literary responses. During the Cold War period, they sensitised a generation of students to preferred codes of reading and interpretation. Priestcraft of whatever kind finds no favour in Crichton Smith's writing, and I take courage from that to propose a reading of 'Deer on the High Hills: A Meditation'[2] as a provocation not only to the competences and assumptions implicit in mid-century Anglo-American approaches to literary structure but also to the Romantic paradigms which they selectively adopted. When, for example, Coleridge in *The Statesman's Manual* defined the imagination as 'that reconciling and mediatory power which, incorporating the Reason in Images of the Sense, and organising (as it were) the flux of the Senses by the permanence and self-circling energies of the Reason, gives birth to a system of symbols, harmonious in themselves and consubstantial with the truths of which they are the conductors',[3] he did more than tease subsequent generations of readers far out of thought. He enabled what his own dialectical procedures elsewhere should have inhibited, namely a perception of literary form as autonomous and self-sustaining.

Subsequent variations on this critical approach, construing the poem as a self-contained and self-expressive artefact, continued to encourage the reading of any poem as a pattern of words for its own sake. Systems 'harmonious in themselves' have proved more attractive than any wider 'truths' they might embody structurally or articulate semantically. For 'New Critics', this developed into an insistence upon the poem as sacrosanct object whose autonomy required a prohibitive recognition of the difference and distance between it and the language which readers might use to describe it.

But what was prohibited, effectively, was any discussion of how, beyond the world it patterns for us on the page, a poem might articulate other systems of meaning in that surrounding context to which it speaks. Under such widely obeyed determinations, history was obliterated. But it is to the problematic intersections between these spheres that 'Deer on the High Hills' directs its attentions, where a central concern is the indeterminacy of cognition and even the instability of perception. So other strategies of reading need to be called into play, for which we might initially be guided by more recent suggestions that the text is not 'a line of words releasing a single "theological" meaning (the "message" of an Author-God), but a multi-dimensional space in which a variety of writings, none of them original, blend and clash'.[4] We would then be reading the poem as an intertextual construct – as a product of various cultural discourses on which it relies for its intelligibility – and we might thereby be better placed to describe some of the meanings it generates. It may not be easy: Crichton Smith has acknowledged that there are areas of the poem he does not understand; and its complexities, confusions even, are part of what it is about. While Paul de Man's claim that literature is 'the place where the possible convergence of rigour and pleasure is shown to be a delusion'[5] might (not untypically) cut twelve ways to nothing clearly, there is a sense of relatedness in that rigour, pleasure and the delusion of similitude are demonstrably constituent elements in Crichton Smith's poem. Unnerving and elliptical, it manages to be a work of celebration which produces both scepticism and pathos from a scripted terrain by turns uncertain and exhilarating. As it tracks the movement of a mind in the processes of creation, self-reflexively examining its own procedures of figuration, ways of looking at deer become ways of looking at language. In writing of this kind, where semantic slippage parallels the deer's essential unknowability, meaning will always exceed any single reading of it, particularly when the production of meaning is itself a primary form of attention. That production of meaning relates as much to the reader's activity as to the poet's invention: 'The reader is the space on which all the quotations that make up a writing are inscribed . . . A text's unity lies not in its origin but in its destination.'[6]

Across the rhythms of 'Deer on the High Hills', both symbolist and imagist precepts are called into question as leaps of faith and the making of fictions become associated procedures. But the initial impulse came from something Crichton Smith actually witnessed. During the time he was teaching at Oban High School, he was travelling home from a visit to Glasgow when he saw three deer on the icy road ahead of him. He began writing the following day, and within ten days or so the poem was finished. A caution appropriate to our understanding of signs in the real world is called for because 'Deer on the High Hills' meditates upon what we *can* know of the natural world, becomes a descant upon modes of knowing that world, and develops into a series of reflections upon the efficacy or otherwise of language as a signifying system and upon the dubious if insistent sufficiency of metaphor as a trope within it. In the process, human and animal realms converge and separate as linguistic construction negotiates an essentially unknowable Other. When Seamus Heaney referred to 'the break into unsettling contemporaneity and phantasmagoria which Iain Crichton Smith has achieved without ever averting his gaze from the crystal of an origin both Hebridean and Presbyterian'[7], he might have had 'Deer on the High Hills' specifically in mind. So, to begin tracing the poem's problematising of figuration in verse, a preliminary linguistic/cultural contextualisation might be useful.

When Sorley MacLean begins one of his best-known poems with the epigraph 'Time, the deer, is in the wood of Hallaig'[8], he attaches it to an established image in Highland writing which adds resonance to the metaphoric repopulation of cherished territory achieved by 'Hallaig'. The figure of the deer carries various associations, and its compensatory sub-Romantic installation as 'monarch of the glen' during a nineteenth century which saw economic, territorial and political displacements in Scotland's status was only one popular diversion. For contemporary writers of Gaeldom, the fraudulence implicit in such a strategy, substituting the regime of an icon for the dispossessing realities of Highland experience, is transparent, and one intertext thus invoked by MacLean is Duncan Bàn MacIntyre's eighteenth-century poem 'Ben Dorain'. At the end of his English-language translation of MacIntyre's poem, Crichton Smith writes:

> When one considers it, it is a very strange poem for a Highlander to write. It is the Gaelic language at its peak. It is the poet writing

before morality. Never again would a Gaelic poet write like this. Never again would the Gaelic ethos allow him to.[9]
About 'Deer on the High Hills', Crichton Smith subsequently remarked:
> What came out of the poem in the end was the distance between us and the animal kingdom. It concerns how, in relation to animal nature, we are a Hamletish, divided people: and I also link it up with 'Ben Dorain' and the strangeness of the deer in that poem . . . In several Gaelic poems in the eighteenth century, including 'Ben Dorain', there are tremendous batteries of adjectives, and I find that in a strange kind of way ['Deer on the High Hills'] is a Gaelic poem, though it's written in English, because of the tremendous number of adjectives running through it. I think I must have borrowed this from the Gaelic world.[10]

'Ben Dorain' as he translates it combines an erotic celebration of deer — 'coquettes of the body,/ slim-legged and ready' (p. 12) — with an acceptance of their slaughter, as it composes a hymn to Highland sufficiency:

> There's no sea or wood
> has more plenitude
> of various good food
> than your boundaries.
> (p. 24)

In its stoical acceptances and lavish ceremonial, 'Ben Dorain' precedes the bourgeois moralism that is implicit in its reference to Hanoverian incursion: 'and every battalion King George can assemble' (p. 18). In the figures of the dogs who pursue, the hunter who slays, their quarry the deer and a sustaining environment, death and desire coexist outwith the reach of subsequent ethical imposition. Derick Thomson makes the point that in a poem of detailed natural observation, Duncan Bàn's eye and imagination open 'above all . . . when he is in sight of the deer. There is not a hint of sentimentality in his attitude: he describes in an equally loving way the antics of the hind or the fawn, and the process of stalking or taking aim or shooting the stag.'[11] And for William Gillies it becomes correspondingly important for us to recognise that in its celebration of the life and the way of life it supports, 'Ben Dorain' constructs 'a continuum — an ecological system — sustained by and on the mountain'.

But this is in turn jeopardised by a different note, obliquely sounded, which Gillies detects in the poem : 'When Duncan Bàn asserts the right of the deer to live on the mountain because her ancestors took possession of it . . . I find it hard not to reverse the figure and think of Duncan Bàn's own countrymen in the 1760s; and at the points where the bardic strains are most insistent, the absence of a lord of the hunt or a husband for the mountain is striking and pointed'.[12] And Thomson hints at something similar when he describes 'Ben Dorain' as 'a song in praise of the deer [and] the foremost praise-song in Gaelic – an ironic reflection, when we consider the generations of bards trained to praise human chiefs and patrons' (p. 187). These disconcerting suggestions feed into 'Deer on the High Hills', but at any rate it seems evident that, after the devastation of the Clearances, such clear-eyed witness as MacIntyre was able to achieve was no longer available in poetry until the very differently-directed reconstructions of Sorley MacLean, of Derick Thomson himself, of George Campbell Hay and of Iain Crichton Smith. Whatever else 'Deer on the High Hills' meditates, it seems initially probable that, sub-textually at least, the fate and future of Gaeldom will be somewhere involved in the parameters of its English-language concerns.

> A deer looks through you and to the other side
> and what it is and sees is an inhuman pride.
>
> (p. 24)

Certainly a transference has been made in this beginning, but in variation upon traditionally accepted senses. Max Black's formulations do not really apply in this case. In his argument that metaphors have two subjects, a principle and a subordinate, Black reconstructs the 'tenor' and 'vehicle' model of I.A. Richards which Crichton Smith here prevaricates. But Black's suggestion that both subjects are better regarded as systems of belief rather than as individual things[13] is more usefully applicable to the notion of seeing deer as they might see us. In these opening lines, seeing and being in the animal realm intersects with being and seeing in ours. The transfer of human attributes to the animal realm which the animal then returns to the human opens a process of destabilisation which characterises the poem's larger movement. Its tentative interest in the possibility of cognitive interaction across the two realms exposes language to its own figurative subterfuges. Both the linguistic structuring of perception and the perception of structure thereby encoded are brought into active conjunction. Any readerly response is already cautioned: our own orientation in and towards the poem is as much its subject as any foregrounded narrative. How we read the poem, and how the poem reads us, will form a central part of our textual encounter. Whose world we are in is already at question and our readerly conventions under interrogation. To inflect a remark made by C. Day Lewis, 'we find poetic truth struck out by the collusion rather than the collision of images'.[14]

If 'Ben Dorain' is characterised by a battery of adjectives, 'Deer on the High Hills' begins with a series of similes the first of which, 'like debutantes', directly alludes to MacIntyre's words in Crichton Smith's translation, followed by 'like Louis the Sixteenth', '[mountains] like judging elders', 'like fallen nobles' and 'like the mind of God'. Though referential displacement in the act of comparison, which is the business of simile, will become part of what the poem investigates, the insurgence of history into this second section brings together France's *ancien régime* and Gaelic precedent to suggest the urgent pressures of social transformation. 'The inhuman look of aristocrats' resonates with the poem's opening epigraph and, for Scottish readers, might already conjure the treatment of crofters during the Clearances. What is being conveyed is the extraordinary fertility of deer in Highland imaginings. The capacity of deer to inspire aristocratic emblem and image leads to a free-flowing association of them with rank, with social hierarchy and with the oppressions and divisions such orderings entail. The deer's 'leaps like the mind of God' suggest an imagination boundlessly extending its parameters as the danger posed by a hungry deer is likened to a beggared noble concealing a sword. The violent overthrow of France's pre-revolutionary order is insinuated, and the verse recognises that, for a displaced aristocracy, domination by the erstwhile oppressed might also appear as tyranny, this time exercised by those 'who do not wear but break most ancient crowns'. The section moves from perception to perception and from groups at opposite ends of the social scale, bridging hierarchies while emphasising their distances. Like and unlike the deer, these structuring similitudes are also 'balanced on a delicate logic'; but whatever clarities were available to Duncan Bàn MacIntyre are here compromised by an almost overwhelming release of cultural/linguistic correlations and possibilities.

In response to these disordering contentions, the third section expresses envy for the deer's distance and separation from social conspiracies and antagonisms, but then suggests that to satisfy our own longings for 'a return as to the mountain springs', we must first become 'soldier[s] of the practical'. Punning phonetically to emphasise a necessary distance between the human 'doer' and the animal 'deer', the section implies that having learned from the animal realm 'a real contempt, a fine hard-won disdain' for prevailing codes of ownership, we might re-enter more fully into possession of a natural world: 'and then go/ back to the hills but not on ignorant feet'.

Difference and desire thus consorting, elisions of the human and the animal produce comedy and pathos in the fourth section's wistful glance at the animal kingdom's detachment from the myths and metaphysics which humankind constructs to preserve and transmit its privileged forms of recognition and identification. There is in Crichton Smith's writing a recurrent suspicion of abstract systems, whether coded as 'history', 'ideology' or any other transcendent mythology, and the injunction to 'Forget these purple evenings and these poems/ that solved all or took for myth, and pointed sail of Ulysses enigmatic' implies his sense of the ways we misread natural iconography and also misconstrue mythic poetry either as offering spiritual salvation or as invincibly separate from the changing circumstances of succeeding generations. Turning Classical epic to its own account, 'Deer on the High Hills' selects appropriate moments. When Hector leaves his wife and child to return to battle, the poem skirts the emotional defences of epic formulation to wonder: 'Where is that other Hector/ who wore the internal shield, the inner sword?' As relevantly, but in a different direction, the returning Ulysses, 'like a rat trapped in a maze', is demythologised into a contemporary businessman. Then, leaping as the deer leap, Crichton Smith's narrative joins classical epic to Highland contemporaneity. Freely associating the sound of colliding antlers, as stags compete in the rutting season, with Olympian participation in the Odyssey's unravelling, the poem refers to its own procedures – 'ideas clash on the mountain tops' – and we move across a scripted territory which no longer deals with a 'simple transfer of words, but with a commerce between thoughts, a transaction between contexts'.[15]

They are contexts of violence for which 'appalled peaks' is apt, picking up as it does a submerged suggestion of making pale, while mist on high ground leads in turn to the 'cloudy systems' – including language as a signifying system – by which phenomena are interpreted and meaning constructed: 'as yesterday we saw a black cloud/ become the expression of a tall mountain./ And that was death, the undertaker, present'. It is an undertaking of 'Deer on the High Hills' to probe the conditions and effects of linguistic similitude – 'and all became like it for that moment' – as, in uncertain dialectic, feeling follows sign and signifier triggers emotional response. 'Signification concerns the word considered in itself . . . sense concerns the word considered in its effect in the mind'[16], but Crichton Smith is confounding our usual categories of objective, subjective and intersubjective. What is real and what is imagined is at question here: the structure of the 'real' is bound up with the figural structurings of thought. Still, his threnody derives from actuality: cloud on a mountain creates the conditions for an 'assumption of anguish':

> and the hollow waters
> the metaphysics of an empty country
> deranged, deranged, a land of rain and stones,
> of stones and rain, of the huge barbarous bones, plucked like a
> loutish harp their harmonies.

From 'the deer roar' through 'hollow waters' to 'the hollow roar of the waterfall', the poem first broaches but then effects a shift away from Rimbaud's advocacy of a subjective derangement of the senses ('dérèglement de tous les sens')[17] and towards the historicising context of place: a depopulated Highlands where Scottish conceptualisations might properly originate. Such linguistic construction of Highland perception must refuse both the romance of history as tartan gallimaufry – 'Prince Charles in a gay Highland shawl' – and the alienation of human value implied in a prescriptive Calvinism's 'mystery in a black Highland coffin'.

The rigours of such a poetic are honed elsewhere in Crichton Smith's work. 'Poem of Lewis' opens a landscape paradoxically recalcitrant and inspirational: 'Here they have no time for the fine graces/ of poetry, unless it fairly grows/ in deep compulsion, like water in the well,/ woven into the texture of the soil in a strong pattern' (p. 3). But the second of 'Eight Songs for a New Ceilidh' confirms for us that such resistance also makes poetry possible: 'It was the fine bareness of Lewis that made the work of my mind like a loom full of the music and the miracles and greatness of our time' (p. 59). In 'Deer on the High Hills', the syllabic music that strikes out its difference in repetition, from 'deranged' to 'rain' and from 'barbarous' to 'harp' to 'harmonies', already encodes an 'incurable numbers' in process of composition. But prescription of any kind is not an attractive option in Crichton Smith's writing, and the imperatives deployed here for the building of a fit poetic speech are accordingly disconcerted: his fascination with an ambiguously undulating 'law' of metre and 'grace' of cadenced utterance signals his preference for forms of freedom corresponding to a poetry which finally seeks escape from any and all prescribed signifying:

> You must build from the rain and the stones
> till you can make

> a stylish deer on the high hills,
> and let its leaps be unpredictable.

For Wallace Stevens, a poet whose work Crichton Smith greatly admires, 'reality is the footing from which we leap after what we do not have and on which everything depends'[18], and Crichton Smith has recently confirmed his own preference:

> I actually think the best poetry happens when two or three things come together which one would normally think of as being totally unrelated. I used to read an enormous amount of Kierkegaard who talks about the leap of faith one has to make whether in theology or in religious life and there's something akin to that in the creation of poetry; a joining together of things that aren't normally joined. Scientists do this too. It's the kind of leap that changes things at deep levels, so that we can start thinking in a new way.[19]

Unpredictability constructs the space for 'Deer' to experiment with codes of meaning. The challenges it offers to inherited determinations of how things signify work also to subvert previously imposed moral codes; an imposition that Crichton Smith's verse elsewhere repeatedly suggests has been most damagingly traced in the legacies of Highland Calvinism. Perhaps that helps to explain why, alluding to Duncan Bàn MacIntyre's intimate knowledge of the deer he memorialised more than two hundred years earlier, section 5 of the poem celebrates a pagan democracy through a series of transfigurings linking MacIntyre with his subject in ways which include a transfer of agency from the deer to the poet:

> They evolved their own music which became
> his music: they elected him
> their poet laureate.

The poem in this section is looking back to a time when perception of and relationship to an environment was not dislocated by the historical, social and discursive pressures which a Gaelic poet writing now in English has to negotiate. It was an environment where, as 'Light to Light' puts it:

> Duncan Bàn MacIntyre, our Gaelic poet
> created from an ordinary place
> a place of genius,
> MacIntyre our illiterate bard
> unable to read or write
> who saw the deer moving waxen-skinned
> in a light that is not our light,

> the light of love.
> That equable happy and cheerful man
> who shot the deer with poetry.
>
> (p. 103)

Without ever learning to read or write (or speak English), MacIntyre produced a body of significant poetry. He can, then, symbolise a lost world of unfallen orality, the lyricist in the forest, and as such a figure of pleasing timelessness. Accordingly, 'Deer on the High Hills' also sees his prelapsarian ecology as uncomplicated by postlapsarian guilt: 'nevertheless he shot them also'. So the poem is able to propose that MacIntyre lived when 'brutality and beauty danced together/ in a silver air,/ incorruptible'. A subsequent moralising and sentimentalising metaphoricity is then repudiated: 'And the clean shot did not disturb his poems./ Nor did the deer kneel in a pool of tears'. The gaps that have since opened up between signifier and signified lead to further play with the distance between perceiver and perceived and between conceiver and conception. Language tricks its graces for the deer in a post-Romantic comedy of dissent: 'What is the knowledge of the deer?/ Is there a philosophy of the hills?/ Do their heads peer into the live stars?/ Do rumours of death disturb them?' Rather than begging sense of metaphysics, the poem prefers a recognition of the animal world based on acceptance of its irreducible difference: 'They inhabit wild systems'. And they simply live through seasonal cycles to which language ascribes meaning. Inseparable from the words which present them, the deer yet remain essentially unknowable, while language as a system of knowing privileges its own coding over them. The poem opens up the gap between the two:

> It is not evil makes the horns bright
> but a running natural lustre. The blood
> is natural wounding. Metaphoric sword
>
> is not their weapon, but an honest thrust.
> Nor does the moon affect their coupling, nor
> remonstrant gods schoolmaster their woods.

Foregrounding metaphor as figure, these lines also expose the mystifying strategies of anthropomorphism: the gods we construct to discipline our forms of attention are nothing to animal existence. That nothing will return, while Crichton Smith's secular rigour expresses a scepticism towards the use of mythic methods for ordering and shaping perception and experience: scepticism because mythicisation can also translate into modes of domination and subjection. Within the framework of a deconstructive bias, the poem suspects metaphysical systems based on specially valued terms or ultimate meaning. Against faith in such systems, it displays a radical free play in language and thought. In place of fixed centres of meaning, it posits the play of differences which offer no easy access to stable identity or certitude. Using metaphor to probe metaphoric signification, the poem traces again the instinctive actions of competing stags, merging their activity with its seasonal motivation (but still including a corresponding figure of human aggression): 'The great spring is how/ these savage captains tear to indigo/ the fiery guts'. Reading different associations into animal behaviour, the hind with her fawn which is traditionally construed as pleasing to the eye is seen as capable of defensive ferocity:

> Evil's more complex, is
> a languaged metaphor, like the mists that scarf
> the deadly hind and her bewildered calf.

The comparison involves both naturalistic observation and a figure of partial impenetrability; 'mists' serve to cloud perception as they separate the hind from the signifying system of language which nonetheless presents her to us. Inevitably, and as the nemesis towards which the poem is proceeding, the lines engage in transference as they propose the unknowable. The prison-house of language is inescapable.

In its versatile transformations, 'Deer on the High Hills' acknowledges the fictionality of all narrative by taking an image that has achieved iconic status in Scottish writing and reading into its historical resonance paradigms of the way we construe meaning in the world. But by treating of the relation of the imagined to the real, the poem is also treating of the problem of belief, and again Wallace Stevens becomes relevant: 'If one no longer believes in God (as truth), it is not possible merely to disbelieve; it becomes necessary to believe in something else'.[20] Subsequently, Stevens was to comment: 'There are things with respect to which we willingly suspend disbelief . . . it seems to me that we can suspend disbelief with reference to a fiction as easily as we can suspend it with reference to anything else'.[21] When Crichton Smith goes on to present god-head as an antlered deer narcissistically enchanted by its own image, the further suggestion is released that it is not the durability of writing which stabilises us in time, but the transience of life: 'as on the ice/ the deer might suddenly slip, go suddenly under/ their balance being precarious'. Leaping still as live deer leap, the poem's next figure, of vital life principle as beautiful woman 'who obscures/ unconscious heavens with her conscious ray', both endorses the poem's preference for lived actuality over abstract systems and is made more arresting by contextual awareness of mutability. The poem is structuring a process of accommodation and assimilation in which verbal symbolism[22] inscribes terms of similitude endlessly contending not only with difference but also with intransigent Otherness:

> As deer so stand, precarious, of a style,
> half-here, half-there, a half-way lustre
>                               breaking
> a wise dawn in a chained ocean far.

That halfway notion will also recur, but when the focus shifts again on the punning echo 'as dear, so dear, Vesuvius, rocket', volcanic eruption as image of specific power is privileged over abstract, deified alienations of potency. 'God may not be beautiful, but you,/ suffer a local wound. You bleed to death/ from all that's best, your active anima.' These are observable moments in a natural ecology where the earlier wounded deer cross-links now to an image of self-wounding earth when volcanos erupt yet from which fertility derives. From both, a 'concordant honouring beauty richly breaks' in the poem's design.

Turning in the widening gyre of its own deliberations, 'Deer on the High Hills' involves in its ninth section different considerations of love and death in Highland history, where a synthesising imagination identifies itself directly with deer, from 'you speak of love' to:

> Your absolute heads populate the hills
>
> like daring thoughts, half-in, half-out this world,
> as a lake might open, and a god peer
> into a darkening room where failing darkness glows.

The capitalised God of the preceding section is refigured as a centaur looking into water which yields, now, no reflecting image but the abyss of an uncomprehending Other. Similarly, 'half-in, half-out' calls back the precarious style of 'half-here, half-there' to link again habitual human constructions of deity with the iconic status achieved by deer in Highland writing. The command structure of belief in either is very much what the poem is about. Transference then moves the other way, from animal to human, as the 'absolute heads' of deer trigger associations with Absolutist heads: 'destructive, ominous, of an impetuous language', whose policies of self-aggrandisement give harder historical edges to other memories of once-populated hills. Animal 'passion' enters the discourse of power more emphatically when the 'honest thrust' of rutting deer associates with a human order 'venomed too with the helpless thrust of spring'. In this ninth sections's fifth tristich, a traditional image of the 'monarch of the glen' variety figures the human in the animal; the sixth remembers deer organically inhabiting their environment: 'Heads like valleys where the stars fed,/ unknown and magical, strange and unassuaged,/ the harmonies humming in a green place', and echoes Marvell's 'green thought in a green shade'.[23] The seventh tristich effects a variation on these elliptical transfigurings when crowned heads and antlered ones imagistically merge:

> So proud these heads, original, distinct,
> they made an air imperial around
> their pointed scrutiny, passionate with power.

The displacing violence of the poem's second section is recalled in this one where 'peasants in the valleys/ felt in their bones disquieting kingdom's break', before an equally disruptive anachronism figures another kind of Reformation associating the birth of Christ with the engendering of an opposing power. Destabilising elements are again at work in language which simultaneously conjures light and darkness:

> in a night honoured with a desperate star,
>
> another head appeared, fiercer than these,
> disdain flashed from his horns, a strange cry
> perplexed the peasants, somnolent, appeased.

Given a persistent sub-text of historical reference, Highland subordination to a religion which kept a peasantry in thrall while absolute power engrossed their substance lends resonance to their perplexity.

But a horned head crying its own appeasement to the confusion of a peasantry effectively demonises these historical transitions, and section 10, in keeping with that theme in Crichton Smith's writing which resists any prior ordination of possibility, opposes to such prescription a libertarian sensuousness. The discourse of dominance is exposed as deceptive, a mirage of promise; and Christian iconography (the forty days which Jesus spent in the desert) is again construed to subversive effect:

> Deer on the high peaks, the wandering senses
> are all, are all: fanatic heads deceive,
> like branches springing in a true desert.

Erotic release and a palpitating, incantatory carnality contest this discursive ground in rhythms which sustain a sensuous incorporation of historical event:

### 'Deer on the High Hills'

> In spring the raven and lascivious swallow,
> migrant of air, the endless circle closing,
> unclosing, closing, a bewildering ring
> of natural marriage, pagan, sensuous
> Return of seasons, and the fugitive
> Culloden of scents, erratic, hesitant.

More explicitly than hitherto, this tenth section then widens the gap between sense and signification as it probes the ways in which we determine meaning. If fanaticism constructs chimeras in the mind, sensuous engagement in a natural world beyond thought might initiate a balancing corrective towards redemptive self-definition. The way we think about the world and the way we write about it have no causal or necessary relationship to the cycles of seasonal occurrence which 'return in spite of the idea,/ the direct reasoning road, the mad Ulysses/ so unperverted so implacable.' Rhyme and reason stand in no self-evident relationship to each other, and yet, by fixing his 'obstinate gaze' on 'a reasoned star', Ulysses 'came at last where his childhood was/ an infant island in an ancient place'.

These rival attractions of order and disorder in the human and non-human universe are pursued in the eleventh section where the 'reasoned star' becomes 'the far and clear/ ordered inventions of the star's going', and stands in marked contrast to earth's 'fierce diversity'. Epic narrative compels kinds of closure which Crichton Smith seeks to avert. A recurrent image of heads reflected in water thematises perception and self-perception and implies that language itself involves a kind of duplicity as the instrument by which we impose order on the world we think we see. More immediately in the present instance, the image of reflection relates to the 'rampant egos' of an aristocracy narcissistically bent only upon preservation of its own uniqueness: '"make me in mirror matchless and the earl/ of such imagined kingdoms as endure"'.

Stones and the seasons, described as 'maenads of necessity', mock these human aspirations to immortality, but still the deer look down and still the ideas they inspire continue to unfold; illusory for the continuities they propose across time, persistent in the illusions they provoke, and sharply contrasted with this multiple facticity of inanimate existence. Self-referentially, the poem acknowledges ordering principles for its own structure, principles which hark back to Graeco-Roman clarifications of the relationship between perceiving subject and the world perceived. This 'obstinate mirage' is one of many systems of signification which we stubbornly cling to as a viable way of shaping and ordering natural plenitude, and which:

> while the deer stand impervious, of a style,
> make vibrant music, high and rich and clear,
> mean what the plain mismeans, inform a chaos.

An inevitable pathos is beginning to make itself felt, but, before it returns to ponder and then accept the intransigent bifurcation of language from the world it seeks to concentrate, the poem in section 12 meditates upon the continuing inspirational fecundity of deer and celebrates the ways in which, as Highland phenomena and as iconic intensification, they seem to transcend the division between world and word, such that each sighting in the hills irresistibly conjures a re-siting in the imagination. As created forms themselves and provoking forms of creation in the poet, they are 'native to air, native to earth both' and so inhabit a 'half-way kingdom,/ uneasy in this, uneasy in the other,/ but all at ease when earth and sky together/ are mixed are mixed, become a royalty none other knows'. Always already in language half-created and half-perceived, deer seem destined permanently to inhabit two worlds, of animal facticity and of linguistic representation, whose fusion remains as elusive and imponderable as it often seems intuitively desirable. Luminous imagery presents deer as entirely self-sustaining – 'the epicures of feeding absolutes' – and the animal is integrated in its own green world while its capacity to trigger in the mind seemingly endless correspondences is preserved and actively disseminated: 'Your antlers flash in light, your speed like thought/ is inspiration decorous and assured,/ a grace not theological but of/ accomplished bodies, sensuous and swift'. So there is, after such voluble elucidations of correspondences, a telling and instructive irony in this section's final reference to 'the image silent on the high hill'. To all the sound and fury of the poem's abundant verbal energies, the deer's inevitable reply is a plangent and echoing nothing.

It is this surviving absence which leads to the poem's closing meditations. Confronted by silence from the animal world it addresses, 'Deer on the High Hills' questions its own prosperity to find figural relationships in image and in myth:

> Do colours cry? Does 'black' weep for the dead?
> Is green so bridal, and is red the flag
> and eloquent elegy of a martial sleep?
>
> Are hills 'majestic' and devoted stones
> plotting in inner distances our fall?
> The mind a sea: and she a Helen who

### 'Deer on the High Hills' 117

> in budding hours awaken to her new
> enchanting empire all the summer day,
> the keys of prison dangling in her hands?

While an analytic reason urges a negative response to these questions, the poem is caught in the affirmative patterning of its own performance. In flight from this impasse, refuge is sought in a gesture of literary solidarity when we encounter lines which shift to transference in another mode, a carrying-over of echo and allusion from one text to another: 'And are rainbows the/ wistful smiles upon a dying face?' The anterior text is Hugh MacDiarmid's 'The Watergaw', an elegising lyric which postpones definition in favour of a less secure but still comforting possibility. Struck by the coincidence of a smile at the moment of death and the play of rainbow, MacDiarmid's speaker is left musing:

> But I have thocht o' that foolish licht
> Ever sin' syne;
> An' I think that mebbe at last I ken
> What your look meant then.[24]

It is the tentative nature of such interpretations that 'Deer on the High Hills' seems to propose, rather than the blank refusal of an alien Other. Its own opening couplet is humanised and softened by the memory of MacDiarmid's lines. The cognitive functions of metaphor may constantly risk semantic slippage, but the alternative of no transference at all is a bleaker and intolerable prospect:

> And you, the deer, who walk upon the peaks,
> are you a world away, a language distant?
> Such symbols freeze upon my desolate lips.

There is, then, as the poem's final section acknowledges, either no metaphor which might successfully 'carry over' from the world of perceived actuality to the world of imaginative cognition, or else all language is metaphorical even when its metaphoric aspect has been forgotten. To say 'the stone is stony' in this context is to derive resonance from the most stripped and pared-down utterance. We conventionally read 'literal' as the opposite of 'figurative', but a literal expression is also a metaphor whose figurality has been forgotten. And if 'there is no non-metaphorical standpoint from which to perceive the order and the demarcation of the metaphorical field', then 'there can be no definition in which the defining does not contain the defined;

metaphoricity is absolutely uncontrollable'.[25] In a gesture of existential courage, 'Deer on the High Hills' culminates in a stoical acceptance – to which its narrative has been inexorably leading – of the contingency and separateness implicit in such a condition:

> The stone is stony.
> The deer step out in isolated air.
> We move at random on an innocent journey.

Accepting the fictivity of metaphor enables the construction of a world of believable connnections, a leap of faith consonant with the secular priorities of Crichton Smith's writing. What we have in the poem is an imaginary self and a reality which is not part of that self, but which for the sake of belief must somehow be made part of it. The etymological derivation of poet from creator, maker, is more immediately preserved in the Scots 'makar', and in that sense all meaning is a result of human *making*. 'Deer on the High Hills' reinscribes uncertainty into the modes of our making. It reinscribes too the pathos of human separateness and of our longing for connecting identifications and relationships. In lines which respond to 'the tigerish access' of an intolerable sense of absence associated with 'The Chair in Which You've Sat' (p. 176), this final section registers a surviving urge to carry communication over to the inanimate if human reaction is unavailable:

> 'You called sir did you?' 'I who was so lonely
> would speak with you: would speak to this tall chair
> would fill it chock-full of my melancholy.'

But the poet who can write elsewhere that 'the true dialectic is to turn in the infinitely complex' (p. 32) is now able to embrace, dancing 'with a human joy', the disconnections of existence since the endless fertility of metaphor will always forge connections beyond the caveats of reason:

> This distance deadly! God or goddess throw me
> a rope to landscape, let that hill, so bare
> blossom with grapes, the wine of Italy.

Not for the only time in Crichton Smith's verse, Mediterranean warmth is invoked to soften native barrenness. In the poem's last collective act of being read, its own shared gesture of community, it throws a rope to us; and in our imaginative attention the hill does blossom and distance is transcended.

### 'Deer on the High Hills'

As a 'poem of the mind in the act of finding/ What will suffice'[26], 'Deer on the High Hills' brings into play relationships between poetry and reality which formed a lifelong concern of Wallace Stevens. In his repeated explorations of 'the flux// Between the thing as idea and/ The idea as thing'[27], Stevens grappled with the problem that all writing is an act of displacement: 'There are no rocks/ And stones, only this imager'.[28] J. Hillis Miller reads him accordingly, in terms relevant to Crichton Smith's poem:

> All referentiality in language is a fiction . . . All words are initially catachreses. The distinction between literal and figurative is an alogical deduction or bifurcation from that primal misnaming. The fiction of the literal or proper is therefore the supreme fiction.[29]

'It comes to this', says Stevens in *Opus Posthumous*, 'that we use the same faculties when we write poetry that we use when we create gods or when we fix the bearing of men in reality'.[30] Both writers exploit the possibilities of mixed metaphor, the very real power of imaginative, illogical, irrational linkages. For both, metaphor is always evasion: all relations between things are created by the human mind; all formulations, the relations of objects to ideas and feelings, are artificial, fictional. And a poem like Stevens' 'The Snow Man' is an early demonstration of his knowledge of the nothingness at the heart of fiction and the compensatory omnipresence of metaphor. Crichton Smith is mired in the same problematic and would no doubt share the hope that Stevens expressed in a letter of 1948, where he speculates that 'thinking about the nature of our relation to what one sees out of the window . . . without any effort to see to the bottom of things, may some day disclose a force capable of destroying nihilism'.[31] In flight from the abyss of metaphor, Stevens writes, in 'An Ordinary Evening in New Haven', of the human desire to 'keep coming back and coming back/ To the real' and for the eye to be 'made clear of uncertainty, with the sight/ Of simple seeing, without reflection':

> We seek
> 
> the poem of pure reality, untouched
> by trope or deviation, straight to the word,
> Straight to the transfixing object.[32]

Perhaps that is why, in its final act of transference, 'Deer on the High Hills', moving towards 'the poem of fact not realised before'[33], strips itself of trope to connect human isolation with that of the deer themselves, now numinously significant in additional ways after such extended explorations, but still ineffably separate:

> for stars are starry and the rain is rainy,
> the stone is stony, and the sun is sunny,
> the deer step out in isolated air.

NOTES

1. Cleanth Brooks, *The Well-Wrought Urn: Studies in the Structure of Poetry* (London 1949, reprinted 1968), p. 157ff.
2. Iain Crichton Smith, *Selected Poems: 1955–80* (Edinburgh, 1981), pp. 42–52. All references to poems are to this volume.
3. *The Collected Works of S.T. Coleridge* (London, 1972), edited by R.J. White, vol. 6, p. 29.
4. Roland Barthes, *Image, Music, Text* (New York, 1977), p. 146.
5. In *On Metaphor* (Chicago, 1979), edited by Sheldon Sacks, p. 28.
6. Barthes, op. cit., p. 148.
7. Seamus Heaney, 'The Regional Forecast', in *The Literature of Region and Nation* (Aberdeen, 1989), edited by R. Draper, p. 23.
8. Sorley MacLean, *From Wood to Ridge: Collected Poems in Gaelic and English* (Manchester, 1989), p. 227.
9. Duncan Bàn MacIntyre, *Ben Dorain* (Newcastle upon Tyne, 1988), translated by Iain Crichton Smith, p. 7.
10. In an interview conducted by the present writer in 1990.
11. Derick Thomson, *An Introduction to Gaelic Poetry* (London, 1974), p. 186.
12. William Gillies, 'The Poem in Praise of Ben Dobhrain', *Lines Review*, 1977, no. 63, pp. 46–7.
13. Max Black, 'More on Metaphor', in *Metaphor and Thought* (Cambridge, 1979), p. 31.
14. C. Day Lewis, *The Poetic Image* (London, 1947), p. 72.
15. Paul Ricoeur, *The Rule of Metaphor* (London, 1978), translated by R. Czerny, with K. McLaughlin and J. Costello, p. 80.
16. Quoted in David Cooper, *Metaphor* (London, 1986), p. 49.
17. Arthur Rimbaud, *Collected Poems* (London, 1962), edited by Oliver Bernard, p. 10.
18. *Letters of Wallace Stevens* (New York, 1966), edited by Holly Stevens, p. 602.
19. Interview conducted by the present writer in 1990.
20. *Letters of Wallace Stevens*, p. 370.
21. Ibid. p. 430.
22. Tzvetan Todorov, *Symbolism and Interpretation* (London, 1983), translated by Catherine Porter, p. 9ff.
23. Andrew Marvell, *The Complete Poems* (Harmondsworth, 1972), edited by Elizabeth Story Donno, p. 101.

24. Hugh MacDiarmid, *Collected Poems* (Harmondsworth, 1985) vol. 2, p. 17.
25. Ricoeur, *The Rule of Metaphor*, p. 287.
26. Wallace Stevens, *Collected Poems* (London, 1990), p. 239.
27. Ibid. p. 295.
28. Ibid. p. 269.
29. J. Hillis Miller, 'Stevens's Rock and Criticism as Cure', *Georgia Review* 30 (1976), p. 29.
30. Wallace Stevens, *Opus Posthumous* (London, 1959), p. 216.
31. *Letters of Wallace Stevens*, p. 602.
32. Wallace Stevens, *Collected Poems*, p. 471.
33. *Opus Posthumous*, p. 164.

# Nine

## The Real Poem

### Carol Gow

In a brief review of W.S. Graham's work in 1979, Iain Crichton Smith offered the intriguing observation 'sometimes the real poem is the dark companion travelling alongside the actually created one'.[1] Like a key casually dropped, its application not immediately apparent, the comment prompts exploration. I intend to shape a definition of 'the real poem' and to argue that the comment is the key which unlocks the major theme of Crichton Smith's work to date. It is a commonplace to say that all artists experience a dissatisfaction with the created work, and that, like Pinter, they see only a kind of failure which provides the impetus for fresh work. Crichton Smith's observation, however, argues not for that kind of perceived ghostly, but unattainable, perfection, but for a volatile relationship: the created poem on the page allows for the 'dark companion' who would otherwise not find presence. Definition of the real poem will involve discussion of the key concepts in Crichton Smith's work; the imagination, self-inscription, interpellation. My thesis is that Crichton Smith writes not individual poems, nor individual collections, but that his work has pursued relentlessly one major theme: the discovery of a self in the mirror of his poems.

Crichton Smith has insisted on the mystery of poetry, the importance of what he calls the imagination. He has frequently discussed the need for the poet to find a balance between conscious control and spontaneity. Two examples will illustrate the point. The first concerns his long sequence 'Deer On The High Hills' (1962), the second the poetry of Hugh MacDiarmid. Crichton Smith's expressed delight in 'Deer On The High Hills' comes in part because the sequence escapes his conscious intention, and, though he senses its significance, he confesses to not understanding it completely. The fourteen sections of the sequence were written with such facility that he suggests 'it might have been written for me'.[2] Satisfaction with the sequence would seem to reside in that mysterious side of the creative impulse which allows the poet to become a reader of his own work, and which Crichton Smith explores as the 'imagination'. Commending the 'hallucinatory quality' of MacDiarmid's 'The Watergaw' in 1972, Crichton Smith insists that

> whatever the imagination is, there is no doubt that it is what we require in poetry at the highest level. How it operates is incomprehensible. What it creates is, strictly speaking, incapable of being managed by the mind.[3]

Is 'the real poem', then, simply that which escapes conscious control in this way, a poem at the highest level? Such a definition can begin to shape an understanding of 'the real poem' but does not, however, embrace the suggestive menace of the 'dark companion' and the important metaphor of the journey. It leaves the poet in the happy and innocent position of reader of his own work. Any definition must encompass the shock of recognition, the poet not just reader, but guilty creator. 'The real poem' embraces not simply that quality which removes poem from creator and allows it a life of its own, but must partake rather of the quality of Frankenstein's monster.

'Self Portrait' offers a 'Free Church face', and the possible discovery, only just held at bay by the ambiguous 'surely', that

> Surely they made you, those secret moral waters,
> in the night when you were not looking, in the day.[4]

The narrative of Crichton Smith's poetry is centred on the construction of a face in the mirror of his poems and the shock of recognition of the monster who has haunted him, the spectre of Calvinism. The movement of Crichton Smith's poetry is a movement away from his Calvinist background but, paradoxically, it is a movement which remorselessly brings him home.

The creation of the self begins as a free, unfettered act. In the loosely autobiographical novel, *The Last Summer* (1969), the adolescent hero, Malcolm, growing up on the island of Lewis, is offered two texts in which to inscribe himself: the Bible and a Penguin *New Writing*. Rejecting the harsh Calvinism of his island, Malcolm turns to the English poets of his reading. In the world of Eliot, Keats and Auden, he flourishes. He seems free to choose the text of his English reading, and the end of the novel sees him leaving his community for university in Aberdeen. 'The real poem' testifies that that freedom of choice is illusory.

The shaping of 'the real poem' begins in 1972 with the publication of *Love Poems and Elegies*. It is at this point that Crichton Smith redefines his language, redefines the portrait. Suspicion of what he calls the 'glitteringly aesthetic' originates in poems which 'sprang directly from the death of my mother'.[5] Here we see an instinctive exploration of the opposition between the poet free to write himself, and the poet inscribed as 'son'. The poet embodies these oppositions as metaphor and the physical fact of death:

> No metaphors swarm
>
> around that fact, around that strangest thing,
> that being that was and now no longer is.[6]

The poet of 'The Long River' who created powerful images in defiance of a bare background now insists on a bare language and desires to strip his language of metaphor. Yet 'No metaphors swarm' is itself a metaphor. In 'The Black Jar', the use of the word 'black' seven times in a poem which, including the title, is just sixty-four words long, is a kind of literary head-banging, revealing the frustrations of a writer who knows we are in metaphor and cannot get out of it alive.[7]

Crichton Smith is a poet who recklessly tests the value of his art. His experience of his mother's death, and his responses to it, begin involvement with a test which threatens to silence the poet, to leave him without justification:

> Everything I have ever done is really eventually coming to this question. What is death? What is a dead person, and in the end what is the value of writing when one is confronted by a dead person?[8]

*Love Poems and Elegies* marks a watershed in Crichton Smith's work, the discovery that 'metaphor can be used to conceal insoluble contradictions in life':

> Beyond the poems of Seamus Heaney, beautiful though they are, the masked men will stand above the draped coffins saluting an empty heaven with their guns.[9]

Seamus Heaney, as if in direct response, argues:

> Art is an image. It is not a solution to reality, and to confuse the pacifications and appeasements and peace of art with something that is attainable in life is a great error. But to deny your life the suasion of art-peace is also an unnecessary Puritanism.[10]

*Love Poems and Elegies* reveals the desire to confront the contradiction. An 'unnecessary Puritanism' is indeed what the poet begins to demand of his life and his work. The awareness of the potentially destructive nature of such a course is explored but not fully recognised in the long poem 'Orpheus'.[11] The Orpheus myth is useful to Crichton Smith at this stage of his career. His mother's death was a real event in his real world which challenged the sense of self created in his poetry. In this long poem, the mother figure is recast as Euridice, Orpheus becomes an Orphean figure in an Oban, a littered, small-town Scottish burgh, where poems are graffiti scrawled on walls. Taking from the legend Orpheus's experience of separation and his questioning of his music-making, the poem casts a backward glance over the poet's career in an instinctive, irrevocable movement. When Orpheus glanced back, he lost his love for a second, final time. There is the same fresh discovery of loss for Crichton Smith at the end of his poem. His lesson is that the human experiences of love and death will redefine and hone his art. The poem explores the oppositions of art and life and ends with ordinary, domestic images which suggest baptism and rebirth and Orpheus's recognition of bittersweet gain: a white-vested man washing, children blowing bubbles, references to the commercial heroes of the wasteland. Orpheus is usurped by the heroes of popular culture: Valentino, Elvis Presley. The 'And so' which opens the lines below offers a poet aware of the terrible gains he has made:

> And so his lyre had a graver heavier tone
> as if containing all the possible grains
> that can be found in marble or in stone.
> What he had lost was the sweet and random strains
> which leaped obliquely from the vast unknown
> concordances and mirrors but the gains,
> though seeming sparser, were more dearly won.[12]

The 'graver heavier tone' replaces the 'sweet and random strains' but the rhyme on the key words, and the limited variation on 'grains', 'strains' and 'gains' enacts the poet's development here: a reworking, an absorbing, the plainer canvas.

The 'mirror' is central to Crichton Smith's poetry: it symbolises the identities reflected in poems written by a poet who has rejected the mirror of his Calvinist background. Here, there is a new linking of 'mirror', 'marble' and 'stone'. The 'marble' and 'stone' come after 'graver' and pick up the images of the elegies for his mother: they suggest gravestones, unreadable, reflecting nothing. The creation of an identity can no longer be a free intellectual process, but is acknowledged now as trammelled and limited by mortality. The gaze of the death's head which has made the poet stutter in poems like 'Sunday Morning Walk' no longer provides an impasse, but has been absorbed into the poetry. 'The vast unknown concordances', which provides the language of a poet with freedom to experiment in an unselfconscious way, have their counterpart in the gravestone, with 'all the possible grains'. Against an image of reflected light, movement and unpredictability is placed an image of a set pattern ingrained in stone. The identity of the poet is no longer a free act, but is created from something already set down. 'Seeming', however, leaves the poet innocent of the destructive nature of his course.

Malcolm's choice between the text of the Bible and the text of English poetry is re-examined in *The Notebooks of Robinson Crusoe* (1975). Both these texts offer a false inscription. The poet seeks, like Crusoe, a bare island, a blank page, on which to inscribe himself. In 'Today I Wished to Write a Story', the poet contemplates a story of his own experiences on the island. Yet instead of writing his history, creating the self, he opens the Bible to discover that the self has already been inscribed — as son:

> written in faded ink on
> the leaf before Genesis the words, 'To my dearest son from his mother'.
> I could not elucidate the date.[13]

Opening the Bible before the beginning, before Genesis, reveals that something has already been written before that beginning, before 'In the beginning was the Word'.[14] 'To my dearest son from his mother' inscribes him as son. 'I could not elucidate the date' subverts the possibility of writing the self. Language colonises. Malcolm's freedom is illusory and his choice is invalidated. The poet of the notebooks must submit to being claimed and named by his society.

Crichton Smith's comments on the way in which social formation claims the individual recognise the benefits of community in a fragmented world. His experiences of his upbringing on Lewis give his definition of the relationship a sombre colouring. Interpellation, answering the call of the community and finding a sense of self reflected in that community, offers the antithesis of self-inscription:

> One is known as the person one is, for ever. One's parents are known, one's grandparents are known, one is in an assigned position.[15]

The 'assigned position', the discovery of the interpellation of 'son', threatens the poet's freedom to write himself. It is something to be resisted, because a Calvinist inheritance is perceived by Crichton Smith in negative terms:

I think I feel it more and more strongly now the older I grow that
it has done harm. And I feel it has done harm to my own
psychology, this kind of – this kind of depressive lack of joy . . .
this kind of uniformity, and I feel that it has done my own writing
no good at all, except as a form of something to fight against.[16]

That fight is dramatised on the stage of the Westerns of his childhood
reading. In the radio play, *Goodman and Death Mahoney*, Goodman kills
Death Mahoney in a showdown which also symbolises the freeing of son
from 'Maw', a God-fearing Christian woman, who is also the Gaelic
matriarch, the spectre of Calvinism.[17] In a poem from *The Notebooks of
Robinson Crusoe*, the gunfight is between 'I' and 'a man in a black hat'.
The villain is representative of the 'hard black hatted' men from
'Highland Sunday', an early poem in which the poet's church-goers are
drowned in the sensuous language of *The White Noon* collection.[18] Here,
the black-hatted figure is recast in a scene from the western 'High
Noon'. The 'I' is the dreamer, the poet; the black-hatted man the
Calvinist opponent. Duel is also dual, the doubleness of the 'I' fighting
for recognition. And the identity of the survivor is left in doubt:

> If I could fire
> just once more
> I'd know who fell.[19]

In a poem which uses the image of a face in the mirror and the act of
shaving, the poet commits himself to 'elucidating' the text of the face:

> Steadily I reaped, clearing the undergrowth, clarifying the
> lines of the face, elucidating its text.
> It is no mean novel sensationally hot from the printers: it is
> true Bible, responsible. On it shall all words be printed.[20]

'Lines', 'text', 'no mean novel' and 'all words be printed' accept that
language colonises, that the individual is constructed in and by his
language. The resolution is towards 'true Bible, responsible'. 'Novel' is
contrasted with 'Bible', and 'mean' with 'true'. These oppositions fall
into the category of the 'vast unknown concordances' and 'all the
possible grains' of the Orpheus poem and offer the same hegemony – a
cold, sober language taking precedence over sensational heat; truth over
lies. The act of shaving is an act of criticising. Clearing the
undergrowth is an act which finds its parallel in Crusoe's work on the
island. *The Notebooks of Robinson Crusoe* are crisis poems because they

explore the conflict between the poem, the freedom of the poet to write himself, and the claim of his background, between self-inscription and interpellation.

When Crusoe leaves his island, he turns his back on a solipsistic isolation and answers the call of community. A quotation from the 1987 novel, *In The Middle of the Wood*, clarifies the choice. The hero, Ralph Simmons, delivered from the fragmented world of the schizophrenic, discovers:

> He knew suddenly why Hamlet needed Horatio as a witness, why Horatio had to be left behind to tell the truth as he saw it, to explain the extraordinary pattern of events, the murders, the accidents. The most terrible thing of all would be to be in a world without witnesses, a Robinson Crusoe on an island. That in a sense was what he had been.[21]

The created self, seen in the mirror of his own poems, is 'homotextual', a Robinson Crusoe without a witness.

For Crichton Smith, answering the call of community, accepting the inscription of son, is to enter into a hostile and deadly relationship. The effects can be seen in the turn towards a new, barer language. He has spoken about a conscious decision to abandon the 'dandyish' language of his early work which was 'a kind of pose in a way' and seek a plainer, barer language which is 'part of what I do, the way I think'.[22] This is a rational analysis by a poet who is no longer innocent reader of own work. The self-portrait has begun to take shape and, standing farther back, he experiences the shock of recognition. Such a rational stance denies how the changes are actually worked through in the poetry itself by an innocent poet, and is in danger of obfuscating our understanding of 'the real poem'. I have argued that 'the real poem' partakes of that mysterious area which Crichton Smith has called the imagination; I have suggested that the poet who creates a self in the mirror of his own poems has written poems of the highest order on the imaginative level. I have suggested that he begins to confront contradiction and to explore the conflict between self-inscription and interpellation.

The volume which follows *The Notebooks, In The Middle* (1977), attempts to negotiate the conflict: writing the self, accepting the inscription of son. The title of the volume and the poems themselves reveal a precarious and schizophrenic balancing act. There is a gap of seven years between publication of *In The Middle* and the subsequent volume, *The Exiles*. The lacuna is significant. Crichton Smith has left the portrait unfinished. He has abandoned the course which drew him back to his Calvinist roots because he has perceived in the mirror of his poems the spectre. Elucidating the text, clarifying the lines of the face, reveals another walking alongside: Frankenstein perceives his monster.

The definition of 'the real poem' can now be attempted. The 'dark companion' is the shadow cast by the created, individual poem, a shape defined clearly only in retrospect, against the accumulating œuvre. Iain Crichton Smith's comment:

> what at the time to me seemed to be a spontaneous gesture or a spontaneous book or a poem turns out to have been part of an overall, fixed developing theme . . . There's an enormous amount of conditioning in what we do[23]

reveals the shock of discovery, his awareness of that larger pattern. When I spoke to him in 1987, he was able to elaborate this point with a quotation from 'Of A Rare Courage', a poem from the 1961 collection, *Thistles and Roses*:

> for he, unlike those others, sees quite clearly
> the fractured failure of the best we are.
> . . .
> and therefore I will praise him like those other
> successful darlings who discover late
> a tang of burning in the acid ether
> and in spontaneous gestures a fixed fate.[24]

The shadow cast by each individual poem reveals a new shape which takes the poet by surprise. His flight from the spectre of Calvinism, his Lewis background and the creation of a free and unfettered identity have begun to shape a reflection that he has sought to escape; he is to be brought face to face with the Lewis self and the innocent, yet terrifying, self-inscription of son.

In *A Life* (1986), Crichton Smith offers this description of the real poem:

> The sacred and abhorred
> real poem has a waspish sting.[25]

'The real poem' is a poem written by a poet who can sense its integrity, its authenticity, its connection with a lived life, and is therefore freed from the charge of homotextuality. It is therefore 'sacred', encompassing the Bible, Calvinism, the whole truth. It is 'abhorred' because it admits into his poetry the very forces which are ultimately destructive. 'The real poem' has a 'waspish sting' because the conflict between the creation of a self in his poems and the acceptance of the inscription of son is developed and explored on the imaginative level; the outcome takes the poet too by surprise.

To have freed oneself from a culture, and then to find that one carries that culture deep within the self, offers fruitful ground for new work. It demands that the lacuna be confronted and worked through, that the portrait be finished. 'Homotextuality' has been abandoned. The 'Free church face' which inscribes him son presents him with the spectre of Calvinism, which seems to deny the poet and lead to silence. But it is in confronting the spectre, in the working-out of this portrait, that Crichton Smith will create the real poem *on* the page. He stands poised, his materials before him, the greatest work not yet begun.

NOTES

1. 'Charts of Poetic Journeys', *Glasgow Herald*, 6 December 1979, p. 12.
2. Interview with the poet, Taynuilt, 1987.
3. 'The Golden Lyric', in *Hugh MacDiarmid: A Critical Survey*, edited by Duncan Glen (London, 1972), pp. 124–40 (p. 138).
4. 'Self Portrait', in *Seven Poets* (Glasgow, 1981), p. 43.
5. *Love Poems and Elegies* (London, 1972), p. 10.
6. Ibid., p. 21.
7. Ibid., p. 31.
8. 'Poet in Bourgeois Land', *Scottish International* (September 1971), pp. 22–8 (p. 27).
9. *Towards The Human* (London, 1986), p. 48.
10. Randy Barnes, 'Seamus Heaney: An Interview', *Salmagundi* 80, 1988, pp. 4–21 (p. 21).
11. In *Orpheus and Other Poems* (Preston, 1974), pp. 10–14.
12. Ibid., p. 14.
13. *The Notebooks of Robinson Crusoe* (London, 1975), p. 70.
14. John 1 i.
15. 'Real People in a Real Place', in *Towards The Human* (London, 1986), p. 27.
16. Taynuilt interview.
17. BBC Radio Scotland, 3 May 1988.
18. In *New Poets 1959*, edited by Edwin Muir (London, 1959), p. 18.
19. *The Notebooks of Robinson Crusoe*, p. 72.
20. Ibid., p. 85.
21. *In The Middle Of The Wood* (London, 1974), p. 183.
22. Taynuilt interview.
23. Taynuilt interview.
24. *Thistles and Roses* (London, 1961), p. 54.
25. *A Life* (Manchester, 1986), p. 48.

# Ten

## The Double Vision: Imagery in the English Poetry

### J.H. Alexander

Every significant poet has a distinctive voice, and their poetry a unique atmosphere or feel to it. Two of the most important elements producing this feel are favourite words and recurring images. Iain Crichton Smith does not often startle or delight the reader with unusual words or ordinary words unusually employed[1], but it is not difficult to identify two sets of constantly recurring terms that give his English poetry its peculiar atmosphere. There are words such as *bare*, *tall*, *pale* and *thin*, which establish the scrupulous, rather attenuated, often delicate tone of the verse 'with its own elegance, intense and sparse' (*Or* 12; see the Abbreviations at the end of the chapter); and then there are the basic colour terms, notably *black* and *white*, *blue*, *green*, *red* and *yellow*, and (less often) *grey*, *orange* and *silver*. These colour terms can accumulate certain thematic significances, some of which will be noted below; but they function most importantly as a basic element in the characteristic verbal texture.

Far more remarkable than Crichton Smith's individual words is his imagery. The first part of this chapter analyses his use of recurrent imagery to create and explore the double vision characteristic of his perception. The second part extends this discussion to consider the imagery of his aesthetics. There follows a recognition of the importance of the isolated, one-off image. The final section takes as close a look as limitations of space allow at the role of imagery in the most recent collection but one, *A Life*.

The titles of two of the early collections, *Thistles and Roses* and *The Law and the Grace*, serve to alert the reader to Crichton Smith's characteristic habit of working with two opposing or contrasting entities. One world, one way of thinking, is set against another; two conflicting ways of seeing are investigated. The contrast is usually clear, but it is seldom rigidly schematic, and opposition nearly always shades into complementarity. The two cited titles indicate one of the main initial oppositions in Crichton Smith's vision, which persists throughout his work: a world dominated by severity, rigidity, hardness and law is set against one of gentleness, fluidity, fragile vulnerability and grace. Each of these worlds is defined and explored by connected groups of persistent images.

The vision of a world dominated by law and imposed order is expressed by a cluster of hard, confining images involving the elements of stone and iron, and derived images of cage, fence and armour. The short poem 'Minister' (*LG* 21) deploys virtually the whole arsenal, somewhat unrelentingly, to define the theologically rigid world of Crichton Smith's childhood with its 'moral cage', 'soul's diamond', nailing to a text, 'naked stone', and a concluding surreal gothicism: 'The wooden pew's iron eyes/ hollowed out his joyful Sundays'. There is more of debate in the haunting dialogue 'About that Mile', where an interlocutor says to the narrator: 'You think me moral like the weighted stone/ engraved on graves' for accepting the loss of Eden and leaving it as foolery to poetry (*TR* 19–20). The weighted tombstone, sometimes linked with an open Bible[2], can stand for any oppressive thinking, perhaps even for abstract thought itself as opposed to living sensation: the angels and devils of orthodoxy apparently wish 'to stand beside/ the stone' they set on the poet (*LG* 38), and a writer is advised:

> To stand so steady that the world is still
> and take your cold blue pen and write it down
> (all that you see) before the thought can kill
> and set on the living grass the heavy stone
> is what you're here for.
>
> (*TR* 32)

As the reader's sense of Crichton Smith's imagistic resonance builds up from poem to poem, he or she will have no difficulty in discerning the implications of mental confinement in such a literal (but not quite literal) statement as that about the islanders: 'Always they're making fences, making barred/ gates to keep the wind out' (*LPE* 16). That futile attempt at fencing resonates with more than a dozen elsewhere in the English poetry, and perhaps most notably with the discerning in New England as in Old Scotland of 'the stiff,/ formal, bristling, fence round brimming life' (*FBL* 49).

Against such harsh constraints, Crichton Smith sets an ardent, glittering world of light and fire, fragile bones, humming life and shifting clouds. In 'The Cemetery near Burns' Cottage', the grey tombs of the Covenanters, servants of 'the heart's immaculate order', seem pale intruders into a fierce vitality:

> This churchyard now
> flickers with light, untameably with Burns,
>
> the secret enemy within the stone,
> the hand which even here stings its hot whip
> in glittering rays from socketed bone to bone.
> (*LG* 42)

That exultant, glittering light is linked throughout Crichton Smith's work with a dangerous fire, destructive and creative at once, whose naked contact is to be feared, yet whose energy is the source of all living art. Of the puritans, he can write: 'That was great courage to have watched that fire,/ not placing a screen before it as we do/ with pictures, poems, landscapes' (*TR* 11) but Orpheus is advised by the god of the underworld:

> You must learn
> to read the flags more closely and compelled
> by an ardour of the spirit always burn
> forward on tracks continually rebuilt.
> (*Or* 13)

(The railway image is a recurrent member of the iron cluster, suggesting here a destiny which need not involve rigidity, and one demanding a living, passionate response.) The island world is itself double, fenced and yet 'humming' with vibrant life, so that the poet's experience of it can be linked with the zest for life at the extreme displayed by the Elizabethans: 'On the axe's edge/ the humming colours hone a sensuous music' (*TR* 40, 51). In an opposition parallel to, and linked with, the theological, the stiff bourgeois who are troubled by 'unsettling clouds' confront the poets who 'walk on clouds', who may indeed be as weak as clouds, and for whom clouds are far from those the bank clerk enters in red in his mental cash-book entries (*FBL* 13, 15, 57, 26).

The basic, opposed image-clusters are supplemented by several subsidiary elements, of which one may be selected for notice here. The world of obsessive order, and its theological preference, is often indicated by reference to watches and clocks:

>     Dressed in its Sunday best the club's assured
>     that God presides at their communion still,
>     holy and perfect and invisible
>     and punctual as the watch that lies obscured
>
>     in an ironed waistcoat on its golden chain
>     ticking so comfortably, taking no queer leaps,
>     but steady, measured, in its clear eclipse,
>     golden and round and perfect in design.
>                                              (*FBL* 31)

By implication, a truer religion is to be found in 'the howling faces of eternity' which the speaker gives in exchange for a retirement presentation watch (*FBL* 44). Conversely, a hideous parody of the light of creative liberation is offered by 'the plague of neon' in the contemporary city (*NRC* 31).

The basic opposition explored above hints at the imaginative world which Crichton Smith sees as the natural home of the creative artist. It is now time to explore this creative world in more detail, to examine some of its certainties and ambiguities.

The guiding spirit of Crichton Smith's aesthetics is John Keats (though the actual feel of his own poetry is in some ways more Shelleyan, silver rather than gold). Crichton Smith is clearly attracted by the combination in Keats of high poetic ambition, a passion for truth and beauty combined with a sceptical intelligence teasing out the connection between them, and a commitment to humanity with its imperfections and its search for perfection. In *A Life*, Crichton Smith refers to 'Keats who died/ in perpetual autumn with the nightingale' (41). This is clearly not to be taken as literary history (Keats wrote his 'Ode to a Nightingale' in the spring, and he died in February); rather, it is an imaginative summing-up of Keats' own transience, of his concern with human and natural transience in general, and of his quest for an art at once alive and monumental, a quest which met with complete success in his ode 'To Autumn' and perhaps only there. Autumn is the most prominent season in Crichton Smith's work, appearing in the title of the collection *Hamlet in Autumn*, where one of his finest and most profound poems is 'For Keats'. Its concluding stanzas bring together several of the words and images associated with Crichton Smith's aesthetic quest:

>     Fighting the scree, to arrive at Autumn,
>     innocent impersonal accepted
>     where the trees do not weep like gods
>     but are at last themselves.

> Bristly autumn, posthumous and still,
> the crowning fine frost on the hill
> the perfect picture blue and open-eyed
> with the lakes as fixed as your brother's eyes,
> autumn that will return
>
> and will return and will return, however
> the different delicate vase revolves
> in the brown mortal foliage, in the woods
> of egos white as flowers.
>
> (*HIA* 33)

These rich lines, which should of course be read in the context of the preceding stanzas, bring together images of the perfect picture (Vermeer is Crichton Smith's favourite artist), of crowning, of pure blueness, of the vase recalling Keats' Grecian Urn, of decaying natural brownness, and of whiteness denoting a sort of fragile purity as well as the pallor of illness, deathbed sheets and the corpse. The egos form part of a larger picture, as Keats arrived 'at Autumn,/ innocent impersonal accepted' and as in Gaelic nature-poetry Crichton Smith admires the impersonal treatment of the natural world.[3]

Like Keats, Crichton Smith recognises that art cannot be made out of spontaneity alone; it also requires discipline. This is where the distinctions explored in the first section begin to be understood as complementary rather than diametrical opposites, almost as Blakean contraries. This is most evident in the poetry's many classical references. Roman discipline is often forbidding and negative: the 'Schoolteacher' of *The Law and the Grace* is associated with blind note-taking and inhumanity (31). But the classics teacher 'Mr M.' represented a distinguished order and taught 'Aeneas and the rest/ dressed in the supine and infinitive/ ghosts of words, ghosts of innocence, language/ beautiful, tough, persistent' (*Lines* 8), and John MacLean's classicism is found wholly admirable:

> Where you burned
>
> exactitude prevailed, the rule of Rome,
> the gravitas of Brutus, and his calm,
> his stoic tenderness, his love of books,
> his principles and practice.
>
> (*HIA* 36–7)

The same poem uses positive images to reinforce this recognition of the positive side of classical discipline – light, wind, steadiness, a grave autumn, as opposed to modern neon and cracking vases – and its final section is a radiant, stoical acceptance of destiny, linking autumn with crown and helmet, the last a recurring image of human endeavour and endurance:

> So with your battered helmet let you be
> immersed in golden autumn as each tree
> accepts its destiny and will put by
> its outworn crown, its varying finery.
>
> (38)

Crichton Smith's aesthetic exploration is at its most complex when involved with images of mirrors and textuality. The mirror perfectly suggests doubleness. A poem may be a mirror, a duplicate world, as the speaker suggests to 'S', whom he has taken into his poems: 'You can sit in front of a mirror on a chair,/ and make the poem look back at you' (*LPE* 56). It is a way of knowing the self, but it may involve a distortion of the self, so that Hamlet is in a hall of trick mirrors distorting like spoons both himself and the other characters at court (*FBL* 18, 25). That very distortion may be a reflection of a disturbing reality in the self, of evil in the unconscious, which the speaker can nevertheless find preferable to superficial bourgeois blandness:

> I say, 'You are so monstrous I would call
> the bells of hell, gassed faces in the mirror,
> to enliven age on age your bourgeois soul.'
>
> (*FBL* 10)

The phenomenal world itself is seen by the speaker of 'The Letter' as a mirror, the letter in question being written 'out of the mirror' to 'God who created us' (*HIA* 57). The final goodbye is 'just/ an injustice of the glass' (61). Complexities are multiplied when Crichton Smith recognises the extent to which poets feed on each other, reflecting 'from each other like mirrors', in the phenomenon which has come to be known as intertextuality (*IM* 58).

Recurrent images of textuality indicate the extent to which Crichton Smith is conscious of the constitutive role of language and of the potential dangers of such role-playing. At the outset of his career, the region of 'It was a Country' 'was a land made to be written on/ with words carved out of the shining sky', recognising a reciprocity between subject and recorder/interpreter (*LR* 11), and in his most recent collection summer is 'leafy,/ just like a newspaper/ composed of coloured paper' (*V* 10). This reciprocity has its limits, as when Crichton Smith contemplates a disaster of the past that attracts his attention more than once, the loss of the *Iolaire* and her complement of returning servicemen in 1919: 'One cannot speak of this/ or ask the illuminating storms/ to write their reasons on a plain coast' (*TR* 44). Even a poet must recognise not only that literature means little to many people, but also that it is not necessarily 'truest', in whatever sense that word may be taken: 'The truest work is learning to be human/ definitive texts the poorest can afford' (*TR* 46). The very next page of this collection images a more radical fear about the status of the poet's own work, despised by the inhabitants of the quasi-normal world of committee meetings with its unpurified language of the tribe:

> And I was terrified lest my world be fake
> and these blunt men who make all words opaque
> should stand like giants by my dwarfish verse.
>
> (*TR* 47)

The modern poet's reaction to the great texts of the past is often sceptical: Keats built an earlier version of that very scepticism into his verse which carries its own burden of the past, but the same may not be true of Milton's 'Lycidas', whose images assert a hallowed but questionable version of reality:

> Too simple an ending that,
> that he should rise as the sun rises
> out of the water where it never set.
> Too simple this pure art's hypothesis
> transforming bones and flesh into light.
>
> (*LG* 58)

Crichton Smith's experience of Hebridean death is not thus; in the actual presence of death, images can seem futile or impossible: the corpse 'will not permit/ the play of imagery' (*LPE* 21–2). Yet, later in the same collection, a carefully distanced speaker ('He said' the poem begins, and it is called 'Argument') enlists imagery in coming to terms with death as a generality: it is 'just a place that we have looked/ too deeply at, not into, as at a book/ held that short space too close', a painting to be seen whole only from a distance (36). This aesthetics of Crichton Smith's is precious, but it is also consciously precarious.

The examples quoted up to this point will incidentally have indicated that Crichton Smith's recurrent images are seldom used mechanically. One of the delights in reading his poetry is to observe the extraordinary resource and ingenuity which make most such reappearances fresh and stimulating. An equal source of delight, and at times of astonishment, is the seemingly endless supply of isolated, one-off images introduced for special effect. These are often particularly effective when they are used to end a poem. All readers of Crichton Smith's work, and a good many of those who have encountered his work only in anthologies, will recall the haunting image that concludes the best-known of his 'Old Woman' poems:

> And nothing moved within the knotted head
>
> but only a few poor veins as one might see
> vague wishless seaweed floating on a tide
> of all the salty waters where had died
> too many waves to mark two more or three.
>
> (*TR* 9)

Many of Crichton Smith's colleagues in the teaching profession will have alerted their pupils to the perfect match here of visual correspondence, verbal fittingness (or 'keeping' in Hazlitt's happy terminology), metrical movement, rhyme and half-rhyme, and appropriately dribbling syntax. These are not lines that one forgets or grows tired of.

The *Exiles* collection has a particularly effective set of unique concluding images, of which two may be singled out for special mention. In the title poem 'The Exiles', translated from Crichton Smith's own Gaelic, the moon (itself a recurrent motif) is promoted from initial cliché to a startling newness that satisfies entirely:

> That sea of May running in such blue,
> a moon at night, a sun at daytime,
> and the moon like a yellow fruit,
> like a plate on a wall
> to which they raise their hands
> like a silver magnet
> with piercing rays
> streaming into the heart.
>
> (*E* 13)

The final 'Envoi', spoken as it were by the dying Hamlet, has a somewhat Stoppardian ending, but one which does not suggest a wholly paid-up post-modernism:

> Tragedy is
> nothing but churned foam.
> I wave to you
> from this secure and leafy entrance,
> this wooden

> door on which I bump my head,
> this moment and then,
> that.
>                           (E 57)

One recalls the lines from an earlier collection which, though spoken by a distanced narrator, must reflect Crichton Smith's own experience:

> the poet knows when he's concluded, for
> there's an exactitude that he's aiming at.
> He knows it by a sense beyond the poem,
> he knows it as he knows a coming home,
> perfection to which nothing can be added,
> nor by the mind can wholly be decoded.
>                           (LPE 34)

Not every unique image will work for every reader, and some of them will be incomprehensible intellectually or will fail to work imaginatively. That is inevitable with so rich an imagist. The present writer can make little, for instance, of the one-off image in another 'Envoi': 'I in my plates of frost go/ among the falling crockery of hills// stones, plains, all falling and falling' (LG 60); but other readers may be able to respond more positively. On the other hand, if a degree of arbitrariness and self-indulgence may be permitted, the following four images stand out for this reader for grotesqueness, grandeur, horror and sheer exuberant fun respectively: 'Time sagged in the middle/ like a sack void of grain' (LR 24); 'Light strikes the stone bible like a gong' (WN 16); 'a woman drag[s]/ her cancer like a creel' (TR 19); 'in the bursting masts a lad, blue-rigged,/ lace at his throat, ready to munch and munch/ clear days like biscuits' (TR 42).

At the outset of his career, Crichton Smith's one-off images (and occasionally his uses of recurrent imagery) were often obscure, and some of them are now obscure even to him.[4] One can understand why he wrote in 1972:

> I too was terrified of words once.
> I was so frightened of where words would lead me
> that I would walk at night over the stones
> (yellow with moonlight) and feel fear beside me
> as palpable as a yellow snarling dog
> or a yellow rat . . .
> I feared each clicking motion of my foot
> and felt below me a huge echoing well

> where language sent each yellow writhing root
> which, had I known it, would grow green and cool.
>
> *(HIA* 15)

Images can be frightening intruders into the upper world from the unconscious, as Coleridge knew well. Crichton Smith's attempts to tame these demonic visitors in the middle years of his career were sometimes too insistent: *From Bourgeois Land* is certainly a unified volume, but its unity is achieved at the cost of an impoverishing schematicisation that at times comes close to caricature. In his most recent work, he has managed to combine a satisfying unity in individual volumes without any cramping of the imagination. His three collections of the 1980s, *Exiles*, *A Life* and *The Village and Other Poems*, are masterful without any of the tyranny often associated with mastering.

*A Life* is a highly complex web of interconnecting images, which any attempt at analysis can only hint at and hope not to distort too brutally. The volume can, of course, be read on its own, but, more than any other of Crichton Smith's collections, it gains by drawing on the accumulated associations of recurrent imagery in the preceding volumes. The twin worlds are already familiar: island and mainland, childhood and adulthood, school and outside world, dream and reality, death and life, reality and a defining or distorting reflection of reality. These are again pervasive in the *Life* collection, and occasionally they are explicitly discussed:

> A winsome boyhood among glens and bens
> casts, later, double images and shades.
> And ceilidhs in the cities are the lens
> through which we see ourselves, unmade, remade,
> by music and by grief.
>
> (10)

And in Aberdeen 'the scholar ghosts/ through a double landscape of new streets, old Greeks' (20). Old resonances are recalled both in insistent repetitions (such as moon and dance in the haunting opening sequence 'Lewis 1928–45') and in isolated occurrences of familiar images. Thus when we read 'The windows of the school are red shields' (15), we are aware not only that the image is a way of describing the actual windows, but also that it links up with school as world of classical discipline encountered in earlier collections, and of course with shields as school trophies. When we encounter Mrs Gray, Crichton Smith's 'iron landlady with the Roman nose' (20), the wider harshnesses of iron and Rome are recalled. And when Crichton Smith writes of his retirement from schoolteaching to commit himself to full-time writing, 'not forgetting human voices too/ in my study of the vases and the stone' (51), he is using a sort of imaginative shorthand, a code to which readers familiar with his earlier work will immediately respond, though not one which will prove arcane to newcomers.

*A Life* has its own unique pattern of images, though it incorporates many familiar from elsewhere in Crichton Smith's work. It links web and thread, by way of marble, grid and cage, with chalk, ash, fire and light in a tapestry of great subtlety. The opening Lewis sequence contrasts memories of magical island youth with the ravages of age as 'our knuckles redden and webbed lines engage/ eyes that were once so brilliant and blue' (9): this last image links up directly with the picture of the once famous footballer, now an alcoholic, who 'kicks right through the mirror' so that 'The spidery keeper hurts him in the rib' (11: the shattered mirror brings to mind net and web). We move by way of the literal net woven by a sailor (13), and the 'thatched roofs, woven by dead hands' (14), to winter Aberdeen where 'God the spider shrinks in his crystal web' (23), then to the complex net of the unliterary school footballers which has metaphysical overtones with its 'ghost with gloves' as goalkeeper (48), and finally to the poet escaped from the stone, rising from the dead, whose 'shroud is palpable/ changed into web' (60). The connections here are intensely imaginative rather than logical, evoking a metaphysical uncertainty, a ghostliness or ghastliness at the heart of human, and possibly of divine, matters; there is in addition the concept of woven textuality, reinforced by the metaphorical 'frayed thread of being' (9) and the primarily literal 'cloth both fine and frayed' (10). The old woman whose thread is frayed 'runs home lightly to her thousand pills,/ her clouded marbles' (9–10), and the emphasis on the pattern of the marble establishes a crucial link between frail or ghostly webs and that type of stone. Marble recurs in a sequence of significations: a sailor's flesh (13); a recalling of tombstones as open Bibles (14); an indication of the 'transient images' of the Odeon (21); a suggestion of classical grandeur opposed — but not wholly opposed — to pale girls on neon roads (34) or of classical control in literature (40); a hard substance through which light may 'sway' (40); and an allusion to earthly immortality paralleling the graffiti which the stone attracts (42). This highly resonant cluster of associations is summed up in the final occurrences, 'the pale-faced girl chained to the changing moon,/ and Venus smiling from her marble text' (46) and the poet's room as 'this cold marble cell which will forgive/ only the best and truest' (51).

Marble, in all its complex linking of worlds, connects in its turn with rigid grids, railway lines and necessary discipline, with school chalk, with the pallor of a ghostly underworld and the ashes of imaginative extinction, and with the erotic paleness of girls and their white legs. There is an inevitable connection between ashes and fire, and between fire and the light which pervades the final section of the collection, where sexual imagery, skirts and bridal fulfilment attain a sort of apotheosis.

In *A Life*, the reader has privileged access to a fully-realised imaginative world, scrupulous, enriching, life-giving, humane and masterful. The experience of reading this collection is a moving one, and not the least moving moment is when Iain Crichton Smith recalls the title image of his first collection, *The Long River* of thirty years earlier, in the process of eliminating himself from his own text:

> The author is not important, the author dies.
> The tale lives on. It is the long river
> heard at deepest midnight, in the day,
> with berries hanging over it, subsumed
> in a sweet water that is not a mirror.
>
> Set out, set out, on your bare autumn sail.
>
> (55)

NOTES

1. Among rare examples of words that catch the attention in their own right, the following may be noted (italics added): 'I walked one day by the *composed* water' (*TR* 42); 'A saw *nags* at a tree' (*WN* 17); 'The sky begins to brighten as before,/ remorseless amber, and the *bruised* blue grows/ at the erupting edges' (*E* 45); 'the stacks of corn are *gossiping* in the field' (*L* 9).
2. E.g. *WN* 16, *TR* 10.
3. See Crichton Smith's Introduction to his translation of Duncan Bàn MacIntyre's *Ben Dorain*, originally published in 1969 and reprinted by Northern House, Newcastle upon Tyne, in 1988.
4. In an interview with Aonghas Macneacail (*Stand*, 30:1 (Winter 1988–9), Crichton Smith says of 'Deer on the High Hills': 'I'm sure many people can't understand much of that poem. There are parts I don't understand now. But I don't think, in a way, that it matters.'

ABBREVIATIONS

LR   *The Long River* (Edinburgh, 1955)
WN   *The White Noon* (*New Poets 1959*, ed. Edwin Muir, London, 1959)
TR   *Thistles and Roses* (London, 1961)
LG   *The Law and the Grace* (London, 1965)

| | |
|---|---|
| Lines | *Lines Review*, 29 (June 1969) |
| FBL | *From Bourgeois Land* (London, 1972) |
| LPE | *Love Poems and Elegies* (London, 1972) |
| HIA | *Hamlet in Autumn* (Loanhead, 1972) |
| Or | *Orpheus and Other Poems* (Preston, 1974) |
| NRC | *The Notebooks of Robinson Crusoe* (London, 1975) |
| IM | *In the Middle* (London, 1977) |
| E | *The Exiles* (Manchester and Dublin, 1984) |
| L | *A Life* (Manchester, 1986) |
| V | *The Village and Other Poems* (Manchester, 1989) |

## Eleven

## Iain Crichton Smith: Cockerel From the Dawn

### Alastair Fowler

There are few obvious rules governing stages of development in a writer's imagination. Keats and Rimbaud ran through their entire poetic evolution in their youth, but John Cooper Powys only began his in his fifties, and Molly Keane began (or recommenced) in her eighties. And Iain Crichton Smith manifests a different pattern again, in that he has been publishing continuously since 1959 and is currently still at his freshest, freest and best. Indeed, with *A Life* (1986) and *The Village and Other Poems* (1989), he may be said to have made a quantum jump in accomplishment. Earlier collections contained stronger individual poems; but these two have more coherence and substance, more cumulative weight as volumes.

Along with the winged gifts of the mercurial poet, Crichton Smith has had to contend with the problems of facility — of excessive speed in composition. His earlier work was brilliantly fluent, and predictably flawed. The flaws must often have been, or have become, evident enough to their author; yet he appeared averse to revision. This may have had something to do, paradoxically, with his self-imposed high standards. (It is not easy to pursue excellence in a country where 'There shall not be excellence, there shall be the average'.[1] And how can an excellent poem come from the lapidary exchanges and compromises of revision?) But it probably had more to do with his Gaelic origins. At any rate, he seems almost to have felt words as interposing a screen — a barrier to be broken through for communication of a sense of being — rather than as parts of being, enjoyable in themselves. It was as if he had in mind other structures of thought than could quite be found an equivalent for in English (and for him, of course, Scots has not been a real alternative).

One way of accommodating or bridging different structures of thought is through imagery; and perhaps that is why imagery has always been for Crichton Smith by far the most important poetic element. The pleasures of his extraordinarily compressed figures – difficult yet richly meaningful – have made him in this regard a poets' poet. Yet his fluency in composition has often worked against this very strength, by facilitating an easy neatness at odds with the complex, ramifying imagery:

> It was my own kindness brought me here
> to an eventless room, bare of ornament.
> This is the threshold charity carried me over.
> I live here slowly in a permament
>
> but clement weather. It will do for ever.
> A barren bulb creates my firmament.[2]

The trim endstopping makes one pause inappropriately, here, over the paradox 'barren . . . creates' – perhaps to conclude that it cannot bear logical examination. Actually, it is only through suspended, incomplete chains of discourse, reaching out untidily beyond the line, that the ideas held in play suggest themselves. For example: 'A bulb constitutes my (similarly spherical but stunted) firmament'; 'A bulb switched on creates my world by its light'; 'bare of ornament . . . A barren bulb bears no shade'; etc. Considered on its own, the line is less accessible, less communicative. To encourage the uptake of ramifying half-connections, Crichton Smith has over the years progressively loosened his metrical and syntactic forms, and so opened up possibilities for more active imagery, depending on ever more distant, further-fetched connections. This is not to say that he has become formally reckless, any more than one would wish to say that of a brilliantly loose painter such as Frans Hals. For the loosening has in Crichton Smith's case oddly made for more strength – much as, in the game of Go, it is often the more loosely strung-out stones that hold their ground most tenaciously.

This comes out clearly enough in *A Life*, where the lines are consistently enjambed in such a way as to minimise line breaks and induce a rapid reading speed, almost like that of prose. The reader is paced, in particular being carried over broken chains of discourse. Many partial meanings are thus held in suspension, as if the virtual present were unusually extended. Crichton Smith is able in consequence to exploit half-registered associations – subliminal, residual effects of phrases recently passed over but not yet determined as to meaning. He can explore beyond implications to weaker and still weaker (but ever more communicative) implicatures.

Some of the imagery is now extremely bold:

> You will not find a Rubens, Rembrandt here,
> nor my revered Vermeer. You will not find
> the velvet-lined
> hound faces of aristocrats: the blind
> blank mask of genius with its gravid stare.[3]

In a way, 'hound faces' is indefensible. If it had to be dwelt on, it might well be pronounced meaningless: 'are the faces "hound" in shape, colour or way of moving?' a latter-day F.R. Leavis might ask. But coming to the phrase on the run, with Rubens and 'velvet-lined' still in mind, the colour of Netherlandish portrait backgrounds flickers on the inward eye. And now associations ramify: family portraits imply lineage (a whole pack of hound faces) and the breeding of aristocrats suggests, perhaps, the breeding of hounds. In context, 'hound' may come to mean something like 'overbred'.

In *A Village* (1989), this method is carried a good deal further. Not only are line breaks commonly overridden by extreme enjambement, but also a new system of indentation is introduced to extend the 'virtual present' even more. For this system increases the pace of reading by reducing eye movement. And sometimes it has the effect of inviting consideration of the indented lines as a unit. The reader is led rapidly through these almost as if they made a parenthesis:

> She walks,
> mumbling to herself
>    down this street,
> big-bellied, round-faced.
> She has found no one
>    other than herself
>    to talk to,
> and her discussions
>    are infinite.
> Beyond her
> the sea keeps its own music
>    obsessive, self-absorbed,
> omnivorous.[4]

Nevertheless, the images are now no less compressed. In the sixth section of the title poem, 'The Village',

> The fox sings
>   his song of slyness,
>   and lopes easily
>     by the hedge:
> and the spare hawk anchors
>     by a cloud.
>   By rabbit-watch
> I walk clothed among the naked.
>   Not by lamplight
> does the harsh buzzard read his book,
>   nor change from black
>   will the ragged crow
> whose language does not frame the No
>   of the soul's delicacy.

The hawk 'anchors' by hovering beside its cloud-island; and presumably it is 'spare' because idle, as well as unfleshy. But reading faster than ordinary sense requires may catch hints of fainter implicatures. Is the hawk also spare because it is additional to those hunting animal prey, and thus not occupied *yet* — so that the cloud becomes a shade ominous, although perhaps no bigger than a man's hand? And how about 'rabbit-watch'? With 'lamplight' and buzzard a few quick words away, are we to recall Dylan Thomas's 'owl-light'?

In *A Life* and *The Village*, Crichton Smith grasps the nature of his art more firmly than ever, drawing from Robert Lowell and D.H. Lawrence forms more appropriate for the notation of felt (as against cerebrated) life. Formally, both volumes, despite their loose semantic structures, are more careful than their predecessors. Douglas Dunn, reviewing the earlier *Selected Poems 1955–80*, regretted 'the absence of an audibly cultivated verse', 'a loss of music' and (increasingly) of memorable 'tune'. This has never been wholly true: in Dunn's own quotation, for example,

>         These defend
> the clattering tills, the taxis, thin pale girls
> who wear at evening their Woolworth pearls
> and from dewed railings gaze at the world's end.

The lingering, sustained stresses of 'from dewed railings gaze' offer not a bad resonance for the sense. No-one, I suppose, would claim that texture and phonic pattern are Crichton Smith's *forte*. Still, his textures and lexical choices have become more considered, perhaps because now more often revised. One example of many must serve:

> In summer
> the blur of warm mist
> over the water,
> and the tall girls in green
> riding horses
> along the level road,
> clip-clop by shop-front.
> Such mornings
> opening like books
> fresh and novel,
> such fresh black shadows
> humming among the leaves.[5]

Here, the riding on level road is well realised by the rhythms, the crisp sound of the hoofs by the junctures of the spondaic hyphenated words. But, even here, the main interest is in more fugitive effects, like 'green' as 'inexperienced', or the momentary collocation 'green . . . horses', which raises the association 'white horses', only to reject it as insufficiently calm, insufficiently compatible with the soft focus of 'warm mist'. And those 'black shadows': why are they 'humming'?

'Humming', a recurrent epithet in Crichton Smith's work, ultimately implies the humming of bees and belongs to his work's georgic programme, as he speaks in his own person and situates his discourse *vis à vis* an observed nature of wonderful details. The apian work is to extract honey from nature: from life and from death. Thus, in an early section of *A Life*:

> ceilidhs in the cities are the lens
> through which we see ourselves, unmade, remade,
> by music and by grief. The island sails
> within us and around us. Startled we
> see it in Glasgow, hulk of the humming dead . . .[6]

Here, the image can be naturalized as the physical humming of the ceilidhs, but elsewhere it may be the sound of the city, the sound of harmonious work, or the sound of life transformed by civilisation and art. Such interaction of distant contexts is more than a device from the Lowell of *Notebook*; it has to do with a visionary aspect of Crichton Smith's work.

The matter of the obvious influence on Crichton Smith of Robert Lowell and D.H. Lawrence, agreed on by his critics and indeed confessed by himself, is far from being so straightforward as it appears. For Crichton Smith is scarcely a confessional poet. In general terms, one may say that the confessional and autobiographical modes are not easily accessible to Scots. (Perhaps the Scots have too much to hide.) Hugh MacDiarmid and Norman MacCaig avoided these modes altogether; and, despite appearances, Edwin Muir virtually did so too, because of his generality. From this point of view, *A Life* represents an important threshold in Crichton Smith's work. Earlier weakness in transition can now be solved by narrative means, for example by memory's natural fragmentation. And vivid autobiographical material can thus be handled — indeed, is handled very effectively. One should notice, though, that it is often treated in a generalizing way, or *very* fragmentarily, or indirectly (though perhaps all the more eloquently for that). The poet's feelings about the memories are seldom confessed directly. In *The Village*, feelings are more immediately represented, so that one can almost speak of a confessional element there. But, if so, it is confessional only in certain limited areas of experience: fear of death, for example, and hatred of false religion ('Sundays, how awful they are'). Crichton Smith's aspires to be a classic art, and his use of D.H. Lawrence has almost to be likened to that of a *repoussoir* or enriching contrary.

Similarly deceptive are the insistently recurrent themes of Crichton Smith's work. These seem at first easily identifiable, and in fact have sometimes been listed in antithetic pairs: Presbyterian *synagoga* (law or false church) versus the grace of the classics; sensuous life and fear of death; simple natural island origins versus the excellence of high art (but also versus the invasive culture of affluence). And one might add others, like tradition and modernism, or young nymphs and dying women. Such themes may never have been more than scaffolding or provisional schemata, and they are certainly inadequate as a basis for interpreting Crichton Smith's later poetry. In the complexity of actual poems, the terms of the antitheses become blurred, and have a way of eluding complete identification. This is not to deny the existence of Caledonian antisyzygies, or of the contradictions that aspiring to high art comes up against, in an over-defined peripheral culture without material wealth. Far less is it to deny Crichton Smith's intelligible horror of bad religious instruction and his frequent impulse to dispel the orthodox bromides with darker truths. The latter struggle undoubtedly underlies the sense of doom in such a poem as 'Graves invent nothing . . . .'.[7] But even here there are discrepant suggestions in the lively description — 'the flicker of birds', the returning 'wheel of crocuses', the Easter hats — and in the unnecessarily introduced 'distant countries' of the clouds' destination. All these details have, of course, their negative function in the persuasion of nature's obliviousness to man's plight; but this hardly seems to exhaust their suggestive potential.

Later poems in the sequence explore and modify the same antithesis of life and death, and some even interchange its terms:

> The old lady is dying
> among the roses,
>   and at night
> she hears the hoot of the owl,
> the fluting of the blackbird,
> the excited cry of the thrush.
>   Doctor,
> she knows well what is wrong,
> she is adjusting her shoulders
> to the stone cloak.
>   She has put out the ashes
> for the last time.
>   And yet, who is dying
> in this summer of stunning splendour
> when the rhododendrons are ablaze
> by the hedge,
>   when the pansies
> are bowed in thought,
>   and the azaleas
> are a constant fire?[8]

Natural death cannot be a matter for sorrow, when nature as a whole is so splendidly alive. The euphemistic periphrasis 'stone cloak', which could easily have been used to grim effect, is gravely, gently employed, as is 'We are part of the earth,/ its blackness nestles about us'. All is natural: 'the rabbit/ runs easily towards its death'. And the old lady's death is part, too, of a summer endless in the 'freshness' of its plots. Her white curtain 'freshens the window', just as the red tractor renews the earth. Worked through like this, death becomes another form of life.

Such interweaving of life and death recurs throughout *The Village*. Section 28 of the title poem, for example, has another (or the same) 'aged lady', whose roots in earth are tenacious ('almost unpullable'),

> so that you have to be tugged
>   out of your chair
> which is burning there
>   in a priceless sunset.

And in the recurrent image of 'ashes', the thematic interchange is still more active, although hardly obvious. Indeed, in Section 14 it is easy to pass over what seems no more than a scrap of quotidian verisimilitude: 'She has put out the ashes/ for the last time'. But the imagery turns out to have many interactive resonances. Ashes or burning (and the same is true of several other images) could be seen as yet another 'obsession' of Crichton Smith's:

>                     Ash
>      badges the rowan tree . . .
>
>      I put out the ashes,
>          and stand amazed
>      beneath the blaze
>          of a million million stars.
>
>      . . . for he wakens early
>          with ash in his mouth . . .
>
>                . . . for the bad
>      an earth converted to ashes . . .
>
>      . . . burning there
>          in a priceless sunset.[9]

But it is a more helpful approach to see these instances as belonging to a deeply implicit half-argument or enthymeme, a tentative construct of implicatures. Is there not a suggestion that, if ashes are dead, the death of the flesh is itself like putting out the ashes — an occurrence as ordinary, that is to say, as a chore? It is a natural event. And not only is it one that freshens and renews the natural world, but it also has a surprising, positive accomplishment, offering a wonderful perspective on the stars.

Like other visionary poets, such as Blake, Crichton Smith sometimes writes with so much haste that he has no time for 'tune'. But, again like Blake, he achieves in compensation sequences of racing thought that carry his lyrics to greatness. There is nothing hurried about the profound meditation on natural death that issues in *The Village*. It is the number of ideas and feelings brought to bear in simultaneity that provokes the rapidity of review. For, besides the individual aspects of death that I have glanced at, death appears in the subtle sub-sequence 21–4 (Dark Ages — 'demented stories' — rational Renaissance) as a cultural process necessary until now, but now to be transcended: 'without me they would not exist', says Death:

>     And as for Greece or Rome,
>     beyond the Dark Ages
>     they shine like jewels of fire.'[10]

But how is the transcendence to be achieved? It seems, by art:

>     Art, how marvellous you are.
>     You bring us a birth,
>     a second birth in reflection,
>     and these reflections
>     seem more real than the real.[11]

To condemn this as aestheticism — to object that it loads on 'art' a weight it cannot bear — would be to take Crichton Smith for a quite different kind of poet from what I think he is. How much 'art' means for him, how much of all civilisation itself it has included and has still to include, can only be arrived at by following out the implications of its introductions throughout the sequence of *The Village*. Art means at least as much as the whole transformation of moving on to the next stage of anything: the next school, next age, next world. Crichton Smith is not, then, 'solid and meaty' in the same way as 'some of our poets', who regard art in a way that passes for more sensible. Nevertheless, like the dog that 'runs away/ with the hen in his mouth', he can feel in his teeth 'the theme of a new world', and 'he will snatch the cockerel from the dawn'.

In *A Life* and *The Village*, more clearly than in previous volumes, Crichton Smith shows himself to be a visionary poet. And this in turn pervasively affects his poetry's accessibility, although in itself it by no means always makes the meaning 'easier'. Indeed, it gives rise to features that increase the apparent difficulty. Yet this occasional difficulty is just what ensures the firmness of his meaning and resists misprision. It is not that words like 'humming' are to be decoded (as if they everywhere had the same meaning), but that their meanings are related, so that we can refer implications from one use to another. The allusiveness that I have traced — for example the internal references to other, perhaps remote aspects of his vision — has the effect of increasing the overall coherence and governing the poetry's openness to polysemic interplay.

NOTES

1. 'The White Air of March'.
2. 'Statement by a Responsible Spinster'.
3. *A Life* (Manchester and New York: Carcanet, 1986), p. 10.

4. *The Village* (Manchester: Caracenet, 1989), p. 10.
5. 'The Village', section 45.
6. *A Life*, 'Lewis 1928–45', section 3.
7. 'The Village', section 2.
8. Ibid., section 14.
9. Ibid., sections 3, 5, 18, 26, 28.
10. Ibid., section 21.
11. Ibid., section 48.

# Twelve

## Iain Crichton Smith: A Rare Intelligence

### Lorn Macintyre

I have to declare a personal interest in Iain Crichton Smith. I had the privilege of being taught by him at Oban High School, and, through regular visits to his Oban home from the late 1950s onwards, of watching his development as one of Scotland's most significant poets.

Crichton Smith's search for an individual poetic voice was complicated by his bilingualism. Gaelic was his first language; yet, by the time he began to express himself in it through his writing, it appeared to be dying. In English, his role as a Highland writer has been complicated by the fact that the literary tradition of that region was largely a nineteenth-century romantic creation of Sir Walter Scott.

Though Crichton Smith was born in Glasgow, he was taken at a very young age to Lewis and raised in a village in the strict Free Church tradition. Island life and the influence of the Church have been enduring themes in his poetry and prose. His reaction against the strictures of his Free Church upbringing has produced poems that have the elegance and lyricism of the metrical psalms. In an interview which I recorded with him in 1971, he revealed that his much-anthologised poem 'Old Woman' was based on an incident he witnessed while on holiday in Lewis, and that the two people in the poem were a sister and her brother, a Free Church elder.[1]

Crichton Smith establishes the old woman's helplessness from the first line, where he uses the image of the old horse, exhausted to the point where even food is losing its meaning. The brother is helping her, and the poet is there as an observer, recording the pathetic scene. The brother asks the 'all-forgiving' God for deliverance for his sister.

The poet is torn between 'pity and shame'. On the one hand, the sight of helpless senility distresses him. But his intellect contemplates a different type of death. In hard classical times, the Greeks and Romans

> pushed their bitter spears into a vein
> and would not spend an hour with such decay.

Douglas Dunn found this verse
> unnecessary or exaggerated, perhaps even banal in its over-explicit reminder of an alternative to charitable humanity.[2]

However, the stress on 'yes' in the line 'and wished to be away, yes, to be far away' does suggest that the poet is aware of his shortcoming through the discomfort of the scene.

But there are other old women in Crichton Smith's poetry who are not helpless and who do not get his pity. In another poem, also called 'Old Woman', he says critically of the stern figure with the creel of fuel on her back:

> Your set mouth
> forgives no-one, not even God's justice
> perpetually drowning law with grace.

Here he appears to be reacting against an inhumanity and a sense of self-righteousness bred out of religion. Though Crichton Smith has rejected the stern Free Church philosophy, clearly he has been attracted and influenced by its tenets of self-discipline and self-scrutiny. Its stoicism is related to the hard simplicity of island life. That is why he is able to assert in the first of his 'Eight Songs for a New Ceilidh' in his own translation from his Gaelic collection *Biobuill is Sanasan-Reice* (1965):

> as for me I grew up in bare Lewis without tree or branch and for that reason my mind is harder than the foolish babble of the heavens.

Again, he closes a poem addressed to his mother with the dogma:

> This only I admire
>
> to roll the seventieth sea
> as if her voyage were
> to truthful Lewis rising
> most loved though most bare
> at the end of a rich season.

As for his mother, so for Crichton Smith. The belief here is that however far he voyages imaginatively, he must inevitably return to Lewis for certain values. In the opening lines of 'The Island' in the 1965 Gaelic collection, he makes this explicit:

> There is an island in the spirit so that
> we can flee there when the way is hard.

Crichton Smith appears to have transmuted his Free Church upbringing into a worship of discipline. There is a connection between poems on old Highland women and historical figures like Lenin. Though the old Free Church woman with her creel may lack intellect, she has the same determination, the same self-discipline and the same self-righteousness that allowed Lenin to engineer a revolution. There are Calvinistic comparisons ('iron' against 'pleasure') in the opening lines of Crichton Smith's poem on the Bolshevik leader:

> In a chair of iron
> sits coldly my image of Lenin,
> that troubling man
> 'who never read a book for pleasure alone'.

The poet recognises that

> the true dialectic is to turn
> in the infinitely complex, like a chain
> we steadily burn through, steadily forge and burn
> not to be dismissed in any poem
>
> by admiration for the ruthless man
> nor for the saint but for the moving on
> into the endlessly various, real, human,
> world, which is no new era, shining dawn.

The truth is that the way is hard, and there are no miracles, whether it be the Lewis crofter hacking a living from the soil, or the intellectual man of action seeking to change the course of history. The struggle is all. The old woman might retain her Free Church faith and find there is nothing in the end; Lenin might make and melt down the 'chain' of his intellect many times, with relentless self-discipline and self-determination, but the end result might not be in accordance with his expectations or efforts.

However, Crichton Smith believes that intense intellectual self-scrutiny can be creative. In his poem on the Danish theologian Kierkegaard, he refers to

> that crucial
> omnivorous intelligence so cruel
> it mocked the pain that made the bare brain howl
>
> Till the new category, the individual,
> rose like a thorn from the one rose he knew.

In the 1971 interview, Crichton Smith told me:

> Another reason why there may be what we might call lack of warmth or humanity in my verse is that I tend to write verse which is perhaps rather intellectual. That is to say, I am concerned in my poetry with intelligence to a great extent.

He also said:

> I think myself that I would prefer to be an analytical poet, a questioning poet, rather than a poet of the heart considered simply.[3]

How many readers have detected that part of Kierkegaard's philosophy is set out in the poem 'Spring Wedding?' The first category in Kierkegaard is the aesthetic:

> Step out, my dear, down the aesthetic aisles
> The wind is pulling at your bridal veils.
> The black wears roses, and the shoes stream out
> dazzle of roses from their mirrors' light.

The second category is the ethical:

> Ethics of minister, and the standing choir
> fix you this moment in your own quiet shire.
> The cameras click for albums to be stored
> of billowing lady and her pin-striped lord.

The third category is what Crichton Smith calls 'the existence of existentialism':

> Existence threatens as in veils you go
> through gales or spring which tug your furbelow
> Neat black, proud white, the angel must be held
> by a black anchor on a shadowy field.

But poetry should not be confused with philosophy. In the same way as Yeats' poems do not depend for their appreciation on understanding the beliefs or 'system' behind them, a poem like 'Highland Wedding' can be enjoyed for its images and movement.

Crichton Smith's Highland background may explain the philosophical content and rigorous craftsmanship of some of his poems. In the 1971 interview, he revealed:

> In my poetry I want to struggle against the fact that the Highlander is naturally a nostalgic person, because he is living in a civilisation which sort of abnegates everything that he has ever stood for, and he thinks that he is finished as a being of the future, and that is tremendous, and Gaelic poetry is full of nostalgia.

Our history encourages this, with Gaelic song and story celebrating the failed Forty-Five rebellion, and the wandering prince never betrayed by those upon whom he had brought calumny. Highland writers have felt obliged to react to the Clearances in poetry and prose, and Crichton Smith is no exception. His novel *Consider the Lilies* (1968) is a distinguished one in which the old woman is allowed to speak of her woes without intellectual imposition. But in his poem 'The Clearances', Crichton Smith's harsh voice comes from his Free Church tradition as he addresses Patrick Sellar, Sutherland's notorious factor:

> Though hate is evil we cannot
> but hope your courtier's heels in hell
>
> are burning.

Such spontaneity of feeling is rare in Crichton Smith's poetry of the 1950s and 1960s. However, 'Deer on the High Hills' (1961) was a memorable exception in which he allowed his emotions to lead him in a new direction. Crichton Smith told me in 1971:

> It is one of the few poems, in fact it is probably the only poem, that I have ever written that I had no intellectual control over at all, and for this reason I am very suspicious of it . . . I wasn't actually sure what this poem was all about. And this may be why it is considered so strange, and perhaps even difficult to place in the rest of the things that I have done.

The poem opens with a description of the deer and their habitat, but Crichton Smith is not a nature poet like MacCaig. In Crichton Smith's poetic landscape, the deer are a shifting symbol. The imagery is of aloofness, the January deer being compared to 'debutantes on a smooth ballroom floor'. Having disdainfully regarded man, they go bounding up to the darkness of the heights. Crichton Smith points out how isolated they are on the hills, under the 'starry metaphysical sky'. Creatures of moods according to the seasons, they come down to accept bread from man, but they are proud and unpredictable. The reference here is both Highland and universal.

> A beggared noble can conceal a sword
> next to his skin for the aimless and abhorred
>
> tyrants who cannot dance but throw stones,
> tyrants who crack the finest bones:
> tyrants who do not wear but break most ancient crowns.

But the deer are symbolic of intellectual as well as social elevation. The poet, Crichton Smith urges, must forget 'practical things' and move into the peace and solitude of the heights, just like the deer, but only after learning

> a real contempt, a fine hard-won disdain
> for these possessions, marbles of unripe children.

Crichton Smith attacks modern materialism and its myths. The old heroes Hector and Ulysses have been supplanted, and Ulysses is now a 'business magnate' in a land that is barren from an imaginative point of view. Crichton Smith laments

> the metaphysics of an empty country,
>
> deranged, deranged, a land of rain and stones,
> of stones and rain, the huge barbarous bones.

What therefore is to be done? 'Seek the beginning', Edwin Muir advised in a poem, and Crichton Smith echoes him. The poet has to go back to first principles, to 'build from the rain and stones'. He has to go into solitude and isolation, imaginatively if not physically, and to use his intellect in creating. But he must not start with science or an 'inhuman music'. He must start with nature, 'in the hollow roar of the waterfall'.

There is a caution, however. Crichton Smith does not want romanticism or nostalgia. He warns against the powers of the emotions as evident in 'a taste of love', and he warns against religion, 'intuitions from the sky above'. And history in the form of myths about Prince Charles or Highland superstititons will not help. The intellect must be in control, but the end product must be imaginative, or, as the poet puts it:

> You must build from the rain and stones
> till you can make
> a stylish deer on the high hills
> and let its leaps be unpredictable!

Here, Yeats' stylish poems and his idea of an intellectual aristocracy come to mind. But Crichton Smith does not extend his argument at this point. Instead, he switches to a consideration of the Gaelic poet Duncan Bàn MacIntyre, who shot deer as well as writing poems about them, and so the stalker was like his quarry, since

> Brutality and beauty danced together
> in a silver air, incorruptible.

It is man who imposes mortality. As for the deer, they have neither knowledge nor philosophy, and are not disturbed by death. In their world of 'wild systems', they engage in combat, and draw blood, but not through will.

> Metaphoric sword
> is not their weapon, but an honest thrust.

Evil has to do with intelligence and the manipulation of language.

> Evil's more complex, is
> a languaged metaphor.

Then Crichton Smith introduces a striking image, the 'branched head' God, narcissist contemplating Himself in the pool He has created. This is the supreme example of the self-regarding intellectual cleverness that Crichton Smith appears to have become suspicious of, because heads can be turned by their own cleverness, and when they turn, they can attack. Addressing the deer, Crichton Smith sees the human comparison and tells them that there have been heads

> as proud as yours, destructive, ominous,
> of an impetuous language, measureless,

such as the head of Hitler with his impetuous language which stoked Belsen. Such heads, Crichton Smith warns us, develop in isolation until they are ready to come down among men to do their work:

> Electric instinct of the high hills
> till later, peasants in the valleys
> felt in their bones disquieting kingdoms break.

Whether they be liberators or oppressors, such 'fanatic heads' deceive and are deadly. It is not poetry through the intellect ripening in isolation that Crichton Smith wants; he wants poetry from the 'wandering senses' in the natural cycle of the seasons that man cannot break.

But nature has its own emotions, its own language hidden from man. Colours cannot 'cry'; black does not 'weep for the dead'. As he nears the end of his poem, Crichton Smith sees that it is all a matter of language.

> There is no metaphor. The stone is stony.

Whatever art creates cannot conceal reality. The poet has to stay down in this world and write about things as they really are, without letting language distort truth. Crichton Smith's philosophy is therefore akin to stoicism, the stoicism of the old Free Church woman who accepts her lot. The same stoicism is to be found in Wallace Stevens, who, after manipulating language brilliantly through a long life, closed his Collected Poems with a poem entitled 'Not Ideas about the Thing but the Thing Itself'. Not only are there thematic similarities between Stevens' poetry and Crichton Smith's poems: the similarity of linguistic movement and music is also striking, in particular the American poet's device of repeating a phrase.

Edwin Morgan was correct in calling 'Deer on the High Hills' 'confused'.[4] But, like MacDiarmid's 'A Drunk Man Looks at the Thistle', Crichton Smith's poem is more a meditation inspired by the imagination than a system of philosophy set out by the intellect. It showed his concern about the function of the poet and the direction and dimension of his own work. In the Gaelic tradition, the bard had high status in society, creating poems about life as it happened. Though the language was under threat, Sorley MacLean had made it a medium for poetry of European reference, and MacDiarmid had achieved national and international prominence, if not notoriety, through his poetry. Crichton Smith was physically, and to some extent intellectually isolated in Oban, which even in the 1960s was no longer a typical Highland community.

He recalled his position thus in our 1971 conversation:

> I had reached a certain stage, and I started analysing whether I could get big subjects in Scotland, and I found myself confronted with an enormous blankness. I think the reason why I found myself confronted with an enormous blankness is precisely because Scotland is bourgeois: that is to say, there are very few people in Scotland who feel intensely enough about anything to do anything about it.

Crichton Smith's attempt to give himself a national voice was heard in his 1969 volume *From Bourgeois Land* in which he scrutinised modern Scotland, with dislike showing through in every line. The land is locked in tradition:

> My Scottish towns with Town Halls and with courts,
> with tidy flowering squares and small squat towers,
> with steady traffic, the clock's cruising hours,
> the ruined castles and the empty forts,
>
> you are so still one could believe you dead.

But there is menace:

> Gauleiters pace by curtained windows, grass
> absorbs the blood of mild philosophers.
> Artists are killed for an inferior art.

Crichton Smith had followed R.H. Tawney in equating the rise of the bourgeois system with Calvinism.[5] Carol Gow quotes a statement by Crichton Smith that the Hamlet figure in *From Bourgeois Land* is

> the vulnerable intellectual and poet . . . fighting to be himself, but people are always trying to find his 'secret'.[6]

Though the poetic prince is overpowered by bourgeois forces in that volume, nevertheless the writing of the sequence allowed Crichton Smith to scrutinise Scottish and Highland society in an international context. In subsequent poems, his sorrow at what has been lost, and his anger at what has replaced it, came together memorably, as in the poem 'At the Highland Games':

> Finished. All of it's finished. The Gaelic
> boils in my mouth, the South Sea silver stick
>
> twirls, settles. The mannequins are here.
> Calum, how you'd talk of their glassy stare,
>
> their loud public voices. Stained pictures
> of what was raw, violent, alive and coarse.
>
> I watch their heirs, Caligulas with canes
> stalk in their rainbow kilts towards the dance.

In 'Dunoon and the Holy Loch',

> The huge sea widens from us, mile on mile.
> Kenneth MacKellar sings from the domed pier.
> A tinker piper plays a ragged tune
> on ragged pipes. He tramps under a moon
> which rises like the dollar. Think how here
> missiles like sugar rocks are all incised
> with Alabaman Homer. These defend
> the clattering tills, the taxis, thin pale girls
> who wear at evening their Woolworth pearls
> and from dewed railings gaze at the world's end.

The poetic form and the contemporary images echo Robert Lowell. But Crichton Smith did not want to become a chronicler of modern society and its decadence. Having worked the 'big poem' ambition out of his system, in the last decade or so he has returned to the theme of the small community. This is in accordance with his ambition, as expressed to me in 1971:

> I would like to deal less with the intellect. Yes, because I think it is only a very minor part of people, much more so than I used to

think. I used to think at one time that cleverness was very important. I don't believe that now.

In recent collections, he has kept the promise he made to himself in 'Deer on the High Hills' to deal more with nature and with life as it is lived at an ordinary level, not on the intellectual heights. *A Life* (1986) is a poetic autobiography from childhood in Lewis to settlement in Taynuilt outside Oban. It has been a long road:

> Such joy that I have come home to
> after all that measurement.

The rigorous verse form has gone; in lines of Pasternakian lightness, sights (the redbrest and the cherry tree) are set down as seen. In *A Life*, Crichton Smith appears to reject his early image of 'truthful Lewis' lying apart.

> There is no island
> The sea units us.

In the last poem, 'Listen', in *The Village and Other Poems* (1989), Crichton Smith assures the reader that he has emerged from the Calvinist thicket:

> Listen, I have flown through darkness towards joy,
> I have put the mossy stones away from me,
> and the thorns, the thistles, the brambles.

Though spontaneously attractive, Crichton Smith's later poems seem to me to be less satisfying than the earlier ones of rigorous form and intellectual questioning. The later poems, like some of his recent prose pieces, appear to have been set down hurriedly on paper, without destinations having been worked out. Some of them are jottings for poems, rather than poems in themselves, in the same way that he has made short stories out of Kafkaesque anecdotes.

Iain Crichton Smith is now in his early sixties, but is as creative as ever. Will he be content to reside mentally in the village, or will he move on, surprising and delighting his readers, as he has been doing for a quarter of a century as one of our most rewarding poets?

NOTES

1. Tape-recorded interview with Iain Crichton Smith for University of Stirling Project, August 1971. Part of interview published in 'Scottish International', September 1971, pp. 22–7.
2. Douglas Dunn, 'Iain Crichton Smith's "Old Woman"', in 'Criticism of Twenty Famous Twentieth-Century Scottish Poems by Twenty Critics', Akros, vol. 17, no. 51, October 1983, pp. 47–9.

3. 1971 interview.
4. Edwin Morgan, 'Poets of the Sixties' – 1: Iain Crichton Smith', *Lines Review* no. 21, Summer 1965.
5. R.H. Tawney, *Religion and the Rise of Capitalism: A Historical Survey*, London, 1929.
6. Carol Gow, 'Bourgeois Land: Another Country', *Cencrastus*, Winter 1989, pp. 3–5.

# Thirteen

## Leaving Oban High School: *Hamlet in Autumn* and *Mr Trill in Hades*

### Ann E. Boutelle

> You were a teacher also: what we've learned
> is also what we teach: and what we are
> cannot be hidden, though we walk black-gowned
> along the radiant corridors. . . .[1]

I have chosen to write about Crichton Smith's *Hamlet in Autumn* (1972) and *Mr Trill in Hades* (1984) for reasons that anyone may recognise as self-indulgent: both works urge me to return in memory to the late 1950s and early 1960s, to my years at Oban High School, where Crichton Smith was a teacher and I was a pupil.

*Hamlet in Autumn* was published in 1972 while Iain was still teaching. (The same year saw the publication of *Love Poems and Elegies*, which mourns the death of Crichton Smith's mother and celebrates a passionate and painful love.) As in *Love Poems*, the tone of *Hamlet in Autumn* is elegiac and death-haunted, the intellect caught helpless before the realities of time and death, turning within its narrow bound, circling, burning. But there is more anger than in *Love Poems*. As the third poem in the sequence which mourns John MacLean's death makes clear, there is as much anger here as there is grief:

> I know that it is waning, that clear light
> that shone on all our books and made them white
> with unanswerable grammar . . .
>
> . . . I know that Athene is wandering now,
> dishevelled in the shrubbery, and the nurse
> beckons at evening to her. Gods rehearse
> their ruined postures and the ruined brow
> reflects from mirrors not of fire but ice

> and that our brute Achilles drives his wheels
> across the gesturing shadows: and that kneels
> to cheering legions Aphrodite: packs
> are watching Ajax hacking with his axe
> inanely the pale sheep: and shady deals
> illuminate Odysseus's tracks.
>
> (p. 36)

The progression in this section is from a quiet accepting grief to a building anger. Each 'and that' shifts the poem to a higher emotional key, which climaxes in the wrenching of the sentence structure as Aphrodite kneels, and in the brutality of the internal rhymes as Ajax hacks away at the sheep ('packs', 'Ajax', 'hacking', 'axe'). A residue of this violent anger is to be found in the final lines, not only in the 'tracks' that connect with the Ajax lines, but also in the weary disgust emanating from the irony that 'shady deals/ illuminate Odysseus's tracks'.

Meanwhile, the formal tightness of the poem (three sestets in iambic pentameter) and the rhyme-scheme here and in the 'John MacLean' sequence as a whole provide a strong, classical housing for the surging feelings. Each sestet uses only two rhymes, in a pattern such as aabbab, or abaaba, or ababba. In each section of the sequence, stanzas one and three use an identical rhyme-scheme, while stanza two uses a different scheme. The overall effect is one of control and order, held in place and maintained with great effort and skill.

The volume as a whole duplicates this effect. Some of the poems are very formal (for example the 'Carol and Hamlet' sonnet sequence). Some use *vers libre*, for example, 'Dead for a Rat', which begins with

> What snarls
> in the corner?
> It wants to live
> It bares its teeth at you.
>
> (p. 12)

And yet this poem ends with a six-line unit which (thanks to the insistent rhyming) seems reined in and tight:

> Will you go Hamlet
> in your shuttling armour
> in your whirr
> of literature
> with your French rapier
> sparkling, veering?
>
> (p. 12)

Similarly, 'On a Summer's Day', the first poem in the book, presents itself as *vers libre*:

> Thus it is,
> There is much loneliness
> and the cigarette coupons will not save us.
>
> (p. 7)

The poem, however, quickly resolves itself into three-line stanzas, with internal rhymes, half-rhymes and alliteration holding it all tightly together.

I have been emphasizing the structure here for the reason that the structural shifts (suggesting degrees of order and disorder) seem crucial in the construction of this volume. The battle throughout (and it is an exhilarating battle) is one between order and disorder, which is presented as a chaotic, frightening and invigorating craziness much like Hamlet's manic thoughts and behaviour in the conversations with Rosenkrantz and Guildenstern, and very different from the restraint and control of *Love Poems*. There is much that is surrealistic about these poems: the wild mixture of references to *Hamlet* and to classical mythology, and the unexpected allusions to Russian literature, Ingmar Bergman movies, Charlie Chaplin, American westerns and Francis Bacon paintings, set against backgrounds which appear real and ordinary: a school, a seaside resort, a Chinese restaurant, a cemetery. 'On a Summer's Day', the introductory poem, catches this dizzying movement from the ordinary to the surrealistic, and uses it to set the tone for the volume as a whole. I quote the entire poem, so that the bizarre shifts of reference can be seen: for example, the way that a window becomes a movie screen or television screen, then flickers (as 'screen' flickers into 'scream') into the frame of a Francis Bacon painting:

> Thus it is.
> There is much loneliness
> and the cigarette coupons will not save us.
>
> I have studied your face across the draughtsboard.
> It is freckled and young.
> Death and summer have such fine breasts.
>
> Tanned, they return from the sea.
> The colour of sand, their blouses the colour of waves,
> they walk in the large screen of my window.
>
> Bacon, whose Pope screams in the regalia
> of chairs and glass, dwarf of all the ages,
> an hour-glass of ancient Latin,

> you have fixed us where we are, cacti able to talk,
> twitched by unintelligible tornadoes,
> snakes of collapsing sand.
>
> They trail home from the seaside in their loose blouses.
> The idiot bounces his ball as they pass.
> He tests his senile smile.
>
> (p. 7)

The poem benefits enormously from being read aloud to hear the sibilants twisting their way through the stanzas: the sound of the ocean, the sound of the 'snakes of collapsing sand' — ominous and insistent. As the reader hastens to follow the speaker through the wild jumps and bounces of his thought, the three-line structure and the tight and ecstatic sound-patterns provide clear and marked paths.

In a similar way, the punning wordplay throughout the volume preserves the manic, surrealistic atmosphere and at the same time suggests a rigour and an artistry that allow the mania to exist. Odysseus' 'shady deals' are a quiet example of this, with 'shady' operating in its contemporary colloquial meaning while at the same time suggesting 'shades' or ghosts, and also playing ironically off 'illuminate'. A more dramatic example is to be found in the final section of the 'John MacLean' sequence:

> If there were pyres
>
> then a pyre you should have had, and lictors too.
> And phantom legions. In this perfect blue
> imagine therefore flame that's amber, yellow,
> leaves of good flame, volumes that burn and glow,
> the foliage of your autumn . . .
>
> (p. 38)

Autumn leaves whirl through many of these poems. In the lines quoted above, the reader is forced into a backward-spiralling reassessment of 'leaves of good flame'. The phrase initially reads as a translation of the flames of the funeral pyre into autumn leaves: the 'October leaves in yellow' were established early on in the sequence, and they fall persistently throughout. But the 'volumes that burn and glow' give a secondary meaning to those leaves, and a second translation from 'leaves of a tree' to 'leaves in a book'.

This swirling of word-place and meaning is a device favoured throughout the volume (and it *is* a volume that burns and glows), with more examples than can be cited here. Perhaps one of the most stunning is the play on 'theatre' in 'The Moon' and 'Oedipus and Others' (the second and third poems in the collection) as Apollo turns surgeon, 'scooping out the eyes' (p. 8) in a theatre which is, at one and the same time, a theatre for Greek tragedy and a brightly-lit operating theatre: 'They're all proud germs the theatre must kill' (p. 9). Another prominently-featured example involves 'crystal' with its multiple meanings involving frost crystals, crystal radios and crystals in watches.

This circling of word and meaning is paralleled by the overarching cycle of the seasons. We progress, in the collection, from the summer world of the first poem, through autumn, to the winter of 'Fairy Story' and 'Christmas, 1971'. This seasonal cycle is repeated in the imagery: the many references to wheels, clocks, circles and repetitions. 'Over and Over' (which I quote in its entirety) is a fine example:

> They came for him at night in the light of Homer.
> Their pistols glittered on the hexameters.
>
> They shot him when the verse was in his mind
> of Hector dying, and the chariot wheels
>
> went click click click. In the black leather
> he saw Troy burning, and a clear small face
>
> with large round spectacles, barrelled in the light
> of the study's genial fireplace. He got up
>
> to pick the book, leathered in black, and then
> there was the knock and they came in again.
>                                                (p. 11)

The clicking of the chariot wheels becomes the ticking of a clock, which in turn becomes the face of a clock, then the face of a person, then spectacles, and finally the barrel of a gun. The nightmarish cycle (held tightly in place by the two-line stanzas and by the echoing sounds and rhymes) ends only to start up, relentlessly, again and again, as the title of the poem instructs us. There is no waking from these dreams.

The psychological risks, meanwhile, which the poet takes in this volume are great. It is as if the strictly formal aspects go hand in hand with the increasingly confessional aspect of the book. In 'Carol and Hamlet: Excerpts from a Sonnet Sequence', the sonnet form holds or contains – or (I would suggest) gives the illusion of control and therefore makes possible – the suggestion of a teacher/student relationship that borders on forbidden territory: the first sonnet begins with 'Small and small-breasted you scribble in your jotter', and ends with 'and I on this unsteady hovering chair' (p. 13). Many of the poems present a speaker who is identifiably close to Crichton Smith himself, middle-aged (he was forty-four when the volume was published), alone, trapped both in time and in his role of teacher, hastening toward death, living and questioning the life of the mind in a century filled with barbarism and violence. Confessional material breaks through to the surface more and more clearly as the volume hurries towards its close and as loss and grief predominate – in the 'oh love, how long ago it all was' (p. 55) of 'Fairy Story', in the lost brother of 'Christmas, 1971' ('We diverge at the road-end in the whirling snow/ never to meet but singing, pulling gloves/ over and over our disappearing hands' p. 56) and in the suggestions of a love affair gone awry, faltering and ending finally in 'In the Time of the Useless Pity' ('Nothing I could do, I had tried everything,/ lain flat on the rug, fluttered my spaniel paws,/ offered you my house like an unlocked crystal' p. 58).

The poet who gave Crichton Smith a model for this combination of form coupled with psychological risk-taking was Robert Lowell, and *Hamlet in Autumn* owes much to a work such as Lowell's *Life Studies* (1960). As M.L. Rosenthal has pointed out, '*Life Studies* gives us the naked psyche of a suffering man in a hostile world, and Lowell's way to manage this material, to *keep it*, is by his insistent emphasis on form'.[2] Just such a statement could be made about material and form in *Hamlet in Autumn*. As Crichton Smith recognises in reference to his work as a whole, 'No particular sources, except that I admire Lowell's work'.[3]

In *Hamlet in Autumn*, the debt to Lowell is acknowledged in a slantingly explicit way: the poem 'For Ann in America in the Autumn' includes the lines 'remember how it is here in this small/ place without air far from New England's Lowell' (p. 45). The poem was written, I would suppose, while I was teaching in a school in New Jersey in 1965–7. I did not read the poem until the *Hamlet* volume arrived with a letter that disclaimed any personal significance: 'The poem re yourself was an attempt to bring Robert Lowell into my poetry and as I knew no-one else in America at the time . . .'. (I am glad that I gave Crichton Smith that opportunity, and I am also glad that now I have the chance to emphasise just how important that debt to Lowell is.) The line reads in a rather mysterious way, as the 'Ann' of the poem is in New Jersey, not New England: 'When the wind dies in New Jersey/ and it is the Fall' (p. 45). (Perhaps Crichton Smith thought that New Jersey was part of New England?) Also, 'Lowell' might well be understood as the town in Massachusetts – or perhaps as other members of the distinguished Lowell family, not necessarily Robert Lowell. Nevertheless, whether or not the reference is clear, it is important, as its emphatic position at the end of the first stanza indicates, and as the echoing half-rhymes throughout stanzas two and three insist: 'fall', 'apple', 'prevails', 'heels', 'Fall', 'wheel'. The final stanza is particularly lovely, with its surge of a feeling which does indeed seem personal (despite the plural 'we' and 'girls'), and with its serious playing on 'leaves' and on the image of the wheel:

> Something regrets us. Something we regret.
> I smell your woodsmoke, it is pure and tart.
> Here by this shore the sea turns round again.
> My head swings dully in its leaves of pain.
> What horses leave me in this frosty Fall –
> the girls ride westward on their rising wheel.
>
> (p. 45)

In 1977, five years after the publication of *Hamlet in Autumn*, Crichton Smith's life was to change dramatically. He married, retired (early, at the age of forty-nine) from teaching, and embarked on a career of full-time writing. (The restless, agonised circlings of *Hamlet in Autumn* are quite possibly a foreshadowing of this change.) His new circumstances could not have been exactly easy: Donalda's two sons by a previous marriage moved in, along with her, into Crichton Smith's small flat in Combie Street. There was not much space or quiet for writing. His life, outside the school, now moved to the rhythms of others. Granted that the circumstances of his life had changed, how did he adapt to this entirely new way of defining himself, as husband, stepfather, full-time writer, retired teacher?

The 1984 *Mr Trill in Hades* answers some of these questions. In it, Crichton Smith looks back on his time at Oban High School and considers the meaning of the twenty-two years of his life which he had spent there. Many of the characters in these stories and some of the incidents are easily recognisable to anyone who knew the school; and there is a particularly savage and exact portrait of the new rector (known in the story as the 'Bingo Caesar') who replaced John MacLean. (The name of Mr Trill himself comes not from Oban, but from a master at the Nicholson Institute, Stornoway, where Crichton Smith had been a pupil; the name offers him wonderful punning opportunities.) While *Hamlet in Autumn* had made use of Oban High School as one of many points of reference, *Mr Trill* never moves far from the world of the school.

The first story provides an obvious link to *Hamlet in Autumn* and establishes Crichton Smith's readiness to provide a close fictional translation of his own experience. (It is a method which he was to pursue ever more closely: the 1987 novel *In the Middle of the Wood* is a compellingly accurate rendering of his breakdown and hospitalisation. The risk-taking which he establishes in *Hamlet in Autumn*, the facing of the psyche's own horrors and terrors, is to continue as an important thread in the works of the late 1970s and the 1980s.) 'What to Do about Ralph?' presents a variant of Crichton Smith's situation after his marriage. This English teacher, Jim (nicknamed 'Sniffy'), finds himself with a stepson who is resentful and angry ('he is not my father'[4]) and who begins to suspect (here the fusing with *Hamlet in Autumn* and a clear departure from Crichton Smith's own situation) that he is in a Hamlet-like situation: perhaps his mother had had an affair with his stepfather (brother to his biological father) before her first husband died. Ironically (and to spell out the literary parallel), the suspicion is planted in the son's mind by Jim's lecture on *Hamlet* and his questions to the class regarding Gertrude and Claudius. Much of the imagery evokes *Hamlet*: Ralph's mother, lying drunk on the bed, resembles Ophelia ('her hair floating down her face, stirring in the weak movement of her breath' p. 20); Jim himself, wearing his academic gown, looks 'like a ghost inside its holed chalky armour' p. 19). The resolution hinges on Ralph's recognition, when he goes to fetch his stepfather from school, that 'tragedy was the thing you couldn't do anything about' (p. 21). Somewhat melodramatically, Ralph calls Jim home, and Jim's ghost face cracks 'as if chalk were a cracking and a human face were showing through' (p. 21). The two leave together, 'almost but not quite side by side' (p. 21).

The handling of point of view in this story adds some realism to a plot which would otherwise strain belief: the point of view flickers from Ralph, to his mother, to Jim, never resting long on any particular character, establishing the full complexity of the situation, and setting each of the characters' intricate worlds side by side with the others. The teenage world of Ralph's crude pals (young thugs in the making) is presented with particularly painful accuracy: 'Old Sniffy's a poof. I always thought he was a poof. What age was the bugger when he got married? Where was he getting it before that?' (p. 16).

Throughout the rest of the collection, point of view is controlled in a deliberate and alternative manner: in one story the point of view will be that of a teacher; in the next, that of a pupil. 'The Ring', the second story in the collection, provides a transition into this pattern, and gives an unusual twist: the point of view is that of the pupil, but told by the adult, with the concluding revelation that the pupil has grown up to be a teacher. From this story on, the point of view settles: 'Greater Love'

*Leaving Oban High School* 173

(teacher); 'The Snowballs' (pupil); 'The Play' (teacher); 'In the School' (pupil); and 'Mr Trill in Hades' (teacher). The overall effect is to provide a wide, multi-dimensional, complex picture of life in a school. We are on the pupil-edge of a teacher's love affair in 'The Ring'. We view a teacher's obsession with the First World war through the sympathetic eyes of a colleague in 'Greater Love'. We witness an angry indictment of corporal punishment through the pupil's eyes in 'The Snowballs'. (This story is set in a small country school, apparently earlier in the century than the other stories. It seems to hark back to Lewis rather than to Oban.) 'The Play' lets us see a teacher puzzling over how to reach a class of fourteen-year-old girls who dream only of becoming hairdressers. 'In the School' takes us on a rampage with teenage vandals. And 'Mr Trill' moves us, in the company of a Classics teacher, to Hades and back.

The collection crests with 'In the School' and 'Mr Trill', which both share the surrealistic atmosphere of *Hamlet in Autumn*. 'In the School' begins in a sinister but realistic mode: three teenage vandals break into the school, carrying a can of petrol. Terry, the ringleader, the 'mad one' (p. 71), may be the same crude and violent Terry who was an acquaintance of Ralph in the opening story. Terry urinates in the maths room, draws obscene pictures on the blackboard, sends Frankie off to get paper from the art room, plays a wild game of football in the empty gym with Roddy, sends Roddy off to find Frankie, and in the Latin room spits on the word 'insula', minces in the teacher's gown, then rips the gown to shreds. The building violence is accompanied by strange hints that something else, unexplained and almost supernatural, is going on: 'a flash of black like a bird's wing passing, but that was impossible' (p. 76). These flashes (which may be hallucinations on Terry's part, or the police closing in, or the ghosts of teachers in their black gowns) culminate in a nightmarish circle of faceless men in black who surround Terry: 'He looked up and he screamed and he screamed and he screamed' (p. 81). We have moved from school to madhouse: nothing is as it seems. 'His hands beat on the floor in the silence' (p. 81).

'Mr Trill in Hades', the novella which takes up about half the book, continues the surrealistic atmosphere. Its opening is deadpan: 'One afternoon Mr Trill, dead classics master of Eastborough Grammar School, found himself in Hades' (p. 85). Crichton Smith has clearly enjoyed following Mr Trill around Hades and watching him as, time after time, Mr Trill's illusions shatter. Myth after myth is debunked: Orpheus is a petulant homosexual who doesn't want Eurydice back;

Agamemnon doesn't 'know his arse from his elbow' (p. 88); Ulysses is 'a thin whip of survival . . . an infection returning home' (p. 149); and so on.

The structure, meanwhile, is tight: an interweaving of memories from Mr Trill's life, memories evoked by the figures he meets. Chief among these are his failures: his failure to engage in battle with the 'Bingo Caesar' headmaster, and his failures in love: the first girl he had ever taken out, whom he did not kiss; Grace, who expects him to marry her after a ten-year courtship, when her mother finally dies; Thelma, the student with whom he becomes infatuated and who mocks him.

What has it all meant? The question applies to the entire volume, as well as to Mr Trill's life, and the answer is clear and triumphant. It means the courage to see and acknowledge disengagement from life, and, given a second chance, to choose differently: to choose ordinary, temporary life, in all its ugliness and loveliness, and to choose to be fully a part of it. The novella and the volume end with Mr Trill's triumphant crowing, as – given the chance to return to life, not as a schoolmaster and 'without shield' (p. 168) – he sells newspapers on the street: 'His boots were yellow in the light, he crowed like a cock, his bronze claws sunk in the pavement' (p. 168).

The trilling bird has been transformed into crowing cock. Hamlet has broken free from his manic frenzy and has chosen life, not death; action, not thought; marriage, not school. And while I have oversimplified the issues here (because it is, after all, life *and* death, action *and* thought, marriage *and* school, that must be chosen), it would seem that in the process of following Hamlet and Mr Trill, Crichton Smith has fought his way towards a more engaged art – a more courageous and committed and dangerous art; a less elegant art, a less schoolteacherly art; an art that has its 'bronze claws sunk in the pavement'.

Courage to move away from the familiar, to choose differently, came, I suspect, from several sources: from the act of leaving Oban High School; from the poetry of Robert Lowell; and from Donalda.

These two volumes are transitional. The consequences of the choices made here are to be found in the works that follow. Read them.

Be like King Duncan. Hang around, and find out what happens in the kingdom.

NOTES

1. 'For John MacLean, Headmaster, and Classical and Gaelic Scholar', *Hamlet in Autumn* (Loanhead, Midlothian: M. Macdonald, 1972), p. 35. Page numbers for the poems refer to this edition.

2. M.L. Rosenthal, 'Poetic Theory of Some Contemporary Poets or Notes from the Front', *Salmagundi*, vol. 1, no. 4 (1966–7), p. 71.
3. *Contemporary Poets*, eds James Vinson and D.L. Kirkpatrick, 4th ed. (New York: St Martin's, 1985), p. 798.
4. *Mr Trill in Hades and Other Stories* (London: Victor Gollancz, 1984), p. 9. Page numbers for the stories refer to this edition.

# Fourteen

## The White Horse: Design and Grace

### Christopher Small

> We are in need of something to take the place of the old order. Not in need of a balance of power, a new arrangement of conquests, but of a League of Nations for the moral ordering of the impulses; a new order based on conciliation, not in attempted suppression.
>
> Only the rarest individuals hitherto have achieved such an order, and never without disorganisation of the ordinary social life . . . But many have achieved it for a brief while, for particular phases of experience, and many have recorded it for these phases.
>
> Of these records poetry consists . . .
>
> The motives which shape a poem spring from the root of the mind. The poet's style is the direct outcome of the way in which his interests are organised. That amazing capacity of his for ordering speech is only a part of a more amazing capacity for ordering his experience.
>
> (I.A. Richards, *Poetries and Sciences*, 1970, pp. 40, 44)

In the first paragraph of Iain Crichton Smith's first novel, *Consider the Lilies*,[1] the reader is offered a striking image. The antagonists in the drama – Mrs Scott and Patrick Sellar, respectively exemplary victim and agent of the Clearances – are tersely introduced, with the mocking detail that Sellar is mounted and that 'he wasn't riding his horse very well, though he felt in his position he ought to have a horse'. We have an immediate preliminary glimpse into the nature of Sellar, the comic-contemptible villain of the piece. The next two sentences, though still speaking about the human characters, perform something a little surprising, turning from Sellar to the nature of the horse: 'He [Sellar] was an ex-lawyer, and horses aren't used to that kind of law. Also it was a white horse which was one of the reasons why the old woman paid such particular attention to it.'

## Design and Grace

I would like to suggest that we too should pay attention to this white horse, not merely as an actor in this particular drama, but as a creature of strong significance for the whole of Crichton Smith's work. That such a steed, not unrelated to Pegasus, should move through the imagination of the writer as a poet may be obvious, even though its actual appearances in his verse are few. But to select it as a key image for his prose fiction as well perhaps needs some justification. It may seem obvious again that a highly 'poetic' prose should be closely linked, for the properly appreciative reader, with the poetry. But though such blending is natural, there are distinctions which should not be blurred, because they have a function in the writer's very method. Not simply the similarity of Crichton Smith's prose to his poetry – in subject-matter, in feeling, in imagery – but their complementary differences are of importance for an understanding of both.

Their relationship may moreover have something more general to say about the nature of poetry, if poetry is the 'record', as I.A. Richards claims, of a particular response, a 'moral ordering' of experience. Such a formula seems to reinforce one traditional view of poetry, still commonly held, and especially among poets, that it is the final product, the essence of expression, and therefore the 'highest form' of all the arts of language; and there is something in everyone who tries to write or simply to enjoy poetry which assents to this opinion. But it is a risky opinion, with traps of blindness and constriction or, to put it bluntly, of artistic paranoia concealed within it; and these dangers – dangers for the artist in any medium – are part of the experience with which the art has to deal, and which, in work such as this, is brought to order. The process can be seen in a writer like Crichton Smith in the relation between his poetry and his prose: the poetry 'grows out of' and comments upon the prose, but the prose also judges the poetry. Out of this intimate, complex, delicate complementarity, the writer's whole view takes shape. You may call it his style if you wish, but the word has become so debased as to be, although not devoid of meaning, unavoidably likely to make wrong suggestions. It is easy to call this writing stylish; so, if a world-view, an 'ordering of experience' of unusual clarity, sensibility and consistency are style, it is. But description in such terms degrades the property it describes to a species of literary real estate. Style is not something which Crichton Smith 'has', or aspires to.

Patrick Sellar, in *Consider the Lilies*, is in poor control of his horse, though otherwise in excellent control of the situation. Frith, the elderly, successful author briefly introduced at the beginning of *My Last*

*Duchess*[1], is admired by the central character, Mark Simmons — who has called on the older man in hope of help — for his early work, 'indisputably great' and full of feeling, which Frith himself disparages. He says, 'My later work *is* better, and shall I tell you why? Because I am in control of it . . . Not to be in control is bad.' Just how bad, the rest of the story, plotting the disintegration of the main character, powerfully demonstrates. Simmons progressively loses control of his life, and, as he recalls the stages of his personal disaster course and enters at last the very antechamber of madness ('Everything could enter him. He was a mirror open to the doings of the universe') (*MLD*, p. 158), the perjink, well-preserved figures of the literary eminence, once capable of feeling, who was fleetingly glimpsed at the beginning, seems to make a comment on the whole proceeding. It delivers a dreadful, double warning. Not to be in control is bad; to be in control, and to make that a principle of conduct or of writing, is possibly worse.

This evidently insoluble problem is thus set down as one of art and of life, without separating the two categories. Especially in this novel, concerned with writers and painters, the dialogue of both — so wonderfully dramatised in Browning's poem of title and epigraph, the warm, live portrait of the dead Duchess and the deadly coldness of the living Duke — runs throughout the story. It is present in many other places in Crichton Smith's work, and is formulated by him specifically in an essay on MacDiarmid ('Hugh MacDiarmid's *A Drunk Man Looks at the Thistle*') in *Towards the Human*[3]: 'Art demands form, but life is formless. To reconcile the two on the highest level is impossible.' The problem, with the powerfully suggestive but unelaborated rider, that 'Life is continually making art appear minor', is not taken much further in this chapter, nor elsewhere in Crichton Smith's published criticism. But it is present, variously but identifiably, throughout all the imaginative making, prose and poetry, which is the substance in his work.

'Life isn't rational', says the adolescent Malcolm in *The Last Summer*[4], making this apparently banal discovery for himself and out of experience. In the early short story *The Black and the Red*[5] — symbolic colours which represent a whole cluster of opposites, English/Gaelic, death-life, chaos/order — the youth is now away from his island home and in the expanding world of the university. New and liberating experience is also perceived as order; even on the train to Aberdeen (the first such rail-predestinate journey of his life), he notices the unfamiliar landscape of the farms, 'geometrical sections . . . very orderly and beautiful, comparing very favourably with the untidy patches at home'.

*Design and Grace* 179

On a subsequent urban walk, he explores a park with 'great wrought iron gates and flowers of many colours arranged very cleverly to read WELCOME'. Nearby is 'a cemetery which is orderly and has some green glass urns containing paper flowers. It is almost too orderly, like streets.' The youth's progress, recounted in confessional letters home, ends in an act of what is known to law as public disorder and a vision in court ('which was like a church') of actual cosmic chaos: 'The sun exploded through the window, drunkenly . . . It swayed the wall diagonally towards the policeman, scything him in two, it made the varnish into a stifling musk, and punched me between the eyes exploding light in my head. The prison fell in like a pack of cards.'

We shall encounter this explosive conjunction of order/disorder again. The point to notice is the violent effect. It is not anything to be taken lightly. The narrator of another short story ('The Prophecy', in *The Village*[6]) finds that 'there is an enmity between consistency and life', a revelation so 'shattering that for a long time I was incapable of working at all'. The apparently elementary discovery, which many take unexamined and in their stride, is truly terrible, and a considerable part of the moral effort in the poems and stories goes towards showing how terrible it is. *My Last Duchess* ends in disorder which is to be understood in the full sense of the word, including the clinical; and over and over again, abandonment of order, with its deathliness, invites the most terrifying disarray. Of this there are many images, which may be culled almost at random: the 'manic pattern' of the falling snow, which is no pattern at all; the drunk 'making his staggering way among the rain and the fog and the neon lights'; the miscellaneous jetsam of the shore which engenders a nightmare reversal of time, backwards to primal chaos.[7] The sea itself, eternal and ambiguous, may be soothing and healing in its monotony and also its 'untidyness', calming a schoolboy ('After the Film', *The Village*, p. 100) out of his fierce, isolated fantasies. But more often, it is not simply dangerous and devouring but beyond thought itself; even when personified, as in the sea-poem for children in *River, river*[8], it is so entirely different that it is 'going mad with loneliness'. It infects all perception with profound disorganisation so that, for the bright young men who have landed 'On the Island' in *Survival Without Error*[9], the whole sea-and-landscape, everything in sight, is snatched out of rational reach: 'The town with its spires, halls, houses, pubs, rose from the sea, holding out against the wind. It was what there was of it. Nothing that was not unintelligible could be said about it.'

The triple negative in which this last thought is expressed, reinforcing its utter bleakness and bafflement, could be described as clumsy. At the risk of pettifogging, it may be worth looking at this apparent clumsiness or infelicity. It would be wrong, I think, to suppose that these 'flaws' – together with many 'factual inaccuracies' of detail – which are to be detected by the carping eye in many of the stories are the result of simple carelessness. Nor, though it is usually effective, as in the instance given, should it be thought deliberate. It is rather that Crichton Smith *allows* his prose a certain laxness, even carelessness, as the price of escaping from tight control. It should be understood at once that saying this is not at all to say that the prose is crude or inadequate to its purpose: the fine sensibility to verbal associations and rhythms and, more importantly, to the feeling and moral discrimination which these endeavour to encompass, is always at work. Indeed, it is because these sensibilities – and, one may guess, the peculiar tensions set up within them by thinking in two languages – are the writer's constant guide, that relaxation is necessary. Carelessness is a word with two different meanings. In a certain context, it is a moral imperative. The reins *must* be dropped on the horse's neck.

Such submission and relinquishing of control is never total, of course; the rider must remain in the saddle, trusting his mount not to lose the way for both. It is easier in prose than in poetry; for though the two modes are, as has been said, very closely related for Crichton Smith, the tasks of marrying form and content and the special problems of order and freedom are different for each. Perhaps it might be said, modifying the equestrian metaphor, that in prose writing, horse and rider are still separate beings: for poetry, the rider must join his being to his mount and become a centaur.

Poetry, the most strict and exigent art, requires precision, clarity and truth. Bad poetry for Crichton Smith arises out of 'bad faith', that is the chronic concealment from consciousness of 'the facts of the case' – the condition, among other misfortunes, to which exiles are prone (*Towards the Human*, p. 17). Poetry that deserves the name is the place 'where truth is imperative' (ibid., p. 35). The enemies of poetry, from Plato to Thomas Love Peacock, and plenty of other later champions of 'hard fact', have claimed that poets are inherently incapable of dealing with it. And poets, in their loyalty to truth, may be inclined to agree: poetry cannot help being untruthful, as it deals in metaphors, not facts, and never speaks of 'things as they are'. Out of this very self-doubt they may make poetry.

So Crichton Smith contemplates the fact of mortality ('On Looking at the Dead', in *Love Poems and Elegies*[10]) and attempts to grasp it, 'the stubborn thing', 'the stubborn place' where 'no metaphors swarm'. It beats the beholder down, it is what it is without 'compromise'; so the poet, loving truth, finds in it the fixed point of 'a real thing', 'therefore central and of major price'.

The long 'meditation' *Deer on the High Hills*[11], though it appears to offer a symbolic account of poetic activity, strives to escape from symbols altogether. The deer with their grace, their 'inhuman pride', their otherness, are seen finally as utterly inexplicable, unpredictable, symbolic of nothing – and what they are, everything else is, each separate thing in its inexplicable kind. The hills and the heavens are nothing but themselves,

> for stars are starry and the rain is rainy,
> the stone is stony, and the sun is sunny,
> the deer step out in isolated air.

Truthfully, the poem recording these 'brute facts' also records the frightful isolation that results from their perception as such, and the poet's longing to 'speak with any/ stone or tree or river', to make some connection across 'this distance deadly'. It is impossible, in practice, for a poet to refrain from connecting (Plato and Peacock were also poets, of course), and if communication with hard facts is impossible, these can be arranged in an imposed order, rather as the constellations are given shape and names. Truth is sought in the connections themselves, in their purity and precision, the shortest lines between isolated points. For Crichton Smith, images of such connection abound, in geometry and physics, in the precise measurement of time (i.e. clockwork, distinguished from the immeasurable way of time flowing like a river). These images, and especially that of time ticked off on a clock, carry at the same time the message that truth conceived in this way, and the strict form which embodies it, the desired perfection of design for purpose, is not only effectual but also restricting; even deathly. Truth-telling, the supreme puritan virtue and the claim with which poetry aspires to disarm puritan hostility, flips over and becomes destructive.

The contradictions engaged with here may be seen in Crichton Smith's repeated and appropriate homage to Dante, in whose 'three-line bars of flame' judgment is exactly and 'thriftily' executed ('In this Pitiless Age', in *The Village and Other Poems*[12]), and whose mathematically and astronomically ordered scheme does indeed go like clockwork. The sense for Crichton Smith as for others of Dante as the supreme standard for and judgment upon their own work finds ominous utterance elsewhere, in one of the pieces of *From Bourgeois Land*.[13] 'What's your Success to me who read the great dead,' he asks, claiming direct kinship with those 'whose marble faces, consistent overhead,/

outstare my verse?' Transitory rewards are nothing under the perfected firmament where

> the hammered poetry of Dante turns
> light as a wristwatch, bright as a thousand suns.

Mathematical precision, chronometric and predestinate punctuality, and light which allows no sheltering shadow meet in the flawless sky described in another poem, 'At the Stones of Callanish'[14] – the 'beautiful blue ball like heaven cracking' over Hiroshima and Nagasaki. The most perfect design, the subjugation of brute fact to order, the sure defence against surrounding disorder, produce the most entire disintegration.

How does art deal with this? That it does deal with it in some way is a fact, for it is evident that works of art, all of which must in some degree accommodate themselves to order/disorder, actually exist; and it belongs to the profound realism of Crichton Smith's work that he is ready to confront the implications and try to elucidate them. The conflict is brought to light in many places, and again examples may be taken almost at random, and appropriately so: randomness, or unexpectedness, is perhaps the key quality of the art which saves. One must stand for many, in the reflections upon order in the explicitly autobiographical sequence *A Life*.[15] These poems dwell especially on the supposedly orderly life of teaching and being taught, and maintains a steady to-and-fro between rule and what escapes from rule and prescription. Nothing valuable, not even the seasons, can be subdued to certainty and prediction: 'The unpredicted that I prize/ blossoms in a furious/ dishevelled spring'. (p. 44). Browning's Grammarian can perhaps be detected in the background, or it may simply be that poets wrestling with similar contradictions between life and learning produce similar exclamations:

> This man decided not to Live but to Know . . .
>
> Here – here's his place, where meteors shoot, clouds form,
> Lightnings are loosened,
> Stars come and go! let joy break with the storm –
> Peace let the dew send!
> (A Grammarian's Funeral)

and:

> To find the way!
> The raindrops glitter,
> Lucretius's idea.

> To let the light
> sway through the marble —
> temporal appetite.
>
> To keep the mist
> about the grammar
> in the amethyst
>
> bloom of violet.
> Sheep's eyes
> cast greeny jets
>
> and grass waves —
> itself how lightly
> over graves.
> (*A Life*, pp. 40–1)

To make so marvellous a conjunction as *mist/amethyst* is poetry's prerogative.

Exercise of this prerogative is an operation of grace, a term so important, for Crichton Smith and at the same time capable of such delicately modulated use that, though one may point to it, pinpointing is perilous. (The mocking warning concerning the precise critic who 'goes looking for a carcass/ that will give him nourishment, that he can dissect' (*In the Middle*[16]) should not be forgotten, and especially here.) What is the grace thrown away by the 'Puritans' against whom the poet states his case?

> I accuse
> these men of singleness and loss of grace
> who stared so deeply into the fire's hues
> that all was fire to them.
> ('A Note on Puritans',
> in *The Law and the Grace*[17])

Set in its orthodox duet with law, theological grace (at any rate in the predestinarian teaching which stands grimly in the wings) seems itself to be tied hand and foot. The poet who explores the old manse to 'sniff again/ the Free Church air' (*FBL*, pp. 11–12) finds only a faint and ambiguous memory of grace in an old photograph of a girl and 'the ancient tints of brown that eat at brow/ and hair and nose, and make her now/ as almost rusted in this world of grace./ How little beauty conscious sins allow!' The poem escapes from the house and its rigid formulas into the garden; but the grace 'gross and fruitful' imagined there is nevertheless reached for through prayer.

Grace is not to be defined in religious terms, or any other; exclusive definition shuts out the quality itself, as in the Puritans who lose what they exclusively seek. Yet the word is not used in that poem with any sort of vagueness; the poet-accuser knows exactly what he is talking about. It may well be that the subject who experiences grace cannot (as in Joan of Arc's justly praised reply to her inquisitors) say whether she or he is in 'a state of grace' or not. But the presence of grace can be recognised. It may be manifest anywhere, in the playing of a melodeon and village dancing by moonlight, in the nifty footwork of a football player, in the workmen who 'sing like birds in the scaffolding' while the wind blows 'as at play' as it listeth (*The Notebooks of Robinson Crusoe*[18], in the fleetness of the deer, explicitly 'a grace not theological but of/ accomplished bodies, sensuous and swift' (*DOHH*, XII). It is in the making of poetry itself; indeed, as already suggested, it has an absolutely crucial part in reconciling the elements of design and freedom at odds within the maker's task. 'It's the law they ask of me and not grace', he protests, knowing that he has attendant angels more persuasive than accusations of 'blasphemy and devilry'. They are 'spontaneous' and act through love;

> They have no design
> on anyone else, but only on my pride.
> (*The Law and the Grace*)

Grace is needful for the poet, as for anyone else; and as for anyone else, it is unspeakable, but the poem, with luck, describes it; it delineates, so to speak, the invisible object. No more than for anyone else can grace be planned for or calculated upon, but its operation can be seen, retrospectively, in the completed poem itself. The process may even to some extent be analysed, as for instance in 'Argument' (*LPAE*, pp. 34–7). This important poem does indeed marshal most of the conflicting claims of Law and Grace, beginning with the proposition that they are in practice dependent on one another: if the 'fine spiritual graces' are denied, 'then there's the terror of pure nothingness' and (with reference to Dostoevsky's forebodings of radical nihilism) 'everything is allowed'. Want of meaning, the possibility (added here to the bleak conclusion of *Deer on the High Hills*) that there is 'nothing behind the morning' would seem to be a rational conclusion. Facts are facts, the stones are stony, there is nothing more to be said. But such a conclusion, however reasonable, is contrary to what human beings do with their experience.

That is not the way we live. There are 'notes/ inside the music' which actually control ('dominate') 'the else unmeaning scenery'; and in the

## Design and Grace

poet's work there is something inside it, a 'sense beyond the poem', known to the maker only by an exactitude, achievement of completion or the sense of an ending:

> He knows it as he knows a coming home,
> perfection to which nothing can be added,
> nor by the mind can wholly be decoded.

The crux of this highly concentrated exposition is in the word 'perfection', which unavoidably reintroduces the ideas of law and obedience to law:

> The Greeks believed the circle was the perfect
> figure. Therefore the heavens must conform . . .

Yet we know that, *in fact*, astronomically speaking, they were wrong; circles had to be adjusted to ellipses. How can this be done? How can we learn to see more correctly, more *justly*?

> It just required a little movement of
> a human mind, a justice as of love –

and the transformation is brought about. Things locked in law ('dull loggish stability', the obedience of the dead) are quickened, 'a brilliant foil which lights a whole stage up', and 'lights flash in all directions from pure faces/ which are as diamonds in their clear excesses'. The junction of contradictory elements and images, especially of diamond-purity and excess, is in truth an illumination.

The whole poem reminds us strongly of G.M. Hopkins, which may indicate how misleading it is to categorise poetry as 'religious' or otherwise. In the final stanza, 'Argument' makes a visible drama from the operation of 'a justice as of love':

> Out of the chaos marches a whole street
> with a church, an inn and houses, people too,
> and the light curves all around them with the shape
> of a woman in her vulnerable hope
> bent over a candle, tucking sheet and shawl
> into an order which is loved and real.

The concluding image would have been acceptable to Hopkins, also perhaps to the master-poet, alluded to so frequently and often with a striking mixture of reverence and revulsion. The last lines of the poem already mentioned, 'In this Pitiless Age', allow Dante to rest, beyond his 'thrifty justice', in 'that tremendous sentence luminous,/ "The Love that moves the sun and the other stars"'.

'Argument' makes many of the connections which are to be assumed between Crichton Smith's poetry and his prose fiction. At one point in *Consider the Lilies*, a conversation occurs between the old woman, Mrs Scott, and Donald MacLeod, opponent of the Clearances, who is meditating at the same time upon his own role as a 'voice' for speechless suffering and the victims of injustice. Much is said in MacLeod's thoughts about communication, its failures and its unconvenanted accomplishments. Mrs Scott has shown him a letter she is sending to her son, and he is puzzled by something lacking in it until he realises that — astonishingly in so pious a person as the old woman — it contains no mention whatever of God. He understands that Mrs Scott has been trying to tell him something, and that this, her abandonment of religious defences, is it. His own responsibility is the greater, and as he stands there 'distracted by the heady scent of flowers', as they are both together 'in the humming day . . . while the summer flowed round them in interpenetrating colour and scent' — just as in 'Argument' '. . . the hum/ of bees in summer harmonises plum/ and grape and apple so that these are notes/ inside the music' — he seeks 'with great patience' but in vain for something to say himself:

> He hadn't found the spell which would release them, the word that he could say and she could understand. And this tormented him. Obscurely he felt that it was important to him to find the word and to be able to say it, so that he would be united with her and what she was. Perhaps only the poets would be able to find that word. Or perhaps it didn't exist. But it must exist. Somewhere it lay concealed under lies and differences, like the soot in a black house which could be used to fertilise the land. Sometimes, if he could tear the beams apart, the dry old beams, he would find it and build a new kind of house. For after all he was a mason. He would find it if he was worthy.
>
> (*CTL*, p. 141)

'Perhaps only the poets would be able to find that word.' At the end of the novel, the white horse on whose back Patrick Sellar is so uneasy a rider reappears, with another horse — a black one — which is the mount of Sellar's superior, the lawyer John Loch. They are tethered outside while the two men enter Mrs Scott's cottage to cajole, bully and deceive the old woman into leaving her home without fuss. Violence and evil are not far off. A thunderstorm is brewing, and the horses become restive; when, having failed to persuade Mrs Scott, the men leave, they mount with difficulty and ride off into the thunder and rising wind on beasts only barely under their control. Somewhere a cock is crowing, potent symbol both of betrayal and rebirth. So the unpredictable powers of poetry, white and black, the light and its shadow, both unamenable to law, plunge into the storm of history.

Clearly, the largest claims for poetry are being made here. They are implied throughout the successive stages of Crichton Smith's work; sometimes they are stated directly. The superb piece 'Poets aren't dangerous, you think' (*FBL*, p. 15) goes on not only to deliver the warning that 'poets can destroy' but also to justify poetic destruction on absolute grounds: poets are

> such birds
>
> as I am member of, impersonal, grave,
> the Parcae of hard honour, single-beaked,
> immune to bribery, however weak,
> and trained to justice by implacable love.

Poetry's claim is not aesthetic (if that is supposed to be a separate category), but ethical; Shelley's *Defence* could not pitch it higher.

Crichton Smith, not less proud of his calling, is very much more aware than Shelley of the pitfalls in wait for those who follow it. The ambivalences of 'implacable love' are already suggested in this poem; a later one ('Slowly', in a collection much concerned with home-coming and taking stock[19]) declares that the ethical and the aesthetic may indeed meet, but that they will do so only where language and the distinctions made by language no longer operate: stage agony and actual agony 'meet where no one has a name./ They meet where all the walls have fallen down.'

In the meantime, poetry must not renege upon its vocation, but must constantly strive to renew and correct it. The corrective, which becomes more explicit as these writings advance in directness and force, is nothing less than life. If it seems banal to say so, the conclusion must be related to what has gone before, in tracing the hard to-and-fro struggle to see life as it is, the brute facts, the 'snake-pit of contradictions' – to see these, and to wait for their transformation in 'those motions of the spirit which see the human being as he is, whoever he is, and really notice him'. (*TTH*, pp. 51, 56). These are the motions, unpredictable but faithful, 'the brief eternal wind that trembles among leaves and is the soul' (*AL*. p. 58), which have been identified with the idea of grace. They do not exclude the stern spirit of the poet as legislator and judge, but they render this (unacknowledged) function more hospitable to human need. 'Inspiration' has its most persuasive advocate in the hilarious and simple-hearted ghost of one of the stories in *The Village*

(TV, p. 27–31), who 'wants to make people happy'. And who are 'people', the ordinary, the common people, who know nothing of poetics? The poet in *The Exiles* 'begins to think' that 'there are no "ordinary" people'. 'O Lord', says Robinson Crusoe, the ultimate isolate and exile, 'let me cast myself on the common waters'. (*NRC*, p. 82). And finally, we may return to the discussion of 'the conflict between art and life' in the essay on MacDiarmid already referred to, and to the simple, devastating statement that in this conflict 'Life is continually making art appear minor'.

The artist, whose claims have been so exalted, seems radically to undercut himself. But in truth, and in the simplest terms, what he has claimed is rendered thereby only more exact and well-founded. For 'art', obviously, is a part of 'life'; unless for the mad solipsist, the eye is no more than the organ through which all the other is seen. But the perceiving eye and the consciousness which it informs are the means of seeing and distinguishing; they are the active part which, susceptible to grace, may discover design and give it form. The amazing capacity for ordering experience, shared with all ordinary people, is ordinary, as the very word suggests. What the poet has, perhaps, in acute degree, is the capacity to feel and express his amazement.

NOTES

Works of Iain Crichton Smith quoted are listed below. Where the same work is subsequently referred to, it is identified by initials (e.g. *Consider the Lilies* as '*CTL*') given parenthetically in the text.

1. *Consider the Lilies*: London (Gollancz), 1968, p. 9.
2. *My Last Duchess*: London (Gollancz), 1971, p. 19.
3. *Towards the Human: Selected Essays*: Edinburgh (Macdonald), 1986, p. 172.
4. *The Last Summer*: London (Gollancz), 1969, p. 101.
5. *The Black and the Red*: London (Gollancz), 1973, pp. 118, 121–2, 157.
6. *The Village*: Inverness (Club Leabhar), 1976, p. 77.
7. From *The Last Summer*, 'God's Own Country' in *The Black and the Red*, 'The Vision', in *The Village*.
8. *River, river: Poems for Children*: Loanhead, Midlothian (Macdonald), 1978, p. 16.
9. *Survival Without Error and Other Stories*: London (Gollancz), 1970, p. 193.
10. *Love Poems and Elegies*: London (Gollancz), 1972, pp. 21–2.
11. *Deer on the High Hills*: Edinburgh (Giles Gordon), 1962; also in *Selected Poems 1955–80*: Loanhead, Midlothian (Macdonald), 1981, pp. 42–52.
12. *The Village and Other Poems*: Manchester (Carcanet), 1989, p. 48.

13. *From Bourgeois Land*: London (Gollancz), 1969, p. 55.
14. *Bibles and Advertisements* (Biobuill is Sanasan-reice, translated by the author), in *Selected Poems*, p. 58.
15. *A Life*: Manchester (Carcanet), 1986, pp. 40–1.
16. *In the Middle*: London (Gollancz), 1977, p. 17.
17. *The Law and the Grace*: Edinburgh (Giles Gordon), 1962; also in *Selected Poems*, p. 15.
18. *Notebooks of Robinson Crusoe* (Gollancz), 1975, p. 23.
19. *The Exiles*: Manchester (Carcanet), 1984, p. 54.

# Fifteen

## Uirsgeul Mhic a' Ghobhainn: Iain Crichton Smith's Gaelic Fiction

### Richard A.V. Cox

Iain Mac a' Ghobhainn is one of the most prolific writers of Gaelic fiction today, and has been producing short stories and novels fairly continuously over almost four decades.

Apart from the collections, which contain a large proportion of items unpublished elsewhere, his short stories have mainly appeared in the periodicals *Gairm* and *An Gaidheal* or been broadcast by the BBC. The first of these, *Am Bodach* (*Gairm* 6 'the old man'), was published in 1953.

The first of four collections of stories, *Bùrn is Aran* (*BA*; 'bread and water'), appeared in 1960, and was closely followed by *An Dubh is an Gorm* (*DG*; 'the black and blue') in 1963. After a comparatively longer gap, *Maighisteirean is Ministeirean* (*MM*; 'masters and ministers') appeared in 1970, followed, again closely, by *An t-Adhar Ameireaganach* (*AA*; 'the American sky') in 1973.[1]

Mac a' Ghobhainn has produced five novels. The first of these, *Iain am Measg nan Reultan* (1970 'John among the stars'), is intended for a younger readership, as is *Am Bruadaraiche* (1980 'the dreamer').[2] The adult novels are *An t-Aonaran* (1976 'the loner'), *Murchadh* (*Gairm* 106-9, 1979–80 'Murdoch'), and the recent *Na Speuclairean Dubha* (1989 'the dark glasses').[3]

The setting for much of Mac a' Ghobhainn's work is the Highlands. Occasionally this is specifically 'island', as in *Clachan Chalanais* (*BA* 'the Callanish stones') where a young boy feels threatened when he sees the stones move; at other times, specifically 'mainland', as in *Am Maor* (*DG* 'the factor') where an old woman is given notice of eviction.[4] However, while Mac a' Ghobhainn's intimate knowledge of island (particularly

Lewis) life is frequently evident, there is generally no specific reference to place within a Highland context.

A number of stories have an urban setting, e.g. *Anns a' Chafe* (*Gairm* 56 'in the cafe') in Aberdeen, *Turus do'n Fhithich* (*Gairm* 45 'journey to the raven') in Glasgow, and the novel *Na Speuclairean Dubha* in Oban and Taynuilt. In the story *An Dubh is an Gorm*, although the young university student writes from Aberdeen, elements of his Highland home are felt via his mother's implied responses.

The same link with a Highland home is made in the 'exile' stories, e.g. *Turus Dhachaigh* I and II (*BA* 'a journey home'), *An t-Adhar Ameireaganach* and *Bràthair mo Mhàthar* (*Gairm* 93 'my maternal uncle'). However, as with the New World, other non-Scottish settings are usually incidental in the relatively small number of stories where they occur, e.g. Elba in *Napòleon* (*DG*), Germany and Poland in *Na h-Iùdhaich* (DG 'the Jews'), and in the 'biblical' stories *Iòseph* (*Gairm* 43), *Abraham is Isaac* (*DG*) and *Is agus Esan* (*DG* 'Adam and Eve').

Many of the stories are set within a very short space of time, from a few hours as in *Aig a' Phartaidh* (*AA* 'at the party') to less than half an hour as in *Am Maor* and *An Duine Dubh* (*BA* 'the black man') in which a Pakistani pedlar tries to sell his wares to an old woman. Some are set within a longer period, e.g. *Maighisteirean is Ministeirean* within a working day, and *An Dubh is an Gorm* and *Pickering* (*MM*), in which the young army conscript commits suicide, within the space of several weeks.[5] The novels are also set within a period of weeks. The past or a passage of time in the past, however, is often conveyed through the recollection of one or more characters: while in *Maighisteirean is Ministeirean* much of the life of Maighistear Trill is recounted in third person narrative, despite the time-setting of a single day, in *Anns a' Bhùrn* (*DG* 'in the water') we have thoughts of the past from a man on the point of drowning, and through the monologues in *Granny anns a' Chòrnair* (*Gairm* 54 'Granny in the corner') we have the accounts by several members of a family of important issues that have affected them during their lives.

In the short stories, it is commonly a circumstance or event in the immediate past which gives rise to the situation in which the character or characters find themselves: in *An Coigreach* (*BA* 'the stranger', Alasdair has returned home from Canada and finds himself lying about his identity when he assumes that his mother (who has gone blind) does not recognise him; in *Briseadh Cridhe* (*BA* 'heart-break'), the death of his girlfriend's father prompts an investigation into the central character's feelings as well as the cause of death; in *Bùrn* (*BA* 'water'), a soldier has found himself unwillingly guarding one of the enemy in the filth and debris of the battlefield; and in *Turus do'n Fhithich*, a doctor has discovered that he is terminally ill. As in *Briseadh Cridhe*, the circumstance or event is often a central element within the plot: in *An Telegram* (*An Gaidheal* LX, 4 'the telegram'), two mothers watch in trepidation as the church elder, War Office telegram in hand, approaches their houses; and in *Na h-Iùdhaich*, a group of Jews is transported unknowingly to their deaths.

At times, Mac a' Ghobhainn makes use of well-known stories for his plot, as in the 'biblical' stories. In a similar way, he introduces the exiled Emperor in *Napòleon*, Defoe's castaway in *Robinson Crusoe* (*AA*), and the psychopathic Mac an t-Srònaich in *Anns an Uaimh* (*DG* 'in the cave').

Occasionally we find an element from one story reworked elsewhere. For example, the central plot of *An Telegram* recurs as a minor episode recollected in *Granny anns a' Chòrnair*, while the same character (Mr Trill) appears, if only superficially, in both *Maighistir Trill agus Vergil* (*Gairm* 53 'Mr Trill and Vergil') and *Maighisteirean is Ministeirean*.[6]

Of the novels, plot is least apparent in *Murchadh*, although the stages and questions raised in the main character's attempt at self-analysis (the initiation of the search; predestination; independence/dependence; a superior being; the shaping of personality) constitute an informal structure. In *An t-Aonaran*, the central plot is the arrival of, the reaction to and the banishment of the loner. As a psychological novel, however, it is Teàrlach's (changing) position which is of importance, and Mac a' Ghobhainn reveals this by introducing, in turn, a number of characters (as well as a dream) to produce responses to this end. In *Na Speuclairean Dubha*, in which Trevor Bailey investigates the cause of a local poet's suicide, Mac a' Ghobhainn at first employs a similar technique. The first part of the novel essentially sets the scene for the dénouement in the second, which is mostly taken up by the rehearsals for a play. Here, Mac a' Ghobhainn symbolises the relationships between his characters by deftly linking them with the characters within the play.

Action within the short stories is, on the whole, severely limited. In *An Taghadh* (*DG* 'the choice'), a mother has to decide which of her three sons the Hanoverian officer will kill, and in *An Carbad* (*DG* 'the car'), the driver has to go back to the person he has just run over. In effect, action is limited to the playing-out of the event. In *An Duine Dubh anns a' Chùbainn* (*MM* 'the black man in the pulpit'), where a woman agonises to her companion over seeing a black minister, real action is almost non-existent — the important action takes place in the mind of

# The Gaelic Fiction

the woman when she decides she knows why the minister was there. Action, then, is frequently confined to the psychological response. Some stories are open-ended, e.g. *Turus Dhachaigh* I and *An Gunfighter* (*Gairm* 141). Most, however, do have a resolution. In *Briseadh Cridhe*, the murderer is correctly identified, and in *An Duine Dubh*, the old woman buys some silk underwear just as the pedlar is about to leave. Such resolutions, however, are distinct from the psychological (often incomplete) resolutions of the characters. In these examples, the important reactions of the characters have already been revealed: in *Briseadh Cridhe* where the central character brings out his feelings of fear, aggression and guilt, and in *An Duine Dubh* where the old woman recalls her lighter self. It is often, in fact, where a character's response coincides with the ending of a story that resolutions proper are most easily perceived, as in *Na Guthan* (*AA* 'the voices'), where the husband comes to terms with the guilt he has felt since his wife's death.

The characters that Mac a' Ghobhainn introduces in both his short stories and his novels are superficially various: from the old woman and pedlar in *An Duine Dubh* to the broken Emperor in *Napòleon*, and from the unemployed joiner in *An Saor* (*Gairm* 122 'the joiner') to the old man finding it difficult to come to terms with the frailty of age in *An Turus* (*Gairm* 140 'the journey'). In terms of physical description, much is left to the imagination, even in the novels. Any description is often the observation of another character, as in *An Coigreach*, where the man sees his rather dishevelled mother standing in the doorway, and in *A' Bhanrigh* (*AA* 'the queen'), where descriptions of the girl arise from the central character's feelings, and where they are enhanced by the contrast of her beauty with the dirtiness of the city around them.

Despite their apparent variety, and despite the lack of physical description, Mac a' Ghobhainn's characters can often be typed. For example, the girls in *Bùrn*, *Aig a' Phartaidh* and *An Fhidheall* (*BA* 'the fiddle') represent a fresh and youthful beauty. (No matter that in stories like *Bùrn* the girl is merely recalled by the main character.) This type is frequently goddess-like, inaccessible and unobtainable.

A second type featured is the male authority figure, such as the policeman in *Briseadh Cridhe* and the drunken father in *An Gaol* (*AA* 'love'). This type often reveals a dangerous quality, as in *Clachan Chalanais*, where the frightening stones are symbolic of feelings about the boy's father, and in *An Carbad*, where the accident and its victim instil dread into the driver. This type is impressive, awesome, uncontrollable, powerful, stern and dangerous, but often only obliquely presented.

The most striking type – the characters in whom it is found being frequently the most tangible – is the mature or older woman, such as the mother in *An Taghadh* and *An Dubh is an Gorm*, or the old woman in *Am Maor*. This type is strong, principled, maternal and reliable.

Along with the above, we have a type exemplified by the boy in *Clachan Chalanais*, the young poet in *Am Bàrd* (BA 'the poet'), the youth in *An Carbad*, the factor in *Am Maor* and the husband in *Na Guthan*. Indeed, this type includes males of all ages. He is usually the central character, and often the speaker in first person narratives such as *An Dealbh-Chluiche* (AA 'the play'), where he, a doctor involved in amateur dramatics, is indirectly the cause of the suicide of his lover's husband.

While in one sense, therefore, Mac a' Ghobhainn's characters are undeveloped, in another they are by virtue of their relationship with other characters. This is most apparent where stories involve an individual (male) with either one or both parents – especially so where the mother is in prominent focus, as in *An Coigreach* or *An Dubh is an Gorm*; but more abstract and ephemeral where the young woman or girl type is concerned. Least developed perhaps is a type not previously mentioned, the brother type, which occurs in stories such as *Fear à Rhodesia* (AA 'a man from Rhodesia') and *E Fhèin is a Bhràthair* (DG 'he and his brother').

Although the majority of stories only involve one or two main characters – on the surface this is certainly true of *An Coigreach*, with mother and son, and of *Anns a' Bhùrn*, with a lone figure in the ocean – reference to other types is nevertheless made: in *An Coigreach* to the father, and in *Anns a' Bhùrn* to the father, mother, brother and girl. Examples of stories including the individual's parents (with or without a brother or girl appearing) are *Turus Dhachaigh* I, *Clachan Chalanais, Bùrn, Anns a' Bhùrn* and *Na Facail air a' Bhalla* (DG 'the words on the wall'), in which a man uncovers the words 'Mary Campbell loves John Campbell' while renovating an old house.[7] Examples where only the father type occurs (with or without brother or girl) are *Briseadh Cridhe, Turus Dhachaigh* II, *An Carbad* and *Jenkins is Marlowe* (DG), in which a would-be mountain-climber uses an imagined, but psychologically real, Marlowe as competitor.

It would be wrong to over-emphasise the question of character types with regard to characterisation, for they belong to the ideas or themes behind the narrative to which the characters are essentially subordinate. Mac a' Ghobhainn is not arbitrarily choosing situations in which he tests for responses from his characters (in *Robinson Crusoe* the admitted experiment to find an alternative ending is a disclaimer that the story has anything to do with Defoe's); rather, his stories are descriptions of the individual's world, i.e. the psychological world of attitudes and beliefs, and of influences in development. It is here that the question of character types has value.

It is not difficult to see the influence of psychoanalytical theory in Mac a' Ghobhainn's work. For example, *Briseadh Cridhe* and *An Carbad* seem to incorporate elements of the Oedipus complex. In the former, the parental authority held formerly by the girlfriend's father (and to which the central character felt subjected) is carried over and continued in the character of the policeman. In the latter, it is possible to assume there has been no real accident, nor real victim (cf. *Jenkins is Marlowe*), and that they are merely symbolic of the threatening feelings which the central character finds undermining his relationship with his girlfriend. As a theme, the Oedipus complex is most successfully treated, however, in Mac a' Ghobhainn's latest novel, *Na Speuclairean Dubha*.

Other thematic elements are equally apparent. The influence of existentialism is evident in many stories. *Abraham is Isaac* and *Is agus Esan*, for instance, exemplify the concept of blind choice, while stories such as *Anns an Uaimh*, where Mac an t-Srònaich decides to set his schoolboy captive free, and *An Taghadh*, where the woman decides which of her sons the officer will kill, present the potential dilemma in the question of choice and point to the concept of responsibility once it has been made. Similarly, the influence of Camus' concept of the absurd can be seen in stories such as *An Rionnag* (AA 'the star'), in which a sportive God portrays irrational existence. On the other hand, stories such as *Bùrn* and *Rudeigin Coltach ri Chekhov* (AA 'something like Chekhov') embody ideas on the hopelessness of communication.

The stern face of Calvinistic religion is often portrayed. On occasion, only its influence is implied, for example by the presence of a Bible, as in *An Duine Dubh*, or, more unusually, by the Bible not being needed in *Robinson Crusoe*. Its restrictive authority is, however, fully expressed in the following passage, translated from the novel *Murchadh*, describing a modern-day Calvin:

> He has a face like iron and sits at the table writing day and night with a large black Bible in front of him.
> He can't bear a candle in the same house as him.
> If he sees anyone drinking or smoking he comes out and starts shouting and jumping up and down on the road, shaking his fist at the man.
> He's also against cars.

If he sees a woman approaching he closes the door and shakes his fist at her out of the window. If she looks at him he shuts his eyes and they stay shut till she's gone by.
Then he washes his face.

(*Gairm* 108, 376–7)

Some stories portray aspects of personality unfettered by the normal controlling influences of society, e.g. *Air a' Bhus* (*Gairm* 55 'on the bus') in which a fear of travelling on buses is described.[8] Such stories, in common with others, often incorporate elements that defy rational explanation or create a preposterous or ludicrous situation. Besides being sometimes surrealistic, the effect of this is impressionistic, producing a larger-than-life picture in which psychological detail is itself enlarged. A sense of this is certainly found in stories such as *Napòleon, Anns an Uaimh* and *Robinson Crusoe*; similarly in *An Rionnag*, where we have the Devil and his colleagues having their plans for earth being spoilt by God.[9] Mac a' Ghobhainn's forte, however, in terms of the 'exotic' must be *Murchadh*, in which the writer who cannot write is driven to ludicrous extremes in his attempt to write. Here, the attempt to write is used in a literal sense within the plot, but also symbolically for the process of self-analysis.

The 'exile' stories have often been singled out from the point of view of theme.[10] Certainly they evoke a sense of attachment to the homeland and the paradox of the exile's position. They go further, however, in that they analyse the attachment and relationship with his family as well. In these stories, the exile's feelings remain largely unresolved, as in *An t-Adhar Ameireaganach*, where chronological and psychological gaps between childhood in the past and adulthood in the present are felt to be unbridgeable.

Mac a' Ghobhainn, then, is predominantly preoccupied with the psychological dimension of human existence, interpreted through broad philosophical frameworks. Frequently he deals with the dominating influences in the individual's (and his own) life, and many stories appear to be a rehearsal of an attempt to present and understand these more fully. Often, however, stories remain partially obscure. This may be due partly to the amount of incoming information (in terms of responses, etc.), but also, I suspect, to an element of resistance on the part of the author.[11]

In contrast to the low levels of action and of character development, there is a great deal going on in the minds of characters. Mac a' Ghobhainn's earlier preference for the use of third person narration allowed him to develop this mental or psychological movement quickly.[12] Besides utilising an all-knowing author and dialogue between characters, he frequently features the internal monologue (or dialogue) of his characters, either in the first or third person. The following is from *Am Maor*, and begins in the middle of the factor's conversation with the old woman, but continues with his recollection of a conversation with the Duke:

'I must tell you why I came,' he began.

'Well,' she said, 'the water's not far off. There's a well beside us here. But how stupid I am – Tormod was lost in Canada.'

When the Duke wanted a factor he put in for it.

'But I know the ways of the people here,' he said, as the Duke laughed. The Duke started thinking (you could tell for he was striking his whip against the leather covering his legs).

'That's right,' he said at length, 'that's right.' And he looked at him in surprise as though he couldn't understand something.

'Oh well,' said the Duke at last, looking out of the window, 'one world's coming to an end. You know that.'

'Yes.' (It wasn't a terribly good world anyway.)

'You must get a horse. If you have a horse you'll be fine. Were you ever on horseback? (In a month or two there'd be no one left in the village anyway: there were only ten houses. And who'd point the finger then?)

'No,' he replied.

(*DG*, 12–13)

It is particularly via this interpretation of thoughts, then, that Mac a' Ghobhainn conveys the mood and attitude of his characters. This technique, which includes the relating of events as if disconnected from a main chronological sequence, causes a slowing-down of time: in effect, the suspension of time (and action) enhances the observation of psychological processes.

In *Maighisteirean is Ministeirean*, there is a detectable, though temporary, change of method in this respect. There is a greater emphasis on the progression of plot and the description of events in sequence, but the result is a lengthy, drawn-out affair. Mac a' Ghobhainn is at his best, as in *Bùrn* and *An Coigreach*, when least concentrating on action within the conventional plot.

His prose style has a deceptive simplicity, unencumbered by verbosity or any heavy turn of phrase, promoting a precision and clarity in his description.[13] Yet, frequently, there is a startling use of imagery, for example *chan fhaigheadh e air carachadh. Bha dà chloich air a chasan* (*An Carbad* 'he couldn't move. There were two stones on his feet') and *dh'òl e e mar a dh'òlas lit bainne* (*An Duine Dubh* 'he drank it like porridge drinks milk'). At first sight, it may seem that the imagery in such instances has simply got out of control. However, the effect of bringing one up sharp is likely to be intentional, in that this use or manipulation of imagery is at once impressionistic and surrealistic.

Mac a' Ghobhainn makes frequent use of colours as symbols in his work — although their application seems to vary — and this is extended to the colour or quality of light. For example, yellow, gold and the sun may symbolise truth or understanding, while white, silver and the moon symbolise falsehood or confusion. The sun and moon are also symbols for the father and mother respectively. White in general also appears to represent the intellect — a pure, sterile colour, in contrast to green of the emotions. The following illustrates the juxtaposition of symbols which sometimes occurs: *Bha a mhac-meanmna a' gul fola, mar ghealach air sgàineadh, 's an duine a' cur charan, 's an carbad mòr gorm a' leum troimh sholus na gealaich* (*An Carbad* 'His imagination was weeping blood, like a moon rent, the man rolling over, and the great dark car leaping through the moonlight').

In conclusion, it would be difficult to argue that Mac a' Ghobhainn's work contains a progressive series of unifying themes, although a proportion of stories within a particular period may hold unifying elements. Rather, he appears to return to his themes again and again. Clearly, there is a strong personal element in his work. As an intellectual, he consciously draws from a wide range of literary, philosophical and psychoanalytical traditions, so that, along with his own innovative style and treatment of theme, his cannot be seen as a traditional Gaelic literary form. This is not to say that he does not reveal a clear insight into a Gaelic cultural environment when required; but it is new to contemporary Gaelic literature, and is an important and significant contribution to it.

NOTES

1. Stories appearing in the anthologies *Dorcha tro Ghlainne* (1970) and *Eadar Peann is Pàipear* (1985) have been previously published.
2. These are not included in the following discussion.
3. The first chapter of *Murchadh* occurred as a short story in the anthology *Amannan* (1979). Indeed, although it was announced as a novel when serialised in *Gairm*, it might be argued that *Murchadh*, like *Maighisteirean is Ministeirean* in the collection of that name, is really an extended short story rather than a novel.
4. *Am Maor* forms the basis for the first chapter of Mac a' Ghobhainn's English novel *Consider the Lilies* (1968), set in the nineteenth century during the period of the Sutherland Clearances.

## The Gaelic Fiction 199

5. In the collection *Maighisteirean is Ministeirean*, the titles for the stories *Pickering* and *Air an Trèin* 'on the train' should be exchanged.
6. Similarly, the character of Ruaraidh in *An t-Iomradh* (*An Gaidheal* LX, 2 'the news report'), who asks questions such as 'What is the Gaelic for *Indian Summer?*', is found in the prose poem *An t-Eilean* (18) in *An t-Eilean agus an Cànan* (1987).
7. This is also the case in *Am Maor*: Does he (the new factor) not want Vera? But will he get her? What if she and her father, the stern Duke, leave for London without him? And must he not throw the old woman out of her home, the old woman whom he really understands so well?
8. A different story entitled *Air a' Bhus* occurs in the collection *Maighisteirean is Ministeirean*.
9. The anthropomorphic essays, *An Tilleadh* (*AA* 'the return') and *Latha nan Leumadairean* (*AA* 'the day of the dolphins'), are the least successful in this respect. In the former, an alien race (of crabs) brings home a human only to find him full of aggression, and, in the latter, there is an attempt to describe a sense of mutual understanding between man and dolphin.
10. Among these are *Turus Dhachaigh* I and II, *An Coigreach, Turus Mhurchaidh* (*An Gaidheal* LXI, 8 'Murdoch's journey'), *A' Dol Dhachaigh* (*AA* 'going home'), *An t-Adhar Ameireaganach* and *Bràthair mo Mhàthar*.
11. It is probable that Mac a' Ghobhainn has met a general disapproval of 'things psychological', as is suggested in *An Fhidheall* when Dolan says: 'Chan eil mi ag iarraidh do chuid "psychology"' ('I don't want your psychology').
12. Since the early 1970s, he has gradually turned to using first person narration slightly more frequently than third. Technically, this is more limiting.
13. Donald John MacLeod, in his synopsis of Mac a' Ghobhainn's earlier work, succinctly and accurately states that 'his writing style has been ruthlessly pared down . . . it is a lean, athletic style, a tool he has created to suit the bent of his mind' (*Twentieth Century Gaelic Literature*, a doctoral thesis, University of Glasgow 1969, 110).

# Notes on Contributors

J.H. ALEXANDER is Senior Lecturer in English at the University of Aberdeen, the editor of *Scottish Literary Studies* and *The Scott Newsletter*, and an executive of the Edinburgh Edition of the Waverley Novels, for which he edited *Kenilworth*. Among his other published work is *Reading Wordsworth* (1987).

ANN E. BOUTELLE currently lives in western Massachusetts and teaches in the English Department at Smith College. Born and raised in Scotland, she went to Oban High School when Crichton Smith was teaching there, and she is the author of *Thistle and Rose: A Study of Hugh MacDiarmid's Poetry* (1980).

STEWART CONN is a poet, a playwright, and currently head of BBC Scotland's Radio Drama Department. Among his published plays are *Thistlewood, The Burning, The Qaurium, I Didn't Always Live Here* and *Play Donkey*, and he wrote the television screenplay for Neil Gunn's novel *Bloodhunt*. His poetry collections include *In the Kibble Palace* and *The Luncheon of the Boating Party*.

RICHARD A.V. COX taught until recently in the Celtic Department of Glasgow University. He served as editorial assistant for the Historical Dictionary of Scottish Gaelic, and is the editor of a Gaelic School Dictionary.

CAIRNS CRAIG teaches English and Scottish literature at the University of Edinburgh. He edited the *History of Scottish Literature* (Aberdeen University Press, 4 vols, 1988–90) and is the general editor of the *Determinations* series produced by Polygon books. He has also published widely on modern poetry (*Yeats, Eliot, Pound and the Politics of Poetry*, Croom Helm, 1981) and on literary theory. He was for many years closely associated with *Cencrastus* and *Radical Scotland*, and a collection of his essays on Scottish culture, entitled *Out of History*, will be published by Polygon in 1992.

GERALD DAWE is a poet and critic who teaches in the English Department at Trinity College Dublin. He is general editor of the review *Krino*, and is currently preparing *Icon and Lares: Readings in Irish Poetry*. His poetry collections include *Sheltering Places, The Lundy's Letter, The Water Table* and *Safe Houses*.

DOUGLAS DUNN is a Professor in the Department of English Literature at the University of St Andrews. His most recent poetry collections are *Elegies* (1985), *Selected Poems* (1986) and *Northlight* (1988), and he also edited *Scotland: An Anthology* (1991) and *The Faber Book of Twentieth-Century Scottish Poetry* (1992).

ALASTAIR FOWLER is Regius Professor Emeritus at Edinburgh University, and co-editor of Milton's *Paradise Lost*. His other books include a *History of English Literature, Spenser and the Numbers of Time, Triumphal Forms, Conceitful Thought* and *Kinds of Literature*. His volumes of poetry include *Catacomb Suburb* and *From the Domain of Arnheim*.

CAROL GOW is a lecturer in Communications and Media Studies at Dundee College, and her book *Mirror and Marble: The Poetry of Iain Crichton Smith* is to be published by MacDonald.

LORN MACINTYRE was taught by Iain Crichton Smith at Oban High School, received his doctorate on Walter Scott and the Highlands from Glasgow University, and is now a full-time writer. He has published three novels in his Chronicles of Invernevis series.

COLIN NICHOLSON is a Senior Lecturer in the Department of English Literature at Edinburgh University. He edited *Alexander Pope: Essays for the Tercentenary* and *Margaret Laurence: New Critical Essays*, and is currently editor of the *British Journal of Canadian Studies*. His book on contemporary Scottish Poetry, *Landscapes of the Mind*, is to be published by Polygon in 1992.

CHRISTOPHER SMALL is now retired, having formerly been literary editor of the *Glasgow Herald* for twenty-five years. His books include a study of Shelley and Mary Shelley, *Ariel Like a Harpy*.

STAN SMITH is Professor of English at Dundee University whose books include *A Sadly Contracted Hero: The Comic Self in Post-War American Fiction, Inviolable Voice: History and Twentieth-Century Poetry, W.H. Auden, Edward Thomas* and *W.B. Yeats: A Critical Introduction*. He is also general editor of *Longman Studies in Twentieth-Century Literature* and co-director of Dundee University's Auden Concordance Project.

DERICK THOMSON was born on the Isle of Lewis and was until recently Professor of Celtic at Glasgow University. His many publications include *An Introduction to Gaelic Poetry*, *The Companion to Gaelic Scotland* and his Collected Poems, *Creachadh na Clarsaich/Plundering the Harp*. Since 1952 he has been editor of *Gairm*.

GEORGE WATSON is a Senior Lecturer in the Department of English Literature at the University of Aberdeen where Iain Crichton Smith was recently Writer in Residence. He has published extensively on both Irish Literature and cultural politics, including 'Cultural Imperialism: An Irish View' for the *Yale Review* (1979). He is the author of *Irish Identity and the Literary Revival*.

# Select Bibliography

POETRY

*The Long River* (Macdonald, Loanhead, 1955)
*Thistles and Roses* (Eyre and Spottiswoode, London, 1961)
*Biobuill is Sanasan-Reice* [Bibles and Advertisements), (Gairm, Glasgow, 1965)
*The Law and the Grace* (Eyre and Spottiswoode, London, 1965)
*From Bourgeois Land* (Victor Gollancz, London, 1969)
*Selected Poems* (Victor Gollancz, London, 1970)
*Hamlet in Autumn* (Macdonald, London, 1972)
*Love Poems and Elegies* (Victor Gollancz, London, 1972)
*Rabhadan is Rudan* [Ditties and Things] (Gairm, Glasgow, 1973)
*Orpheus and Other Poems* (Akros, Preston, 1974)
*Poems for Donalda* (Ulsterman Publications, Belfast, 1974)
*The Notebooks of Robinson Crusoe and Other Poems* (Victor Gollancz, London, 1975)
*The Permanent Island: Gaelic poems translated by the author* (Macdonald, Loanhead, 1975)
*In the Middle* (Victor Gollancz, London, 1977)
*Na h-Ainmhidhean* [The Animals] (Clo Chailleann, Aberfeldy: 1979)
*Selected Poems, 1955-1980*, compiled by Robin Fulton (Macdonald, Loanhead, 1981)
*Na h-Eilthirich* [The Exiles] (Dept of Celtic, University of Glasgow, 1983)
*The Exiles* (Carcanet, Manchester, 1984)
*Selected Poems* (Carcanet, Manchester, 1985)
*A Life* (Carcanet, Manchester, 1986)
*An t-Eilean agus an Cànan* [The Island and the Language] (Dept of Celtic, Glasgow University, 1987)
*The Village and Other Poems* (Carcanet, Manchester, 1989)

NOVELS

*Consider the Lilies* (Victor Gollancz, London, 1968)
*The Last Summer* (Victor Gollancz, London, 1969)

*My Last Duchess* (Victor Gollancz, London, 1971)
*Goodbye Mr Dixon* (Victor Gollancz, 1974)
*An t-Aonaran* [The Hermit] (Dept of Celtic, Glasgow University, 1976)
*An End to Autumn* (Victor Gollancz, London, 1978)
*A Field Full of Folk* (Victor Gollancz, London, 1982)
*The Search* (Victor Gollancz, London, 1983)
*The Tenement* (Victor Gollancz, London 1985)
*In the Middle of the Wood* (Victor Gollancz, 1987)

SHORT STORIES

*Bùrn is Aran* [Bread and water] (Gairm, Glasgow, 1960)
*An Dubh is an Gorm* [The Black and the Blue] (Aberdeen, 1963)
*Iain am Measg nan Reultan* [Iain Among the Stars] (Gairm, Glasgow, 1970)
*Survival Without Error and Other Stories* (Victor Gollancz, London, 1970)
*an t-Adhar Ameireaganach is sgeulachdan eile* [The American Sky and Other Stories] [Club Leabhar, Inverness, 1973)
*The Black and the Red and Other Stories* (Victor Gollancz, London, 1973)
*The Village* (Club Leabhar, Inverness, 1976)
*The Hermit and Other Stories* (Victor Gollancz, London, 1977)
*Am Bruadaraiche* [The Daydreamer] (Stornoway: Acair, 1980)
*Murdo and Other Stories* (Victor Gollancz, London, 1981)
*Mr Trill in Hades and Other Stories* (Victor Gollancz, London, 1984)
*Selected Stories* (Carcanet, Manchester, 1989)

CRITICISM

*Towards the Human* (Macdonald, Loanhead, 1986)

# Index

A' Bhanrigh, 193
'A' Chailleach', viii, 2–3
'A Clach', viii
'A' dol dhachaigh', 2
'About that Mile', 42, 132
Abraham is Isaac, 191, 195
accident, 14, 15, 17, 22–5
Actor, The, 29–30
Adam and Eve, 191, 195
'After the Film', 179
'Agig Clachan Chalanais', vii, 182
'Aig a' Chladh', vii, 2
Aig a' Phartaidh, 191, 193
Air a' Bhus, 196
'Air Oidhche Foghair', viii
'Airson Deòrsa Caimbeul Hay', 2
Alba, 1
alcoholism, 8
'All Our Ancestors', 77
Am Bàrd, 194
Am Bodach, 190
Am Bruadaraiche, 190
'Am Faigh a' Ghàdhlig Bàs?' ('Shall Gaelic Die?'), 43, 87
Am Maor, 190, 191, 194, 197
American Sky, The (An t-Adhar Ameireaganach), 190–6
An Carbad, 192–5, 197–8
An Coigreach, 193, 194, 197
An Dealbh-Chluiche, 194
An Dileah, 2
An Dubh is an Gorm, 190, 191, 192, 194, 197
An Duine Dubh, 191, 193, 195, 198
An Duine Dubh anns a' Chùbainn, 192–3
An Fhidheall, 193

An Gaidheal, 190, 192
An Goal, 193
An Goigreach, 191, 194
An Gunfighter, 193
An Rionnag, 195, 196
An Saor, 193
An t-Adhar Ameireaganach, 190–6
An t-Aonaran, 190, 192
An t-Eilean agus an Cànan, 8–9
'An t-Oban', 5
'An t-Uisge', vii
An Taghadh, 192, 194, 195
An Telegram, 192
An Turus, 193
'Anecdote of the Jar', 124
Anns a' Bhùrn, 191, 194
Anns a Chafe, 191
Anns an Uaimh, 192, 195, 196
anticlimax, vi–vii, 21
'Aon Nighean', viii
'Argument', 137, 184–6
Arnold, Matthew, 96
art, 152, 188
ash theme, 151
'At the Cemetery', vii, 2
'At the Firth of Lorne', viii
'At the Highland Games', 162
At the Party (Aig a' Phartaidh), 191, 193
'At the Sale', 39, 56, 64–5
'At the Stones of Callanish', vii, 182
Aubrey's Brief Lives, 98–9
Auden, W.H., 79, 94
  influence, 56, 69, 73
autobiography, 77, 149
'Autumn', 92

autumn theme, 134–5, 168

Baudelaire, Charles Pierre, 56
Beckett, Samuel, 80–1
'Ben Dorain', 104–7, 142
Bersani, Leo, 42
'Between Sea and Moor', 55, 65
*Bibles and Advertisements* (*Bìobull is Sanasan-Reice*), 4–6, 58, 155
biculturalism, 8
bilingualism, 8, 58–9, 154
Black, Max, 106
*Black and Blue, The* (*An Dubh is an Gorm*), 190, 191, 192, 194, 197
*Black and the Red, The*, 178–9
*Black Man, The* (*An Duine Dubh*), 191, 193, 195, 198
*Black Man in the Pulpit, The*, 192–3
Blake, William, vi, 135, 151
*Bràthair mo Mhàthar*, 191
*Bread and Water* (*Bùrn is Aran*), 2, 4, 58, 190–1, 193–4
*Briseadh Cridhe*, 191–5
*Burn*, 191–2, 193, 194, 195, 197
burning theme, 151
'By Ferry to the Island', viii
*By the Sea*, 27–9, 68, 69

*Callanish Stones, The* (*Clachan Chalanais*), 190, 193, 194
Calvinism, 16, 42–3, 80–1, 110
  influence, 123, 126–7, 128–9, 130
  in writings, 17, 109, 162, 163, 195
*Car, The* (*An Carbad*), 192–5, 197–8
'Carol and Hamlet' sequence, 166, 169
'Cemetery near Burns' Cottage, The', 133
'Chair in Which You've Sat, The', 118
characters, 15, 193–5
'Chinese Poem', 56
*Choice, The* (*An Taghadh*), 192, 194, 195
'Christmas, 1971', 169, 170
*Clachan Chalanais*, 190, 193, 194
classical references, 135, 149
Clearances, 107, 158, 176, 186
'Clearances, The', 60, 61, 158
Coleridge, Samuel Taylor, 102
colour imagery, 124, 131, 178, 198
compassion, vi
condensed verse, 56
Conrad, Joseph, 90
*Consider the Lilies*, 11, 12, 17, 26, 58
  plot, 24, 176, 177–8, 186
contemplation, v–vi

Corkery, Daniel, 45
crisis plot, 12
culture, 43–4

Dante, 90, 181, 185
*Dark Glasses, The* (*Na Speuclairean Dubha*), 10, 190, 191, 192, 195
'Dè tha Ceàrr?', vii, 3–4
'Dead for a Rat', 166
death, 40, 82–101, 137, 149–51, 154–5, 165–6
  'Sunday Morning Walk', viii, 11, 125–6
'Deer on the High Hills', 56, 61, 102–21, 122–3, 184
  'metaphor, 40, 87
  style, ix, 77, 158–61, 163, 181
'Do bhoireannach aosd' ('To an old lady'), 2–3, 4
'Do mo Mhathair', viii
'Do Ruaraidh MacThòmais', 6
Donoghue, Denis, 48–9
*Dream, The* (novel), 12–13, 16–18, 22–3
'Dream, The' (poem), 84
*Dreamer, The*, 190
'Drowned, The', 96–7, 99
Dunn, Douglas, 147
'Dunoon and the Holy Loch', 162

*E Fhèin is a Bhràthair*, 194
*Eader Fealladhà is Glaschu*, 6–7
'Earth Eats Everything, The', 88–9
'Eight Songs for a New Ceilidh', 4–5, 109, 155
Eliot, T.S., 18, 20, 54, 90, 102
emotions, 158, 159
*End to Autumn, An*, 18–19, 21, 22
endings of poems, 138–9
enjambement, 145, 146
'Entering Your House', ix, 39
'Envoi', 60–1, 70–1, 97, 138–9
exile theme, 7–8, 9, 12–15, 191, 196
*Exiles, The* (collection), 7–8, 45–6, 128, 188
  death, 91, 92, 94, 97, 99
  imagery, 138–9, 140
'Exiles, The' (poem), viii, 138
existentialism, 195

'Face of an Old Highland Woman', 38, 39
*Factor, The* (*Am Maor*), 190, 191, 194, 197
'Fairy Story', 169, 170

# Index

father, death of, 84, 85
Faulkner, William, 49
*Fear à Rhodesia*, 194
*Fiddle, The*, 193
fluency, 144–5
'For Ann in America in the Autumn', 170
'For George Campbell Hay', 2
'For Keats', 134–5
'For Poets Writing in English Over in Ireland', 45–6
'For the Unknown Seamen of the 1939–45 War Buried in Iona Churchyard', 59
Free Church, ix, 63, 74, 154–7
free verse, 4, 145, 166–7
Freud, 5–6, 37, 44
Friel, Brian, 48
*From Bourgeois Land*, 61–7, 71, 161–2, 181–3, 187
imagery, 133–4, 136, 140
*Fun and Glasgow*, 6–7

Gaelic fiction, 190–9
Gaelic language, vii, 13, 74
importance, 43–5, 47–9, 104–5, 110–11, 157–8
Gaelic poetry, 1–10
Gaelic Renaissance, vi
*Gairm*, 1, 2, 58, 190–3, 196
*General, The*, 29
Gillies, William, 105–6
'Girl and Child', 41
'Glass of Water, The', 77
'Going Home', 2
'Good Place, The', 54, 59
*Goodman and Death Mahoney*, 31, 127
grace, 183–4, 187–8
*Grammarian's Funeral, A*, 182
*Granny anns a' Chòrnair (Granny in the Corner)*, 191, 192
'Greater Love', 172–3
*Gunfighter, The*, 193

haiku form, 7
Hamilton, Ian, 64
Hamlet, 79, 83, 162
'Envoi', 70, 71, 97, 138
*Hamlet in Autumn*, 82, 134–6, 140, 165–74
Hay, George Campbell, 2, 106
*He and his Brother*, 194
Heaney, Seamus, 40, 42, 104, 124
*Heart-break (Briseadh Cridhe)*, 191–5

Highland English, 60, 63
'Highland Wedding', 157
Highland writing, 11, 37, 43, 104, 157
Hiroshima, 2, 4–5, 37, 182
history, 12, 38, 107
Holocaust, 61–2
home theme, 92–3
Hopkins, G.M., 185
horse imagery, 176–7, 180, 186–7
'How Often I Feel Like You', 78–9
humming usage, 148
humour, 7

'I Build an Orange Church', 42
'I Thought I Saw You', 86
*Iain am Measg nan Reultan*, 190
'If Ever I Loved You', 79
'If You are about to Die Now', ix
imagery, vii-viii, 68, 131–43, 145–8
Gaelic, 2, 197–8
imagination, 38, 42, 102, 122–3, 128
'In Luss Churchyard', 39
*In the Cafe*, 191
*In the Cave (Anns an Uaimh)*, 192, 195, 196
*In the Middle* (collection), 90–1, 128, 136, 183
'In the Middle' (poem), 90–1
*In the Middle of the Wood*, 14–16, 19, 23–5, 128, 172
*In the Person of ...* , 29–31
'In the School', 173
'In the Time of the Useless Pity', 170
*In the Water (Anns a' Bhùrn)*, 191, 194
'In this Pitiless Age', 181, 185
indentation, 146
'Innocence', viii
inspiration, 58, 187
*Iòseph*, 191
Ireland, 45–9
*Is agus Esan*, 191, 195
'Island, The', 155
*Island and the Language, The*, 8–9
island life
influence, 80, 155
theme, x, 16–17, 43–4, 132–3, 190
'It Was a Country', 136

'Jean Brodie's Children', ix
*Jenkins is Marlowe*, 194, 195
*Jews, The (Na h-Iùdhaich)*, 191, 192
*John among the Stars*, 190
'John MacLean' sequence, 165–6, 168
'Johnson in the Highlands', 78

Joiner, The, 193
Joseph, 191
Journey, The, 193
Journey Home, A (Turus Dhachaigh), 191, 193, 194
Journey to the Raven (Turus do'n Fhithich), 191, 192
Joyce, James, 48

Kant, Immanuel, 33
Keane, Molly, 144
Keats, John, 42, 134–5, 137, 144
Kierkegaard, S.A., 110, 156–7
Kinsella, Thomas, 49
Knox, John, 99

language, 13, 43–8, 49
Larkin, Philip, 56, 60, 64, 67, 69
Last Summer, The, 123, 178
Law and the Grace, The (collection), 31, 60, 184
  imagery, 131–2, 133, 135, 137, 139
'Law and the Grace, The' (poem), 42, 81
  poetic truth, 56–7, 60, 61
Lawrence, D.H., 81, 100, 147, 148, 149
'Legend, The', 93
'Lenin', 60, 61, 70, 156
'Letter, The' (poem), 136
Letter, The (radio play), 32
Lewis, v, vii, 60, 73
  influence, 35, 53–5, 126, 129, 154
  in writings, 37, 43, 109, 155, 163
'Lewis 1928–45', 140
Librarian, The, 29, 30
Life, A, 129, 134, 140–2
  death, 91–2, 94–6, 97–100
  style, 144, 145–6, 147, 148–9, 152
  themes, 68, 70, 163, 182–3
'Light to Light', 10–11
Lines, v, 135
'Listen', 71, 163
Literature of Region and Nation, The, 58
loneliness theme, 28, 61
Loner, The (An t-Aonaran), 190, 192
Long River, The (collection), 58, 136, 139, 142
'Long River, The' (poem), 124
Love, 193
Love Poems and Elegies, 56, 123–4
  death, 84, 86, 165, 180
  imagery, 132, 136, 137
love theme, 84, 113

Lowell, Robert, 74–5, 77, 79, 162, 170
  influence, 56, 64, 73, 147, 148
lyrical cry, vi

MacAulay, Donald, 45
MacCaig, Norman, 149, 155
MacDiarmid, Hugh, 37, 55, 178
  style, v, vi, 117, 123, 161
MacIntyre, Duncan Bàn, 5, 37, 110–11, 159
  'Ben Dorain', 104–7, 142
MacLean, John, 165–6, 168
MacLean, Sorley, 59, 104, 106, 161
MacNeice, Louis, 51, 66
Maighisteirean is Ministeirean, 190, 191, 192, 197
Maighistir Trill agus Vergil, 192
Man from Rhodesia, A, 194
'Man Without a Name, The', 92
marble imagery, 141–2
Masters and Ministers (Maighisteirean is Ministeirean), 190, 191, 192, 197
material life theme, 68
metaphors, 40–1, 87, 106, 119, 180
metrical structure, 4, 9, 63, 109
  effects, 57, 65, 71 145
Miller, J. Hillis, 119
Milton, John, 137
'Minister', 132
mirror imagery, 125, 127, 136
  'Deer on the High Hills', 112–13, 115
'Mo Bhardachd', viii
moon imagery, 23, 138, 140
Morgan, Edwin, 55, 161
mother, death of, 83–5, 87–8, 124–5
Mr Trill and Vergil, 192
Mr Trill in Hades (collection), 33–4, 171–4
'Mr Trill in Hades' (story), 173–4
Muir, Edwin, 54, 149, 159
Munro, John, 2
Murchadh (Murdoch), 190, 192, 195–6
Murdo, 32–3
Murray, Les, 49
'My Brother', ix
My Last Duchess, 177–8, 179
My Maternal Uncle, 191
'My Poetry', viii

Na Facail air a' Bhalla, 194
Na Guthan, 193, 194
Na h-Eilthirich, see Exiles, The (collection)
'Na h-Eilthirich' see 'Exiles, The' (poem)
Na h-Iùdhaich, 191, 192

# Index

*Na Speuclairean Dubha*, 10, 190, 191, 192, 195
Nagasaki, vii, 182
*Napoleon*, 30, 191, 192, 193, 196
'Neochiontas', viii
'New Criticism', 102–3
*New Poems*, 58
'Next Time', 92
'No One At Home', 86
'No Return', 92–3
'None is the Same as Another', 71, 91
'Note on Puritans, A', 42–3, 75–6, 183
*Notebooks of Robinson Crusoe, The*, 56, 134, 184, 188
    real poem, 126, 127–8
'Nuair a Bha Sinn Og', viii

Oban, 5
'Oban 1955–82', 68–9, 70, 99
objectivity, 76
'Ochd òrdain airson cèilidh ùir', *see* 'Eight Songs for a New Ceilidh'
'Oedipus and Others', 82
Oedipus complex, 95, 195
'Of a Rare Courage', 129
'Of the Uncomplicated Dairy Girl', ix
'Old Highland Lady Reading Newspaper', viii
old lady theme, 3, 141, 150, 194
*Old Man, The*, 190
'Old Woman', viii, 59, 138, 154–5
'Old Woman, The' ('A' Chailleach'), viii, 2–3
'Old Woman ("Overwhelmed with Kindness")', ix
'Old Woman (Your Thorned Back)', viii
'On a Summer's Day', 70, 167–8
'On an Autumn Night', viii
'On an Icy Day', 79–80
'On Looking At the Dead', 40, 87–8, 89–90, 180
*On the Bus* (radio play), 27
*On the Bus* (story), 196
'On the Island', 179–80
'one', use of, 59
'One Girl', viii
'Orpheus', 124–5
*Orpheus and Other Poems*, 83–4, 131, 133
'Over and Over', 169

passion, vi
Pasternak, Boris, 79, 80
*Patient, The*, 30
*Pickering*, 191

'Play, The', 173
*Play, The (An Dealbh-Chluiche)*, 194
plots, 23–4, 192
'Poem in March' 60–1
'Poem of Lewis', 38–9, 42, 53, 56, 109
'Poems for S.', 84, 86
*Poet, The*, 194
poetic truth, 51–3, 56–7, 66–8, 71–2
'Poets aren't dangerous, you think', 187
politics in poetry, 51
*Portrait of the Artist, A*, 91
Powys, John Cowper, 144
'Prophecy, The', 179

*Queen, The*, 193

radio theme, 65–6
radio work, xi, 26–36
railway imagery, 133
'Rain, The', vii
rainbow imagery, 117
reading material, 55, 73
'Reading Shakespeare', 94
'Real People in a Real Place', 39, 44, 45, 55
reflections, 125, 127, 136
    'Deer on the High Hills', 112–13, 115
religion, 80, 112, 114, 134, 186
    influence, 74, 75–6, 149
    *see also* Calvinism; Free Church
'Returning Exile', 91
*Review, The*, 56
rhyme-schemes, 166–7, 171
Richards, I.A., 106, 176, 177
Rilke, Rainer Maria, 71, 72
'Ring, The', 172, 173
*River, river*, 179
*Robinson Crusoe*, 192, 194–5, 196
*Rudeigin Coltach ri Chekhov*, 195
'Russian Poem', 78–9

Sartre, Jean-Paul, 72
'Schoolroom Incident', 60
'Schoolteacher' (poem), 135
*Schoolteacher, The* (radio play), 30–1
Scott, Sir Walter, 12, 154
sea imagery, 99, 179
*Search, The*, 15, 20–1, 23, 24
*Selected Poems*, ix, 38, 56, 68, 147
'Self Portrait', 173
*Seven Poets*, 74
sexuality theme, 97–8, 142
Shakespeare, William, 56

'Shall Gaelic Die?', 43, 87
Shelley, v, vi, 134, 187
'Skye', 77–8
'Slowly', 41, 187
*Smile, The*, 33
'Snowballs, The', 173
*Something Like Chekhov*, 195
'Space-Ship, The', 84
'Speech for a Woman', ix
spontaneity, 158
'Spring Wedding', 157
*St Columba and John Knox*, 26
*Star, The* (*An Rionnag*), 195, 196
Stevens, Wallace, 102, 110, 112, 119
  style, 56, 99, 160–1
'Stone, The', viii
'Story, The', 101
*Stranger, The* (*An Goigreach*), 191, 194
suffocation imagery, 84
'Sunday Morning Walk', viii, 56
  death, 11, 39, 125–6
surrealism, vii, 79, 167–8, 173, 196
*Survival Without Error*, 179–80
'Survivors, The', 97

Tawney, R.H., 162
'Taynuilt 1982–', 69–70, 98–100
*Telegram, The*, 192
television theme, 7
'Tha thu air Aigeann M'Inntinn' ('You are at the Bottom of my Mind'), vi, 2, 4
*Thistles and Roses*, 58, 129
  imagery, 131–2, 133, 137, 138, 139
Thomson, Derick, 45, 53, 59, 105, 106
time span in writings, 191
'To an old lady', 2–3, 4
'To Autumn', 134
'To my Mother', viii
'Today I Wished to Write a Story', 126

'Torches, The', 79
*Towards the Human*, 75, 180, 187
tragedy, 16, 22, 70–1
*Turus Dhachaigh*, 191, 193, 194
*Turus do'n Fhithich* (*Journey to the Raven*), 191, 192
'Two Girls Singing', viii, 60

Valéry, Paul, 58
'Village, The', 146–7, 148, 150–2
*Village and Other Poems, The*
  death, 91–2, 96–7, 99, 101
  imagery, 137, 140, 187–8
  style, 71, 144, 146–7, 149–52
'Villagers', 97
*Visitor, The*, 34
*Voices, The* (radio play), 32
*Voices, The* (*Na Guthan*) (story), 193, 194

wake theme, 93–7
'Wandering Jew', 92
*Water* (*Bùrn*), 191–2, 193, 194, 195, 197
well imagery, 53
'What is Wrong?', vii, 3–4
'What to do about Ralph?', 172
'When My Poetry Making Has Failed', 93–4
'When We Were Young', viii
'Where Are You Tonight?', 89
*White Noon, The*, 127, 139
*Words on the Wall, The*, 194
Wordsworth, William, vi, 95

Yeats, W.B., 93, 40, 157, 159
'You are at the Bottom of my Mind', vi, 2, 4
'You Told Me Once', 84, 85–6, 91
'Young Highland Girl Studying Poetry, A', viii